INIQUITIES 1.

Book 2

Walking Alone

INIQUITIES TRILOGY
Book 2

Walking Alone

Carolyn McCrae

Matador
9 De Montfort Mews
Leicester LE1 7FW, UK
Tel: (+44) 116 255 9311 / 9312
Email: books@troubador.co.uk
Web: www.troubador.co.uk/matador

www.carolynmccrae.com

ISBN
Paperback: 978-1905886 51-7
Hardback: 978-1905886-52-4

Typeset in 11pt Stempel Garamond by Troubador Publishing Ltd, Leicester, UK
Printed in the UK by The Cromwell Press Ltd, Trowbridge, Wilts, UK

Matador is an imprint of Troubador Publishing Ltd

This book is for my mother,
Joanna Homan, 1920-1971
and my step-father
Edward (Chris) Homan, 1919-1999

Acknowledgement is again due to my husband Colin.
For all the meals he has cooked and all the hours he has
spent talking about people he did not know until he read this
book.
And for the cover images. He has a vision I don't.

Iniquity

The word has two meanings according to the *Shorter Oxford Dictionary*:

1. Immoral, unrighteous or harmful action or conduct; gross injustice, wickedness, sin.

2. Inequality, inequity, unfairness. (obsolete).

Something by Way of Explanation

Ted phoned this morning to tell me Max was dying.

Perhaps I should have been more saddened than I was at hearing this news of the man who had been my friend for so long, but I have not seen him for some years and he was very old.

"Is he in hospital?"

"No. There's no point. He's back at Sandhey and Monika is looking after him."

It seemed strange to hear the names spoken again. I had lived in Max's house, Sandhey, for many years and Monika, his housekeeper and friend, had looked after me for all the early part of my life.

But Ted hadn't called just to keep me informed; he wanted me to do something for him.

He told me he had been writing the history of my family, introducing the youngest generation to their parents and grandparents as they would never have known them; trying to make sense of all that had happened in our lives. He left the words 'before it's too late' unspoken.

"I can write about the early years, in fact I have done so." He spoke without emotion. "But I know little of your lives as you all grew up and rebelled in your different ways against what your parents had made you."

Ted had always been in the background, the old family friend, the trusted lawyer, always available when we needed him. But he was right; he could have known very little of what really happened.

"Charles, you must know I am not the person to write about that time."

I was reluctant to agree to do as he asked so I started to tell him how busy I was, how my life was full enough. I had no time.

"Those are excuses, Charles, not reasons." He spoke quietly; it had never been his way to raise his voice.

I tried to give a better explanation.

I would find it difficult to rake over the events of those years that followed the death of my Mother; the memories would be hard to bear, I'd tried to forget much of it for long enough.

"Sometimes facing up to your failings makes them easier to bear."

So he agreed I had failed.

There is a quotation 'The only thing necessary for the triumph of evil is for good men to do nothing.' Was I the 'good man' who had done nothing? Evil had certainly triumphed. One way or another.

I argued that by writing it all down I would make it real and unchangeable but Ted countered my points one by one. "It was real. Those people existed, those events occurred. Not accepting that won't undo history."

Perhaps my biggest problem, I tried to put my fears into words, was that the people about whom I would be writing would read my version of what had happened. Perhaps they would remember it all differently.

"Of course they will remember it differently." Ted was dismissive. "No two human beings remember the same event in the same way. They are necessarily looking at it from different perspectives, they have views of themselves that are often totally at odds with those of others."

There would be so much I would want to change, conversations I would remember with embarrassment, circumstances I should have handled differently. I would be tempted to write about events as I wanted them to have been, not as they were.

"You will write about those years as you saw them. Just because you see only your part of the picture doesn't necessarily mean it is wrong. It is still the truth, even if it isn't the *whole* truth it is *your* truth."

It wouldn't be objective. My last throw of the dice as I knew I was losing the argument.

"Who said anything about objectivity Charles? What is needed is *your* knowledge of what happened, what *you* knew, what *you* thought Holly and Linda believed. Your view of why it all happened the way it did."

"I can't do it Ted."

"If not you, who?" Over the many years I had known and liked him I had never seen Ted lose his temper. Whenever he wanted to persuade someone to a course of action he just made simple points in a straightforward manner. Sooner or later they gave in. "That part of the story needs to be told or the whole is incomplete."

So I agreed to dig out my memories of that time nearly 30 years ago, to make contact again with Carl and Susannah, to check the accuracy of my recollections with those of Holly and Linda.

I will have to write it all down for the others to read.

And judge.

I am reminded of something my father once said: "Do not judge me too harshly for things I could not know." I begin to understand what he meant.

Charles Donaldson
Sevenoaks, Kent
August 1998

Chapter One

To anyone who may have been watching them, the three figures illustrated the less glamorous aspects of international travel. They must have travelled a long way and have been very tired, because the middle-aged woman, although somewhat dishevelled, was far too stylishly dressed to be sitting on the kerb with her feet in the gutter. She yawned as she ran her fingers through her hair.

"When I do that I get told off." her daughter complained, continuing in a voice mimicking her Mother *"You should always put your hand in front of your mouth when you yawn."* She was silenced by a look from her father.

It was only just past lunchtime but Speke Airport had a middle-of-the-night feel about it as no more flights were expected for some hours. The family had had every opportunity to know this since there had been only the Arrivals and Departures screens to entertain them while they had waited for their bags to appear on the conveyor belt. Their fellow passengers on the flight up from Heathrow had had only hand baggage and had all quickly disappeared through the hall.

The middle-of-the-night feeling was emphasised when they had eventually wheeled their luggage trolleys outside to be met by an empty road with no sign of a single cab waiting for a fare.

They stood for a while by the taxi sign before deciding it was to be a long wait and making themselves a bit more comfortable. Holly perched herself on top of the cases on the trolley, Mary sat on the kerb, her legs stretched out in front of her while Matt tried to lean as much of his weight as possible on the handle of the trolley without tipping his daughter onto the pavement.

"At home there'd be hundreds of cabs." Holly wound her long hair around her fingers and sucked on it.

"Don't do that! How many times do I have to tell you?"

"A cab will be along soon just hang on in there a few minutes more. We're on the last leg." Matt tried to sound encouraging but there was no sign of any vehicle let alone a taxi cab.

"At least it's not raining." Mary had been expecting it always to be raining in England, even in July, but the sun was shining and it was pleasantly warm.

"What time is it?" asked Holly "I'm ready for a shower, though I bet

1

they don't have such things as showers over here."

"Of course they have showers." Matt sounded rather more confident than he felt. He hoped that the hotel he had been assured was the best in Liverpool would live up to its reputation. "You'll be very comfortable here, Sir," the reservations clerk had said "we have lots of Americans staying here. We're used to your special requirements." 'Whatever that means' Matt had thought at the time. Still a shower shouldn't be too much to ask.

Holly was not only tired, she was sulking because she didn't want to be in England. She hadn't wanted to leave her friends and her school to come to England for God knows how long – a few weeks, a few months, years, forever? Especially Paul. She hadn't wanted to leave him when she'd only just managed to get him to notice her. She was determined to write to him every week, as she had promised. She was pretty sure he would write back.

"I bet they only have bathtubs. I hate them. Why did we have to come?"

"You'll be OK tomorrow, right now you're just tired. You always act way below your age when you're tired." Her father had a way of putting her down that she could never argue against.

There was no way either of her parents would have answered Holly's question truthfully and explained why Matt had uprooted his family.

The simple answer was that her Mother had been persuaded to leave her job in Boston to take up a post as visiting lecturer in the Department of Statistics and Computational Maths at Liverpool University. 'Why can't they just call it 'Computing' like the rest of the world?' Holly had commented when she had first been told.

But it was more complicated than that.

It had all been Matt's idea and Mary felt he had never really explained why he had insisted on the move.

It took over half an hour before a cab finally appeared. It was small and an undistinguished colour of pale green but at least they could finally be on their way into the city. The driver got out and spoke loudly and quickly in what sounded to them all like a foreign language.

"I think he's telling us not to worry – he'll fit us and all our bags in the cab." translated Matt. "I'm not so sure."

As they drove towards the city the driver kept saying something that was probably an apology but none of his passengers could understand what he was saying.

"Can you speak slower?" Matt had decided we must try to communicate with the driver.

"Sorry wack! Keep forgerring you don' speak English you know

2

warr I mean like you being yanks an' all youknowwarrImeanlike."

"Is that English? I'll never understand anyone." Holly moaned and slouched against the door.

Matt and Mary settled back as best they could amongst the bags on the back seat.

"He's driving so fast." Mary was used to more gentle speeds and the way they were being driven was almost the last straw. She felt as though she would soon break down in tears and she couldn't do that until they were in their room and Holly wouldn't know. She hoped Holly couldn't hear her with the noise of the car and the driver who was still talking to no one in particular. "Oh Matt are we doing the right thing?"

"It'll be fine Mary, it'll all work out OK you'll see."

"Sure, it'll all be OK. I'm just tired." She didn't sound convinced. "I'd thought that England would just be like home only wetter and, just, somehow, greyer. I thought the people would be just like us, and the language just the same. But it's all so different. It's all so foreign."

Holly had regained some of her energy when they arrived at the hotel. She ran up the steps, turned round and looked out at the crowded city streets, her tiredness and bad mood forgotten. "Wow. Liverpool. This is so neat!"

"Tomorrow, Holly, you can explore tomorrow. Meanwhile don't wander away while I check in." Matt, having shepherded his wife and daughter across the Atlantic, had just about had enough. He was ready for a shower and bed.

As they crossed the foyer Holly bumped straight into two men who were deep in conversation. Normally she would have just pushed on, she was used to crowds, but she made a thing of this collision because she thought one was pretty nice-looking. She noticed him because he was exactly as he had hoped English men would be, with long hair tied in a pony-tail and wearing a black polo necked sweater with a brown leather jacket and denim jeans.

She stopped and rubbed her arm as if hurt.

"I beg your pardon." She had got what she had wanted, a longer look at him, but he didn't seem to have noticed her other than to make the automatic reaction of apology.

"Oh no, Holly got in your way – it's not your fault at all." Mary knew she was in England when people apologised for things that were not their fault, and she hustled Holly out of their way.

"Mom! He walked into me. It wasn't my fault." Holly turned to watch over her shoulder as the hunk walked away, talking animatedly

3

with his older companion, engrossed in their own business as they left through the revolving door.

"He was kinda smart."

As Matt had a bath Mary unpacked, bemoaning the lack of drawer and cupboard space. She sat down on the side of the bed, hit by the realisation that there was no going back.

For at least a year they were stuck here, in Liverpool.

She repeated to herself the question her daughter had asked earlier.

"Did we *have* to come?"

Chapter Two

It had been just over two years earlier, in the spring of 1968, when Matt had first mentioned his idea of going to Europe. He had asked Mary, apparently nonchalantly, whether they should go to Europe on vacation that summer. "Just you and me. Holly can go to camp."

It seemed like an innocent enquiry at the time and Mary had no reason to question his motives. She had agreed with surprise but little hesitation. All their vacations had been family ones and since she had always been looking after Holly and her friends they had not really been vacations for her at all.

In the week that followed Mary bought guidebooks for all the capitals so she could make sure their time would be well spent and she dreamed of staying at sophisticated hotels in Paris and Rome. She and Matt could spend time together, sitting at pavement cafes and sightseeing, doing those tourist things that they could never do with Holly.

They needed time together, to restore something of their marriage, perhaps even to get to like each other again.

"Austria? Innsbruck?" She was shocked when the following weekend Matt told her he had bought the tickets, arranged the hire car, and booked the hotel in a place she had barely heard of.

"What happened to Paris and Rome? I thought going to Europe meant going to the cities, the culture, not some remote place in the middle of nowhere! What do we do in Austria? Couldn't we even discuss this?"

The argument was not easily resolved. Matt had decided where they were going and was used to getting his way but Mary was unusually determined that she was not going to miss seeing Rome and Paris.

She tried to compromise "Well, Rome only this trip – we can do Paris next year." But he was adamant. "We fly to Innsbruck. It is all arranged. I'm not going to change anything."

She had asked him why he was so determined to go to Austria. Did he know anyone there? Was there something he wanted to learn for his work? But Matt was not forthcoming and simply shrugged, repeating that the tickets were bought and the arrangements made.

He had always treated her like this. Throughout their 18-year marriage he had made all the important decisions about their lives. She knew she should have stood up for herself more but she hadn't, she had gone along with whatever Matt said with never more than token resistance.

In 1948 Matt had had a good job as an assistant librarian at the University in Toronto, lived in a small but adequate apartment and had been swiftly improving his English. But he knew that if he were to truly integrate into his chosen country's society he would have to marry. With a Canadian wife his status could never be questioned.

With that end in mind he carefully observed the students who used his library. He needed to identify one who was not always surrounded by a group of friends, who might be lonely and vulnerable. It was important to him to find someone who lacked confidence and would give him respect and obedience. He would have to be careful as he had quickly realised that most Canadian women were headstrong and expected to have their own way.

That sort of woman wouldn't have suited him at all.

As he observed Mary over a period of weeks he never saw her speak to anyone. She would often spend whole days working alone even when there were major ice hockey games and the library was more than usually empty of students. He began to engage her in brief conversations, never intrusive, but enough to make her think he might be interested in her.

He learned that she lived with her parents who she disliked and who had little time for her as they worked in their family business. The O'Dwyers were old-fashioned and insular, keeping to their own people having moved to Canada from Ireland when Mary was a baby. He discovered that, although she was modest about her ability, she was realistically expecting to graduate amongst the top of her year.

Matt began to pay Mary attention at a time when she was worrying what she could do when she graduated. Her parents didn't want her to have her own life. They said her place was with the family, taking over their business, looking after them as they grew older. That was not what she wanted to do at all but she had no idea how she could break away. She wanted to go to The United States, to work in the newly developing world of computers. She knew it would be hard to escape the life her parents had planned for her, but she felt the battle would be worth it.

When Matt first asked her out she had found excuses to turn him down; her parents needed her at home, she had assignments to complete; but he had persisted and eventually she had accepted his invitation. He didn't make advances too quickly and she was beginning to think he didn't like her after all when, on their fourth date, he put his arm, apparently tentatively, around her shoulders. Playing the long game he gained her trust and when she relaxed and smiled he thought she could be quite pretty.

They had been going out for nearly a year before he finally managed to get her into his bed. He knew then that she would marry him. Matt had found someone who needed marriage as much as he did.

After their wedding he changed.

Matt made sure he was amusing and gentlemanly when there were other people around but when they were alone his mood would swing without warning to anger or a surly belligerence. He always flattered her and was attentive and considerate in public, but when they were on their own he was a bully, using force or insidious emotional blackmail to get her to do as he wished. After a very short time she knew her marriage had been a mistake.

She had thought marriage meant she could lead her life her own way. She had been wrong. She had simply exchanged the constraints placed on her by her parents for those imposed by her husband.

She thought about divorce but she had never believed it was right. In marriage she had promised herself to this man 'for better or for worse'.

When her daughter, Holly, was born on Christmas Day 1952 Mary finally accepted that she could never again have a life of her own. She would just have to make the best of everything.

Holly had been only a few months old when Matt had announced that he had given their notice to the landlord and they would be leaving the apartment in Toronto at the end of the summer. She had asked for information 'Why?' He had given her no explanation. 'Where are we going to live?' Boston. 'Why Boston?' He had never explained. 'Shouldn't we have discussed this first, just a little?' But in the end she had to do as he wanted.

Now Holly was 15 years old and was to go to camp leaving Mary to have what she felt was a long overdue summer that she could enjoy.

But she really did not want that holiday to be in Austria.

"I'm going to Rome. I've read the guidebook on Innsbruck and it seems lovely but not for two whole weeks, and you don't want to go to Innsbruck itself anyway, you want to tour around the country. Well I don't want to spend my summer in a car. If I go to Europe it'll be to Rome."

After several weeks during which Mary, uncharacteristically, did not back down, they came to an agreement. Mary would go to Rome.

7

She would spend some time there before joining Matt in Innsbruck where they would have a few days together before flying home.

Mary's thoughts, as she walked across the airport tarmac responsible only for herself, were of freedom. She would have two weeks of being herself. She turned towards the departure lounge where Matt was waiting for his flight and waved with a great sense of relief.

Matt's thoughts as he sat at the bar were surprisingly similar. His time would be his own, he wouldn't have to lie and prevaricate, he could just do what he had to do.

He was sickened by forever playing second fiddle to his wife and living off her money. Everyone who knew them was aware that all he had was because of Mary. As that became increasingly hard to bear the idea of going to Austria, to trace what inheritances were due to him, took hold in his mind. He had been thinking more and more often about going back as each year that passed meant his task would become more difficult.

It was already 30 years since he had left.

He wondered what had happened to his father's farm. There was never any money in farming but the land itself must still be worth something. Perhaps his parents had survived the war and Rebecca was now living there, on land that should be his. His Uncle Maximilian, had been a lawyer and there were no such things as poor lawyers. If he had survived the war he would have money. Matt was sure there had to be a way of getting hold of some of it for himself. He wasn't sure how but there had to be a way.

That first year he had driven out of the city, up into the mountains, with an increasing sense of familiarity. He had parked the hired car in front of one of the many hotels that now occupied the main street of what had once been a small agricultural village. As he checked in he wondered whether he would have known the middle aged man who called him 'Sir' when they were both young. Perhaps they had been at school together, learned the advantages of their sex together, marched together in their uniforms to save their world in the war against the Jews.

On his first day in the village he walked the short distance to what was left of his old home. There was nothing left but ruined walls on an abandoned hillside. No one wanted to farm the land, it was too difficult in these more affluent days when there were easier ways to make money. He walked the fields he had once worked remembering the hatred he had felt for his family. His father had worked them so hard, for nothing. Even if he could have proved his right of ownership Matt recognised the land was worthless.

It took no time at all to get used to the language again, even though he had left the village before he was 18, but he was careful not to let on to anyone that he understood their words. It was far better they thought him the 'uncomprehending American' as he spent time in bars, listening to the conversations, picking up names of people and places he had once known. On the fifth day of his visit he heard the name 'Max Fischer'. Listening without appearing to, he learned that this Max Fischer lived in England, was a lawyer of some kind with his own firm in Liverpool. Max Fischer had visited the village alone every summer since the late 1940s. No one was quite sure why. They were talking about him because he had been there the previous week.

Matt had missed him by just a few days.

When they met up in Innsbruck Mary had so much to tell Matt. She talked enthusiastically about Rome. She told him every detail of her hotel room, every sight she had seen in the city, the squares, the fountains, the motor scooters, the ruined city within the city, the food and wine she had enjoyed in small restaurants with red checked tablecloths. She had had a wonderful time.

Of course there were things she didn't tell him. How for the first time for many years she had been able to get out of bed when she wanted to; eat when, where and what she had wanted to; bathe, sit, walk, do anything and everything she wanted to, when she wanted to, without having to negotiate with husband or daughter.

"I should have had a holiday on my own years ago."

Matt asked her no questions simply letting her talk on, and he volunteered nothing of what he had done.

"Did you do any walking? What were the hotels like? What was the food like?" He answered her in monosyllables giving away no information that mattered.

If she hadn't known how much he had wanted her to be on his trip she would have thought he had been with another woman.

Those days in Innsbruck were not comfortable ones. Matt let Mary do the ordering at restaurants and bars which she did by speaking English slowly and clearly or, when that didn't work, by reading from a German phrasebook. She thought this unusual because at home he would never let her talk to waiters or barmen and when he saw other men's wives ordering he would say sharply how ugly it was for women to put themselves forward, how demeaning for their men.

She was relieved when they were in the air on their way home. All that week Matt had been withdrawn and uncommunicative and Mary had an overwhelming sense of anti-climax.

"I'm sorry you didn't have a good time." Mary tried to soften the atmosphere as the no smoking light went out and they undid their seat belts.

"What makes you think that? It was fine. I did things I'd always wanted to do."

But she wasn't convinced and summoned up the courage to ask the question that had been on her mind "What *did* you do?" But before he could answer, even if he had been going to, the stewardess interrupted offering plastic glasses half filled with a fizzy wine which probably was not champagne. Their conversation turned to the safe ground of Holly and how she would have enjoyed her summer.

Although he had learned many useful things he was frustrated that he would have to wait another year to meet Max. He had not been able to hide his mood when Mary had arrived in Innsbruck. The days they had spent together he was preoccupied with how he was going to be able to get back the next year.

Mary was surprised when, the following spring, Matt raised the subject of Europe again.

"Will you come with me to Paris this time?"

"You had such a good time on your own last year." He had said without directly answering her question.

"Are you going back to Austria? You seemed a bit disappointed last year."

"There're things I'd like to do," was all he would say in explanation "and you'd probably have a better time on your own."

"You want to go alone? Again?"

Mary was still sure it wasn't another woman.

They had had a good year, one of their best. Mary's research was going well, the world of computers was opening up and she was thrilled to be a part of it. Matt was working on a new cataloguing system in the library that was going to revolutionise access to information and make life so much easier for students and faculty alike. Holly was doing well at school and was popular with her classmates, a fact that was especially important to Mary, who sometimes blamed her early marriage on her lonely childhood.

She should have had a wonderful week in Paris, that summer of 1969, doing all the things she had carefully planned from reading the guidebooks. She should have relaxed and enjoyed herself visiting all those places she had only read about or seen in the movies. But she couldn't resurrect the feeling of freedom she had experienced the previous year.

She could not free herself of the thoughts of Matt. What was he doing? Why was he obsessed with Austria?

If he had wanted to go back to his past, she worried as she sat at a stylish café on the Isle de la Cité, surely he would have gone to Switzerland.

Matt had gone straight back to the village spending the week on his own as he had the year before, not talking to anyone, just listening in the bars. He heard nothing of the man called Max. With only two days left he had risked talking to a group of local men in badly pronounced, stilted German. He asked about a man, Max, he had met the previous year.

"We know no one of that name."

"If we did we have not seen him for many years."

"Perhaps he is dead."

Matt realised that these summer trips to the village were never going to be a certain way of finding Max.

To have any chance of doing that, and of getting his hands on any money, he would have to go to England, to Liverpool.

How different so many lives would have been if, when Matt had been leaving the hotel the previous year, he had not noticed a small mistake on the bill. He had questioned it and, failing to get the apology he felt appropriate, had lost his temper with the manager. Being rude and overbearing, he had using language that showed him not to be American.

The manager had immediately written to Max.

'I must warn you, Maximilian my old friend, that a man who pretends not to understand our language has visited the village searching for you. I am very afraid that it is that bastard Mattieu risen from the dead. Do not come next year at your usual time for he will undoubtedly be here waiting for you. Be assured we, your friends, will tell him nothing.'

When he met his wife's train in Innsbruck, Matt was smiling. It seemed to Mary as if a great weight had lifted from his mind. He was relaxed and thoughtful, almost as he had been when she first met him.

And he spoke German.

"Have you been studying the language on the quiet all year?"

"I thought I might as well."

"And you never told me."

"Why would I?"

"You're so fluent." Mary said admiringly as he held conversations with people in the bar, making jokes and telling stories, much as he did at the club at home.

But again he told her nothing of what he had been doing.

Her mood was very different from the previous year when the aircraft's no-smoking lights went out, seat belts were unbuckled and the sparkling wine was handed round.

"Are we coming back next year?"

"Would you like to?"

"I'm getting quite used to Europe in the summer."

They talked about Holly, they ate their plastic meals and Mary watched the uncontroversial film with a sense of well-being she had not experienced for years. They slept and read the hours away as they crossed the Atlantic.

It was as they were making their approach into Boston that Matt asked her, quite casually "How about going to live there?"

"Where?"

"England."

She couldn't find the words to say what a stupid idea it was before he continued. "Any of their universities would love to have you, it would broaden Holly's mind, be good for her education. We could all go over to live there for a year or so, see how it goes."

Still she couldn't think what to say as their fast descent meant that her ears popped and she could hear nothing but the engines. She dug her nails into the palms of her hands, trying to think of the answer to what should have been a very simple question.

Why?

Chapter Three

On their first morning in Liverpool, while Holly was allowed to explore the city on her own, Matt and Mary carefully went through the list of properties that the university had supplied. They only had a few days in which to find somewhere to live and Matt was very particular. He bought a map of the city and the surrounding area and had the concierge tell him which were the better areas. 'Where would, say, a well-off businessman live?' Any properties outside that area Matt rejected out of hand. He soon reduced the list to two possible properties, one in Formby, to the north of the city and the other across the river Mersey on the Wirral.

After a heated discussion with Holly 'we're going by train, you can do the *ferry 'cross the Mersey* some other time', that afternoon they headed for West Kirby. The man who checked their tickets told them that their stop was the end of the line so they could enjoy the journey without worrying every time the train pulled up at a station, which seemed to be quite often. Mary and Holly spent the short journey enjoying the view, nudging each other and joking together about the rows of houses, the narrowness of the roads and the smell of the chocolate factory.

As they walked through the small red brick station out into the sunshine of West Kirby Mary felt a little less worried about their move, maybe it wouldn't be so bad after all.

They would have to walk to the house, Matt said, but it wouldn't take long and it would give them the opportunity to see the town that might be their home. Map in hand, Matt headed in the direction of the promenade.

"I like this town. I don't want to live in the city and the sea will be good for Holly. There'll be a yacht club won't there?"

"I should think so. Do you like the look of it?"

"It seems OK. There seems to be a lot going on. Let's wait until we've seen the house."

"Ice cream!" Holly ran on ahead, heading for a shop well-signed with a number of hand written blackboards.

Matt was uncharacteristically willing to listen to the wishes of his wife. It had not been difficult for him to steer Mary towards applying to Liverpool University with its important department of Computing but now they were here, he wanted her to be happy so she wouldn't worry too much about why he had brought them to England.

And what he would be doing with his time.

They caught up with Holly outside the ice cream shop.

"Dandelion and what?" exclaimed Holly "What is that! Dandelion popsickles!"

"I'm sure they're not actually made of weeds." Mary couldn't believe that, even in England, that would be allowed.

"Do you want one?"

"They're really nice you know." A rather chubby girl of around Holly's age, wearing shorts and a red t-shirt that clashed violently with her almost orange hair, confidently entered into their discussion. "And it is made of weeds; real dandelions and burdock leaves, but it tastes really nice. I'm Linda, Linda Forster. Terrible name isn't it? What's yours?"

"Butt out!" Holly reacted to the friendly approach as she would in the States.

"Holly, I'm sure she's only trying to be friendly." Mary admonished her daughter gently.

"Why would she want to be friendly?"

"Because I'm not American!" Linda answered acidly "I just thought you seemed a bit lost and I was only trying to help. I'll leave you to it if you want." Linda Forster took a long lick of her green lolly ice and turned to leave them.

"I'm sorry, my daughter doesn't mean to be rude. She's just not used to strangers talking to her. You understand?"

"That's OK. I suppose it's different in America. I've always wanted to go there. Your name's Holly? What's that short for? I'm always 'Linda' though it's short for Rosalind. No one's called me Rosalind for years."

Holly was allowing herself to be won over.

"I'm Holly Eccleston. Holly isn't short for anything. I was born on Christmas Day and Mom wanted my name to something to do with the holidays. Can I try one Mom?"

"That's horrible, being born on Christmas Day I mean, you'll get only one present." Without waiting for approval Linda led Holly through the shop door.

"What colour do you want?"

"Don't you do flavours?"

"OK" Linda started to list the options. "Orange, lemon, lime, blackcurrant, cream soda..."

"What's that?"

"No idea, but it's bright green, that's the one I've got."

14

"No I'll have the dandelion." She added a hasty 'please' as the old lady behind the counter raised an enquiring eyebrow.

"You'll need sixpence, that's half a shilling, a fifth of half-a-crown, two threepences, a twelfth of ten bob or one twenty-fourth of a pound. A bob is a shilling a quid is a pound,"

"You're just trying to mess me up!" Holly tried to concentrate. She knew that if she were back at home and Linda was the visitor she would do just the same. She took a handful of English money out of her pocket. She looked at them mystified. "Six pennies?" Holly felt overwhelmed by this strange girl who seemed so confident. She wasn't used to being teased.

"Here, this one," Linda picked out a strange shaped coin "that's a threepenny bit, and these, they're pennies." She picked three of the largest "That's sixpence altogether. Don't worry, we're changing our money soon anyway so sixpence will be two and a half pence and instead of twelve shillings to the pound there'll be 100 pence."

"What'll happen to shillings?" Holly wanted Linda to realise she had been keeping up.

"They won't exist any more."

Holly decided she liked Linda, she just wasn't used to people she didn't know talking to her like this. "At least the new money seems sensible, the same as 100 cents to a dollar, that'll be easy."

"You'll be able to teach me then."

They were laughing together licking the lolly ices as they came out of the shop, already knowing they were friends.

"It's delicious!" Holly was licking long sweeps of the dark browny purple ice. She knew she should act with more sophistication, she was nearly 18, but Linda was so relaxed, so natural and friendly she couldn't be standoffish.

"Aren't there any normal ices?" Mary was laughing looking at Holly's brown ice and Linda's green one. "No orange or lemon or chocolate ice cream?"

"There's everything in there."

Mary walked into the tiny shop and looked around at the shelves lining every wall, all were occupied by jars filled with sweets of every size and colour imaginable. Along the bottom shelf were glass bottles of pop of every colour from clear to dark brown, and bright green. This was the England she had imagined, she felt as if she had stepped back to her childhood. She was grinning broadly as she gave Matt his choc-ice and bit into hers. "Wow! That's good." Then, looking around her, "Where's Holly?"

She was heading down towards the beach, Linda's red head clearly visible in the crowd.

15

"They seem happy!"

"So do you."

"This town feels right doesn't it?"

"Yeah. Funny how a visit to a candy store changes everything."

"A 'sweet shop' not a 'candy store'. We must start to learn the language."

They turned to follow their daughter towards the sea. "Let's hope the house is as nice."

An hour later they weren't so happy.

"It's so small, Matt, we couldn't all fit in that. It only has two bedrooms, and no den and you couldn't get a table in that kitchen, and there was no shower, no place even to put one in."

Linda had attached herself to them as their guide, waiting outside as they were shown around the house. When they came out, disappointed and deflated, she led them back to the beach where she made it her business to explain everything, pointing to all the landmarks and describing all the places they could see along the coast and across the river.

"That's Wales over there. It's a whole different country with its own language and everything. Those islands are called Hilbre and the tide comes in *very* quickly and it's *really* dangerous. *Loads* of people are drowned every year. A man was drowned yesterday though not going to the islands. He nearly drowned his *children* but they were saved. It's in all the papers. But if you're *really* careful and don't do anything completely stupid it's safe to walk over to the islands." She spoke quickly and dramatically, keeping Holly enthralled as Matt and Mary talked.

"I love the town, and it'd be wonderful having the sea so close but I couldn't live in that house."

"There aren't any others in West Kirby on the faculty list."

"I'll get a paper and look in the ads. We don't have to go through the university. Stay here with Holly and I won't be a while." Matt left them, dusting the sand off his trousers.

"What's the problem?" Linda was concerned, suddenly seeming a lot older than she had all afternoon.

"We're here to find somewhere to live not just laze around in the sun on the beach."

"And you've got to be in West Kirby. We've just got to know each other. I'll help."

Mary had a quick feeling of gratefulness to the God who had introduced them to Linda. She just knew she would be a good friend for Holly.

When Matt returned with the papers they each took a page and sat circling houses, referring to Linda to find out where they were.

She rejected most 'Up on the hill; fantastic views but its miles from the station', 'grotty road', 'backs onto the railway line'. But when Mary read out one address she shrieked "Yeah! That backs onto our road. Perfect!"

"How far is it? From here I mean. We could go and see the outside. Matt! Wake up! We're off to see a house."

But Matt hadn't been looking at properties in the paper. He had seen a photograph on the front page and was engrossed in the story that went with it.

"Matt! Come on!"

He folded up his page of the newspaper and put it in his pocket. It was all falling into place quite nicely.

"I'm right behind you."

"Linda you are a genius. This is lovely." The road was quiet, tree lined, with red brick detached houses, all slightly different from each other, with drives and garages, the front gardens with their striped patches of grass separated from each other by carefully trimmed hedges. Perfectly English.

They went up to the door and rang the bell.

The woman who answered had not been expecting viewers but, when they explained their circumstances, she said she didn't mind, they should have a look round, get the feel for the place. She made a pot of tea trying not to be too hopeful that at last she had found someone to take over the house.

An hour later they were all gathered around the table in the kitchen with their second mug of tea as they finalised arrangements. They had the house for a year, with the possibility of extending for longer. "I'm going to live with my sister in Spain but I don't want to sell up until I know that I won't ever came back." She explained. "I hoped a happy family would live here. We had four children here and it was a happy house until they all grew up and left and then my husband died. I'll enjoy knowing that it's alive again."

By the time they left 'Number 16' an hour later they had agreed to talk to the agent immediately so that they could move in the following week.

As they travelled back to Liverpool the three members of the Eccleston family each had different thoughts about the successes of the day.

Mary thought about the house, looking forward to making it their home and spending time in the yard that had been rather left to grow wild. She loved the English idea of grass lawns and beds of flowers but she wondered whether she would have a real chance to get it into shape, if she was only going to be there for a year.

Holly wondered at how easily she had made a friend. She had never known anyone like Linda before, she was a child and an adult at the same time. All her friends back home gave up anything remotely childlike at the age of 11. Linda didn't seem to mind that she acted five years old one minute and 20 the next. Holly hoped Linda would help her learn about living in England and that they would be friends for a long time.

Matt thought about the picture in the newspaper.

He had known the moment he saw the photograph. He hardly had to read the article to know, but he had. Words had sprung at him from the page, *rich, mysterious, foreigner, lawyer.*

He had found Max.

Chapter Four

The week after the Ecclestons moved into their new home Carl Witherby was sitting in the garden that backed onto Number 16 quietly talking to Linda's parents. Pat, her mother, had wanted to ask Carl about important subjects like what had really happened when his sister Susannah's husband had drowned. The story still occupied many column inches of the local newspapers with innuendo and gossip but very little in the way of real information. She wanted to know if he had seen Susannah, or their brother Charles, but the young man only chatted inconsequentially with her husband Jeff about the cricket and when, if ever, the Open Golf would return to Hoylake.

She was wondering at men's ability to talk about nothing for hours, with such important things left unspoken, when they were rudely interrupted.

"Carl!" Linda yelled as she ran up the lawn. By the time she had reached him he was standing so he could catch her in his arms and swing her around as if she were a little girl. That was how he still saw her. Linda was the baby of the family, she couldn't possibly be 17 years old.

"Hello Afterthought!" He put her down and hugged her in a brotherly fashion. She hated it when he used the nickname she had been given by her brothers just because they were so much older than she was.

Linda kept her arms round Carl's chest and refused to let him go. "You never said you were coming!"

"I didn't know."

"Come on you, help me with this lot." Pat was bringing out plates of scones, chocolate cakes, freshly baked bread and jugs of home made lemonade "I've made a proper tea. Where's Holly?"

"She went straight home. To freshen up." Linda realised how dishevelled she looked and ran her fingers through her hair to try to straighten the mess that resulted from a day on the beach.

"You look just like Linda should." Carl had always been aware of her adoration, he had dealt with it by ignoring it and treating her exactly as her brothers did. They had never made any allowances for her being a girl, a situation she had encouraged until she was 15. Then she had decided she wanted Carl to look at her as a young woman.

19

There was nothing she could do about her appearance now, it would be too obvious if she went upstairs to change into a skirt and the blouse that was just a little too tight for her. It wasn't fair thàt Holly would soon appear fresh, clean and tidy.

It was worse than she could have imagined when Holly came through the gap in the hedge at the bottom of the garden. She had showered and her blonde hair was brushed straight and shiny, her white t-shirt emphasising her tan and her cut-off jeans showing off her long brown legs to their best advantage. Linda ran down the garden slope to intercept Holly.

"Who's that hunk?" Holly whispered.

"Hands off. He's mine. At least he will be when he realises I'm not a kid any more."

"It's the famous Carl."

One of the first things the girls had done to cement their friendship was tell each other the most important secret of their lives. It had been Holly's idea, she said it was the equivalent of pricking their fingers and mingling their blood; it would make them blood sisters. Linda thought it rather an odd American idea but went along with it anyway.

Holly told Linda that her parents hated each other, she knew they only stayed together because of her and she felt so guilty about it. "They argue all the time, Dad's so *horrible* to Mom and I know she would have left him if she hadn't had me. If I hadn't been born Mom would have left him and have been happy. It was all my fault that she's so unhappy. They think I don't know they argue, they think I don't see him making her cry. They think they're so clever keeping it all from me. They must think I'm completely stupid."

Linda had no idea how Holly felt. Her own parents were happy, had always been happy, so had she and, as far as she knew, so had her twin brothers Crispin and Oliver. She couldn't imagine what it was like to have parents who didn't like each other and could think of nothing to say that would comfort Holly.

The hostage to fortune Linda gave in return was how she felt about Carl.

"He's so *beautiful.* I loved him the moment I first saw him. He's so *tragic.* His father drowned when he was walking over to Hilbre but he'd done the walk so often for years everyone reckoned he'd killed himself. Then a couple of months later, that was all, a couple of months, his Mother went to live with this dreadful divorced man who was her lover and they got married. Carl fell in love with his step-sister, that's Susannah. I've seen her, she's OK but why he fell for her I can't imagine. Anyway there was this terrible row when his stepfather told him that he was, actually, his real, biological, natural father so Susannah was his sister! He was so angry that they'd lied to him all those years and never ever told him the truth that he left and came to live with us. He was in Crisp and Olly's class at school. They didn't know him very well and had no idea why he had chosen us, but he did, and for that I'll be *eternally* grateful. He's sort of lived with us on and off ever since. You know that story the papers are full of? That's Susannah's husband. Everyone says he was trying to rape the nanny and then kill the children. But Carl hasn't had anything to do with them for years."

Holly had listened enthralled as Linda talked about Carl as if he was the most wonderful person in the world.

"Wow. When do I meet him?"

Linda wasn't going to say that, if she had her way, Holly, tall slim Holly, with the blonde hair and the brown legs; clever, pretty, American Holly would never, ever, meet Carl.

Holly stared at the young man sitting cross-legged on the ground, contentedly leaning against a chair. His hands were clasped behind his neck, his long dark hair tied behind his head in a rather old-fashioned, 1960s sort of way. He was totally at ease, laughing at something Pat had said and his teeth shone white against the brown face.

"Wow!" she whispered to Linda as they walked up the garden "He's gorgeous. You don't see teeth like that too often over here!"

"For Christ's sake stop saying Wow." Linda knew she was going to get very irritated with Holly.

"And who's this?"

"I'm Holly. Hi."

"Ah the American. I've heard all about you and how you and your family were kidnapped. How are you all settling in?"

Through the long afternoon as they talked Holly was transfixed, she could not take her eyes off him, yet he was relaxed and friendly, treating her as he did Linda, as a young sister.

Carl soon realised he recognised Holly.

"In another life? In my dreams?" she suggested when he mentioned having seen her somewhere and wondering where it might have been.

"Now I remember. You were in the Adelphi a fortnight ago. We bumped into you in the foyer."

"You were those guys!"

"I know what you mean. Yes, I was with my brother, Charles, and we rushed passed you and your family. We did apologise didn't we?"

"You were very polite, my Mom was real impressed!" Holly couldn't help noticing that Linda seemed annoyed that Carl had remembered her from two weeks earlier.

"You and Charles?" Linda asked, happy to be able to put one over Holly by knowing more than she did about his family.

"Who's Charles?" Holly wasn't going to let Linda hijack the conversation by talking about people she didn't know.

Carl answered Holly's question simply. Now was not the time for complex explanations about his family tree. "Charles Donaldson, he's my brother, well half-brother really." He turned back to Linda "We met in Liverpool, a complete accident. We didn't recognise each other at first."

"That would make him Susannah's brother as well?" Holly interrupted, ignoring Linda's frantic warning pinch.

"Half brother." He corrected her in a voice that stopped her from asking any more questions far more effectively than Linda could. She changed the subject. "Do you live round here?" She asked the question determined to hold his attention though she already knew the answer.

"Oxford, though I'm moving to Cambridge soon."

"Fed up with Olly and Crisp always bumming off you?" Again Linda was pleased to exclude Holly from the conversation by talking about people she did not know. Holly, however, was not about to let Carl go.

"What do you do there? You're too old to be a student."

"I lecture."

"Wow! I'm impressed!" What do you lecture in?"

"History."

"Wow! I'm going to do History. It's one of the courses that I've covered a lot of back home."

Linda wished Holly would stop saying 'Wow' all the time but she was happy as it seemed to be annoying Carl as well.

Carl had managed to deal with the crush he knew Linda had had on him for years, but this pushy American friend of hers was not so easy to ignore. He turned to Pat. "I'd better go now. I'll call. Thanks for tea, smashing as usual!" And he was gone.

"Wow!"

"Oh shut up!"

It was the first time a bad word had been spoken between them. And it had to be over Carl.

Through the summer they spent most of the time together listening to records, trying on each other's clothes, talking about their lives, their hopes, their fears and making a bond between them that would not be broken for years.

When the school year began they found themselves, thanks to some string pulling by Jeff, in the same class for their final year before A levels and university.

Linda was enthusiastic. "It'll be great, I've only been at this school a year, we've been living in London for years and everyone already had their friends when I came. Pick my subjects and it'll be a doddle."

Holly helped Linda as much as Linda helped Holly, the competition between them generally genuinely friendly.

They spent the year working together, sharing each other's clothes, reading the same books, watching the same films. They found they were alike in so many ways but Pat and Jeff saw the differences. Whether it was because of the life she had led or traits inherited from her parents, Holly was more independent, harder and more self-contained than Linda.

"That girl's not happy." Pat had said one evening as she and Jeff watched Holly walk back down the garden to her home. "She puts a brave face on it but she's lonely and she's frightened. If she and Linda hadn't made friends I hate to think what would have happened to her."

Through the year they discovered there were things they didn't like about each other. Holly thought Linda could sometimes be rather bossy, determined that her approach to something was always the best way and Linda grew to be aware of Holly's black moods. There were times when Holly seemed to act as though they didn't know each other at all.

In the long hours they discovered that, although they disagreed on topics ranging from the merits of the current top of the hit parade to whether American television was better than English, they agreed on more important things like the war in Vietnam, religion and sex.

"Have you? You know. Have you ever?" Linda hadn't necessarily expected an answer, she wasn't sure she would have answered honestly if Holly had asked her the same question.

"Yeah. Once. At camp before we came here. It wasn't great really. We'd all been drinking and this guy, I don't think I ever knew his name, Scott or Snot or something like that."

"What was it like?"

"Well, it was hot and he was all clammy, his stomach stuck to mine and it hurt when he moved, like someone pinching me."

"No, silly, what did it feel like?"

"I guess I wasn't really ready, it hurt for a bit and then it just felt like, I can't think how to describe it, like it should have felt nicer."

"Not so great then?"

"Don't know what all the fuss is about."

Through the year it became obvious that if they were going to continue to be friends they must keep off the subject of Carl. Linda thought she had ownership rights on him and she didn't like the way Holly was getting to know so much about him. Whenever he came up in conversation, which had been quite often in the early days, they argued, Linda always warning Holly not to venture into her territory 'I like you Holly but keep your claws out of Carl', with Holly responding that Linda didn't own Carl. 'I like you too Linda, but if push comes to shove I'll probably do what I want'.

Usually, after several minutes of silence, they would get back to work.

The day before they were to find out the results of their A level exams Linda was sitting on the grass in the back garden, leaning against the white wicker chair. Her eyes were screwed up against the bright sunlight as she tried to read to take her mind off what was going to happen the next day. Tomorrow. Results day. Tomorrow she would find out whether all her years of education had been worth it, especially this last year when she and Holly had worked so hard. She had escaped into the garden as the house was full. Crispin and Oliver, had come back home from Oxford 'to celebrate' they said. She'd asked them what they'd do if she didn't get the right grades and they'd laughed, saying success was a certainty. They'd put money on it.

But what if she didn't? What would she do if she didn't get the grades for her first choice university?

'What do you want to do Sociology for?' they had asked her with the teasing tone they reserved for their young sister 'It's not a proper subject.'

They hadn't listened to her argument that she had to find a subject she liked the sound of that no one else in the family had already done. It was difficult being the last and least academic in a clever family. 'It would be so awful to compete with you all. I don't want to do that. I want to do something new, something that's mine, learn things that I can tell you all that you didn't already know.' She thought she had persuaded them, but it was a popular course and she needed good grades to get in. She wouldn't be able to bear it if she failed and she had to go somewhere else to do something normal; or worse, if Holly got the grades and she didn't.

She wanted them both to do well so they could do the same course and share the adventure of being away from home.

Linda's thoughts were rudely interrupted. "Hi. You reading?"

"Hi Holly. Not really. Worrying about tomorrow, grades, the rest of my life. You know, silly things like that."

"What time are we supposed to be in school?"

"9."

"It'll all be over by 10."

"We'll have said goodbye to everyone, found out whether the last 14 years have done their job. Know what we'll be doing for the next 40."

"An important day. What are you going to wear?"

"Nice to know you've got your priorities right."

"Yeah right! At home everyone dresses up for the last day at school. We hire stretch limos, escorts, you know, make a real thing of our last day before College. Lets do that. Go formal. Everyone else'll be in jeans. Let's be different."

"Posh frocks! Brilliant!"

"How'll we get there?"

"Olly and Crisp'll be chauffeurs, they're up for the celebration party they think will be inevitable. They won't mind and matching red sports cars would be so neat."

"Wow! No one will forget us!"

The day that Holly Eccleston and Linda Forster arrived for their A level results in off the shoulder evening dresses, made up to the nines and escorted by two good looking young men with red sports cars became something of a legend in the school.

It even made the papers. The local newspaper had sent a reporter to capture the happy smiles of successful pretty pupils and the tears of the less attractive ones. The editor was very happy with the photographs of Holly and Linda.

They loved the headline when they saw it. '*Star Pupils*'. They each bought several copies of the paper, cutting out the photographs and sending them to everyone they thought might be interested.

"2 As and a B. I can't believe it. All that work was worth it!" Linda had done as well as she had hoped.

"3 Bs I can't believe it either."

"Brilliant!" Oliver and Crispin hugged and kissed them both and any other girl they came across.

After a few minutes they had said their thanks to their teachers and their goodbyes to their schooldays.

Crispin handed Holly into the front seat of his car and sprinted round to settle into the driving seat. "I can drive a little faster now it doesn't matter if your hair gets all messed up."

Holly smiled, took the pins out shook her hair out, "That's better, can we get some air into it?"

Crispin took that as the OK to drive the long way home. He turned out of the school gates and headed towards the sea front, three miles of road that would have little traffic on it at this time of day. He put his foot down and they sped down the promenade. He pulled over to turn around at the end of the road where the concrete gave way to sand. Putting his arm on the back of the seat to help him reverse he touched Holly's bare shoulder.

The tide was in, the sun was out and the moment demanded that he kissed her.

He only pulled away from her when he heard the stern voice of a uniformed nanny telling off the giggling young boys in her charge.

"Sorry." He was embarrassed. "I shouldn't have done that."

"Why not? It was nice, you're a great kisser and no harm done." Holly leaned back against the leather seat "Nice as that was we'd better get back. They'll be wondering where we've got to."

It didn't seem to matter one way or another to Holly whether he ever kissed her again. But it did to Crispin.

From that moment it mattered a great deal.

The champagne was flowing and the celebration party was in full swing when they returned.

"Somehow with it all depending on exams it seems so special." Mary spoke proudly to Pat and Jeff. "Back home you know before you take the final tests what grades you'll get, it's all done on course assessments. I don't know how you've stood the tension of going through this with three children."

"Four if you include Carl. I trust them to do as well as they can, and if they are disappointed we always know they've done their best."

"Lovely philosophy but likely only to work when you know your kids are real clever."

"Come on you two, fill up your glasses and congratulate these two geniuses." Oliver and Crispin were doing the rounds with the bottles.

"Is this a private party or can anyone join in?" A voice from the French windows interrupted them.

"Carl! Magic!" Linda ran over, all thoughts of elegance gone as she flung her arms round Carl's neck.

"I wasn't going to miss the celebrations was I? You look good enough to eat! And you too Holly."

There followed what they always remembered as one of the best parties ever. 'You can have whatever music you want and as loud as you like' had been Jeff's rash promise, one he regretted for four hours.

Matt and Mary's reward for Holly, that she could spend two weeks with Linda and her brothers in Oxford, had rather longer reaching consequences.

After the party the Ecclestons sat around the kitchen table at number

26

16, Holly had come home to replace her long evening dress with jeans ready to go out for the evening with Linda and the boys but Mary had stopped her rushing out of the door, telling her to sit down at the kitchen table where her father was waiting, his hands firmly wrapped around a mug of coffee.

"Why have neither of you asked me about it?" Mary asked her husband and daughter. "What is wrong with you both? You're so tied up in your own worlds you don't think do you? I can understand you, Holly, you've had all that work to do and all your exams but Matt, what have you been doing? What have you been so wrapped up in that you haven't even thought to ask me?"

Matt and Holly sat looking at Mary wondering what she was talking about.

"My contract. It was for a year. You're making all these plans. You haven't once asked what's happening? You've left it all up to me, like you always have, like you always do."

Matt said nothing. He didn't rise to the bait. He let Holly answer her Mother.

"But..." Holly couldn't find the words to describe her sense of panic. "I don't want to go back! I won't know what to do. I've got a place at University here. I *can't* go back!"

Matt had time to think and had decided that an argument was the best way to divert attention from either of them asking what he had actually been doing in the year they had been in England. "I told you months ago to go for an extension, don't blame me if you didn't get it."

He nearly managed to disguise how important it was to him that they stayed, but Mary knew him too well. "Why do you want to stay so badly?" She closed her eyes, pursed her lips and gently shook her head, a signal that Holly knew meant they were going to argue and she should leave.

"Well I don't care what you two do I'm staying here. I'll live with Linda, at least her bloody parents talk to each other without always bloody arguing!" She stormed out of the kitchen.

Matt had had time to recover himself "Holly needs some stability, you've messed up her education once it wouldn't be fair to do that again."

Mary did not point out the obvious fact that it was Matt who had engineered the move the previous year. "I'm asking why *you* want to stay so much." She wanted the real reason, but somehow knew she wasn't going to get it.

"I like it here." He knew it sounded a very limp and unconvincing answer. "I like the people and I like the place. I like that Holly's happy. I like that you're happy and not so tired when you get back from work."

"Well it's lucky I got offered the extension then isn't it. But you'll have to find a job. I don't earn as much here as in the States, we're nearly through our savings. I don't know what you've been doing all this time, you certainly haven't been earning anything."

The argument that followed was a familiar one.

Mary would explain why they needed more money than she earned; Matt would go on the defensive explaining how he had tried to get jobs, it wasn't his fault he hadn't, what did she want him to do? Clean the streets? Be a garbage collector? There never was an answer.

Certainly he never gave one.

"I'm going to the pub. At least I have friends there, blokes I can talk to, have a laugh with. No chance of a laugh here."

Matt had spent a lot of time in the pub through the year.

He had started by sitting at a table in a corner watching people, just as he had in the hotel bars in Austria a couple of years before. After a few weeks he had realised that if he got to the pub at opening time, when he was the only customer, he could talk to Glenda the barmaid.

She told him a lot about the people in the town and, thanks to the continuing gossip in the newspapers about the attempted rape and drowning, it was quite natural that they would talk about the household at Sandhey.

It was Glenda who first introduced him to a young man who also seemed interested in Max Fischer and the Donaldsons.

They soon found they had a great deal in common.

Chapter Five

The twins had been given instructions by Pat and Jeff to use those two weeks in Oxford in the summer of 1971 to show Linda and Holly something of what their lives as students would be like. They took this to mean that their job was to get them used to spending most of their time in pubs.

"Funny how Americans don't know how to act in pubs." Oliver began to explain a game he and Crispin played. Spot All the Things Americans Do Wrong in Pubs.

"SATA DWIP we call it."

"They ask for a pint of *your finest ale.*"

"They sit down at a table and expect to be served."

"They call the spotty youth behind the bar *Landlord.*"

"They want ice in their whisky."

"They expect a tab and get shirty when asked to pay for each round as they buy it."

"Hang on," Holly tried to speak up for her fellow countrymen "I don't do any of those things."

"But you're not really American any more." It was meant as a compliment.

"It's a pity you're not coming up to Oxford, all this local knowledge will be wasted." Crispin commented as they left the ninth pub in their first night's tour of the city.

"Leicester's not that far away. You'll come to visit won't you?"

Holly and Linda had chosen Leicester University because it wasn't Oxford or Cambridge but it was easy enough to get to both. The course was incidental. Pat and Jeff couldn't argue with Linda's reasoning 'You all do serious stuff, even Olly and Crisp did a proper degree, but they don't use it do they? What's bio-chemistry got to do with car mechanics? I don't want to teach so I might as well just get a degree in anything. Bee-keeping wasn't on offer so this'll be great'.

Crispin made sure he was always alongside Holly, always being careful to walk on the outside of the pavement whilst keeping up a running commentary about the buildings they passed in the short distances between the many pubs they visited on that first night.

Linda was having such a good time she didn't notice. But Oliver did.

As they moved from pub to pub they collected friends and acquaintances but Crispin still stuck to Holly. At closing time a large group went back to the twins' flat and the rest of the night was spent talking and drinking coffee.

"Is it always like this?" Holly asked Crispin as they stood in the kitchen waiting for the kettle to boil as it was beginning to get light.

"Like what?" He leant over and lazily flicked some of her hair out of her eyes.

"You know. Booze and talk and no-one getting any sleep."

"Well we've solved all the world's problems haven't we?"

" I do think Gerry's ideas about Russia are a bit far-fetched. I mean .."

"I don't think you were supposed to take him seriously."

"I suppose not. He seemed very upset about people playing cricket in pyjamas with a white ball so I don't suppose you can take too much about what he says seriously!"

"But that is serious! That is the end of life as we know it!"

He intercepted her hand as it aimed a mock punch in his direction and, holding onto it, pulled her towards him and kissed her.

She hadn't thought of Crispin in that way at all. The kiss as he had been turning the car around on the promenade had been a one-off, it had just seemed the right thing to do at the time. This second kiss was different. She let herself enjoy it. Perhaps it was the way he gently held the back of her neck with his hand, and the way his head had to bend down for their lips to meet, but her overwhelming feeling wasn't of desire it was of being looked after, being safe and secure.

She was just relaxing into him when he was pulled away.

Oliver had been increasingly worried through the evening about his brother's attention to Holly, he had been watching them, trying to make sure they had no chance to be alone. He told Linda so they could both keep an eye on them. Neither thought it would be a good idea for them to get together, even though Linda thought that it would mean Holly wouldn't pursue Carl. When she had seen Crispin follow Holly out to the kitchen, she had nudged Oliver to intervene. Just in case.

"Now now now! None of that! Holly's off limits Crisp. Don't take advantage, we're supposed to be looking after her."

"I was."

"It's OK!" Holly laughed it off "We weren't doing anything, just a bit of fun."

But it hadn't been just a bit of fun for Crispin.

The next afternoon the four sat around reading the Sunday newspapers, Linda and Holly nursing unfamiliar hangovers. Any bad feeling between Crispin and his brother had disappeared as they whispered together before Crispin laughed and disappeared. They heard the front door slam and then a short time later open and slam again.

Crispin appeared in the room with six tins of Baked Beans.

"This is a scientific survey," Oliver explained "we're going to count the beans in each tin, measure them and identify which gives the best value." He looked down at the sceptical faces. "No. Seriously. It's a proper experiment!" Linda didn't seem too enthusiastic but Holly joined in with the spirit of the game. "Come on you two, get Gerry and Steve from downstairs and we'll do a tin each."

"They'll be watching the box like any sensible person on a wet Sunday afternoon."

"Who said they were sensible?"

"I'll get them." Linda wasn't too reluctant to go downstairs, she quite fancied Gerry.

What started out as an organised attempt to grade the various makes of baked beans quickly descended into a bean fight. "He started it!" cried Holly as she flicked beans in the direction of Crispin with the fork she had been using to carefully separate out individual beans.

Linda took advantage of the mayhem to pour some of her tin down Gerry's back and then thoroughly enjoyed his attempts to reciprocate.

Oliver and Steve sat back watching as beans went everywhere "It's a good thing she's off with Crisp not you isn't it?"

"Why's that?"

"Well if she was yours it'd be Olly and Holly!"

Steve's self-congratulatory laughter was silenced by Oliver's scowl. "They're not off with each other."

"It bloody well looks like it to me."

Oliver had to admit Steve had a point as he watched Holly trying to lick beans and tomato sauce off his brother's face as he tried to clean hers.

"Leave her alone Crisp." His brother warned him later that evening. "She's Linda's best friend. It won't work. I thought you realised that last night."

"Too close to home you mean?"

"Something like that."

"I do fancy her though."

"If you really like her you'll leave her alone. Give her some years when she hasn't got a heavy relationship. Let her have fun, but not with you, you're too involved. You don't just fancy her do you? You really fancy her. You hate it when she's with anyone else, you hate it when she ogles Carl, you are beginning to act as if she's yours and you can't. Not when she's got three years at university and she's got to grow up. When she graduates, if you're both still interested, have a go then."

"She'll think I've led her on."

"Do a diversion. What about that girl in the pub last week?"

"Liz?"

"Yeah. Spend time with her, Crisp, she's more your age anyway."

"I thought he fancied me." A week later Holly and Linda were sitting on the pavement outside the pub watching the tourists and the traffic. "He's avoiding me. He spends all his time with that tart Liz."

"Don't ask me. I'm not my brother's keeper. He can get off with anyone he likes."

"But not me."

"Not a good idea. I'd hate it if you got off with him, it would be so embarrassing. You don't fancy him do you? I mean he's got freckles and red hair. You couldn't possibly fancy someone like that."

"He's got lovely eyes and what's wrong with freckles? He's nice."

"No he's not. He's my brother. He can't be nice. Not like that."

"He's always been nice to me, all year he's talked to me and asked me how work's going and how I like living in England, and do I miss home. He's always listened to me."

"There're so many gross things I could tell you about him! And Oliver."

"Like what?"

Linda wondered what she could say that would really put Holly off.

"Well they only wear one pair of underpants a week."

"What? Between them?"

"No silly, each."

"What about socks?"

"You're not taking this seriously are you?"

"No, still," Holly continued after a pause, "I'm not making any promises. About any of them."

And Linda knew exactly what she meant.

They sat on the pavement in self-conscious silence for a while, watching the parade of tourists and foreign students who stayed in the city through the summer.

"I wonder what it's like to be pregnant." Holly nudged Linda out of her sulk.

"What makes you say that?"

Holly pointed to a woman who looked as if she was going to explode.

"Oh God! How Gross! She's vast!"

"Shut up, she'll hear you. It must be horrible. Something growing inside you and there's only one way out! It's gross! I'll never get pregnant! It's too yuchy for words!"

"Talking about sex..."

"As we weren't..."

"Well nearly. Anyway, you know when you told me about having sex with Snot."

"Or whatever his name was."

"Well, how did you get into the situation? How'd you get alone with him, you know, how did it start?"

"Why? You thinking of someone in particular?"

"Well I can't go to University a virgin can I?"

"I'm sure one or two people do."

"Well I don't want to so I've got to do something about it this summer. I'm running out of time."

"Got anyone in mind?"

"Hey you guys, want another drink?" Gerry sat down next to Linda and put his arm around her shoulders. "Talking about anything important?"

"Nope." Linda and Holly both giggled. "Nothing important at all."

Chapter Six

"How many do you think will come back?"

"I have no idea, that's the problem with funerals isn't it? It's very good of you to have Alicia's people to stay and then have everyone back here."

"Ted, it's the least Charles and I can do."

"Weddings, birthday parties and now funerals." It seemed odd how many of our family events over the years had been held at Sandhey.

It was early January 1972 and I was sitting with Max and his old friend Ted Mottram. We were seated in comfortable leather armchairs around the fire in Max's study. Ted wore the grey trousers, checked shirt, paisley tie and tweed jacket that were the informal uniform of his generation and his short hair was receding and turning grey at the temples, but it was the way he was slumped in his chair that made him seem more than his 53 years.

I felt out of place even though it was my Mother's funeral we were discussing.

Perhaps I felt like that because I was the only one who had not loved her.

"How's Susannah?" I reluctantly asked Ted about my sister.

"Shocked, Charles, shocked It's set her back again. She was just beginning to recover from..." he hesitated "the events of two years past." I thought that a rather feeble description of her returning home from having an abortion to find her husband attempting to rape Monika and then watching him die while he was trying to drown the children. "She was just beginning to learn that her Mother wasn't the dreadful woman she had thought she was. They were quite close these final months but they argued at the end." I heard him add quietly "*We* argued at the end."

"Susannah must come here." Max spoke firmly, breaking into the embarrassed silence. "It isn't suitable for her to be with you whereas I am old and there is Monika in the house. We will look after her well." Max spoke kindly but Ted seemed hurt, as if Max had been criticising the care he could give. I tried to divert their attention.

"When's my sister finally going to take responsibility for the children?" I argued "She can't expect them to live with that Nanny forever, surely she's got to start facing up to life?"

They ignored my intervention.

"We can discuss her moving here this evening when she comes over for dinner. I'm sure she will agree, she must realise it's inappropriate for her to stay with me and she really doesn't have anywhere else to go."

"Have you heard from Carl?" I asked Ted; whenever Susannah was mentioned in conversation thoughts of Carl were never far away.

"He's back in the south I think. I saw him last month but he doesn't really keep in touch." Ted had more time for my half brother than I did. "He's a very unsettled and unhappy young man in many ways."

"Hardly surprising."

"As you say, hardly surprising."

"To get back to the original question about tomorrow. I can't see that many will be at the church. It's a long time since her life was here. There are the three of us, Susannah and Monika of course and Alicia's mother is travelling up." He looked at his watch and out through the windows at the rain and the mid winter evening already drawing in. "They should be here soon."

"They?"

"Yes she's coming with a grandson, Graham. He'd be your cousin Charles."

A grandmother and a cousin I had never met. I knew my Mother had married against her parents' wishes and had lost contact with her family years ago, perhaps this would be a chance to find out some of details.

"There won't be many then."

"Probably not, though it was in the paper and you never know how many people will come either for old times sake or simply because they're curious. She was a very popular lady in her time, what with Arnold's politicking." I thought that an appropriate dismissal of my father's ambitions.

I answered the doorbell as Monika was busy in the kitchen cooking the formal dinner we were having that evening.

"I'm so sorry we're late." The old lady spoke breathlessly. "We had a bit of trouble getting the car. They wouldn't give us one. They said Graham had been drinking and David was too old. So Maureen had to hire it. It was so lucky we met her on the train otherwise we wouldn't have been able to get here. It all took so long. You must be Charles."

I tried to take in all that she had said and ushered the group into the hall, taking their coats and bags.

"Can we start again?"

We had been expecting my grandmother and a grandson. I was not sure who the old gentleman was, or the other woman who seemed vaguely familiar. My grandmother must have seen the enquiry in my face as she immediately explained, but her explanation begged more questions than it answered.

"This is my husband, David McKennah, my grandson Graham Tyler, and this kind lady is Maureen Shelton. She was not only an old friend of your Mother's but is also related. She is your step-aunt, we have been talking about it on the train. She is Kathleen's sister."

I was still trying to take in all the relationships as, with the detached good manners that had been instilled in me for years, I asked them to make themselves comfortable while I sorted out the additional rooms that would be needed.

I walked across the hall to Max's study where we had been sitting so securely a few minutes earlier unsure how I was going to explain our additional guests.

"Our guests have arrived," I began "but they appear to have multiplied. My grandmother is here, with her grandson who, I should warn you, seems rather drunk. There's also a man who was introduced as her husband and a woman who is apparently not only an old friend of my Mother's but also my step-mother's sister."

"Maureen?" Ted seemed intrigued "I wonder where she sprang from."

Max looked thoughtful but not overly enthusiastic to meet them "Show them to their rooms will you Charles, I will meet our guests at dinner."

Ted, Susannah and I were in the drawing room promptly at seven o'clock.

Maureen was the first to appear. She was elegantly but unostentatiously dressed. I tried to remember what my step-mother had been like and whether there was any similarity between them. I found I could hardly remember her. It had all been a long time ago.

"I am so sorry to land myself on you tonight, it certainly wasn't planned. I was on the train and couldn't help hearing the conversation of the people sitting behind me. They were talking about Alicia. For many years I had been her friend, possibly her only friend until Ted came along." She paused and smiled in Ted's direction. "I wasn't at all sure whether I should make myself known. I mentally tossed a coin; heads I'd talk to them, tails I would stay quiet. As the coin twirled in my mind's eye I wanted it to land 'heads' so I didn't worry about finishing the image, but just leaned round to talk to them." I had heard of this way of deciding which of two courses of action to take before, I was sure Carl had described it to me. I had rather liked the idea. "So they asked me to join them. I'm afraid we spent most of the journey talking about old times and Graham, well, I'm afraid he seems to have spent most of the journey in the buffet car."

My grandmother and her husband joined us and they took up the story talking good-naturedly, finishing each other's sentences in the manner of people who were comfortable with themselves, each other and their surroundings.

"We had been decided before we even got to Crewe that Maureen would share our hire car…"

"… and would direct us here."

"I had been worried about how we would find the house on a dark and wet evening, even though Graham said he knew where the house was."

"He's been studying in Liverpool for nearly three years now."

"It was an arrangement that really suited us all, especially when the hire company wouldn't let Graham drive because he was too drunk…"

"…or me because they said I was too old."

"So Maureen drove by default. The least I could do was offer her hospitality. I realise it was presumptuous of me."

"I hope you don't mind, but she really has been very helpful."

When I heard Max's footsteps on the polished parquet floor I turned to introduce him to our guests but he didn't come in the room immediately, he stood in the doorway for several moments before joining us.

"You must be Edith. How do you do? I am so pleased to meet you despite the occasion."

"Do call me Edie" she replied as David stood up and shook Max's proffered hand. "David McKennah". He had spoken oddly, emphasising his surname. Max glanced at me, it seemed like he was checking whether I had noticed anything. I had, but I had no idea what it was.

Some while later Graham appeared still dressed in the scruffy jeans and sweater he had arrived in. He could easily have changed but it seemed he wanted to be deliberately defiant.

He ignored the others in the room and came to within two feet of me as I poured glasses at the drinks table. "Been looking forward to talking to you, cousin Charles. I've heard a lot about you. I've met queers before but never actually been this close to one, not knowingly anyway. Better not turn my back on you had I?" He laughed as though he felt he was being very clever. I sincerely hoped no one else heard what he was saying to me above the general conversation.

I wasn't sure how to answer and hadn't responded when he continued "How old were you when you came here to live with an old man? 13? 14? That can't be right can it? Not proper at all. And only with your old nanny to keep you apart. Fancy living with your nanny."

I shouldn't have credited his insinuations with an answer but I had to say something. "She's not a nanny any more. She hasn't been for years. She's our housekeeper." I spoke through clenched teeth, trying not to gain anyone's attention.

"Well it's obvious isn't it? Old man, young man, 'housekeeper'. It can't be normal can it?"

"Of course it can!" I was stung into arguing with him when it would have been best to have ignore his rudeness.

"Yeah. Right." I didn't know how to react to Graham's sarcasm.

I had known for years what people thought of my living in Max's house and the nature of our relationship but no one had been so crass as to mention it to my face. I had never thought how I would respond if someone had.

"Yeah." He repeated, laughing as he made a point of sidling away from me to sit down next to Susannah. "Hi coz, at least I'm safe with you."

Ted poured drinks and as I handed them round I was thinking what a strange group we made.

Throughout the meal the atmosphere was subdued. I spent most of the time telling my Grandmother and Maureen about my love of birds and answering their questions on how I had managed to make something of a living by writing and giving talks. They seemed interested to hear about it and let me talk on. Graham behaved himself through the meal, saying little and using approximately the correct cutlery.

Monika normally ate with Max and I, as she was our friend as well as our housekeeper. This evening, though, she didn't join us until after she had served the coffee and Max was walking round the table, his left arm behind his back in almost military fashion, carefully pouring deep yellow wine into the last unused glasses. A lengthy after dinner session was obviously anticipated. As he poured I noticed the year on the bottle. 1934. It must have been one of his most special wines.

It appeared David had noticed as well. "A rare trocken-beerenauslese Max." he said appreciatively. "1934, a difficult year."

Max nodded but said nothing, just returning to his place at the head of the table.

He did not sit down.

"I would like to propose a toast to Alicia. At one time the most beautiful and the most frustrating woman I have ever known."

We all followed Max's lead, even Graham who seemed to be observing us as if we were animals in a zoo. We all stood and raised our glasses somewhat self-consciously as Max effortlessly dictated what we should do and how we should act. "We must now each spend a few moments sharing our memories of her."

Max had once told me that during the war he had refused to accept the custom of ignoring empty places in the mess when someone had failed to return. He believed it was disrespectful and had made a point always of speaking for a few minutes of the missing comrade. 'If a life is not worth five minutes then what's it all for?' he had asked rhetorically. He rarely referred to his life before he had bought the failing law firm in Liverpool and moved to the Wirral in 1941 so I had felt privileged to be given a rare insight into his past.

"You start Charles. Be truthful. She is dead and cannot be hurt."

It took a few minutes for me to think what I could possibly say.

I had heard of my mother's death when Ted had telephoned just a few minutes afterwards. I knew she had been living with Ted but I did not really know why and, although she had only been barely half a mile away across the golf course, I had never visited her.

'Too much history Ted. It would be a waste of time.' I had said when Ted had told me that I should talk to her before it was too late. 'What would we say to each other? What could we say to each other? I've not been part of that family since Max took me and Monika under his wing.'

'She is your mother.'

But I had argued with him. 'She may be, but I don't think she ever thought of me as her son.'

'You're very bitter Charles, but also very lucky that Max has looked after you.'

I had been defiant. 'Yes, I've been very lucky. What I am, who I've turned out to be, is no thanks to her.'

Ted had put the phone down after responding coldly 'I wouldn't say that.'

So I hadn't visited my Mother. And now she was dead.

I looked around the table before I eventually stood up. That seemed to be the right thing to do and I was rewarded by a slight but encouraging nod from David.

I sipped the wine. I was not sure I wanted to share my history with these strangers, especially with Graham. Although I was going to be careful with my words, I felt I owed it to Max to honour the spirit of what he was trying to do.

I cleared my throat and began.

"I hardly knew her. I don't suppose we've spent more than a few hours in each other's company my whole life. When we were little, Susannah and I, we were kept in the nursery, only brought out for a few minutes on display to our parents and their guests, they always seemed to have guests. We had to be clean and tidy and behave ourselves like little adults. I can remember nothing else of the time before she left other than a sand pit and a big teddy bear underneath a large Christmas tree in the hall at Millcourt. Then she went to Switzerland. I was 6 when she left, Susannah was 2. I don't remember her ever saying goodbye and I heard my father say he didn't believe she had gone to Switzerland at all. When she came back from wherever it was she'd really been she didn't live with us so Susannah and I only saw her for odd holidays. Those were always dreadful and we spent as much time as possible out of her company. The one day she did come back to the house I had a long talk with her and quite liked her. But it was partly because of what she did that day that led me to leave and come here."

I glanced at Graham who was smirking as he sat back, lounging casually in his chair. 'Yeah right' he mouthed silently.

"The next time I met her was at Susannah's wedding but that was only for the few minutes she could be bothered to turn up and then briefly last year when I had had no idea she was living half a mile away. That's how close we were. She hadn't told me she had moved from Surrey. Neither had you Ted. So there we have it. I'm 29 years old and I hardly ever saw her. She was my Mother but I hardly knew her."

I heard Graham muttering 'diddums'.

Max waited until I had sat down.

"There's a lot of her in you, you know. You have much of her look. You have a lot of her selfishness and self-centredness. You go your own way, she went hers, they just weren't the same way."

"I didn't know her either, until the last few months." Susannah began speaking very quietly, so quietly that we had to concentrate hard to hear what she had to say. "I had thought she was a bloody selfish cow. I had always thought she left us because she wanted more than us, we weren't enough for her and I thought we should be. I hated her because she left us but I didn't realise until recently that it wasn't us she hated, it was everything. In her head she imagined what her life would have been, what it should have been like if she hadn't had the accident, if she hadn't married Dad, if she hadn't had us. She blamed life for not being what she had wanted it to be. It wasn't our fault she was unhappy, it was hers because she could never accept what life was, she spent her whole life wanting it to be something else."

"Well she really wasn't much of a Mother was she?" I didn't want to hear about another side of her.

"Harsh. But you're probably right. But then she was a bit of a victim herself." Max wanted us to remember a different Alicia. "Don't forget that no one ever comes into anyone else's life with a clean canvass. From the day we are born we have the baggage our parents leave us. God knows you have yours but remember she also had hers. All you can do is try to live down the legacy your parents leave you. You should try to understand her a little."

When Ted spoke we all turned to look at him. He was looking hard at me as he quoted *"Don't hold your parents up to contempt. After all, you are their son, and it is just possible that you may take after them."*

"Evelyn Waugh I think." Max nodded towards Ted. "Very apt."

As we paused for glasses and coffee cups to be refilled I wondered whether my grandmother was at all affronted by Max's words, she didn't appear to be. When everyone had settled down Max began his story, addressing himself to Susannah and myself, ignoring all the others around the table.

"I first met Alicia when she was barely 21, pregnant, frightened, lonely and sincerely regretting marrying your father. She left him as soon as she had a legitimate reason. She was very ill for years, but she survived. She had to keep herself once your father's money dried up, a situation for which she was ill prepared. She had to do many things that she found distasteful and difficult, but she survived. Through these years I met her regularly in London and tried to give her a taste of the luxury she needed."

It had never occurred to me until that moment that my Mother and

Max could have been lovers but that was the clear implication. I couldn't interpret the look on Susannah's face, either she didn't care or had known for a while. Ted looked devastated.

Max continued "She was a most articulate, intelligent and stylish woman. She was also a fighter who battled with that awful disease until she could fight no more. For complicated reasons our relationship changed to friendship some years ago but I continued to visit her and keep her informed about her children. In all those years she never lost her concern for you. For all her strengths she didn't possess the confidence to get back into your lives and would never had had that last chance had it not been for Ted."

If he wanted me to feel guilty he succeeded.

Ted may have wanted to talk of the woman he had loved for 30 years, to explain something of the Alicia he had known but he said nothing. Perhaps he couldn't.

Monika broke the short silence that followed.

"I knew so little of the mother of my Susannah and Charles. I believed for many years she must be evil, or mad, to leave such a wonderful home and such lovely children. I knew her only through the people who had been in her life. Now I realise she was a very lucky woman, from what you have all said, and not said, in some way you all loved her. Not many people can be loved by so many people."

The silence was broken by Graham

"What's the point of all this? It's morbid shit. She's fucking dead isn't she?"

It was David who recovered the quickest speaking with dignity and authority "Funerals are as much about the living as the dead. This is something you may learn in time. It is cathartic for people who have suffered the loss of someone they love to talk about that person, to learn details they didn't know, to try to understand that person as others saw them. You will sit down quietly or you will leave."

"You can't tell me what to do."

"We're not arguing with you Graham, either behave like an adult or leave."

"Before I go do I get my say? You've all indulged yourselves. Well I never met her. I didn't want to. She knew what side her bread was buttered, she saw money and grabbed it. If she had to sleep with someone for two or three years what did that matter? When she left him she would be rich and free. Nothing more than a pro, that's what my Dad says, prostituted herself for money. She left them all soon enough didn't she?"

42

Edie came to her daughter's defence countering her grandson's assumptions with dignity. "We don't know why she did that. We must trust that she did the only thing that was possible for her. We must believe that he gave her no choice."

"When I get married my wife won't dare leave me. I'd bloody well make sure of that. No question. I'd fucking kill her first."

His resentment of everything we stood for was clear as he pushed back his chair and walked unsteadily to the door. He seemed to be doing everything he could to show his contempt for our way of life, our mores and manners, just like a bad tempered child.

I made a mistake that evening. I underestimated my cousin and thought him a fool.

I had no idea at the time how much of a threat he would turn out to be.

Edie broke the silence that followed. "I'm afraid all my sons were brought up with violence. Their father was not an easy man to live with. I tried to soften his aggression, but it was a bitter household and they have passed that violence on to their sons. Perhaps I need to tell you some things about Alicia. Perhaps if I don't tell you now it will be too late."

As we all listened to my grandmother I believed that, for all the years Ted and Max had known my mother, neither had known any of it.

"My first daughter died before she was a week old. The nurse took her away as if she had never existed. But times were different then, it was 1919 and it wasn't only babies that died so a baby's death was not important. There was no mourning, people moved on, they had another." She spoke with resignation.

"Bert knew, of course he did, that that dead baby wasn't his. He had been in France until two months before the birth. So when I fell pregnant again he had his suspicions. He couldn't be absolutely certain but he was pretty sure, especially when Alicia was so artistic, so beautiful, so unlike him. Or me. I wanted to call her Alison but Bert insisted she was christened Alberta. She never liked the name, she never was an 'Alberta'. She was too sensitive, artistic and beautiful to be 'Alberta'. She was too like her father." With barely a pause she continued "I had met David during the war..."

Her meaning was clear.

"I wasn't sent to France. I stayed in London."

"I bumped into him in the street. I was hurrying to get, somewhere, I can't remember where, and I bumped into him. I was carrying a shopping basket and all the contents spilled on the pavement."

"I helped pick them up and took her to tea at the Lyons Corner House."

"And that was it."

"We met as often as we could from then on."

"For about 40 years."

"No one knew."

"After the war I stayed with Bert, away from David, another war came and went before Bert finally died. Then David and I were free to marry. But it was too late for Alicia. She never came to see us. I was never able to explain."

After a few moments she continued, none of us had thought to interrupt.

"Alicia got married on her 21st birthday. Bert wouldn't give his approval so they had to wait until they didn't need it. She was pregnant, with you Charles, but it was wartime. Things were different then. However she did it, and whatever she did to do it, Alicia did the only thing she could and got away from her family."

"She was my daughter," David spoke firmly, "and I couldn't acknowledge that to anyone until it was too late. Though, and this is something you didn't know Edie, I did speak to her once. It was four years ago at the Savoy. She was there with a beautiful young man, they were quite involved in conversation. I listened in as I was sitting at the table next to theirs. She was very poised, very articulate and very beautiful. She looked ill but happy and at ease with herself, and with the young man. I said 'Good evening' as I brushed against their table when I left. She looked at me very briefly, returning my greeting with an abstracted smile. So I did see her, that once."

"Oh David. I'm so sorry."

I looked across the table at Max. It was difficult to interpret his look. He was thinking, I could recognise that, but there was something else. He was looking at David trying to read something in his face, in his words, that was not there for the rest of us.

"Should funerals always be like this?" Susannah asked "History being dug up and raked over?" Perhaps she was thinking of eighteen months earlier, when her husband had died. There had been no valedictory dinner, no family gathering. He had been drowned trying to kill his children. He had tried to rape Monika and she, defending herself, had stabbed him with the bread knife. We had all come under investigation and his funeral was conducted with as little ceremony as possible.

44

"They are usually a time for reflection and memory, yes, certainly." Maureen answered her. "A time for families to get together and say things they could never say at other times."

"Why did Graham come? He seems to hate being here."

Edie began to answer "I was surprised when he phoned and offered to come with us. I can only think it was curiosity. It was one of the less attractive characteristics of my sons that they were very jealous of their sister. They thought she had a far easier time of things than they did. They believed she married into money and lived a life of luxury. The boy's father will have laid it on thick, and I think he must have pushed Graham to come so he can report back."

Or, I thought, to see if there was anything in it for him.

"Also, he's at college in Liverpool, so this way he doesn't have to pay his own fare." David's attempt at lightening the conversation didn't distract Maureen from what she had been saying.

"But she had such a terrible time for so much of her life! Don't they know that? What about her accident? Don't they know her career was ruined by one moment's stupidity?"

"We knew Alicia had had a dreadful marriage, had been ill for most of her adult life and hadn't been happy for years, but the boys, they always thought that because she had money she must be happy. To them it would be impossible to be unhappy if you were rich. Money was, is, their answer to everything."

"But after the divorce she didn't have any." It seemed important to Maureen that we understood her friend.

"They never listened to anything they didn't want to hear and they wanted to feel hard done by."

"So you think Graham came to delve around a bit?"

"He probably wants to see if there're any skeletons in the cupboard."

"That seems a bit harsh."

"I don't like my sons a lot, there's too much of their father in them and their sons are just as bad."

"But Alicia was different?"

"Yes. Alicia was different."

Chapter Seven

The next morning the church was almost full.

I wondered who all the people were and why they had come. They couldn't possibly all have known my mother. I had heard that some people turned up to any funeral as a way of getting free food and drink at the wake. I recognised one or two journalists otherwise I knew very few.

Most members of the congregation were in formal black, or at least generally subdued colours. Most of the women wore hats or dark scarves knotted tightly under their chins and looking from the back of the church it was a drab sight. I wondered what the Alicia I had heard about the previous night would have thought about it.

I think she would have hated it.

As we left Sandhey that morning Ted had handed out a variety of ties for the men and scarves and hats for the ladies so we all exhibited splashes of bright colour in the general funereal uniforms. Ted's tie was yellow, mine red, Max's purple and David wore a multi coloured bow tie which many of the more po-faced strangers in the congregation probably felt was better suited to the circus. Susannah, Monika, Maureen and Edie also drew whispered condemnation.

But we weren't the only people standing out from the drab crowd.

Two young women sitting near the back of the church appeared to have had a better idea than most of my mother's character. The large bright green hat one was wearing should not have looked good on a redhead but I thought it looked extremely appropriate. The head of the young woman sitting next to her was crowned with an interesting creation of net and feathers almost the exact colour of her friend's hair. I thought they looked wonderful whatever others may have thought.

I glanced at Ted and saw him smiling at them with approval. There was a nod of the green hat. Perhaps Ted knew them.

There were two recordings to be played at the service. The first, introduced by Max as one that was of particular significance to my Mother, was her singing, very lightly and quietly a song by Nöel Coward. I noticed my grandmother weeping quietly into the handkerchief David had handed to her.

I'll see you again, whenever Spring breaks through again,
Time may lie heavy between, but what has been, is past forgetting

He, too, looked close to tears as we all listened to the beautiful voice. I had never known that about her.

Susannah introduced the second tape saying Alicia had recorded and re-recorded the poem until it was exactly as she wanted to be remembered. The congregation was silent as we listened to the perfect diction.

'There's a breathless hush in the close tonight,
Ten to make and the match to win.'

It was a poem I knew well. I wondered why it had been important to my mother.

It was a relief from the tension of listening to those recordings for us all to stand to sing the first hymn.

An hour later I stood in the hallway at Sandhey welcoming the large number of people who had come back either out of respect for my Mother or simply out of curiosity about our family and the household at Sandhey which had frequently been the centre of local gossip and scandal.

I was pleased when the two girls walked through the door. I was interested to know who they were and why they had come.

"Thank you for coming." I began and barely listened as the usual pleasantries were exchanged, 'Such a sad day.' 'Even when you are expecting death it is no easier when it actually happens.'

"I know this is dreadfully rude" I interrupted "but how did you know my mother?"

"Oh I didn't." the redhead replied enthusiastically. "I'd better explain. I'm Linda Forster. "

"Ah." The penny dropped very quickly. "Carl asked you to come."

She spoke quickly with confidence "Obviously, he couldn't come himself though he wanted to because he really liked your mother. He spent quite a lot of time with her when she was first ill, you know, in Surrey. But he couldn't could he?" She answered her own question in a rush. "Not with, you know, your sister, and everything."

"So I suppose you will be reporting back to him?" I asked, not sure whether to be annoyed or amused. She was unashamed. "Afraid so. He wants to know exactly what happened, who was here and everything." I decided to be amused, I hoped my smile expressed generosity and understanding though I probably simply looked pompous and condescending.

"I hope you don't mind. I brought my friend Holly, Holly Eccleston." I wished I could talk longer with these two but I was conscious of the line of people lengthening behind them so, distracted, I spoke the hurried clichés of the moment. "Of course, nice to meet you Holly, thank you both for coming. I hope it wasn't too much of an ordeal." I tried to move on to the next in line but Holly didn't move, she answered my rhetorical question in a gentle voice with a noticeable American accent. "Oh no, thank you. It's the first funeral I've ever been to and it was so beautiful. I really wish I'd known her, she must have been a lovely person, she had such a lovely voice."

"Yes. Yes she did." I had to move on down the line. "Help yourself to food and drink won't you?"

"Don't worry, I'll look after them." Graham, who must have been amongst the first back from the church, and certainly amongst the first at the wine, pushed past me positioning himself between them with an arm on each girl's shoulder "I'll make sure they're well fed and watered." He barely glanced in my direction.

"Perhaps they would prefer to look after themselves." I was rewarded by a look of gratefulness from Holly but there was little I could do as he steered them away from me and I had to turn my attention to other guests.

Some while later I was standing with a group of women whose gossip I had no interest in when I heard the gentle American accent and began to listen to their conversation.

"At least we've got rid of him now. He's disappeared. I hope we managed to put him off."

"Such a boring question, you know 'What do you do?' and he wasn't really interested was he?" Linda began.

"Although he'd asked me," Holly interrupted trying to be light-hearted but there was an edge to her voice, "it was you who always answered."

"He seemed pretty pissed to me."

"Then why did you chat on and on about what we were doing and where? If it had been up to me I wouldn't have told him anything. Why did he keep asking me how long I'd been in this country and why my family were over here?"

"He hardly seems the type to want to make polite conversation, more the type that wants something."

"Then you made the mistake of asking him about himself. That was just plain stupid! Well you don't get a degree from a Poly so that was a lie. So he's not only rude and ugly he's a liar."

I was rather pleased they hadn't liked him either.

By the time most people had left it was dark. Just those who were staying overnight at Sandhey remained in the drawing room, subdued and exhausted by the day.

I was talking to Maureen when I noticed Graham leaving the room. He had been drinking pretty steadily all afternoon and his absence was understandable, but I didn't like the idea of him wandering around the house, despite it being highly likely he had taken every opportunity to do just that in the 24 hours since his arrival.

I was surprised how much I liked Maureen. I had re-appraised my view of my mother, perhaps I should do the same for Maureen's sister, my father's mistress, who had eventually married him to become, briefly, my step-mother.

I was beginning to doubt all the fixed ideas I had had of the people in my life when Maureen pointed out that Graham had been gone for a while. She said she didn't trust him. Perhaps he was having a nose around where he shouldn't. She spoke as if she knew there were things he should not find.

"Go and check, Charles, that one's a nasty piece of work."

I walked into the hall and was immediately worried to see a light under the door of Max's study.

As I opened the door I saw Graham sitting behind Max's desk, he seemed to be putting something in his pocket but there was no way I could be sure so I said nothing. The pale blue blotting pad was covered with scraps of paper and photographs.

He looked up, unembarrassed, and deliberately sorted through the papers to pick a specific one that he began to read aloud.

"Ted, I leave it up to you whether or not you destroy these papers. My advice is you should not, despite their content. These are important and should not be lost. It is the testament to the very brave person you have known as Monika Heller."

I said nothing as he picked up another sheet, written with a different pen and in different ink, but in the same tight almost italicised handwriting.

"Monika, I should have told you myself. I should have told you before. Somehow the appropriate moment never came...."

49

"What the hell are you doing?" I had finally found my voice. "Get away from there! I can't believe you're doing this!"

He didn't jump up, ashamed at being caught, as I'm sure I would have done; he just leant back in the chair as if he had every right to be there

"Do you know what these are? I found them last night. You all thought I was pissed but I thought I'd have a look around. Spent hours in here I did and no one found me. You all thought I was sleeping it off but it takes a lot more booze than that to make me lose it. I've spent most of the afternoon in here too. Very interesting it's been. And not just for me. I know someone who'd be very interested in what I've got here."

I could say nothing, watching as he sorted through the papers again and found the one he wanted. He began to read in a forced cartoon of a pseudo-German accent that I found extremely offensive.

"Monika, I should aff told you myself. I should aff told you before. Somehow ze appropriate moment never came. I have lovved you as any fazer might for all your life. Your name is not Monika Heller, it is Rebecca Rebmann. Your mozzer vas my sister. You are my dear niece – but I could never tell you for all ze memories I knew it vould bring. As ve grew to know each other ze detail of our true relationship could not make us any fonder of each other zo I let it be."

I was stunned. I could not find the words to stop him though at least when he continued he began to speak more normally.

"It was not by accident that I found you in Audierne at the end of the war. I had always hoped you had kept that map I had drawn. I prayed to whatever God still existed in those times that you would follow it and I would find you there. Ours was not a close family, but over the years I couldn't lose touch with you..."

I had had enough. "Put those down! Get away from the desk! You have no right.... I can't believe you're doing this!"

"But you had no idea did you? If I'd lived in this house I'd have read everything, I'd know everything. You must have had enough chances."

"I would never do that. They're private. If Max had wanted me to read them he would have shown them to me. Get up and get out!"

He didn't move. He just sat in Max's chair and smiled. "Perhaps you were too busy doing other things!"

I tried to grab his arm to pull him up but I wasn't strong enough and he had no difficulty in shaking me off.

"Go and call your boyfriend to help you."

Whether it was the emotions of the day or the tone of voice I hit out. I flailed with my fists with more anger than skill. I hadn't been in a fight since I was a young boy at school. I was taller, and my reach must have been longer, but Graham was far stronger and, although quite drunk, an instinctive fighter. He must have had a lot of practice. He stood up facing me and, ducking under my attempts to punch him, he landed a single blow on my face that knocked me back. I had neither the brute strength nor the experience to hurt him back.

"You're pathetic! A pathetic little ponce." He pushed past me leaving me holding my bleeding nose.

After a few moments during which it was all I could do to hold back tears of frustration and pain I started to clear the papers up, putting them together, back into the envelope.

"I suppose you can explain this."

Max stood in the open door.

"What are you doing with that envelope? You're bleeding. What in hell's name is happening here?"

"Graham. He was in here. I saw the light. He was reading. I tried to stop him but…."

"He hit you."

"I'm afraid I'm not very good at fisticuffs."

"Thank goodness for small mercies. There is nothing to be proud of in being good with violence." He was looking at the envelope in my hand. He seemed to be weighing up what to do. Whether to take the papers without explanation and ignore anything I may have learnt or to find out what I knew and control that knowledge.

He sat down and I began to think he was going to talk to me, actually tell me some of these secrets.

I had seen how he had reacted the previous evening when he had recognised David. He hadn't acknowledged that he knew him, he had said nothing all day that would indicate he knew him but I had seen that he did. I certainly didn't think I needed to know everything about him, everyone had the right to privacy and Max's generation, the generation that lived through the war, seemed to have a great many secrets that were better kept.

Since the previous evening I had been doubting my long held preconceptions about people; my mother, my step-mother. Now did I have to think again about Max?

"How much have you seen?"

"Not much – these," I handed some sheets of paper to him. "He began reading them to me. I couldn't stop him."

51

"So what do you know from them?"

"That Monika isn't Monika and she's your niece."

"I suppose that puts it in a nutshell." Max's face was grim.

"That's why you gave me a home wasn't it? You didn't give a home to Monika because of me, it was the other way around, you gave me a home because of Monika."

"This is not about you Charles. I gave you both a home because of your Mother and because it was the right thing to do."

"Why didn't you ever tell me? Why haven't you ever told her?"

"If you know the truth you will keep it to yourself. If you know the pain behind that truth you will understand better why you must hide it. And hide it you will. You must keep it to yourself. Always."

It was obvious he was struggling to know what to do, a situation I had never seen him in. I wondered who else knew of the relationship; obviously not Monika herself, perhaps only Max and me; and now Graham.

"You had better read these." He slowly pulled the papers from the envelope, sorted them and then handed a few, perhaps one tenth, to me. "Perhaps I should have told you more, years ago, but while things were getting on so well it seemed I shouldn't upset our applecart. But maybe now is the time. Sit. Read. I will bring you some wine."

Max took a small key from his waistcoat and, removing two books from a shelf, inserted and turned it, revealing a hidden cupboard. The shelves, lined with real books, hid a door. In the years I had lived in the house I had never known of its existence.

"When I first moved here from Millcourt I undertook many renovations." he spoke conversationally, as if nothing unusual was happening. "I installed this store where the temperature is regulated and my wines would be secure." I saw him looking around the cupboard as if looking at something I could not see.

"Some of what you will soon learn," he continued "I had expected only to be known when I am gone. For 30 years I have given nothing of this away to anyone. I have allowed people to think what they wanted about me, about why I brought you and Monika into this house. Now I must give some of these secrets to you, Charles. I trust you to treat them well."

Choosing a bottle from the bottom rack he lifted it carefully, unscrewed and checked the cork and then carefully poured the dark liquid into a crystal decanter. I watched the ritual, aware that this was a symbolic, almost religious, act of Max's to show the importance of what

I was about to learn.

"You will need this." He placed the decanter and a glass on the desk by the papers. "I will leave you to read what you can."

I turned the sheets over in my hand, they were filled with Max's tight handwriting with many crossings out and words written at angles around the edges of the variously sized pieces of paper. It seemed that this was not a completed work, many of the crossings out and written amendments had been made in different inks and some seemed quite recent.

I turned to the first sheet and soon lost myself in a world I could not recognise.

When I first talked to Monika I asked her name. She answered 'Fotze'. I said that could not be her name. It was not a name. I asked what else people called her and she gave me another word 'Hexen'. Again I said that could not be her name. I asked what her mother was called, she answered 'Mutter', and her father? 'Vater' she replied as if she could not understand how I could not have known that. I asked what other people called her parents and she looked at me blankly. She knew neither her family name nor the names of her family so I gave her the name Monika Heller.

Monika had been born in September 1930 in a farmhouse outside a small village in western Austria. She did not leave that house for the first eight years of her life.

She was an unwanted, unexpected and unprepared for child, perhaps they even hoped she would not survive. Despite the harshness of her life she grew through childhood accepting without question her position in the household. 'Mädchen' they called her when they called her anything. Girl. She did much of the household work from a very young age while her family were in the fields. She had been told always to do as she was told without question.

That much she remembered.

The farmer drove his family hard. His eldest son had some incentive as he would inherit, but the other was less interested as he would have to find his own way. The girl would find a husband as soon as she was old enough. There was no need for her to go to school as long as she learned the ways of the house. In many ways it was a backward community.

When I talked to her of these days what few memories she

53

had were vague and unformed. She talked of herself as if of another person, without emotion. It was I, who understood what she meant by the words she spoke, I who felt the pain.

The summer when Monika was seven years old the brothers did no work on the farm, instead, despite the arguments of their father, they spent their time with new friends playing at being soldiers. They wore uniforms, mud coloured shorts with leather belts and heavy buckles with shirts with shiny buttons and badges. She remembered them shouting at her.

She remembered other things that I wish she had forgotten.

She told me how they would take her into the barn and make her watch as they unbuttoned their shorts and showed off to each other in front of her uncomprehending eyes, demonstrating what they could do to themselves, to each other, and to her. She could not argue with the power that came with their masculinity, their approaching adulthood and their uniforms. Each took their turn, laughing at the others, the brothers included. She understood the times in the barn to be just one more chore to do around the house. Why would she tell anyone? She did not know that what they were doing was wrong.

She had no memory of individual experiences, simply the feeling that sometimes it hurt, sometimes it didn't. Her main memories were of temperature. She remembered the cold times more than the warm ones. They hurt more.

Even if anyone had known what was happening to her could they have done anything? The power of these young men stretched far beyond the control they had over her. They had guns, old shooting rifles, and they marched through the village with them on their shoulders, terrorising the older people who had known war. They practised shooting, first at bottles on fences then at any animals that got in their way. What could anyone do against them? What could their parents do? They were old and tired. They were not strong, and had no power to stop these young men from doing what they wanted.

Their mother's brother was the only visitor to the farm. He could have noticed what was going on and, perhaps, changed things. But he didn't. He was much younger than his sister and lived and worked in a city many miles away. His visits were short and infrequent and didn't interrupt the normal pattern of life.

Then they left the farm.

The brothers hadn't been on the farm for weeks and weren't with them when they left. She never knew what happened to them. They weren't spoken of again. She did not know she was leaving the farm forever.

Over the next days their cart met up with others and they trekked in a line, like the wagon trains she watched on the television years later. She remembered little except the cold and a beautiful lake with deep blue water that reflected the snow covered hills. She did not remember, even if she had ever known, why they had crossed the mountains.

I hadn't poured any of the wine as I read. But at this point, as I reached the end of a sheet, I looked away from the tightly written sheets of paper, poured some of the dark red liquid into the glass and drank it. I sat looking at the empty glass for a few moments as the implications of what I was reading began to sink in. This was Monika I was reading about. This was Max who was writing so dispassionately, though obviously with difficulty. I knew that this was not the final document he would have left to be read after his death. Perhaps there were things he would change, leave out. Add.

I poured another glass and turned to the next sheet.

They survived by doing odd jobs on farms, doing those things for people with money that no-one else would do. She was told never to speak. If she spoke outside their house people would know they came from a different country and in those times to be from a different country was to be an enemy. Soon no words were spoken inside the house. She said nothing when her father came to her bed each night. She said nothing. It was the way.

She soon found that the men of this country were no different from the boys she had always known. They had the power and the ability to do what they wanted with her. So they did.

She was eleven years old when she was cutting kindling in the woods near the village and felt pain in her stomach. She ignored it until she could ignore it any longer. She hurt with a pain such as she had never experienced. She screamed with the pain but it didn't stop. No one heard her, no one interfered as her body ejected an unformed bloody mess. The pain continued all through the night and all through the next day. She thought the bleeding would never stop. As the sun set she stared at it knowing she would never see another. But she did not die. She slept. The next morning she did wake up and returned to her home to carry

55

on as if she hadn't seen the end of the world.

I drank again. Monika must have told all this to Max, yet she had never said anything to me. She would have told me if she had wanted me to know, maybe she had wanted to forget; perhaps she had forgotten.

Perhaps the mind eventually shuts out those things that are too difficult to comprehend.

I had to keep reading, though part of me wondered how I could intrude on this intensity of pain.

She could say nothing. She could ask no one about the pain and the blood. She did not know what had caused it so she could not stop it happening again.

She had bled once, between her legs, but it had not hurt. She had thought it was because of what the men had done. Months later her father found her trying to wipe away blood. He had muttered something angrily and had gone away and never again came to her as he had done most nights since they had left the farm. Never again did he come into her room, lie next to her for a short time, then roll on top of her, thrusting into her for a few seconds before leaving her to her sleep.

She rather missed it.

It was not long after that that he left forever. She never knew what happened to him. For several hours there had been the sounds of guns and shouting, noises that were not unfamiliar but which seemed to go on for longer than normal. The next morning her Mother took her hand and they walked away.

I began to understand something of why Monika was as she was. I had wondered why she had never married, never left us to set up her own home, never wanted all the things that women are supposed to need. Now I thought I knew.

They eventually stopped walking in a village larger than the other and they kept themselves to themselves. As she grew in size no one cared enough about her story that her husband was dead to disbelieve her. She was 14 years old, although small for her age even in those times, and it was not unusual for girls to be in her situation. When the pains started her mother took her out of the village and held her hand as the hours passed. She watched as her mother pulled the baby out of her and strangled it with the cord before burying it under a tree.

Some time after she was walking through the village, which was bright and noisy as people talked that the war would soon be

56

over. She was faced in the square by a group of drunken men who taunted her, called her simple, said what was good for some unknown dead boy was good enough for them and had bundled her into a barn. One by one they had taken what they wanted from her, lining up one behind the other to take their turn, several going back for more as they swigged alcohol from large dark bottles and celebrated the coming end of the suffering of the war.

I had always known that men did this to women, that they were unfeeling and unloving as they dealt with purely physical needs. I had known that women sometimes turned the tables and used men for their own ends. I had never wanted to have anything to do with it. I had childhood memories of the power games played out by people in the name of 'love'. I had never associated 'sex' with 'love' and I doubted I would ever have experience of either.

One day the men of the village were rounded up and shot against the wall of the church in the square. She did not know why they had been shot, she did not know whether all the people shot had been killed, she did not ask, nor did anyone tell her. She was pleased they were dead.

In the summer another baby was born. It was alive for a short time but now she knew what to do. She did as her mother had done, tying the cord around its neck until its crying stopped, burying it before it could know a world of pain.

That evening her Mother gave her a small parcel, an envelope wrapped up in brown paper and tied with string. She told her never to lose that envelope. She didn't tell her what it was, simply that she should never lose it. Monika sewed the envelope into the hem of her dress. The next morning her Mother was gone. She never knew what had happened to her.

She walked away from the village with no idea of where she was going.

She knew nothing of the world. In all her life she had never made decisions. She had gone where her father and mother told her to go, done what others made her do. But now she was alone. She saw young men returning to the village and she knew she did not want to stay.

For the next two years she survived. When she found her body swelling there would be a woman who would get rid of it for her. If the hot baths, the alcohol and the knitting needles didn't work then she would give birth alone and, without feeling, would strangle and bury the bloody mess.

She moved across the country invisible and unhindered, her actions unnoticed by anyone in the world. She was as near to invisible as she could be – a homeless, stateless individual in a chaotic world.

I had always thought my childhood unhappy, it was part of my view of myself, I had been so centred on my own perceived loneliness. But I had always had a roof over my head, there were always people who loved me and who fed me and made sure I was comfortable and well looked after; no one had tried actively to do me harm. Yet I had still thought myself unbearably unhappy.

As I read of Monika's childhood I realised something of what real misery could be and I was ashamed.

It was a ritual for her that whenever she obtained new clothes she would cut the thin parcel out of the old hem, would look at it and would sew it into the new. The familiar lines comforted her, they gave her the feeling that there was somewhere safe in the world.

Through those times she acquired no knowledge other than that required to keep alive. She could neither read nor write, if she had ever known how to she had long since forgotten. She could understand some English, French and German but she didn't like to speak at all.

By the time I found her, in the summer of 1947, she was nearly 17 years old. She had had at least three children who were all dead as were, as far as she knew, all the members of her family.

But she had survived.

As I turned the last of the sheets of paper Max had given me I poured the dregs of the wine into my glass, drank it and leaned back.

This was not the whole story. I knew enough of Max to know this was just the minimum he accepted I must know. Only part of the truth it may have been, but it was enough to change everything for me.

In the years I had known Monika I had understood she had not had an easy life. But she had never told me anything of this. I had only been a young child when she had first come into our home as Nanny, but that had been nearly 25 years ago. Why had Max never told me? Why had he never trusted me with any knowledge of all this? Would he ever have told me if he hadn't had his hand forced by Graham?

He had sheltered me as he would a young and vulnerable child.

I suppose I had never given him any reason not to.

I had let the years pass taking advantage of the security and ease of life at Sandhey. I had never had to grow up; I had never needed to earn a living, had never been asked to do anything I didn't want to.

I had done nothing, achieved nothing, been nothing.

How Max must despise me. How everyone must despise me.

I was in a black mood as I switched out the lights and closed the study door behind me.

"Where is everyone?" Susannah was alone in the drawing room and my question was meant to be casual. Under normal circumstances it may have caused no offence but I suppose the pain of what I had just been reading had given an edge to my voice that she chose to misinterpret.

"If it's of the slightest interest to you I've spent the last hour with our grandmother and grandfather and that little shit of a cousin of ours. Where've you been?" Susannah's response showed her irritation as she continued without waiting for any reply from me. "He's a nasty minded little pervert. He went on and on about the things he had heard through the afternoon. How women were gossiping about 'poor Alicia' and 'the husband's bastard son'. He must know something. He kept winding me up about what they said about him. How 'very clever' he was 'doing so well', 'so good looking' blah blah blah. Then he cut to the nitty gritty. He was positively glowing with pleasure as he put on a stupid female voice imitating those bloody stupid and ignorant women 'didn't he spend a lot of time with Alicia when she was so ill?' 'I heard that they were *unnaturally* close.' I wanted to hit him."

"Well that's something we've got in common at last little sister." I said, trying to make the peace.

"Don't be so bloody sarcastic." She shouted at me. "Where've you been anyway?" she was working herself up into a state just as she had when she was a young child.

I couldn't tell her. When I didn't answer, she goaded me "Running away again?" Perhaps I did run away from things; I had run away from school but she had no idea why; I had run, with Monika, to Max's house but there had been good reason. "You don't know anything." I spoke as unemotionally as I could but it didn't stop the inevitable argument.

"Well, where were you when you should have been helping? I know you didn't care about Mother as much as I did."

"Oh shut up Susie, you don't know what I thought about her."

"Don't call me Susie! Only Carl can call me that.

"OK. Shut up Susannah, you don't know what I thought about her."

"*Thought*! I don't care what you 'thought' I wanted to know whether you actually felt anything."

"You don't know what I feel."

"Do you ever feel anything?"

"What? Like you feel? You have a monopoly on feeling have you?"

"Well at least I can care."

"For the most unsuitable people."

"Shut up!"

"Are you saying Carl's suitable?"

"Shut up"

"Your wonderful Carl. Where's he today then? Where's he ever been when you needed him?"

"Shut up"

"Forget him. Get on with your life. Do something with your life."

"That really is the bloody pot calling the kettle black! What have you done with yours?"

"Well I haven't married a complete waste of space and had four children who I haven't seen for years and have left to others to look after. I haven't abandoned them just like our Mother abandoned us. I haven't completely wasted every opportunity given to me. I haven't…"

"Shut up! At least I've loved someone. You never loved anyone but yourself."

"You're a nasty minded selfish little bitch!"

The argument descended into the small-minded niggles of resentment.

"What have you ever done for yourself?"

"You've always had everything handed to you on a plate."

"You've never done a day's work in your life."

"You only want Carl back so he'll look after you now Joe's dead and you can't face up to having to do it yourself."

"You're so bloody jammy. You've got all the money you need. You don't need to work. You can't call your stupid bird-watching work."

"Well I do. And it's not stupid. I work at it and I'm good at it. I earn money at it, which is more than you bloody do. You've got to get your life together Susie."

"I've told you. Don't call me that."

"Don't wait for Carl to call you Susie. He can't call you anything! He never sees you. He'd see you if he wanted to. But he doesn't want a weak, selfish, stupid failure."

"Don't call me stupid!"

"You are. You failed at university, you failed in your marriage. For

60

heavens sake Susannah get your act together! Well here's some news for you. If you don't do it yourself no one's bloody going to do it for you. We're fed up with looking after you like one of your bloody children. We're all fed up with you moping around like the world's let you down."

I knew I had said some pretty hurtful things so I deserved the slap but I winced as she had hit the same spot as Graham.

"I'll bloody show you."

"What? You'll show us what?"

"I'll show you I can bloody do it. Can you? I'll get that bloody degree, I'll show you what I can do. I'll bloody show you. What'll you do? I'll get back in three, four years with a first and I'll get a bloody fantastic job and show you what I can do and what'll you be doing? Still living here a kept boy looking at your stupid bloody birds and looked after by your nanny."

"What about your children then while you're swanning off re-living your life or are they so unimportant?"

"Sod them! You look after them if you care so much about them. Monika can. I don't care! I never wanted them in the first place."

"Well it's a bit late for that!"

"They were a mistake."

"Everything you've done has been a bloody mistake hasn't it? And none of it has ever been your fault."

"You've never done anything because you're so bloody frightened of leaving your nanny."

"Shut up about Monika, she's had to put up with more than you could possibly imagine."

"Putting up with you all these years you mean."

"No. You've never understood. She's…"

"I know …"

"No you don't …You can't possibly know that she…."

We had been so wrapped up in our quarrel we hadn't heard Max come in. He interrupted me. He was as angry as Susannah and I were, but whereas we were shouting he was quiet and controlled. "Susannah, you look very tired, I will thank you to go upstairs to your room now." When faced with the authority of Max's voice she did as she was told.

He turned to me, as severe as I have ever heard him. "What you learned today is for no one's ears. You disappoint me Charles. I had thought you could be trusted, now I realise you can't. If I find that you have ever told anyone, anyone, what you have learned today; if Monika learns anything of her past from you; if I find that you have broken one

61

confidence, to one person, be assured you will regret it. Do I make myself clear?"

I went to my room as though I were a child told off by an angry parent. I felt misunderstood and misjudged. I gazed out across the blackness of the estuary to the distant lights of Wales. I hated everything. I hated the life Monika had lead, I hated Susannah for goading me, Max for seeing how close I was to giving away secrets that weren't mine, my Mother for dying before I could get to know her but most of all myself.

I hated to admit it but what Susannah had said was true. I had never done anything for myself. I had had a sheltered and easy life.

Knowing how they must all despise me I decided I must leave.

Susannah would say I was running away. Again. Perhaps I was, but I didn't care, too much had happened during the funeral for me to stay.

I had no idea where I would go, or for how long, but I had to get away.

Chapter Eight

When the house was finally dark on the night of Alicia's funeral Max sat at his desk staring at the envelope that had caused so much trouble.

The sheets were out of order, jumbled and untidy. Graham must have read most of them. How much time had he had?

Max was angry with himself for letting down his guard. He should have realised that strangers, any strangers, even members of Alicia's family, could be a threat. He certainly hadn't allowed for Graham.

He tried another drawer in his desk.

Max thanked God that Graham hadn't opened this drawer as well. Locating a small key on his key fob he unlocked the drawer and pulled out a folder crammed with notes and photographs. The pages of familiar uneven blue type were scarcely readable in places on the yellowing paper. Fancifully he imagined the words wanting to disappear, tiring of the pain they caused. The ribbon on the typewriter had needed changing, the tops of the letters were red and some were missing altogether and she had been grateful when he had sent her two new ones.

He re-read the hand-written letters wondering yet again whether he should have done anything differently.

He had thought it was all history, never to be resurrected. He would let Carl see all the papers when he was dead. Not before. But now he knew he had been living in a fool's paradise. Perhaps he should never have thought his secrets could be kept forever.

He had been burying Alicia that day, but the past had been resurrected. Two spectres from his past had appeared signalling in their separate ways that the past would never allow itself to lie dormant forever.

Carefully putting the folder away and re-locking the drawer, he turned back to the album on his desk, leafing through it until he found a particular photograph.

No one would recognise David McKennah in the small group of uniformed men laughing at the camera as they waved their caps in the air celebrating... he could not remember what... it had obviously seemed important at the time. Max only recognised David because he knew the tall, smiling, young man was him. He hadn't been called McKennah then.

In any case, in the manner of the day, he had always been known by his nickname. Max remembered his, Kipper, because someone had thought it a clever pun on his name. David's had been Ginger, which always was remarked on by people who didn't know him well, because he didn't have red hair.

Next to David was Jimbo, the man Max knew as Elizabeth's husband. Within a week of this photograph he was dead. Would he still have been laughing at the camera if he had known? Probably.

The young man on the right of the group, in a uniform of a different colour but still joining in with the hilarity of the moment, he could scarcely recognise as himself.

Thirty years had changed Ginger and Kipper into David and Max. He knew Jimbo had died, he wondered if any of the others had survived.

Turning the pages of the album, back through time, he saw Rebecca, standing awkwardly in the sunshine, her hands clasped behind her, her head to one side. Her long blonde hair was in plaits curled, like a halo, around the top of her head.

Would Monika recognise herself in it? Max felt safe, she could not know what she looked like when she was young. She would not have looked at Holly and seen her young self.

As he had.

The similarity was immediately obvious to Max as he had watched Holly walking into the church that morning. Was it the roundness of the face, the particular colour of the hair? How could someone be so like someone else and not be them, somehow reborn?

He would try to keep them apart though, to be on the safe side.

Max had been expecting Matt to contact him for some time, ever since the letter from his old friends in the village. Now he recognised his daughter, who had somehow become friends with the Forsters. Had Matt engineered that? Max dismissed that, Matt could not be that clever.

But Graham may be. Graham had seen Holly, he must have seen some photographs. He would find Matt. If they weren't already, they would soon be working together.

And Matt with Graham was a very different matter. Especially with the knowledge Graham must now have.

Holly was his family too and although he knew he should do his best to protect her he had more important concerns. It was not Holly in these photographs; Holly was young, strong and seemed well able to look after herself.

She would probably have to.

Max put the photographs away, as he did so wondering how much time Graham had had, how much had he read, what photographs had he seen? He did not like not knowing. Not knowing made it more difficult to protect Monika.

And he must protect Monika.

In protecting Monika he protected himself.

Max took a sheet of writing paper from the stand on the desk and began to write.

Charles,

It is the night after your mother's funeral and perhaps I am feeling a little maudlin but there are some things I think you should know.

Maybe not now but when the time comes.

It was after six in the morning when he finished writing though both the finished letters were only two pages long. Every sentence he wrote brought back vivid memories he had thought long forgotten. He put each letter in an envelope, wrote *Charles* on one and *Ted* on the other.

He pushed his chair back and walked stiffly to the fire which had died away hours since. He tried to resurrect it with some of the wasted sheets of paper.

It was some time later, just as a quiet glow of red appeared on the coals he heard steps in the hall. Charles's leather soles on the parquet flooring.

Max wondered if he should make some attempt to stop him, but he stayed, staring into the small flicker of flame. The front door opened and shut again and a few minutes later he heard the sound of the Daimler accelerating down the drive.

"Goodbye young Charles." Max said to the flame.

He knew he would never see the same man again.

Chapter Nine

I left before it was light. It didn't occur to me that there were people I should talk to, who would want to talk to me. Even if it had I would still have left, I had no intention of meeting Graham.

I didn't bother with breakfast, Monika would be in the kitchen and I didn't think I could trust myself to see her. I could stop for coffee at a café when I knew where I was going. Wherever that was.

During the night I had thought about the Lake District but decided against it. Father had lived there, with Kathleen, and although they were both dead I felt awkward about being in an area they would have known so well. I wanted to go somewhere with no connections with the family, where there was no chance I would be recognised and where my name couldn't raise any difficult questions.

At the roundabout where I had to make the first decision I turned right, towards Chester, and drove along the familiar roads south through the Wirral. As if in automatic pilot I turned right, off the main road, towards Queensferry and Wales, I passed the sign welcoming me to Wales, *Croeso u Cwmru*, the sign I had always dreaded when going back to boarding school. At the next roundabout I turned left, south; north had always meant 'school' and even after all the time that had passed the pain and unhappiness of the year I had spent there was very raw.

I drove down through the marches of Wales, the prosperous market towns each with their hotel called the 'Feathers' or 'The Prince of Wales'. There were few other cars on the road but for once I took little enjoyment in the driving. I crossed the Severn into Gloucestershire and headed south, past Bristol across the Somerset levels and into Devon. It had been dark for a while and I began to feel the need to find a room for the night.

Years before I had stayed at a large hotel with Mother and Susannah on one of the awful forced holidays we had had together. Although I'd hated the holiday I'd liked the hotel, I remembered it overlooked a lake with rhododendrons. There had been pairs of Wellington boots lined up in the hall and large dogs drying themselves in front of the fire, even in the summer. It was peaceful and comfortable, at least it had been 15 years earlier. I tried to remember the name of the town.

After Exeter I headed towards Dartmoor. I recognised nothing so I kept going. 'If I find it I find it.' I said out loud, partly to keep myself awake. 'If I don't there'll be somewhere else signposted.' I was tired, too tired to be driving on unfamiliar roads, but I carried on, concentrating hard to keep awake. The few towns I drove through seemed dark and closed. I saw nothing like a hotel or even someone I could ask directions of.

The road was very narrow now, climbing up onto the moor, there were no more trees, no more houses, just blackness pierced by the infrequent headlights of oncoming cars. I hated driving in the dark. It as something I hadn't had much practice at and oncoming headlights multiplied in my glasses making it even more difficult to make out where the road was. I was beginning to panic, regretting my impulse to leave home so unprepared, when at last I saw a group of lights that were not oncoming vehicles and was extremely relieved to find a hotel with a full car park.

After the loneliness of the road across the moor any sign of civilisation was welcome.

It wasn't a proper hotel, just an old fashioned inn, but I was happy to accept the offer of a sandwich with my pint of beer.

I sat eating and drinking in front of one of the roaring fires that had a sign saying it hadn't been out since 1845 watching the people in the bar. For a week day evening in January in the middle of nowhere there seemed to be a large number of young people. Some of the drinkers enjoying their evening seemed to be bird watchers, I was not too tired to notice the binoculars and one of the magazines I wrote for on the table in front of a particularly large and noisy group. I wanted Susannah to be here to see that not all people who loved studying birds were the fossils she seemed to think we were.

I had thought of them as 'young people' yet they were probably at least my age, or even older. I was suddenly conscious of feeling a generation older. My green cord trousers, checked shirt and cravat would not have looked out of place worn by a man of 70 and contrasted horribly with the jeans and sweatshirts worn by the men and women laughing and joking in the bar. I felt as old as Ted.

Would I ever get to know people of my own age? I realised I had never tried. I was not yet 30 but I looked, and probably acted twenty years older.

Although they all seemed friendly no one spoke to me.

I knew Carl, had he been in my position, would not have had to sit the evening out on his own. He would have had the confidence to speak to them, he would have used shared interests to open a conversation. Carl wouldn't have sat for two hours speaking to no one except the bar maid each time he asked for another pint.

It was a perfect clear sunny morning as I drove across the moor the next day. The sky was a deep blue, any signs of the mist had cleared and the colours of the heather and gorse contrasted completely with the dark and mist of the previous night. At Tavistock I turned towards Plymouth. On that holiday in Moretonhampstead, too late I remembered the name of the town I had hoped to find the previous night, on that holiday we had been into Cornwall, across a bridge and into what seemed like a foreign country. Even the buses had 'Cornwall, Near England' written on the back.

So I headed for Cornwall. The road was narrow and as there was no chance of overtaking any of the few other vehicles I settled down to enjoy the winter sunshine at a sedate 30 miles an hour.

As I drove I conjured up images of the 'Perfect Fishing Village'. Images from magazines and the television worked themselves into a picture of steep cliffs tumbling into a small harbour filled with brightly coloured fishing boats protected by a stone wall. The cottages would be climbing up the steep roads, clinging to the hillsides. There would be cheerful signs welcoming visitors to cream teas and Cornish pasties. There would be quiet, unspoilt pubs and cafés where I could enjoy the sea and my own company. I had no idea whether such a perfect village existed, but I would try to find it if it did.

I decided to let fate guide me. At the first road junction I turned left, at the next one right, then left, then right. It worked. A little more than half an hour after crossing the Tamar I dropped down a steep hill towards the village of Polperro. Ignoring the signs warning drivers to leave their cars in the car park at the top of the hill I drove down the ever-narrowing street. Still turning 'left, right, left' I stopped at the harbour. I had to, the next right turn was a flight of steps.

It was perfect.

Reasoning that in the middle of winter it wouldn't be a problem, I pulled up next to a No Parking sign. It seemed to be what everyone else did as several other vehicles seemed to be parked across similar signs, including an elderly Rolls Royce. I wondered how that had negotiated the narrow turns. As I walked around the harbour I noticed that practically every cottage had a picture in the window saying 'Holiday

68

Cottage To Let'. There would be no difficulty in finding a place to stay.

"I don't suppose you'd know of anywhere to stay would you?" I asked the man behind the bar of the pub at the end of the quay.

"Don't suppose I do." Was the unhelpful response.

"Don't listen to Scrumpy. He's in one of his moods." An impossibly dark haired elderly woman wearing an incongruous red poncho and holding an empty cigarette holder stood down from her bar stool and pulled a card off the beam where it had been pinned. "Dani'll look after you. Just say you've been sent from The Smugglers".

"That's very kind of you, though it sounds quite mysterious." I tried to sound as informal as everyone else appeared to be, but it must have seemed pompous. Until I had accommodation settled I would not relax, but even then I doubted if I could ever be quite as free from stress as the men and women sitting around the bar. And it was only just past eleven o'clock.

"The pub. It's the Smugglers."

"Thanks."

"Just up the steps here, turn left onto the cliff path and it's the last house on your right."

"There aren't any houses on the left you silly cow, there's only the cliff." The man behind the bar commented as he concentrated on wiping a dishcloth around a glass.

I left them and climbed the steps as they had directed. After 30 or so, I gave up counting and paused for breath. I was at a bend in the path where I could look down over the harbour. It was exactly as I had imagined. The tide was out and the yachts and brightly coloured fishing boats in the harbour were resting at drunken angles on the mud, there was a makeshift landing stage at the bottom of the cliff I now realised I was half way up. I felt completely detached from it all, high above the beach no one would know I was there.

Having got my breath back I walked on up the cliff path, thinking I must have missed the house but, rounding a small bend, I saw the gothic grey stone building set into the cliffs looming above me. There were only 15 more steps to the front door.

After I had rung the bell I turned to look across the outer harbour. The village was out of sight, the bend in the path had taken me around the headland enough so that all that could be seen was cliff and sea, and a few houses in the trees on the other side of the harbour.

"Can I help you?"

"I'm looking for Danny." I managed to say as I tried to catch my breath, handing the card towards the young woman who was walking down the steep path at the side of the house.

"I thought I heard someone. I'm Dani. The bell's useless, it's the salt."

"Yes, I suppose it is. I was expecting a man," I continued "the lady in the pub said 'Danny'."

"Dani. With an I." She explained in a patient, not unfriendly, way. She had obviously had to make the explanation many times before. "Danielle really."

"What can I do to help?" she repeated. "Do you need a room? We usually only take couples, same trouble as one but twice the money."

"Well I am looking for a room, but there's only me. But I'll pay for two if that helps. Charles Donaldson, by the way." I thought I had better introduce myself.

"How long for?" As she asked the question I realised I had absolutely no idea. If I turned and went home now I would have been away three days. How long did I need?

"I'm not sure. Until Sunday?"

"Only two nights? Stay until Monday. You'll find driving anywhere a lot easier if you leave on Monday rather than Sunday even at this time of year. We'll leave it open, you might find you want to stay longer." She didn't wait for an answer before continuing "Well Charlie, I'll come down with you and help with your case. Those steps can be a bit much until you're used to them. Where's your car? I'll bring the key to the garage. It's quite a long walk I'm afraid, but you'll get used to it."

I let her talk on, comfortable that I had found exactly the right place, though I wasn't so sure about being called Charlie.

An hour later, the Daimler safely garaged at the top of the village, I sat sipping a blue and white striped mug of tea in the garden looking out to sea. On the way back from the car we had stopped at the bakers. "Hi Chalky, this is Charlie, two pasties please." Turning to me she added "For lunch". Chalky handed me the white paper bag that was already glowing transparent with the grease from the warm pasties.

I had never been shopping with Monika. I tried to remember when I had ever been in a food shop. I couldn't imagine being introduced to a shopkeeper or ever calling one by his nickname.

As I relaxed in the garden Dani sat down in the chair beside me, putting the plate of pasties on the table in front of me. "Do you mind or would you rather be on your own?" I was happy enough for her to sit with me but I had no idea what to say to her, she didn't fit any of the types of people I knew. She didn't seem to need to talk, just sitting silently looking out at the waves rhythmically beating against the rocks. Eventually she did speak, though it seemed more to herself than to me. "I love it when elements meet, the wind on the water, the water on the rocks, the wind in the pines. There's always something to watch and sounds to hear." So I watched and listened to the elements as Dani went back to the house to refill the mugs.

The gulls were completely different from the ones I was used to, these wheeled and glided in the air currents with far more abandon that they did on the flat estuary sands at home. I knew they were feeding but somehow they looked as if they were just having fun.

I relaxed, wondering when, if ever, I had felt like this.

Perhaps it was that the village was a holiday resort rather than a dormitory town for Liverpool that made the difference, but I had never really watched the sea before. I had watched the birds and the people, but rarely the sea itself. I had lived by the sea all my life but it had never made such an impact. It was the reason why the birds I loved came to my garden but my life had never been related to the sea in anything like the way it seemed the lives of the occupants of this village were. I could have lived in Orpington or Leicester for all the real wetness and saltiness of the sea had influenced my life.

Perhaps it was the magic of the village but I stayed in that garden all afternoon watching the tide coming in, counting the waves as they advanced over the rocks and joined the pools together.

After supper, which we ate together in the kitchen, I sat gazing down at the lights of the fishing boats as they approached the harbour.

"This is such a lovely view, it's like being a bird, looking down on everything."

"I call it Brigadoon." Dani said as she emptied the last of the wine into my glass and picked another bottle from the shelf behind her, handing it to me to open. "It's as if we appear in the summer when the world notices us and comes down in droves, then in winter we disappear, perhaps not for 100 years, but off the face of the real world for a few months."

"It's beautiful."

As I poured Dani's wine I asked as casually as I could about something that had been bothering me. "Am I your only guest?"

She seemed not embarrassed at all "Oh yes. When I'm here there's only one room really, that's why we like couples. It's not a problem."

"Won't your parents worry, I mean you alone with a stranger?"

Dani laughed, and waved her left hand towards me.

I noticed for the first time a paleness on the ring finger. "You're married?"

"Just. Separated, nearly divorced, just a matter of time really."

"You look far too…"

"young?" she finished his sentence for me. "People always say I look like a teenager. I suppose there'll be a time when I'm glad I look young but it has been the bane of my life. People still ask me to prove I'm old enough to drink. Flattering really, but a bloody nuisance."

"Are you going to tell me or do I have to guess?"

"I'm 27, 28 next month."

"Don't for God's sake tell me how old you think I am." Although I knew I was not going to be flattered I did want to know what she thought.

"Wild guess?"

"Go on."

"This is dreadful! I'm going to be hopelessly wrong, insulting you one way or the other. 40?"

"Ouch!"

"I knew I'd upset you. Don't take any notice, I'm always hopeless at judging people like that."

"I'll be 30 in May."

"Which date?"

"28th"

"Snap! Twins! Well two years different but twins! That's great."

I couldn't reply. I was two years older than this 'slip of a girl' as I knew Max would have called her. The previous night in the pub on Dartmoor I had felt old before my time, I felt I had missed out a generation. Now I knew I had. Everyone saw me as 40, middle aged, old.

"I've upset you. I'm sorry. What can I do to make up?"

"Don't worry, nothing. There's no need. Honestly you've no need to worry"

She topped up my glass, and drank more from hers.

"What do you do? For a living?"

"Ah, that's something I've been thinking about. Not much really. I write, I give talks, I've broadcast a bit, all about birds. I'm an ornithologist, not properly trained or anything, it's just that I know a lot about them." I felt I had to explain.

"I've never met an ornithologist. Will we have anything of yours here?" She reached behind her for a pile of books and magazines. "There, those are the bird ones."

I leafed through one of the magazines until I found one of my articles, turning the magazine to face her on the table I tried to grin but it probably seemed to her more of a leer. "There, that's one."

"Not a very flattering photograph."

"They were surprised at how young I was. The magazine wanted an old bald or white haired chap peering over half moon glasses. They wanted me to look more distinguished I suppose."

"Do you do anything else? There can't be much money in writing about birds."

I was embarrassed. I had never expected to talk so openly about things that were normally kept private. "Man of independent means?" I said the words as if they were a question and in quotes.

"I've never met one of those either."

I found myself beginning to tell Dani something about my life until I realised how dreadful it sounded; living with an unrelated older man, with the housekeeper who was my old nanny, not needing to work, contributing nothing to any thing or any body; so I turned the question round. "What do you do?"

"You mean when I'm not house-sitting while I wait for my divorce to come through?"

"Do you work? I know it's not a particularly good question to ask these days all women are supposed to work aren't they?"

"No I don't I always wanted to but Pete said no. He thought I should stay at home and arrange flowers and clean and wait until I had babies and while I was waiting I could treat him like one, feed him and service him on demand. Have his scotch ready when he got back from work and practically warm his slippers for him."

"You sound bitter."

"I am."

This time I topped up our glasses. "What did you want to do?"

"What *do* I want to do? What *will* I do? I'll have my own business, I don't know what doing but I'll be my own boss. If I'm going to make any money I'm going to make it for me not anyone else."

I could find no answer to the determination in her voice.

It was a few minutes before she broke the comfortable silence.

"You know what makes you seem so much older, Charles?"

"My clothes? My hair? My speech? My manners? Everything?"

"Well, yes, you have something there, but even if you grew your hair, wore scruffy denims and swore like they do down at the Smugglers you would always seem old because you think old. Spend more time with young people. It sounds like your friend Max is very old fashioned as well as being old and Monika's not going to help. You've got to be with young people Charlie, lighten up. Learn to chill out. When do you have to be back?"

So I decided to stay a while in Polperro.

The next day I rang Max. I had expected him to be angry, to tell me I had let them all down, that he had had to explain my absence to everyone. I could imagine Susannah smirking that I had run away again, and Graham triumphant that I could not face him. Max simply said that my grandmother had been disappointed that she hadn't talked to me more as there hadn't been much opportunity the day before. It was enough to make me feel guilty, as I suspect it was meant to.

I gave him the address and told him how he could get in touch if he needed but I was staying a short while to 'think things through'. He didn't ask about what, if he had I'm not sure I could have answered. He said he'd send my binoculars, and I asked for two particular reference books and for him to forward any correspondence. I was going to have a working holiday.

This time, in running away, I was going to do something positive. I was going to change.

I was going to watch, listen and learn to act my age.

I soon settled into a relaxed routine.

I would get up early and walk along the cliff path watching the sun coming round the eastern headland. Then I'd have breakfast with Dani at the kitchen table overlooking the harbour noticing, day by day, the changing levels of the tides.

The parcel arrived from home, with it there was a note telling me to enjoy my holiday, everything was fine, they understood why I had gone away when I had, funerals were always a time for re-appraisal. I read the letter carefully, making sure there were no hidden messages. I could find nothing written between the lines.

I had initially intended to spend the mornings working, but the books remained unread on the table. I had only one article to write by the end of January, so there was no urgency, though I was conscious that had I been at home it would already have been written and posted. More often than not I just sat watching the birds and the elements beating against each other.

At lunchtime we went down to the Smugglers where we would take turns to walk round to the bakers to buy the pasties for lunch. Whenever I walked through the narrow streets of the village more people would say 'Hello' 'Good morning' and 'How are you today?' than I ever had walking around the streets of Hoylake or West Kirby.

In the afternoons we would do some gardening if it wasn't raining or read if it was. I loved sitting in the broad arc of the window in my bedroom looking out at the water running down the glass, and beyond it the million shades of grey of the sea. When it was raining everything was grey; the sea, the garden, the cliff on the other side of the harbour, but when the sun shone the colours were Mediterranean in their brightness.

When I had been there just over a week Dani broke the routine, saying she had to go out for the day. She wouldn't be back till late so could I manage supper without her.

Although we hadn't been spending most of the days together I missed the feeling that she was just inside the house or just down in the village. I wondered what she was doing. I worried about her.

I was sitting in my window watching the waves in the moonlight when I heard "Hello, I'm back!" I glanced at my watch, it was nearly eleven o'clock. "Wanna drink?" Dani was shouting up the stairs as if it was a perfectly sensible time to start a bottle of wine. Before I had roused myself she had sat down next to me and put the bottle and glasses on the table. "Do you mind? Me being here I mean? I love watching the waves crashing over the rocks, there are some storms when the waves hide them completely." She pointed to a picture on the wall, an atmospheric brooding grey and brown picture of the rocks in a storm.

"I've got to go back to London, just for a week or so."

I wasn't sure what to say, I suddenly didn't want to think about leaving, so I said nothing as she continued "You can stay if you like."

"Could I?" As I spoke I realised what had been odd about the day. I couldn't remember ever having spent so long alone. At home on the days Max went into the office Monika would be around, and if she went out it would never be for more than a few minutes. I had certainly never spent a night alone in a house.

I thought that too ridiculous to mention.

"Of course. You're not going to wreck the place and it's always good to have the lights on at night."

"Is it good or bad? The reason you've got to go?"

"Good really. I've got to clear out all the stuff from my old flat. My divorce has come through."

I realised that she wouldn't appreciate congratulations or

commiserations so I tried to be practical. "Will you have to meet him?"

"Hell no! He's away, America I think, He's taken everything he wants leaving me to take what I want and get rid of the rest. Quite honestly I've already got what I want out of this divorce."

"What's that?"

"My freedom."

"What…?"

"…went wrong? I can't blame anyone but myself. I just married the wrong man for all the wrong reasons. I thought being married would give me all the things I needed, like security, I thought I would never have to be lonely or alone."

"It didn't work out like that?"

"Nope. 'fraid not."

"I'm sorry."

"I'm not, I've long ago put it down to experience. It'll make me more mysterious won't it? Divorcee is much more interesting than spinster don't you think?"

"My parents divorced."

"Well that's something, at least we didn't have any children to mess up. Did your parents mess you up?"

"Do I look messed up?"

"Well yes to be honest. You are an odd mixture of old man and young boy, you just haven't sorted out who you really are. You're trying to be what you think other people want you to be. Am I right?"

"Probably."

"Sorry."

"What for?"

"Being too blunt. Not being fair. Being rude. I don't know your life do I? I don't know what you have to go through so it's not for me to make comments. But I bet you something."

"What?"

"I'm the first person who's ever talked to you like this."

"You'd win."

"Come on." She grabbed my hand and pulled me out of his chair, leading me to a cupboard on the landing. She unlocked it and handed out two suitcases.

"Go on open them!"

I did as I was told and found them to be neatly packed with a man's clothes.

"There was one thing you could say for my husband, ex-husband.

He has, had, good taste. He'll never need these again. You have them."

"I can't possibly."

"Yes you can. They'll fit you and they're just what you need to lighten up your wardrobe. They're all good stuff."

"I can see that."

"Go on. They're no use to me and he'll never come down here again. Take it as payment for you looking after the house while I'm away. You will stay and look after it won't you? I'd really like you to be here."

"Really?"

"Really."

The week Dani was away was another step in my education. I had never had to fend for myself, feed myself, remember to turn the emersion heater on and off, remember to turn the lights out and lock the doors before I went to bed.

It was the first time I had been so responsible.

And I loved it.

I was left entirely to my own devices. I wrote my article, tried on all the clothes, even the shoes fitted, did some hoovering and dusting around the house and some weeding in the garden.

I didn't leave the village once but my horizons were widening. I talked to people I would never have spoken 'at home', I always found someone to chat to in the pub. Back in Hoylake when I had gone into a pub, as I did very occasionally, I would have a single half pint sitting at a table on my own, maybe saying 'Hello' to Glenda who had worked behind the bar for years, but I had never chatted to any of the regulars. Here, I was included in conversations, my opinion was asked about anything and everything, my assistance demanded to solve crossword clues and help untangle word games. I found their acceptance relaxing, and I knew I was becoming less stuffy by the day.

The Daimler remained in the garage until I had a phone call from Dani. Could I pick her up at Liskeard station that evening?

I had enjoyed my time alone, but I was really looking forward to seeing her again as I drove through the unfamiliar narrow country lanes.

She said nothing as we drove back, she didn't want to call in at the Smugglers. She said she just wanted to get home.

That night Dani knocked on my bedroom door when I was just dropping off to sleep. "Can I come in?" It sounded like she was crying. I put on the dressing gown that had been her husband's and opened the door, she walked straight across the room to a chair in the semi circular window. I followed her, sitting down in the other. We both looked out, the sea was calm and there seemed to be a silver path from the land to the moon which was nearly full.

"Sorry, I was just lonely." And she burst into tears.

I had no idea what to do. What did she expect of me? Should I reach over and hold her hand? Should I stand up and put my arm round her shoulders to comfort her?

"Do you want a drink? Should I..."

"Oh Charlie it was awful."

I decided to reach across and take one of her hands in both of mine.

"It was bound to be painful." I tried to find the right words. Everything that came to mind sounded trite. "It's all over now." "There there."

I had to let go of her hand when she needed to wipe her eyes and blow her nose with a soggy handkerchief. I felt so awkward but I really wanted to help her. She had been so good to me.

"Tell me what I can do."

"Give me a cuddle? Hold me?" She had stood up and walked over to the bed. She clearly expected me to follow. It was as she walked over I realised how few clothes she had on. She lay on the bed. Did she want me to make love to her? She hadn't given me any idea that she was interested in me in that way. She had only said 'a cuddle', perhaps, after all, that was all she meant so I sat rather awkwardly on the edge of the bed and self-consciously put my arms around her. "It was so awful" she was sobbing.

I let her cry. I had never kissed a girl, not properly, on the lips. It seemed ridiculous that I had never wanted to. Anyway this wasn't the time. I held her awkwardly, hoping that she would get some comfort from my just being there. I couldn't do anything else.

Eventually her sobbing slowed down so it was more of an intermittent hiccough. I manoeuvred a clean handkerchief out of my pocket and used it to wipe her eyes.

"You OK?"

She nodded. "Sorry. I'll go now. I didn't mean anything."

"I know."

"When I do mean something you'll know it." She was making a joke of it. Trying to smile I went along with the moment. "When you do, I'll not be such a gentleman."

The next morning I woke early intending to ignore the events of the night before. By the time Dani came downstairs I had laid the table, squeezed the oranges and the coffee was bubbling in the percolator. I was determined that neither of us would be embarrassed. Dani, however, was not going to ignore it. "Thanks for last night, I needed to know I wasn't a total shit."

"Was it that bad?"

We talked easily. I had expected awkwardness but there was none.

"I think the worst thing was that I called on our old next door neighbours and they didn't even ask me in! We'd been best mates and they didn't even ask me in! They said they felt it would be disloyal to Pete."

"Some friends."

"I don't think I've got many now, they all seem to have gone with him."

"There're all the people here, in the village. They're your friends."

"Not really, we drink together, they look out for me if I'm on my own, send strange young men up to stay with me, that sort of thing..." she was feeling better, she was teasing me.

"I haven't any friends. I don't think I've ever had anyone I would call a friend."

"Have you got any family, brothers? Sisters?"

"I don't think you could have asked a more difficult question. I've got a sister, her husband died. She's left with four children...."

"Four!"

"Yes, that's what we all thought, she just had one after the other, and she's only 24. It was all rather complicated really."

"How did her husband die? He must have been quite young."

"He drowned. It was the best thing that could have happened really, his dying I mean." She let me leave that unexplained.

"What about the children? How does she cope?"

"She doesn't. She's left them to be looked after by a Nanny..."

"Those 'independent means' come in useful then?"

I shrugged my shoulders and continued as if she hadn't interrupted "...who probably loves having sole control of them with no parents interfering with her regime. We go over every week or so to keep in touch."

"Anyone else? I'm looking to find you a friend in your life."

"I have a half-brother, Carl. He was my father's son but I suppose he's also my step-brother since my father married his Mother. He's all right, but I don't see him very often."

"You sound like you don't really want to."

"I try to like him, but I can't feel anything but suspicion and latent dislike. He's probably funny and undoubtedly clever but we've far too much history to be real friends. Anyway I have no idea where he is now, he was around for a few weeks around when Joe, that's Susannah's husband, died and then he disappeared."

"So where are we going to find you a friend?"

"I've got one. You."

She smiled as she poured another cup of coffee.

After a while I did something else I had rarely done before, I asked someone about their life "What about you?"

"A brother, he's a lot older than me and I haven't seen him for years." Her tone of voice didn't encourage me to enquire further.

"So here we are, two lost and lonely souls!"

Dani ripped up a sheet of paper into two bits and gave me one piece with a pen. She kept the other for herself.

"Right now, write down everyone you know between the ages of 20 and 30."

"That's a bloody short list!"

Carl Susannah

"What about the children's nanny?"

"Aged. Even by my standards." She caught my eye and we both smiled. Dani was doing me good. Not only was I getting used to being teased but I could begin to laugh at myself.

"Come on rack your brains. There must be others."

Linda Forster

"Who's she?"

"When Carl left home he went to live with some school friends, Linda's their young sister."

"How old?"

I crossed her out. "She's probably still at school. No. Hang on. She's just gone to university but that still makes her too young."

"Leave her on the list. She's close enough."

"She's got twin brothers, they're older I'm not sure of their names."

"Well put Linda's twin brothers"

"That's it then. Apart from Holly, I think her name was."

"Who's Holly?"

"A friend of Linda's I only met her for a few minutes."

"Put her on the list. You're going to have to meet people you know, if you're not going to wither and die an old man at 35."

"How am I going to do that?"

"Leave it with me. I'll think of something. Come on time for a walk."

When we got back John the Post had delivered the mail. There was a letter from Monika.

You have been away nearly four weeks and they have been busy times. I have visited the children. Josie asks where you are and I tell her you are having a holiday so she keeps asking questions. Where? Why you didn't take her? You must send her a postcard. Send me a postcard too.

I felt guilty. I had been so wrapped up in myself that I hadn't thought about anyone else.

Take care of yourself; we look forward to seeing you home soon.

"Time to go home?" Dani was watching me as I read.

"No. Not yet. Can you put up with me for longer?"

"Of course. It's good to have you here."

So I stayed.

As the weeks passed I noticed more and more trippers appearing at weekends until they seemed to be everywhere all the time. Shops that had been closed through the week were now open every day, the weather grew warmer and sunnier, and the days longer and still I stayed up at the house on the edge of the village. Easter came and went noticeable only by the increased crowds of people were queuing along the beach for the 'half hour trips along the coast' that were touted in a loud Lancastrian accent every few minutes.

The intimacy we had shared the night Dani had returned from London was never repeated though most people in the village seemed to assume we were sleeping together.

My series of articles *A Different Coast* were well received, it had given my career a necessary boost, but in the regular letters I received from Max and Monika it became increasingly obvious that I was expected home.

At breakfast one morning in early May I must have had a particular frown on my face because Dani asked "Problem?".

In reply I read from the letter "*Josie and the boys keep asking where you are and I have to keep saying you'll be back soon. Please, Charles, you've been away nearly four months now. When are you coming home?*"

81

"Sounds like time for you to go."

"Sounds like it."

"I was hoping you'd be here for our birthday."

"We could've had a joint party. I could have invited that long list of people I know, and there's lots of friends from the village eating our food and drinking our booze."

"Lots of people *who call themselves* friends from the village eating our food and drinking our booze. Most of them would go anywhere for a free nosh and drink "

"It looks like I'll be having a dinner party on my birthday, just a few dressed up people sitting stiffly round a table eating delicious food, drinking good wines probably wishing they could be sitting around watching television and not having to be polite."

"No music? No band? No dancing?"

"No music. No dancing. Just conversation."

I began to realise just how much I had changed in the months I had been away. In January I would have looked forward to the formal dinner. "I've got to go back sooner or later, I can't live in Brigadoon for 100 years."

"But it's a different Charles going back now. They won't recognise you, you're tanned, you've lost weight, your hair's positively hippie length. They'll wonder where the old Charles has gone."

"Why don't you come too? I've visited you for a few weeks, you could come up north and stay with me."

"No, thanks Charlie, I'd love to but I'll stay here. Brigadoon has its attractions."

As I drove the Daimler through the gates of Sandhey late on the following Sunday evening I knew Dani had been right, I was a different person from the Charles that had left, and I knew my life was going to have to change as well. I was looking forward to seeing Max and Monika again, but not Susannah. I didn't know how I was going to handle my sister.

As I let myself into the house I found them waiting for me in the hall like a reception committee. I shook hands with Max and gave Monika a hug. Luckily Susannah wasn't there.

"Your hair! It is so long, we must get that cut. And you are so brown!" Monika exclaimed as she released me, bombarding me with questions. "Where did you get that shirt? I do not recognise it. Have you been eating enough? You are so thin!" Max kept quiet as he waited for Monika to finish her greetings. He must have sensed that the changes in me went far deeper than the length of my hair and the colour of my skin.

"Let the boy get his clothes unpacked and have a wash and brush up after his drive. He can answer all your questions at dinner."

"Where's Susannah?"

Max and Monika exchanged glances and it was Monika who answered. "She left, when she knew you were coming home she said she didn't want to see you and since this was your home she'd go. She said she'd write to let us know where she was. She's a lot better now, we think she can look after herself."

"But she isn't with the children."

"No."

To change the subject I spoke with somewhat forced enthusiasm "I've got some photos, I'll show you where I've been and what I've been up to. They'll do a far better job than I could in words."

As I ran up the stairs two at a time I could hear Max's voice, a mixture of enquiry and sadness "He's changed."

Over dinner I told them about Dani and the house and the village, showing them some of the photographs I had taken.

"A pretty girl." Max was asking far more in his seemingly innocent comment.

"Dani? I suppose so, she's really nice, a bit mixed up at the moment but that's because she's been going through a divorce."

"Divorce? The slip of a girl hardly looks old enough to have a boyfriend let alone an ex-husband." Max frowned over his glasses at me as I smiled at his description. "She hasn't got a new boyfriend then?" I didn't think he was making a joke.

"If you mean what I think you mean no, neither of us was looking for anything like that. She gave me all her husband's old clothes though. Not that they're old old, just the clothes he'd left behind."

"What did you do with all that time you had on your hands?"

"We talked, walked, read, cooked, ate, cleaned the house, did the gardening, just pottered about really. I got my articles in each month on time, just, and it was interesting to study a different coast, they seemed to like the different angles. It really is wonderful down there. Otherwise it was a real holiday."

"It sounds like it with all that housework and gardening. But what a lovely spot to be doing it in."

83

We were being so stilted and polite. I had got used to teasing, argument and laughter at meals, the formality began to grate and I wondered that this had been normal for so many years.

"It was, and the villagers were really nice, those that I met anyway, and friendly. I met and talked with more people in these last months than I ever did here."

Monika had failed to spot the beginnings of impatience in my voice and asked "What sort of people?"

"What do you mean *sort* of people? They probably weren't our *sort* of people, they were butchers, bakers, fishermen, retired hippies, people running away from things, sick people, children, work dodgers, skivers, all sorts of people. Though there was one retired millionaire. Would he be our 'sort'?"

"I didn't mean anything." I shouldn't have snapped and Monika was hurt.

"I'm sorry. I didn't mean to say all that."

"No, Charles, of course you didn't."

I should have been quiet then, Max had warned me and I should have taken notice, but I was determined not to let them make me what I used to be.

"But it's true isn't it? We only meet the 'right sort of people', we only mix with people the same as us and there aren't many of them either. Susannah went outside the circle when she married Joe but it didn't change anything. We just widened the circle and temporarily invited Joe in. We were so arrogant that we thought we could change him into one of us. But we couldn't could we? We hadn't changed him one bit and look where that led."

"We will not talk about Joe." I would previously have obeyed the authority in Max's tone that brooked no argument "I am shocked you should mention his name in front of Monika. Monika, Charles will apologise."

But I didn't. I just carried on. "But Joe *happened*. We look after his children, Susannah's gone completely off the rails and hasn't got over it all."

"We do not talk about it."

I continued to ignore Max's warning. I had thought a lot about this, I had even talked about the situation, hypothetically of course, with the very mixed bunch in the Smugglers. 'What would you do if…' None of them could understand a family where none of it had ever been mentioned since.

84

"But we can't ignore it. It's nearly two years ago and we have *never* talked about it."

"There is nothing to talk about."

"But there is. There is. Can't you see there's *everything* to talk about? What happened to each of us that day, how we feel about it, how we'll get over it. Doesn't it seem strange that we've never talked about it?"

"No it doesn't seem strange and I think you've said enough."

"Are we arguing?" I was so frustrated at the politeness and knew neither of them understood a word I was saying.

"No Charles, we are not arguing. *You* are arguing. And you are going to stop. I don't know what's got into you."

"Perhaps I'm having a belated adolescence."

"I think you're tired after your long drive. Apologise to Monika."

I obeyed like the dutiful child they seemed to think I still was. "I'm sorry if I've upset you Monika, I didn't mean to." But I couldn't leave it there. "But I really think we should know each other well enough by now to talk about things, to try to understand each other. I think I know more about the lives of some of the people in Polperro than I do about you."

I was remembering why I had left.

"We all live in the same house and we know nothing about each other really."

Max got up from the table and walked round to pull Monika's chair back, an old fashioned gesture from an old fashioned gentleman. "Come my dear, we will have coffee in the lounge while our adolescent friend gets some sleep and recovers himself."

I understood myself dismissed.

It had not been a successful return home.

I sat at my desk and looked out at the familiar view, the waters of the sea meeting the estuary, the islands with the mountains in the distance. I realised how much I had enjoyed my time away and how difficult it was going to be to adjust back to what had been a comfortable life.

I undressed slowly but did not pull on the paisley pyjamas that I knew without looking would be neatly folded under my pillow. I knew what the problem was. Max had said so in so many words. I had never been young. Dani was right. I had to do something to stop being buried in this house, however much I respected Max and loved Monika, and I really was truly grateful to them, I could no longer live the way I had been living.

My life was going to have to change.

At breakfast the next morning nothing was said about the previous night's conversation. As always with anything that might upset the smooth running of the house, it was swept under the carpet.

Instead of mentioning any disagreement Max began to talk about my birthday party as if nothing had happened to change things. I interrupted.

"I know it's pretty much a fixture on the calendar but would you mind terribly if we didn't do the usual dinner this year?"

I looked from Monika to Max, there was puzzlement in both their faces.

"But we always..." Monika began.

"Monika so enjoys ..." Max added

But I interrupted them both. "I was thinking more along the lines of a barbecue. I'll find some bricks and build one at the bottom of the garden. I'll cook hamburgers and sausages and with some French sticks and some salad stuff everyone will have enough to eat. Josie and the boys can come, they can invite some of their friends."

I had been very wary of suggesting such a change in our normal household routine but neither had said anything so I felt bold enough to continue. "I'll invite Carl, if Susannah's abandoned ship then he may well come, along with the Forsters, the twins, whatever their names are and the sister. And there was another girl in January, a blonde American, we'll find out who she is and invite her too."

I was surprised when Max seemed to want to put me off inviting the American.

"I don't think that would be a good idea. There is no connection, just that she came to a funeral with her friend. Now what about your young lady in Cornwall?"

Monika seemed very doubtful about the idea of a barbecue. She asked was I sure she couldn't do anything to help. I assured her it wouldn't be up to her standard but I wanted to give her the chance to enjoy a party for once. She allowed herself to be convinced, but only on the condition I wasn't too proud to ask her anything if I got stuck or changed my mind.

Max sat back while Monika and I talked. I tried to interpret his expression. It seemed to be concern, even disappointment.

86

Was that because I had disrupted the normal birthday arrangements?

Or was he recognising that he no longer controlled me and that life at Sandhey would never be the same again.

Chapter Ten

When I said I would do all the arrangements for the barbecue I had no idea what I was letting myself in for, and I had allowed less than a week.

I spent the first day on the phone inviting anyone who was likely to come, emphasising the informality of the afternoon. I found myself having to confirm that, yes, this was me, Charles, and yes, it was a barbecue, and yes, they could come in shorts. As I made the calls I began to realise how people had seen me.

"Yes, it's going to be a fun afternoon, lazing around in the garden, eating hamburgers and hot dogs, drinking wine, doing whatever you like."

Everyone I wanted to come accepted, except Dani. She said she had a houseful of guests and couldn't get away but she wished me luck and said she'd send a parcel of a dozen pasties 'just in case'.

The second day I built the barbecue, copying as closely as I could the design of Dani's in Polperro. It wasn't the best built structure but I reasoned it only had to work once. I tested it out, producing a sausage and a hamburger. It took over an hour but it worked.

I did ask Monika's advice on which shops to go to, though I resisted her offer to do the shopping with me. I accepted her insistence that she peel the potatoes for the potato salad. But everything else I did myself. By the Saturday I was exhausted, but buoyed up with anticipation for the next day. I watched the television weather forecast with trepidation.

After a Sunday morning putting out croquet hoops, setting out the tables and chairs around the garden, getting the barbecue running, setting out the food, I sat back with a glass of lager. The weather was good and I was exhausted. But I had done it.

Even if no one but Max and Monika turned up I felt I had achieved more than I had ever done before.

Susannah's children along with several of their friends shepherded by the aged nanny arrived first, as arranged. I wanted to overcome the problem of the first guest arriving to an empty garden, and awkward conversation. I thought if the children were there, playing croquet or French cricket, they would make the garden feel alive. I spent a difficult ten minutes persuading the nanny that it was perfectly OK for them to run around shouting and enjoying themselves. Usually when they visited us they were kept under strict control, having been firmly warned that they must be on their best behaviour, but now they were enthusiastically taking advantage of their unusual freedom to be children.

When Carl arrived full of adrenalin having driven up from Cambridge that morning he immediately joined the children, organising them into teams and diverting their boundless energy into a competition. Carl seemed to be enjoying himself with Susannah's children. I wondered at first whether he knew which were hers, but then I saw Josie shyly introducing her three younger brothers Jack, Al and Bill. "I just said I was a friend of yours." He explained to me later.

I had never met the Forsters though, of course, I had heard about them from Ted. As I sat down with them with a jug of Pimm's it was they who were putting me at my ease rather than the other way around. Linda soon left to join Carl with the children as Pat and Jeff asked me about my time in Cornwall, how I had come up with the idea of the barbecue and how my writing was going. They seemed genuinely interested. I had the feeling they didn't think much of wasting time simply making polite conversation. I found I was telling them some of the things I had hoped to be able to tell Max and Monika about my months away. They were relaxed and comfortable people to be with and I found myself jealous of Carl for the years he had spent with them.

When the Ecclestons arrived I was surprised that Holly and her parents didn't immediately join us. "Linda and Holly spend such a lot of time together, it's probably no bad thing" Pat Forster commented as she watched them settling down at a table on the other side of the garden. "We'll go over later."

Trying to be a good host I went across to the Ecclestons and said hello to Holly. They seemed a family in complete contrast with the Forsters. Where the Forsters interrupted each other's conversations and rarely stopped smiling the Ecclestons were quiet and it was all I could do to get Holly to answer any question with more than a monosyllable. They seemed tense with me and with each other. Matt Eccleston barely spoke a word, he simply sat staring through me, never meeting my eyes. I wondered how two friends could come from such different families.

Other guests arrived and were welcomed, but my job was chef and I spent most of the rest of the afternoon cooking behind the charcoal. I worked on the principle that my guests could see the food, the drink and they could help themselves.

I began to enjoy myself watching my guests as they moved around the garden as if in a relay race.

Carl and Linda eventually left the children to their games and went to join the Forsters. As he remained with their parents, Oliver and Crispin went to talk to Holly. As they approached the table Holly's father went inside the house.

I noticed Max following him. Remembering Graham at the funeral, less than five months earlier, I left the heat of the barbecue and followed just in time to seem Max ushering Matt into his study. In those few moments they stood together I began to understand something. There was a similarity I couldn't define. There was something in Matt's movements that reminded me of Max, as he had been years before.

I knew if I was in the dining room I could overhear their conversation in the quiet house.

I heard it, but I didn't understand it.

"Why Mr Eccleston, of course." Max was being polite and affable though he sounded a little offended. Matt didn't answer directly but spoke shortly and sharply in German. I had no idea what he said.

Max's response did not surprise me. He spoke firmly and in English. "I do not speak in German. I prefer English now, and have for 30 years."

"As you wish. You know of course who I am."

It was some time before Max answered. When he did he sounded relaxed and at ease. "Of course. I have been expecting you to make yourself known for some time."

I heard the scrape of chair legs against the wooden floor. I thought that quite clever. It was like the interrogations in war films where officers moved slowly, performing some mundane action such as moving to a chair and sitting down, creating valuable moments in which to work out an answer. I had always admired those skills. My father had learned them as a barrister. He had had that same ability to think fast without showing any sign that that was what he was doing, the ability to give nothing away by the look on his face, and, most importantly, the ability to analyse all options and select those that were most likely to succeed.

Max didn't lead the conversation, he said nothing that would help Matt who obviously could think of nothing to say. Perhaps he had expected Max to cry out, to ask questions, at the very least to be shocked and angry. Instead Max was quiet. I imagined him sitting authoritatively at his desk, Matt, still standing, awkward and ill at ease.

I was just thinking I should return to the barbecue, realising I shouldn't be listening but intrigued, when Max broke the silence. "Mattieu, for you could only be Mattieu, your brother would have been more clever, you fall into the trap of youth, though you are no longer young. You see life only from your own perspective. You believe that what you do is everything and that what others do is nothing. When I met Holly at Alicia's funeral I saw immediately the resemblance to the family. I saw things, not of you, for you are an oaf, but of her Mother. You will know that I have returned to our home village each year and was intrigued to find that an American had been there asking questions about me. You have no subtlety. So, yes, Mattieu, I do know who you are."

"What are you going to do then?"

"About what?"

"About fulfilling your family responsibilities."

"What responsibilities would those be? Ah." Max spoke as if the answer had only just come to him "it is money you want."

"Of course. You owe me Uncle Maximilian."

"I do not think so. I owe you nothing and I need do nothing."

"But what about your other family?" Matt spoke as if producing a trump card.

Max again was quiet while he thought what exactly Matt knew to say that.

"That Graham's a sharp boy. He spotted something at that funeral and came to me. He showed me a photograph, it could have been Holly, but it wasn't, the photo was 40 years old and it was in that desk, that drawer. We both know now who I am, and that Holly is your flesh and blood, but what about your housekeeper?"

He must have known that this would be harder for Max to deal with.

"What about her?"

"That photograph was of her. Only she wasn't called 'Monika' then was she?"

A chair moved, creaking against the wooden floor and Max said something I could not hear above the slight scraping, rather like a clicking of heels on the parquet flooring.

"I will do nothing. I will wait and see. A very English habit you would do well to learn."

I wanted to hear how the conversation was concluded but they seemed to be moving towards the door and I had to return to my cooking before either of them could suspect I had overheard their conversation.

I wasn't sure which man I should be more afraid of.

In a lull in the demands for food Linda came over to the barbecue. She sat down on a stool next to me. "You've changed." She said with no preliminary. "Possibly." I replied. "But then you probably don't really know me do you?"

"You were an old fogey, you're not now."

"How?"

"Your hair's a lot longer, you're much more casual, you're smiling and you're actually quite attractive."

I ignored the compliment "You wouldn't expect me to wear shorts at a funeral would you?"

"You know what I mean. You wore formal clothes as if they were the only things you ever wore."

"They were then."

"So I'm right," she proclaimed triumphantly, jumping down from the stool and returning to her parents, and Carl. I wondered what all that had been about.

As we had been talking I noticed Matt leaving the house.

He didn't go back to Holly who was sitting on a tartan rug laid out on the grass with Crispin and Oliver, nor did he join his wife who was standing alone by the wall looking out across the estuary. He stood for some moments on the terrace looking around the garden as if trying to remember every detail of who was there, as if making sure that everyone would see him. We held each other's gaze for a few long moments before he turned to march down the short drive and away. He wanted me to see he was leaving of his own free will.

A short while later Linda came down the garden again.

"Crisp and Oliver, my brothers, want to know why you don't get a proper job."

"No they don't, you do." I wondered what I would have replied if I hadn't had those months in Cornwall.

"OK. Maybe. But they'd like to know, as well."

"I don't see why I should tell you but I do."

"You don't do as much as Carl does. You're never on the television, you don't teach all the time."

"True. But I'm going to be learning all the time." I'm not sure why I thought I should tell this pushy young woman anything but I did feel the need to justify myself, I was never comfortable when compared with Carl. "I'm doing a training course. The magazines are fed up with my writing so they've told me to learn to type. So that's what I'm going to do."

" But you're a man."

"I'm glad you've noticed."

"But learning to type?"

"What's wrong with that? With computers and things everyone will have to type."

She didn't leave this time, she sat helping me with the food, handing it down to Josie to take round to her friends.

Eventually, the sausages exhausted, it was time to let the barbecue die down. Still Linda didn't leave me. "Come on," she had jumped up on the wall and sat down with her back to the garden dangling her legs mischievously inches above the heads of trippers walking along the coast path. I climbed up next to her.

I couldn't resist asking whether she thought I was like Carl. I probably shouldn't have asked but I was curious.

"Pretty much." Her answer told me nothing.

"What does that mean?"

"In January you seemed 30 going on 50, more like Carl's father than his brother."

"Thanks."

"But," continued Linda firmly ignoring me "now you are very alike. You're both really lovely…" she must have seen the look on my face she added swiftly "…and interesting."

"Thanks, I think I'd rather be 'interesting' than 'lovely'."

"You're both interesting."

"But there are differences. Firstly Carl's good at something people are interested in and I'm good at something that most people find incredibly boring."

She smiled at me and mouthed the word 'true'.

"Carl's younger, knows far more people, had a far more interesting life, and…."

I don't know why I told her so much. Perhaps she was a good listener. Perhaps I just felt relaxed in her company. She seemed rather like Dani in some ways.

I told her how I had thought I had been happy but now I realised I had only been avoiding making any decision that might cause risk. I had been so averse to unhappiness that I had avoided doing anything that might lead me away from my comfortable safe home. I told her how my world had changed in the past year and, surprisingly, I was glad. I finished by looking at her "The changes have only just begun."

As Linda talked to me through the afternoon I noticed Holly

watching us. I thought they were friends yet I didn't see them talk once through the afternoon.

Holly had spent a long time talking to Carl, perhaps Linda was jealous and that was why she paid me so much attention.

I'm not sure the afternoon was entirely a success. People seemed to enjoy themselves, the children certainly had a lot of fun, but the party was over long before I had expected. I suppose I had thought it would be like the barbecues in Polperro that had lasted long into the evening. When the children were rounded up by their nanny before six o'clock and ushered away the other guests seemed to take that as a sign to leave. They were all very polite with their thanks but as I was left in the garden alone I felt a depressing sense of anti-climax.

As Monika helped me clear the detritus of the party while Max and Ted watched from the table on the terrace, I wondered if it had been a mistake. Perhaps I should have stuck with the traditional dinner party, at least then it would not have been such a disappointment.

"I think everyone had a good time." She said, in a voice that seemed more intent on cheering me up than saying something she really believed to be true. "All your hard work was worth it."

"The children certainly did. I'm not so sure about some of the others."

"Max and Ted have always enjoyed your birthday evenings. It is a time for them to think that perhaps the world hasn't changed as much as they fear."

In an hour you could not have known there had been a party in that garden and Monika and I sat down with Ted and Max.

"Did you get anything to eat yourself?" Ted broke the uncomfortable silence "I noticed you cooking for all you were worth but I didn't notice you eating anything."

"I had bits and pieces."

"It is easy for the cook to go without." Monika was teasing me "I'll go and get something for supper."

"Well, my boy, was that what you expected?" Max asked as if he thought he knew the answer would be 'no'.

"I hope people enjoyed themselves."

"I don't think people know how to. They sat around and talked to each other much as they would any other day. No one spoke to anyone they wouldn't normally speak to, the family groups barely broke up. There was no sense of occasion."

"That's exactly what I wanted, informality, relaxation."

"But people don't go to parties for 'informality' and 'relaxation' they go for something special. Something out of the ordinary."

Perhaps he was right. Perhaps it had been a mistake. Perhaps I was trying to be something I was not. Perhaps it was best if I just accepted I was never going to have friends my own age, never going to be anything other than what I was. The legacy of Polperro had been an illusion. I wasn't cut out to have a life with people my own age. I had tried, and I had failed. I would just now revert to type.

"Perhaps you're right." Was all I actually said, but Ted must have seen something in my face that said more.

"You were right to try. It is important not just to accept oneself as others see you but to try to be something different."

I was reminded of the evening before my Mother's funeral and the view of Ted I had had then, of someone who had spent a lifetime being what he had fallen into rather than what he had wanted to be. He had loved my Mother but, because of the way she and others saw him, he could never do anything about it. He had become the respectable, reliable, dull dogsbody for my parents when he was about the age I was now.

"Did you ever want to rebel Ted? Did you ever want to say 'the person you all think is me isn't. I am someone else entirely'."

"Of course I did."

"Didn't you try to do anything about it?"

He was quiet for a while. Obviously the question was too close for comfort.

"My mother. She needed me to look after her. My father died just after the war, the first war that is. He died of influenza, not war wounds so somehow it was more ignominious. I looked after her. I got a job, I couldn't fight during the second war and then I was tied in. I did well. I did far better than anyone could have expected, but I always had Mother to look after. I didn't leave home. I didn't marry."

"But you fell in love."

"Of course I did. Anyone who met her fell in love with Alicia. She was beautiful, and vulnerable. She just expected it."

"But you never did anything about it."

"Of course not. How could I? She was out of my league."

"Why? Why was she? I don't understand. You loved her, why didn't you do anything about it?"

Ted looked helpless as he looked out to the estuary for help.

"Times were different then. I was not of her class."

"That's ridiculous."

"No it's not. Times were different then. Alicia, whatever 'class' she started in, married your father. That put her out of my reach. She never saw me as a person in my own right."

"Do you regret it? What would you have done differently?"

"Oh Charles, you do ask questions that are unanswerable. Of course I regret it. I loved her, I thought she was the most precious and beautiful of women. If she had seen me as anything other than me, if she could have seen me as anything other than … Oh I don't know how she saw me, perhaps someone who could help her when she had nowhere else to go, perhaps someone who would look after her when there was no one else. Perhaps I was her person of last resort."

I had never heard Ted so open with his answers, maybe he had had one or two too many wines that afternoon, maybe he had seen how hard I was trying not to be me and wanted to give me courage.

"I am so sorry I didn't go to see her those last months."

"Thank you. I needed to hear that."

"What should I do Ted? I'm a bit lost."

"Like you were when you were a boy?" He reminded me, without actually saying anything, of the time I had run away from school and he had rescued me.

"No Ted, like I am now."

"Well, do you want me to say what I would do if I were you? What I would do if I were 30 again? I would change. Without a doubt. I would change. I would become the person people didn't expect me to be. You tried today. You tried to do something that was different and you did a good job. Don't expect it all to happen in one day though. It will take time for that lovely red-head and the American to recognise you as anything other than the stiff person they saw at the funeral. "

"I should change then?"

"Of course. And you made a good start today. I admire you Charles, many people wouldn't have had the guts to do as you did, especially against the strength of Max. Well done."

"I should carry on then? Rebelling?"

"If that is what you want yes. He will understand, she will understand, they will understand. One day."

"What should I do?"

"You're asking me? I who failed so miserably to change? Thank you Charles. I appreciate that, more than you could possibly understand, but I can give you no answers. Trust your judgement and act on your instincts. Perhaps that's all the advice I can offer as throughout my life I have done neither."

"I want to be my age you know, I want friends of my age."

"I know."

"Ted."

"Yes?"

"Thanks."

I hadn't noticed when Max had gone inside. It was only Ted and I who sat watching the sun sinking.

"Where's Max? And Monika?"

"They're inside, sorting out your birthday dinner I think."

"Oh dear."

"No it hasn't been a waste of time. You have made a sign to them you are changing. That is good. You mustn't give in, Charles. Don't give in. You have a chance to be you. Be you."

Max came out to join us, just as Ted left to go inside.

"I'm sorry Max, I didn't realise how much our formal evenings meant to you."

"No reason why you should." He seemed detached.

"Yes there is, I have lived in your house all these years I should know you by now."

"Indeed you should."

But it seemed that Max was not going to help me in that understanding.

Chapter Eleven

"Hello, Holly isn't it? Fancy seeing you." The scruffy man in black jeans and greasy blue anorak pulled up a chair and sat between Holly and Linda without asking. It was a week after they had got back to Leicester after the funeral. They were in the pub hoping to meet up again with friends from their first term.

"Pardon?" Holly looked blank, she had no idea who it was but they had made a lot of friends in their first few months at Leicester so she assumed she must just have forgotten this one. He seemed eminently forgettable. His hair was greasy, his finger nails dirty and overall he gave the impression he could do with a wash.

"Don't you remember me?" He asked.

"Why on earth would we?" Linda replied, trying her most severe put down.

"I wasn't talking to you, I was talking to Holly, here. You remember me, don't you darling?" He moved as if to kiss her and she smelt the beer and tobacco on his breath.

"Bugger off! I've never seen you before."

"Perhaps you don't recognise me with these clothes on?" He suggested with a smirk Linda and Holly found equally unattractive.

"I don't recognise you. You're right."

He must have decided his planned approach had failed so he changed tack. "The funeral? My aunt's funeral? You remember me now. Graham Tyler."

They did.

"What the hell are you doing here?"

"That's not a very nice welcome."

"Well, what do you expect?" Holly couldn't have sounded less enthusiastic.

"I was nearby and I remembered you'd said you were at Leicester so I checked out the usual drinking holes and here you are. This is only the fifth I've tried. Do you want to go out with me tomorrow." He had turned speaking to Holly.

"I don't know what Linda's got planned."

"No I don't mean you plural, just you, singular."

"Why would I want to do that?"

He ignored the coldness in her voice.

"Have you ever been motor racing? Not actually doing it. Watching it."

"No, I can't say I have."

"We could go to Silverstone, it's not far."

Holly thought she could use Linda as an excuse. "I'll have to ask Linda."

"Why, when she's not invited?" Graham's voice changed. He was past the point of rudeness.

"She won't go without me you know, though why either of us would want to go with you is beyond me."

"Come on, you'll enjoy it. It'll be a chance to learn something about your family won't it?" He continued talking to Holly, his back to Linda.

"What's that supposed to mean?"

He didn't answer the question directly, instead he gave them another reason for going with him. "You'll see what your precious Carl gets up to."

"OK. I suppose so." Linda replied for both of them, showing no sign of enthusiasm as she gave him their address.

When Holly woke the next morning and looked out of the window it was raining. It looked cold and windy. She just knew it was going to be a miserable day.

Graham picked them up at 11, opening the passenger door of the Cortina for Holly and leaving Linda to settle on the back seat amongst a mess of old cigarette packets, beer bottles and maps. The silence as they drove was only broken by the irritating scrape of the windscreen wipers. The car radio didn't work.

"Do we have to go to Silverstone, can't we just find somewhere dry for a drink, a bit of lunch, and then go home?" Holly asked after they had turned off the motorway.

"We're going." The shortness of his reply was slightly threatening, and somehow it was easier to do as he decided. "You'll love it when you get there." It seemed to Holly that he was giving her an order. Linda sat in the back just wishing they hadn't agreed to come.

They were both dressed for the weather, jeans and proper shoes, with heavy sweatshirt and anorak, gloves and scarves, but neither could imagine how they could be so cold as they stood by the fence on a bend next to a strip of empty tarmac in what looked like an abandoned airfield. After a few minutes a stream of cars passed by in a cloud of spray.

"That's it is it?" Linda asked sarcastically after the noise had died down. She got no reply and some minutes later they came round again, far more strung out. The last car had barely passed before the

99

faster ones had caught up. She counted them past ten times and then it went quiet again.

"So interesting. I wouldn't have missed that for the world." She said to no one in particular.

"Well piss off back to the car then. Except I'm not giving you the key am I?" So Linda walked away anyway, towards what looked, through the mists of lingering spray, like a coffee stall. She wanted something warm. If she didn't find them again it didn't matter, she could hitch a ride home.

The rain didn't ease up. Holly stood grimly with hands in pockets and water dripping down the back of her neck.

"What on earth do you see in this?"

"It's a shame it's raining, but I like the sound of the engines and the battles that go on. Just think how wet the drivers are getting."

"Can we go home now?"

"We've only just got here. The best part of the day has yet to come."

"I'm going to find Linda." She decided it couldn't be difficult, there were hardly any other people stupid enough to be standing around in the rain watching cars going round in circles. She caught up with Linda at the coffee stall and they stood, their hands around the paper cups, trying to get some warmth.

By the time Graham had joined them Linda had lost patience. "Graham. We're cold and we're wet. This is completely boring. Can we go home? We're not enjoying it one tiny bit."

"Not yet. Not until we've seen someone. That's why we're here."

"Him." Linda and Holly looked across the wet tarmac to where Graham was pointing and saw a man they both recognised despite his bulky coat and the hood that half covered his face in the rain.

Carl was with a group of other men, surrounding the front of a car, laughing and apparently arguing over the lump of metal he was holding.

"Hello Carl Witherby isn't it, or should I say Donaldson?" Graham walked over and interrupted their discussion before either Holly or Linda could stop him. They followed him. It was the only thing they could do.

Carl saw Holly first, recognising her without knowing who Graham was.

"Holly?" He was so surprised to see her he repeated "Holly!" He handed the shock absorber to one of his friends and walked over to her and hugged her. "Sorry I'm so wet, but then aren't we all! What're you doing here? And Linda!" He hugged her, apologising for getting her even wetter. "Not possible." She had answered miserably. He pulled away a little and dropped his voice "and who's he?"

100

"Graham Tyler." Graham held his hand out towards Carl who automatically shook the proffered hand.

"Tyler?"

"Yes. Tyler."

"Ah."

Holly and Linda didn't understand what was going on between the two men but tried to pick up the threads of meaning behind the conversation.

"Alicia was my aunt."

"So?" Carl was giving little away.

"We are, I believe, related."

"No. I don't think so." They could hear the coldness in Carl's voice, a coldness neither had ever heard, as threatening in its way as Graham's more overt aggression.

"Well nearly. I mean your *father*" Graham stressed the word knowingly "was my uncle so we are practically cousins."

"By marriage perhaps."

"Though you being a bastard I suppose makes it's even slighter a relationship."

"I suppose." Carl was holding his temper, trying to work out where this conversation was going. The friends he was with busied themselves with something at the back of the car. "What is it you want?" He waited a few moments for Graham to answer, but when it came the answer was oblique.

"Are you very rich?"

"What sort of question is that?" Carl was surprised into answering.

"I just wondered. What I mean is your brother doesn't work for a living and you've got a very expensive hobby. I just wondered where the money…"

Carl interrupted him "Why I should explain I don't know. I work for my living and that," Carl gestured towards the mud spattered car "I share with a friend."

"Oh would that be *friend* in your brother's sense of the word?"

Carl didn't answer. He took an oily rag from his pocket and wiped his hands. Ignoring Graham he turned to Holly and Linda. "What are you doing with this scumbag?"

Before they could answer Graham grabbed Holly's arm and steered her away. Linda shrugged her shoulders helplessly at Carl and ran after them. She couldn't leave Holly alone with him.

"That's why you brought us here wasn't it? There's something going on and you needed to make Carl speak to you. You knew he would only do that if you were with someone he knew! What are you up to?"

"Haven't you enjoyed it just a bit?"

"No. We're cold. We're wet. We want to go home."

Again Linda spoke for both of them.

Graham couldn't have been nicer on the way back. He drove more carefully than he had in the morning and talked, apparently quite frankly. "I'm sorry if you feel used. I didn't mean it to be like that. I've been looking forward to seeing you both again and getting to know you, really I have." He spoke to Holly, Linda was huddled in the back seat occasionally wiping the steamed up windows to see that there really was a world out there.

They didn't notice him turning off the main road and driving down country lanes until he stopped at a pub by a canal. It had stopped raining and the sun warmed them almost as much as the large brandies Graham bought them.

He didn't mention Silverstone or the racing, or Carl. He spoke about canals and locks. He seemed to know quite a lot about them. Holly reluctantly found herself listening; he could be quite interesting.

Linda interrupted to ask why he had wanted to talk to Carl.

"I was curious." He then changed the subject back to the canal, the locks and, for a reason they never understood, Roses Lime Juice.

As he talked Holly found that she was enjoying herself far more than she had expected despite Linda's continuing hostility. Graham was not such a bore as she had thought. He seemed to like the same music as she did, and the same films.

Or at least that was what he led her to believe.

Holly felt vaguely annoyed when he said he was heading back to London that evening, as soon as he had dropped them off. "I've enjoyed our chat Holly," he had said whilst looking defiantly at Linda, "I'll give you a call. Perhaps we can have a drink together." 'Without Linda' was left unsaid.

"I'll look forward to that."

It surprised her that she almost meant it.

Linda couldn't understand why Holly had accepted Graham's invitations and had gone out with him a few times. "Just don't let him come back to the flat." Linda had said "He gives me the creeps and I can't understand why he doesn't give you the creeps either."

"He's OK." Holly would say but could offer no evidence.

She couldn't say that Graham was stringing her along with snippets of information about her parents. She couldn't admit to anyone, especially Linda, that she was not only listening to what Graham told her but that she believed it.

He had started, that first weekend after Silverstone, by hinting that he knew more about her parents than she did.

"You know your Dad's not Canadian don't you?"

When she had argued that of course he was, he and her Mom had met at University in Toronto. He had been the librarian and they fell in love during her last year.

"Have it your own way." Graham had said dismissively in a way that really annoyed her.

It was on another date, a week later, that Graham spoke out of the blue. "He didn't get to Canada until after the war."

"Why would you say that? You're lying."

"Have it your own way."

"He's Canadian. Why would he lie?"

"You tell me."

Graham kept asking questions. Knowing that, because she could not answer them, they would sow seeds of doubt in her mind. What did she know of her Father's family? What did she know of her Mother's parents, the O'Dwyers? Didn't they have nothing to do with them because they hadn't approved of her Dad? What about her Eccleston grandparents? What did she know of them? They seemed the sort of questions a boyfriend might ask of a girlfriend he was trying to get to know better. She answered them honestly. She had no reason not to.

It was when he contradicted her answers, saying he knew better, that she began to argue with him.

"I've been through the records. He didn't get to Canada until he was 27 years old. He wasn't born there."

"Of course he was!"

"Have it your own way."

The snippets he fed her week after week preyed on her mind. She couldn't ask her Dad anything and it would only cause problems if she asked her Mom. So she let the seeds of doubt fester.

It was the only reason she kept seeing him. She hated what he had to say, but some of it had the ring of truth.

"How do you know all this?" She asked one afternoon. She was trying not to believe that Linda might be right about Graham after all. She did not realise that by asking that question she was showing him she believed what he said was true.

"That's for me to know and you to find out." She had stormed out of the pub at that, but when he called and asked her out the next week she knew she would go.

The scraps of information he gave her of her family made Holly wonder about her parents and how much she actually did know of their past. It was the details she did have, and told Graham, that proved to be very useful to him.

She couldn't tell Linda why she kept seeing him and Linda, not understanding, felt excluded. And by the time they had finished their first year exams and were heading home Linda and Holly had had enough of each other's company.

"How did you meet?" Holly asked what she thought would be seen as an innocent question when she was having her first supper with her parents after getting home for the long summer holiday.

"Why do you ask?" Her Mother seemed OK with the question.

"I just wondered, you know. I don't know much about you when you were young. I mean we never see my grandparents. I don't know anything about your parents Dad."

Her parents looked across the table at each other and she saw the enquiry in her Mother's eyes.

"Well Matt, we knew she would ask sooner or later."

"You're not going to say I'm adopted or anything. Are you?" Holly panicked. She hadn't been prepared for that.

"No. No. Of course not Darling."

"What is it then?"

"Your Dad had a very difficult childhood. He lost touch with his parents when he was just a boy. He had to find his own way in life. He taught himself everything he knew and got a good job at the university. That's where I met him. He hasn't got a family. Only us."

The phone rang and Matt answered it, seemingly relieved that the interrogation was interrupted. Both Mary and Holly listened to Matt's side of the conversation even though he seemed to be speaking quieter than was natural.

"Not really but carry on anyway."

"Too fucking right." He sounded interested

"Yeah. I'm going."

"How much?"

"OK. Probably. Tomorrow. I said OK." And he put the phone receiver down.

"What was that about?" Mary asked when Matt came back to the table.

"Nothing." They both knew he wasn't going to tell them.

"Dad you were telling me about your family."

"No I wasn't. You were asking about it."

"You met Mum in Toronto. Is that where you came from?" She realised she was playing a dangerous game by pushing her Dad further. He had never liked too many questions.

Mary answered for him. "Don't keep on Holly, your Dad doesn't like thinking about it."

104

"I met your Mother, married her and we had you. That's all you need to know." Matt wanted an end to the conversation but Holly needed information to contradict the picture Graham had painted.

He had told her of a man, no longer young, arriving in Canada after the war with no past. He got a job in the library at the university. His knowledge of languages, especially German, had helped him. He had wanted to marry so he could never be deported. He found an isolated student, rather as a predatory hunter searches for its prey amongst the weak and the marginalized on the plains of Africa.

"But where were you born? What did you do before you got the job in Toronto?"

In Mary, Graham had said, Matt found someone who hated her parents, had no friends and spoke to no one.

"Mum? What happened to your parents? Why don't we ever hear from them?"

Graham said he persuaded her that if they married they could go to America. She had graduated top of her year, any university would snap her up. Then she wouldn't have to look after her parents as they grew old.

"Why do I never see any of my grandparents? Are they all dead? Where do we come from?"

Holly looked at her parents, having had no answer to any of her questions, she asked one final question

"Did you ever love each other?" The silence that followed was answer enough. "So why are you still together?"

She knew her parents had never been happy, she had heard the arguments through the years; her Father's shouting and her Mother's tears. She'd seen the broken furniture and her Mother's bruises. But she had always thought there must have been a time when they loved each other.

"It's because of me isn't it? I've always known you've hated living together and you've only stayed together because of me." Her Mother shook her head but said nothing. "How do you think that makes me feel?"

It seemed that everything Graham had told her was true.

It did not occur to her at the time to ask how he could possibly have known.

The next day the members of the Eccleston family were barely speaking to each other when they went to Charles Donaldson's birthday barbecue.

105

Chapter Twelve

Holly had a miserable summer.

She spent the first weeks alone, Linda seemed to be as happy to avoid her as she was to avoid Linda. She had been looking forward to spending most of the summer in the States. But she had no more fun there. She had tried to meet up with her old friends but after spending two afternoons listening to them talking about their lives she found she had nothing in common with them any more. She realised how much she had changed in the two years since she had left.

She thought about Graham and whether she missed him at all but decided she didn't. If there was anyone she would have liked to talk to it was Crispin. But he hadn't shown any interest all year, not since that first evening in Oxford, and the bean fight. It would have been nice if he'd asked her out.

She had had such hopes of her year at university and it just hadn't turned out like that.

While the Ecclestons were away Graham did what he had wanted to do for months. He broke into number 16.

He spent a long time in Holly's room, going through her clothes, smelling them, lying in her bed, imagining doing the things he wanted to do to her. He would start soon, taking little tasters, just a quick one here and there to keep her interested. But in time, yes, in time, he would let full rein to his imagination and get all he needed of her.

But he hadn't broken into Holly's home to have sexual fantasies in her bed, he was there to find out more about Matt. It seemed Matt had kept everything about his past from his wife and daughter. They didn't know and their not knowing gave Graham his chance.

And it seemed Matt knew nothing about the O'Dwyers.

Graham looked everywhere in the house, there was nothing about Mary's parents. There was nothing in Matt's desk about them, only the carefully written note books showing how much Max was paying him.

It had been Matt's idea to get a regular income from Max but it had taken a while to get him to pay up. He'd only started paying in June, £100 a week Matt had said, and he was giving Graham £50 of that. 'Fair shares' he had said handing over the notes in the pub each Monday night but Graham had thought Max must be paying Matt more than that. A paltry £100 a week was nothing. As he looked through Matt's carefully written notebooks he could see he was getting £250 a week. 'Shit. The fucker's pocketing two hundred quid a week'. That made him angry.

He'd given him all that information about the photographs and the nanny. He'd given him all the proof he needed and he had cheated him out of the best part of two thousand quid.

He decided he wasn't going to get away with it. Life would have to be made a bit more difficult for Matt. He'd make Mary and Holly ask questions, he'd nudge them into knowing what a shit Matt really was.

And he wasn't going to tell him what he'd found out about the O'Dwyers.

He'd go along with Matt just as though they were still working together, but when it came down to it he'd stall on Matt's plan while working on his own. Matt would get nothing. Serve the cheating bastard right.

At the beginning of October Graham called Holly, offering her a lift down to Leicester. She was glad to be going back, even if it did mean putting up with Linda's sarcastic comments again.

"Where's your parents?" He asked her as he loaded his car with Holly's bags.

"Mum's at work. Dad's probably at the pub."

"That's a pity. I'd like to have met them." Holly couldn't think why he would want to meet her parents and was horrified at the idea. She really didn't want her mother to think Graham was her boyfriend.

"I've bought a car." Graham said after they had driven in silence for several minutes.

"What's wrong with this one?"

"No I mean a racing car." She wasn't sure what reaction he had expected but it probably was different from the one she gave.

"Why?"

"What do you mean why?" He had hoped she might be a little more impressed.

"Why? What for? For what reason? What do you think I mean by 'why'?" Holly wasn't in the mood for games. She was regretting accepting his offer of a lift. Graham chain smoked, filling the car with a stinking fog.

"Alright alright, keep your hair on."

"OK. What are you going to do with it?"

"Race it."

"You?"

"Yes me. What's so funny about that?" His voice had that dark threat that sometimes he could not control.

"I'm sorry, I don't mean to laugh. It's just such a strange thing to do! How can you afford it? It must cost a fortune. How do you learn what to do? It can't be that simple – just buy a car, turn up and race can it?"

He spent the rest of the journey telling her how he had done his research, how he had spent the time since they had met in Oxford going to meetings at Brands Hatch, Mallory Park, Lydden Hill and other circuits around the country, how he'd spoken to people with cars that he thought he could afford and talked to them about how they started. They'd been very helpful. They'd shown him how to apply for his provisional licence, they'd sold him second hand fireproof overalls and pointed him in the direction of a suitable car.

She couldn't even attempt to sound interested so she soon stopped listening, just occasionally wiping the steamed up windows and peering out at the rain-sodden countryside.

As they pulled up outside the flat she realised she didn't know when Linda would be getting back, or even how she was coming. It didn't look like she was here yet.

Holly unlocked the door and turned on the light. Even in early afternoon it was gloomy. It didn't help her mood.

"Want some help Doll?"

He had helped her carry her bags up to her room, dropping them just inside the door.

"Will you come with me, you know, racing?" He quietly closed the door behind him, watching her as she put her load on the floor by the bed.

"What would I have to do?" She was concentrating on some books that had spilled out of her bag.

"Not a lot. Stand in the pits with a clipboard, look gorgeous." He pulled her round towards him and kissed her hard, pushing her down on the bed.

Before she could stop him he had his hand between her legs and was kneading her roughly. He was hurting her and she began to wrestle against him but he was strong and he already had his jeans open and her pants pushed aside.

For a few moments she wished she had worn jeans, it wouldn't have been so easy for him, but then she thought 'Hell, why not? No one else cares a shit so what have I got to lose?'

He didn't say any words of endearment or of encouragement. But then she hadn't really expected him to.

As he rolled off her a few minutes later she thought it had been almost as uncomfortable as the first time.

"He never said anything about push starting the car and sitting around for hours in the freezing cold waiting for the fog to lift so they could go out and drive round in circles for half an hour, or the completely awful hamburgers and the filthy freezing loos." Linda listened as Holly told her everything about her day.

Graham had picked her up just after five o'clock on the following Sunday morning. A white Ford Anglia was on a trailer behind a car she knew wasn't his. She'd had to squeeze into the front seat between Graham and Martin. Martin, she was informed, was Graham's mechanic, but from the way he gave Graham directions she thought the race car was actually his and Graham was just showing off. They drove for what seemed like hours but was probably only two, eventually parking on a piece of sloping tarmac surrounded by ghostly figures and car shapes. She couldn't see a race track, she couldn't see anything much in the fog.

"We had to push the car everywhere until half way through the morning. Apparently there's a church near the track and they don't like the noise from the engines. I just seemed to spend all day pushing that bloody car and talking to Martin. Graham had a great time! In the ten hours we were there he got to drive the car about half an hour. But he wasn't last. He'd started at the back but other people fell off and so there were two cars behind him when he finished. He's so proud of himself! He got a signature on his licence. He really enjoyed himself."

"Oh good." Linda said sarcastically asked when she could get a word in. "What about you?"

Holly ignored Linda's tone of voice but still sounded less than convincing. "Yeah. I didn't think I would but I did."

"You won't be going again will you?" Linda hoped that the answer would be 'no'.

"Probably. I saw Carl today." Holly hoped Linda wouldn't assume the two points were connected.

"Yeah?" Linda feigned indifference.

"Yeah." Holly mimicked

"How was he?"

"He sends his love. I didn't see him for long – he was pushing a car in the opposite direction and we couldn't hold things up. I think he was in a garage, we lowly souls were out in the open. He didn't come to find me later, even if he had a chance I'm not sure he would have done anyway. I don't think he likes Graham very much."

"Sensible man."

Holly threw a cushion in Linda's direction.

Holly didn't see Graham at any other time than every other weekend, he was still working in Liverpool and she made it clear that she needed the non-racing weekends to catch up with other things.

"We don't sleep together you know." Holly felt she had to clear the air. "It's not really possible in the car, and Martin is always there."

"What a shame." Linda had replied sarcastically. "He looks like such a good shag."

Holly had thought Graham would make opportunities for them to be together alone on their weekends away but since that first time at the flat they had only had one or two opportunities, snatched minutes which Holly found completely unsatisfying. She wanted to take time over it. If they were going to have sex he should try to make it halfway decent for her. She wanted longer at it, time for him to warm her up, time to get into a state where she could possibly enjoy it. But they were never alone long enough.

Perhaps that was what Graham wanted.

Holly went home at Christmas on her own.

Linda was joining her family in Oxford and Graham hadn't mentioned anything about his plans so she hitch-hiked up the motorway alone.

Her mother and father were as distant from each other as they had always been and she felt uncomfortable with the knowledge that neither wanted to be there with each other, or with her. They did seem to want to make an effort for Christmas though, her 20th birthday.

"You won't be a teenager any more."

"No thank God!"

"You're growing up. We hardly see you any more." As if they cared.

They were surprised when the doorbell rang on Christmas Morning.

"I'll go." Holly who had been clearing the wrapping paper and boxes that were strewn around the floor of the living room.

"Graham! What the hell are you doing here?"

"Don't I get invited in?"

"Well, it's…" She couldn't find the words to put him off.

"Who is it Sweetie?" her Mother called her.

How was she going to explain him? She hadn't told her parents anything about Graham and her weekends away. Whenever they asked about 'boyfriends' she always said 'No one special'. What was she going to say? How was she going to explain him?

"My name's Graham." He had pushed past Holly and walked towards the voices, his hand outstretched to introduce himself. "Graham Tyler. I'm a friend of Holly's, I was in the area so called in to wish her a Happy Birthday. I hope I've not intruded."

It all sounded so respectable but it didn't seem as if he cared whether he intruded or not.

"No. Of course not. We're happy to welcome a friend of Holly's aren't we Matt?" Mary spoke quickly, nervous at this young man's confidence. It reminded her of Matt when they had first met, absolutely charming but with something going on underneath that she couldn't put her finger on. Matt looked as unwelcoming as he could.

After they had all sat down with glasses of champagne Mary tried to make conversation, asking if Graham's family were local.

"No. We come from London but we do have local connections. Quite close connections really."

"But you don't live here?"

"I work in Liverpool but I spend a lot of time in Hoylake. My aunt lived here for some years, though she died a couple of years ago." The politeness and inconsequentiality of the conversation raised, rather than lowered, the tension.

"And your uncle?" Matt decided to join in the game.

"I believe he died some years ago. It is my cousins I have been looking forward to getting to know."

"Would we know them?" Mary had no idea what was going on.

"I believe you do."

"Matt? Do you know who he's talking about?"

"Oh yes."

Mary knew Matt so well. She knew how he spoke when he was trying to pick an argument with her, how he asked short questions and gave short answers as he waited for her to fall into the traps he laid. She realised that that was what he was doing now, with this friend of Holly's.

Graham changed tack "You come from Toronto don't you? Originally I mean."

"Yes, why yes I did."

"How long ago did you leave?" Only Matt realised this was not a natural development of their polite conversation.

"Oh years ago, just after Holly was born."

It was when he asked Mary "Do you have much contact with your parents?" and he caught Matt's eye, that Graham realised he had gone too far.

Mary was watching them both. "You two know each other don't you." She turned to Graham, "You're not here for Holly's birthday at all are you?"

Holly looked at her Mother. What was going on? How could her Dad know Graham?

"Of course I am." Graham's lie was unconvincing.

"You didn't say you were coming. Why are you here?" Holly was remembering the warnings Linda had given her 'Graham is devious.' 'Graham knows a lot more than he should' 'Graham wants something, I don't know what, but he wants something from us.'

"I'm sorry, I shouldn't have come. I just wanted to wish Holly a Happy Birthday. I'll leave now." Graham could do a very good contrite act when he chose.

"Oh no, don't leave yet." Mary ignored the fierce looks her husband and daughter were giving her, she wanted to know what this young man was really after. "Have another drink. She looked at her watch. "It's Holly's birthday until noon and then we have Christmas. Silly really, but it means that she gets some time to celebrate and open her presents before the rest of it all kicks in. Stay till our Christmas begins. We haven't got off to the best of starts have we?"

"Happy Birthday Holl." Graham walked across the room, his back to her parents and, kissed her on the mouth. He handed her a small parcel wrapped in silver paper.

"Thank you Graham. Do I open it now or after 12?"

"Now."

"Is it OK? In front of ..." she spoke quietly and shrugged towards her parents who were watching closely.

He nodded and so she undid the tape. Inside was a jeweller's box and her imagination raced. He couldn't be giving her a ring? Could he? That would be stupid, especially in front of her parents. She didn't want to open the box in case it was something she wouldn't be able to accept or explain, so she hesitated. Graham took it from her hands and opened it, signalling with his hand for her to turn around. She did.

She felt uncomfortable, and for a moment she felt fear, then she realised he was fastening a silver chain around her neck. She lifted the charm, looked at it, and seeing it was a swastika, rapidly tried to undo the clasp of the chain.

"What's that for? Graham! How could you?"

Graham smiled condescendingly. "It's not what you think." He briefly caught Matt's eye and seemed to challenge him to react as he kept Holly from undoing the hook. "It's an ancient Hindu symbol of well-being Holly, a good luck charm. I wanted you to wear it to keep you safe when you're not with me."

"I think you'd better go." Mary thought she spoke for her whole family. Holly realised what Graham was doing. He was proving to her that what he had said about her father's past was true and the fact that he must know even more than he had told her. His presence was unsettling them all.

"I've got to go now anyway. Thank you for the drink Mrs Eccleston.

I'll see you in the New Year." He was polite, acting as if nothing untoward had occurred.

Matt stood up but Graham had let himself out.

Holly removed the chain from her neck and tried to explain to her parents that she wasn't interested in Graham. "I hardly know him. I met him at that funeral in January."

"So how do you know him?" Mary turned to Matt. Holly silently echoed her mother's question and waited for the answer.

"I've seen him in the pub. We have a few drinks together now and again. Just a coincidence he knows Holly too."

It almost seemed reasonable.

Because they had been away at Christmas the Forsters invited the Ecclestons to lunch on the first Sunday in the New Year.

Matt didn't want to go and did the one thing he thought would save him the trouble, he got drunk. As soon as breakfast was finished he helped himself to a beer from the fridge and when Mary asked him not to he swore at her and so she left him alone. She would see how he was in a couple of hours.

Pat was not surprised that only Holly and Mary appeared. Matt's drink problem was almost taken for granted. As they were about to sit down for lunch Mary slipped out and through the gap in the hedge to check on Matt.

She was surprised to hear voices in the kitchen.

"You're so fucking fixated with the Austrian you haven't looked any closer to home have you?"

"What're you talking about?"

"What about the fucking O'Dwyers?" They were talking about her parents.

"What about them?"

"I told you. I knew you were pissed but I thought you'd remember the small matter of a few million."

Mary was amazed at the way Graham was talking to Matt. He was swearing at him, bullying him. She couldn't believe anyone could talk to him like that.

"Irish bloody losers. Scum of the earth the fucking Irish."

"Did you know them? Did you do anything other than piss them off marrying their daughter? Did you never bother to find out anything about them or did you just think 'Irish' 'rubbish' 'no use to anyone'? Everyone reckons I'm an insignificant, thick pisshead but I did find out about them, I did bother to find out and they are loaded. Millions, they've got fucking millions and when they pop off it'll all go to your dearly beloved wife." Mary knew her parents had money, they had always worked so hard, had invested all their time in the business. But 'millions'? Yes, she could almost believe that.

"How? I don't understand. What do you mean 'fucking millions'?"

"I told you last week. They've got property. They own property, apartment blocks, office buildings the whole bit."

"I didn't understand. I didn't remember."

"Well if you weren't out of your head all the time you might remember. If you don't get yourself together and do what you promised to do you won't get a fucking farthing. I'm getting a little impatient waiting."

Mary backed away and slipped back through the hedge before her husband, or Graham, could see her. She tried to make sense of it. Graham and Matt were up to something. She had just got back into the room and shrugged her shoulders at Pat's unspoken enquiry when the door bell rang.

It was obvious to everyone that Matt was the worse for wear but he seemed to be doing his best to behave. She wondered if the look he gave her meant he had spotted her in the garden and knew she had overheard them, but he didn't say anything so perhaps it was just her guilty conscience.

Conversation was limited during the meal, but no table could be entirely quiet when the twins were around. Oliver did his best to keep Matt from making too great a fool of himself by talking to him almost non-stop in a steady calming voice, by handing him the cutlery and taking his glass from him so it was never in danger of spilling. Crispin made it his job to keep Mary and Holly occupied so that they would not notice too much and would forget their embarrassment and enjoy themselves as far as possible.

After lunch Linda, Holly and the twins were sprawled out on the floor playing Monopoly. Gradually Holly relaxed, joining in with the shrieks of 'Ooh' and 'That's not fair' and 'You can't do that'.

"I like Christmas and the New Year," Crispin said to no one in particular, "we can act like childish idiots and no one complains."

The cries of 'Mayfair! That's loads of money!' kept reminding Mary of the conversation she had overheard between Matt and Graham. She had realised on Christmas Day that they knew each other but it seemed that it wasn't friendship between them and whatever it was had everything to do with her and her parents.

She hadn't thought about her parents for years, they might be dead for all she knew. She was wondering what time it was in Toronto and what they might be doing this New Year's Day when she saw the face in the window. She tensed and stifled a squeal of surprise, glancing around the room to see if anyone else had noticed. Pat had

114

her back to the window, all the others, except Matt, were absorbed in their game of Monopoly. Matt was sitting opposite her asleep, his eyes shut and his head bent slightly forward. She really didn't want Graham to make a scene so she left the room. She hoped no one would see them in the dark of the garden.

But Matt had not been asleep. He opened his eyes at Mary's barely audible exclamation and had seen the face in the window. Standing unsteadily, he followed his wife out of the room determined to hear what Graham had to say.

"What do you really know about your husband? Do you really know where he comes from? Ask him about August, your really should ask him about August."

"What do you mean 'ask him about August'? What did he do in August? Which August?" Mary was bewildered, she had no idea what this man was implying. "If you want to know something about my husband you should ask him, why are you asking me?"

But Graham had seen Matt stumbling out of the kitchen door and he wasn't going to stay around to answer any of Mary's questions.

"He just arrived from nowhere." Mary told Pat, clearly upset. "He didn't want to see you Holly, he wanted to see me. He just ranted on at me about Matt and how much he knew about Matt that we didn't. I don't know what he was talking about. He kept going on about August and I should ask him about August."

Their pleasant afternoon was brought prematurely to its end.

In the days before returning to Leicester Holly decided that she had to continue going out with Graham despite Linda's attempts to persuade her that he was dangerous to know. She would have to keep seeing him if she was going to find out what was going on between him and her parents.

Through that spring he phoned her regularly to make arrangements which he never fulfilled. Four weeks in a row he said he would be in Leicester to take her out on the Saturday and each Saturday afternoon he rang to say that 'something's come up' or 'sorry, Doll, can't make it after all'. She was upset each week, not so much because he had stood her up but because it meant she had to spend the weekend alone as Linda spent more and more time in Oxford. Every Sunday evening Linda would flop down in a chair with a large mug of coffee and tell Holly what a great time she had had and every Sunday Holly felt more and more left out. But every week, when Graham phoned to say he would see her at the weekend, she believed him and stayed in Leicester alone.

When Linda asked what she had done at the weekend Holly lied.

She could never admit that she was being strung along by Graham and that he hadn't turned up for even one of their arranged weekends. She kept saying 'yes' to him, she had to if she was ever going to find out what it was he knew about her family, but it rankled with her that he didn't seem interested in her any more.

During her weekends in Oxford, when she and Gerry weren't locked in his bedroom for hours on end, Linda talked with her brothers about Holly and Graham.

"We get on so much better now I never have to meet him."

"Is she happy though?" Crispin knew that however much he wanted to tell Holly she was making a mistake having anything to do with Graham, he must wait.

"She seems to be though she never gives me any details about what they do together."

Oliver laughed. "Well what do you expect! Do you tell her what you get up to with Gerry?" He regretted saying that as soon as he saw Crispin's face.

"Give her time," Oliver told his brother, "she'll see sense in the end."

"And if she doesn't see through the little shit she doesn't deserve you." Linda added, giving her brother a hug.

"I know it makes sense to wait, you're always telling me why I have to, but I don't have to like it."

"We're going round to Number 16 for Easter Sunday anyway. You'll see her then. Mum and Mary have got it all arranged. Mum invited them round but Mary suggested we should all go round to Number 16. Something about Matt finding it less of a strain if he's on his own territory." After Christmas they were all aware that Matt's regular visits to the pub had developed into a real drinking problem. "She's doing a proper roast turkey, all the trimmings. 'Just like Thanksgiving' she said. I think we'll be doing them a favour. Mum said Mary was looking forward to having a house full and some laughter."

On Easter Sunday morning Carl and the Forsters walked round to Number 16 prepared for anything.

"Crispin, please don't sit all the time staring at Holly with that hang dog expression you had at New Year." Pat warned her son.

"That's not fair Mum." But he knew it was going to be difficult not to stare at Holly, it was a long time since he had seen her.

"And don't just sit there brooding because we didn't invite Gerry up." Pat thought she should include Linda in her admonishments.

"I'm not!" Linda missed Gerry and was looking forward to the next weekend.

"And me? What mustn't I do?" Oliver asked innocently.

"You mustn't look so smug and self-satisfied all the time." Linda answered for her mother. "Just because you don't have a love-life to go wrong."

"Now now children." Jeff tried to stop the good-hearted bickering "best behaviour."

"You mean we've got to ignore the fact that Matt will be pissed?"

"Maybe he drinks because no one ever talks to him?"

"He never has anything to say. He's always pissed."

"Catch 22."

"I'll ask him about his book."

"What book?"

"Mary said he's writing a book. She doesn't know what about but she says it explains his long absences from the house, and his inability to get a job."

As Mary put the finishing touches to the meal they settled down with drinks, Linda making sure Crispin wasn't alone with Holly for one moment and Oliver helping Mary in the kitchen.

"How are you getting on with your book?" Pat asked Matt to break the uneasy quiet. She was unprepared for the anger her seemingly innocuous enquiry caused.

"What do you know about a book? What's that fucking bitch told you about a book?"

Pat had learned from her work with young delinquents that the best way to cope with this sort of excessive behaviour was to remain calm and polite, to ignore the details of what was said and to pay compliments to the ego of the angry person.

"She has told me that you have been working very hard on your research, spending a lot of time in the library, and in Liverpool."

"OK so I'm writing a book. Big fucking deal. All those years I've catalogued every cheap little shit who can string two words together. I want the name 'Matthew Eccleston' to be an entry even if it's just once. I want every other sodding library cataloguer to have to put me on their lists."

Other conversation in the room stopped but Matt immediately calmed down. His outburst forgotten, he continued in a perfectly calm voice "Now you all know it'll be that much more pressure on me to finish it and to get it published. If you hadn't known it wouldn't be so bad if it had come to nothing."

Mary had taken great care about where everyone would sit around the table, she had discussed this with Pat and they had agreed to make sure that Carl had neither Holly nor Linda next to him. Just in case it caused a problem with the other one when they seemed to be getting on so much better, and they couldn't put him through the ordeal of having one on either side.

"Too many men!" Mary laughed, rather falsely, as she ushered everyone into the dining room. "Holly, Linda, you go on either side of Jeff at that end. Mary, you sit next to me; Carl, since you are the rarest of guests, you come and sit on my other side." That left Matt, Crispin and Oliver to occupy the other seats.

It seemed very contrived but no one made any comment as the door bell had rung and, as Mary went to answer it, the conversation focussed on who would be rude enough to visit this time on Easter Sunday.

"Not another refugee from home I hope." Jeff joked, looking meaningfully at Carl, who had appeared at their house at Sunday lunchtime nearly ten years before.

"You had pork not turkey."

"And there was no crackling left."

Holly was wondering what had happened to her mother. Several minutes had passed and she was getting worried. Surely, surely, Graham couldn't do it again.

As the minutes passed she was not the only one who was worried. "I'll see how your Mother's getting on, perhaps there was no one at the door and she's struggling in the kitchen!" Carl left the table. Oliver and Crispin were telling Holly how Carl had come into their lives, playing up their chivalry and playing down Carl's misery. It was a story she had heard from Linda before so she didn't listen carefully, instead she was straining to hear what was going on in the hall.

It was some time before Mary and Carl returned.

"That was really odd."

"Who was it?"

"It was Graham Tyler. He said he was in the area and had called in 'on the off-chance' to say 'Hello'. It took all my charm to make him go away!"

"Are you all right Mary? You look like you've seen a ghost!" Jeff was not the only one around the table who had noticed how shocked Mary appeared.

Carl came to her rescue. "He's an odd bod that Graham. I've seen him quite a lot around the race circuits. He always comes up to talk to me, even when he's got nothing to say." Crispin caught the look Linda gave Holly whose face registered only dismay. "Anyway," Carl continued "I've sent him away. Told him it was a family meal and he even had the cheek to ask if there was room for another one! He really didn't want to take 'no' for the answer."

"What on earth could he possibly want this time?" everyone

118

turned to look at Holly.

"Well I didn't ask him. I didn't know you were all coming round until yesterday, how could I have told him?"

"No one's blaming anyone for anything. Come on. Someone help me get it all in from the kitchen before it all gets cold and all my hard work goes to waste."

"I don't think he comes to see me." Holly eventually raised the subject of Graham at breakfast the next morning. "We don't have that sort of relationship."

"Well what sort of relationship do you have?" Matt wanted to know.

"What's happening in August?" Mary interrupted before Holly could answer her father.

"I don't know! How should I know? It's months away."

Matt was more restrained in his response "Why?"

"Graham always asks me to ask you about August. It's what he said back in January, he kept saying it yesterday."

"What exactly did he say?"

"He keeps going on about August, and someone called Rebecca. That's twice now. I'm getting fed up with it."

"What exactly did he say?" Matt repeated, his voice was cold and threatening.

"He just talked about August and Rebecca. He seemed to think it was something I should know and I should do something about. He said if I didn't know I should ask my daughter. 'Holly should know' he said."

"What did he say *exactly*?"

"If you don't know you should, Holly should know. Why haven't you been told? Yes, that was it."

Matt realised far more clearly than his wife what Graham had meant. He hadn't meant, as Mary thought she had understood, that Holly knew something and hadn't told Mary. He had meant that both Mary and Holly had a right to know something that neither had been told.

Matt knew exactly what Graham was threatening to tell them. And what he had to do about it.

Mary changed the subject. "The lawn mower's broken, the weather's so nice I'd like to get going on the garden again." She had persevered with the push mower she had found in the garden shed when they had moved in nearly three years earlier. She had been proud of the stripes on the lawn. 'English lawns must have stripes' she had said with deliberation. "We need a new one."

119

"OK OK I'll go get one of those orange things, you know, the electric ones that just fly over the grass cutting it with no effort required." And Mary agreed, even though she wondered if the lawn would lose its stripes. "Well if you can't cut it there won't be any stripes anyway."

The next morning was the first lovely day of Spring, the sun was shining and because there was warmth in it for the first time for months the kitchen door and windows were wide open.

Holly had been reading about the Watergate scandal in the newspaper that was spread out on the kitchen table.

"Coffee Dad?"

Matt was standing at the window watching his wife walk up and down the lawn. She had started at the bottom of the garden, so that he could see that the cable was long enough, and she was gradually working her way back towards the house.

Just as he had suggested.

Holly leant past him to fill the kettle and she glanced out of the window and watched her mother who seemed to be concentrating hard on the straightness of the lines she was creating in the lawn.

"No prior knowledge! I don't believe a word of it," she said. Her father didn't answer or make any comment, though she would have expected him to. He had always liked Richard Nixon.

As Holly watched the kettle boil, getting three mugs down from the hooks and carefully measuring out the instant coffee and the sugar, she realised that to an outsider this was a 'normal' family scene; the image of domestic contentment.

Anyone watching would not have seen the tensions that lay just under the surface. She resolved that when, if, she could get alone with Graham she would ask him just what it was he thought he was doing. What was all this about Rebecca, who was she, and what was so important about August?

As the noise of the boiling kettle died away she realised that the only sound she could hear was the radio.

'When you walk, through a storm, hold your head up high...'.

For a few moments she thought her Mother must have stopped to come in for her coffee, she expected to see her any moment in the doorway, but as she turned she caught sight through the open door of a figure lying on the ground, the new mower on its side.

Her father had not moved from his place by the window.

Holly knew he must have seen what had happened. He must have seen the cable and how close Mary was to running the new lawnmower over it.

He must have watched but he had not cried any warning.

He still did not move as Holly phoned 999.

As the ambulance-men took the body away they reassured Holly that her mother would have known nothing. She would have died instantly.

It was a ghastly, tragic, accident.

The police arrived and took statements and made measurements, carefully noting everything down. But there had been nothing suspicious about this death. There had to be an inquest, they said, but the result was a foregone conclusion. She was unfamiliar with using an electric mower, there was no safety cut off in place, she had had no idea of the danger. She had simply pushed the mower onto the cable and electrocuted herself.

There was no reason to doubt it had been a completely unavoidable accident.

But Holly believed she knew better.

She saw that her father had not tried to stop the accident. He had not warned her or tried to save her.

She believed that she had done exactly what he planned for her to do.

Chapter Thirteen

We read about the accident in the newspaper.

I wanted to contact Holly, ask her what we could do to help. So I called Linda.

"There is something actually. It's not directly to do with Holly but it would get us out of a problem."

"Whatever we can do to help."

"Holly's grandparents are coming to England to, what do they call it, 'repatriate' their daughter's remains. It sounds gruesome but they want her to be buried in Canada."

"I can understand that."

"Well they're coming over in a couple of days and will need somewhere to stay. We can't put them up and it seems miserable for them to be in some hotel or other. Could you? Would Max mind? Mum's spoken to them on the phone and they seem very nice."

"I'm sure that will be fine. Anything else? Shall I pick them up from the airport? Won't they want to see Holly? Her father?"

"They've said they want to see Holly but not, and they were very definite about it, 'absolutely not that awful man'."

Two days later I drove her to Speke Airport to meet her grandparents. I was pleased to see Mrs O'Dwyer give Holly a reassuring hug as we met in the arrivals hall. Mr O'Dwyer's handshake was firm and I liked him immediately.

"And who are you son? Holly's young man?"

"Just a friend. I hope a good one." I replied, rewarded by Holly's smile. "If there's anything you need or I can do while you're here you must just ask."

"Sure will son." Mr O'Dwyer spoke quietly, seeming to protect his wife from any questions. "It is good to know our grand-daughter's got a friend, they're much more important than having a 'young man' don't you think?"

I felt the O'Dwyers, for all the sadness of the occasion, were going to be very pleasant houseguests.

Ted was dealing with the legal aspects of the repatriation and so there were six of us at dinner that evening. As I watched Holly and Monika in the same room together, I realised how much I had asked of Max in welcoming her into our home.

After dinner Max repaired to his study with Ted and Mr O'Dwyer 'business that need not distress you ladies' he explained to his wife and granddaughter. I was designated to look after Holly and her grandmother. Monika, as was her habit, retired immediately after clearing away dinner.

I had very little entertaining to do as the conversation did not falter. Bridget, as she insisted we both call her, asked Holly to tell her everything about her life and everything she could say about her Mother. "I need to learn everything about her life in such a short time."

Holly spoke self-consciously at first, perhaps aware that I was in the room, but soon she was speaking freely about her mother's love of gardening, her enjoyment of English television, her belief in the importance of computers, her passion for her work.

She seemed to know so much about her mother's life.

Eventually Holly asked the question that she had obviously been wanting to ask since she knew her grandparents were coming over to this country. "Why did we never have any contact? Why didn't Mum take me to see you? Why didn't you visit?"

Bridget began carefully "I have to say we didn't give Mary a happy childhood. Michael was always working, he started from nothing when we arrived in Canada, that was during the depression. It was a very hard life and we had nothing. We both worked every minute there was and it meant we neglected Mary."

She paused as if regretting what she was going to have to say. "We wish we could change what has been, of course we do, but at the time even survival was difficult. We were so very proud of our Mary, she always did well at school, she was so bright, so clever and we had such hopes that she would come into the family business. But we had neglected her, as she grew up we found we didn't know her at all. When Michael mentioned her joining the firm when she graduated she told us she wouldn't think of it. She said she didn't want to spend the rest of her life looking after us. She had a horrid argument with her Father. She said she never wanted to see us again. The last thing she wanted to do with her life was to keep us by working in the business and look after us as we grew old."

It was obviously distressing so I got up to fill her glass. She seemed grateful for the interruption but after sipping at the drink she continued in a darker tone. "It wasn't our Mary talking. She had met that Matthew and it was his words she spoke as she argued with us. He'd set her against us." The anger in her voice subsided, though the pain was obvious. "We never saw her again after she married. She never came to visit us. We got a phone call to say she was having a baby, and a letter saying she had had a daughter. I think Matthew stopped her contacting us. I don't think he liked anyone to have any affection for Mary. I think he lied to her about us and I'm sure he stopped her replying to my letters. She would have written. I know she would." Bridget paused only to dab at the corner of her eye with her handkerchief. "The last letter we got was saying she was coming to England. I don't think she wrote it. It said such horrid things."

As I listened to the mother's view of losing contact with her daughter it was obvious that she didn't blame Mary. Not one word did she say against her. She was just filled with guilt that she hadn't done the right thing, that she and her husband had let Mary down, that they hadn't been good parents.

There were no recriminations against their daughter, there was just unconditional, unjudgmental love.

I left them to talk. They didn't need me to intrude.

I walked down the garden and sat on the sea wall, legs dangling over the rocks below, looking out across the darkness of the estuary to the few twinkling lights on Hilbre Island and to Wales beyond.

I thought of my relationship with my own mother and wondered how many similar emotions she had felt because of me. I had some thinking to do before driving Holly home.

In the car I asked her whether she was going to be seeing more of her grandparents now. "Probably not, it was Mom they really wanted to know. I'm my father's daughter. They hate him too much to see me without seeing him."

"If they got to know you they may see past that."

"Probably not. There's not enough of her in me."

I couldn't think of anything to say that might cheer her up.

After the O'Dwyers' visit was over Max and I sat together in his study.

"Thank you." He said, rather surprisingly. "Thank you for inviting them."

"I was going to thank you for letting them stay."

"I want to tell you what I've learned. It relates to those wretched men Graham and Matt, and therefore to young Holly Eccleston and her friend Linda Forster."

"I hardly know them, you could hardly call them friends."

"You should read this."

He leant down and unlocked the lower drawer in his desk, taking from it an envelope which he handed to me.

As I began to read he spoke to me and I listened to him rather than reading the note he had given me. I rather assumed they had the same message.

"Matt Eccleston. He wanted money from me. He asked for 'a regular income', if he didn't get it he would put certain information into the public domain that I would prefer to keep private. He was not specific as to which of my many secrets he was to make public but I agreed to pay him. In paying him I hoped to protect others."

So he was being blackmailed. He ignored my gesture of surprise.

"It is not costing much, he is really very bad at it. I had thought that as long as he was getting something from me others would be safe. I hadn't thought he would kill his wife. I don't think he would have done if it hadn't been for Graham."

He spoke so easily of murder. "You say he murdered Holly's mother?"

"Undoubtedly. It was no accident."

I was shocked as much by his calmness as by the information itself.

"Can't you do anything about it? Have them investigated, arrested? You can't let them get away with it."

"I have no proof." He spoke as if that was the end of it, as if proof were necessary before he could bring any action against Matt and Graham.

It was only later I knew he had been disingenuous. Max was well able to bring about justice without having to depend on anything so awkward as proof.

"After Alicia's funeral Graham Tyler had evidence that Matt Eccleston was most happy to see. I considered it then only a matter of time before they joined forces, if they had not already done so. After that day Graham had in his possession a number of photographs that linked people together who should not be linked, which anchored people in a place and time they have no right to be. I knew then they would undoubtedly make trouble."

"They started with the aim of getting money from me using the information Graham learned at your Mother's funeral along with what Matt himself knew. Then, I believe, for whatever reason, Graham took control. He learned something about Holly's family that was going to

125

make them more money than I could ever give them. This was the part I didn't know until my discussions with Michael over the past few days. Michael O'Dwyer started a business in the depths of the depression and has developed it over the years."

"Yes, it was the reason they had no time for Mary when she was growing up."

"Exactly. Their business grew. He invested in property. He's retired now, obviously, he sold the business when there was no one to hand it over to. He had hoped Mary would succeed him but she didn't. There is a very great deal of money. This, I believe, is what Graham learned."

"That's why he's with Holly all the time, getting close to her."

"Quite probably."

"That's why they had to kill Mary, so Holly will inherit."

"But I have no proof. Motive is not sufficient for conviction despite there also being the means and the opportunity. There was no reason for the Police to doubt it was an accident. He has been surprisingly clever."

"What will they do next?"

"I think there will be a wedding before too long. If I read these men correctly they will make it impossible for Holly to do anything but marry Graham. Some kind of accident will then befall the O'Dwyers and Holly will inherit. Graham will have control of his wife and the money, some of which he will be obliged to pay his father-in-law."

"That's all a bit far fetched isn't it?"

"I don't think so."

"We must stop it then. We can't let Holly be used like that. You know as well as I do that that would be a disaster. They did meet in our house, he's my cousin, we must have some sort of responsibility?"

"We have no responsibility for Holly Eccleston." Max spoke firmly.

"Can't we warn her, tell her to have nothing to do with him?"

"I don't think so Charles. But if it makes you happier I will make it my business to find out more about Graham."

Max had told me so much.

He had told me of the O'Dwyer's wealth and the plot he believed Matthew and Graham had hatched but he did not tell me the most important thing.

He did not tell me what he thought I did not know, that Matthew Eccleston was his sister's son, and Monika's brother. That they were his family and that he had a great deal of responsibility for Holly.

But he didn't say a word.

As we sat in the comfort of his study we both knew we were

126

sacrificing Holly's happiness to keep Monika safe.

Although I felt uncomfortable with it, I understood his reasons and knew I would do nothing.

I wish I had argued more.

But I didn't.

Chapter Fourteen

Within a week of Mary's death Matt had given his notice to leave number 16 and moved into a flat above a shop by the railway station. He had made it clear there was no room in his life for his daughter. Their last conversation confirmed to Holly all she needed to have known about her parent's marriage.

"There's no room for you in the flat you'll have to sort something out for yourself. You're not my responsibility any more."

"I never was, was I?"

"As long as your Mother was alive I did my best for you both."

"Like shit you did."

"You're nearly 21 years old, no longer a child to be looked after and I don't need to provide a home for you any more. So you can fuck off and sort yourself out. I've got things to do."

That evening Holly went round to Linda's to say she was going back to Leicester.

"Term doesn't start for a week." Linda argued. "You can stay here if you like, you don't have to be in the house if you don't want to." The Forsters offered any help she needed, but there was nothing Holly wanted them to do.

"A week ago I had two parents and a home. I might as well go back, I've got nothing here now."

Through the short weeks of the Summer Term Linda hardly let Holly out of her sight. She regularly phoned Carl, the twins and her parents to talk to them asking what she should do. She really wanted to help but Holly always shut her out. Exams meant that there was no question of Holly going away at weekends and at least, Linda thought, there had been no sign of Graham.

"Perhaps he's showing some sense and keeping away from her." Linda told her Mother during one of their weekly discussions on 'what to do about Holly'.

"Perhaps he's busy doing other things."

"We can hope!"

"You don't like him do you?"

"Nope. Conniving greasy piece of work. He's after something. And I don't mean sex." Linda continued hurriedly. "They're all after that,

128

but he's after something more. He seems to be working his way into her life but sometimes I don't think he even likes her that much."

"Well she'll have to come here and then you can take her to Oxford when you spend your fortnight with the boys. Has she said anything about going back to visit her grandparents in Canada?"

"She's taking it too calmly. She hasn't said anything. I don't know her at the moment, I mean we've got over hating the sight of each other like we did last autumn, but we don't talk that much and she's never said anything about her mum. It's like that never happened. I mean they wanted to give her special dispensation about her exams but she wasn't having it. She just studies and does everything else just as if nothing has happened. Her mum had just been killed for Christ's sake and she's been acting as if nothing's happened!"

"Some people take grief in different ways, darling."

"But if it had been you. And me."

"As I said, darling, grief takes people in different ways. I don't think you can doubt she loved her mother very much."

Graham hadn't phoned to offer them a lift back to the Wirral as he had done at the end of every term since he had wheedled his way into their lives so they lugged their bags to the railway station.

Holly was put out by Graham's lack of interest. He hadn't even been in touch to ask her how her exams had gone. It was as if he didn't want to see her again, and it annoyed her that he hadn't had the guts to tell her to her face.

If he didn't care, she wouldn't.

"What?" Holly had been dreaming as she gazed out of the train window when she realised Linda had been talking to her. "Sorry, I was just wondering what to do this summer. I should have stayed in Leicester, the only reason I'm going home is to clear the house. The agents wrote to say Dad hadn't been near the place and the notice runs out next week. I've got to clear all our stuff out, all Mum's clothes, her books, everything. It's got to be done."

Linda wondered why she hadn't said anything about this before now.

"Stay with us Holly. You can clear the house from there, you don't have to stay there. Don't worry about having to be nice and polite all the time to Mutt and Jeff. You've got to make it your own home where you could be in a bad mood and let everyone know it, where you can have tantrums and arguments and storm out of rooms, knowing that you can come straight back home and no one will say a thing. Just like I do." She realised Holly wasn't finding her funny so she finished rather lamely. "You wouldn't have to think you're living in someone else's house."

129

Holly carried on talking as if she hadn't heard anything Linda had said.

"I'm not going begging to Dad. He made it clear that there was no room for me in his life. He wasn't even interested in my results. He wants nothing to do with me."

Linda tried another tack.

"Do you realise this is our last summer of freedom, next summer we'll be looking for jobs even if we're not working already. Let's forget everything and just enjoy ourselves."

Holly looked at Linda as if she was only just realising how much her life had to change.

"I'm not sure I like the idea of freedom."

Linda wondered how she would have coped if she had lost her mother and her home.

Three months of the summer seemed wonderful to her, filled with her family and doing the things that she had always done; but for Holly it must stretch out ahead frighteningly empty, a full three months before she would be back for her final year at Leicester.

Linda heard Holly humming gently, eventually she recognised the song and the words went round and round in her head *Freedom's just another word for nothing left to lose.*

They didn't speak for the rest of the journey home.

"You must be so tired darlings, all that work and then lugging all these bags home. You should have let Jeff meet you at the station. Come in, sit down and we'll have a cup of coffee." Pat was all enveloping in her welcome. "Holly, darling, you are so welcome," she gave her an extra hug. "for as long as you like. The boys are coming up next weekend to take you down to Oxford. That's if you want to go Holly? They're expecting you both. They say you can spend as much time as you like down there now it's your last summer before having to get jobs. They said it was your last summer of freedom so you should enjoy it!"

"That'd be nice." Holly didn't sound enthusiastic but Linda did all the talking "How are they? They sent us good luck cards for the exams but never bothered to call to find out how we'd done. Have they got girl-friends yet? They're far too old to be on their own. What are they up to now?"

As ever she kept the most important question to last.

"Will Carl be with them?" Her interest in Carl had resurfaced after Gerry had decided, after all, she was not his type.

"They're fine. Doing something really interesting at work I think. They've decided to leave their jobs and set up their own business

130

though I haven't a clue how they're going about it. No, Carl won't be coming up but he phoned last weekend and sends his love, to you both, and says he'll see you down there."

Holly didn't seem to be listening. "I don't think I can go to Oxford. I'd like to but I've got to clear the house out. Dad won't have done it. Then I should get a job. I need to earn some money somehow."

"Time enough to do that when you get back."

Linda did her bit to try to cheer Holly up "I know it's going to be a long hot summer and we're going to get brown and read lots of trashy novels and meet loads of dishy guys and have fun! It's our last summer..."

"Oh shut up about freedom! What's so great about being able to do anything you want without anyone caring what you do?" And Holly burst into tears. "I can do anything I want now. There's no one to tell me not to. I always thought it'd be great to be able to do what I wanted. But it isn't."

Half an hour later she was sobbing quietly, her head resting on her folded arms on the kitchen table. Pat was gently rubbed her back whilst handing her tissue after tissue.

"Do you want to talk?"

Holly shook her head.

"Linda is very fond of you, you know, even if it may sometimes seem that she doesn't. You know we all are. You must know you've always got a home with us." She continued as there was still no response from Holly "I have no idea what you are feeling, how can I? Nor can Linda or anyone else. You have a lot to come to terms with and you've just worked your guts out for your exams and you're worn out. Just know that you have got people who care about you. You aren't on your own, however much it must feel like it now. We've cleared out the spare room for you, it's usually got some of Carl's stuff but he's said he's not coming back up for a while so you're absolutely no bother at all. Just get some rest, some sleep, build up some of that resilience I know you've got."

By the time Crispin and Oliver arrived a few days later Holly was beginning to take more of an interest in the holiday. She had slept late every day while Linda had gone swimming or taken the dogs for long walks on Thurstaston Hill. She had begun to eat at mealtimes after several days of simply forking the food around her plate.

"But Mum, she's indulging herself. She's wallowing in it."

"She's finally facing up to it," Pat explained to her daughter "give her time, she'll be the old Holly soon enough."

"It's months since the accident, why's it hitting her now?"

"Only two. And she will have pushed it to the back of her mind while she had exams to worry about but now she hasn't got them as a prop. Now she looks out of her window at night and sees the garden where it all happened. She sees the garden where she was happy and where it all went wrong. I think you're being a wee bit harsh saying she's being self-indulgent."

"Maybe," was all Linda would say.

The morning the boys were due home Holly got up before five o'clock. It was going to be a hot day and she wanted it to be over with. She'd left it to the last moment, which was so unlike her. She crept out of the house, down through what was left of the gap in the hedge into 'her' back garden. The garden looked unkempt, she made herself not think about all the time her Mother had spent making the garden look nice. She sat down, cross legged and stared at the grass where her Mother had died.

Linda had heard Holly leave the house and had been going to leave her alone reasoning that she needed her space. But after she had watched her sit down on the grass and not move for several minutes she decided to go down to her. She would probably tell her to bugger off but she might just need a friend.

She sat down on the grass beside Holly who looked across at her and smiled grimly.

"Do you want some company? I'll piss off if you want to be alone."

"No. I mean yes. Company would be good."

"I'll help if you want."

It was some minutes before Holly stood up. "Come on, let's get this over with."

They peered through the windows and saw that, although some things had been removed, there was still a lot of stuff in the house.

"Shall we break in?" Linda tried the window and the back door, wondering how they would manage.

"We don't need to. I've got this." Holly took a key from her pocket and put it into the lock. "I hope no one bolted it on the inside." She turned the key and turned the doorknob, pushing gently. The door opened.

They walked around the house, looking at the rooms that had been a home just a few weeks before. Linda followed Holly as she went up the stairs and into her parents' bedroom. "It's all empty," she sounded devastated, "he's emptied all the wardrobes and drawers. I wonder when he did it. What's he done with all of mum's stuff? When the agent wrote he said it was all here."

Linda, wisely, said nothing as Holly turned round and walked across the landing to what had been her bedroom. They had had so much fun there.

"All the posters are still here. Nothing much seems to have changed."

"I wonder what he thought would happen to all this stuff." Holly checked the drawers of dressing table. They hadn't been touched since six weeks earlier she had thrown what she needed for the term in a rucksack and left, refusing to admit to herself that she would never be coming back.

"We can sort out what you want and you can keep it in your room with us. Anything else can go in our loft.

"Most of it's rubbish. I suppose I'll have to get a house clearer in and all this will get dumped. There's some stuff I'd like though."

"I'll go up to the house and get some bags." So Linda left Holly alone.

It took Linda only a couple of minutes and when she got back Holly was ripping down the last poster from the wall. "I remember when you stuck that one up. I always liked Marc Bolan." She watched Holly screw it up in a ball and throw it behind the door to join the others. "Silly really, look at the mess it's made of the wall. Mom," she hesitated "Mom, always told me not to put them up, she told me it would ruin the wall when they came down. She was right."

"Someone else's problem."

As Holly sorted through the drawers she threw more stuff behind the door than she handed to Linda to put into the bags.

"You can't throw all those books away!" Linda argued. "I'll have them if you don't want them." So she put them in the bags. "And what about all your A level notes! You might need those, you never know, you might end up teaching and they'd be useful."

"Me? Teach? Never." But she allowed Linda to put them in the bags anyway.

As they left her room she shut the door behind her with finality.

"I'll take these up to the house." Linda wasn't normally tactful but she realised Holly needed a little time on her own.

When she got back Holly was downstairs looking into the sideboard.

"All our good plates and glasses. Dad hasn't taken anything. I remember when we bought them. She was so pleased with them, she thought they were so English."

"You can't leave them for the clearers. I'll go and get some boxes, you can't leave all these. Your Mum loved them."

So Linda left Holly alone again in the house.

When she got back there was another pile of rubbish behind the door. There had been ornaments on their shelves, gathering a thin layer of dust, and pictures on the walls. They were all in a heap of broken china and glass. "Dad hated photographs, so we never had any. These are all crap. Cheap crap. Bought to fill gaps on walls. Why haven't we got any photos of us? There's none of me and Mum and Dad as a family. Not like you've got all over your house. You can't move for photos of you and Crisp and Olly, even Carl and he's not even proper family."

"We've got ones of you. Look through the ones the boys have taken, Take whatever you want."

"What I want to find is something that is *Mum*. Something small that I can always carry with me, that's her, something that I can always hold on to when I need to feel close to her, something personal, precious and important. You know what I mean?"

Linda nodded. "You've smashed all the ornaments. How about a book, here, there's a small book of poetry here."

"Something small." Holly ran her finger along the rows of orange and turquoise paperbacks that filled most of the shelves. She stopped at a guidebook of New York.

"We took a trip when I was about ten. We went on a boat trip around Manhattan, just Mom and me. I can't remember where Dad had gone. Mom paid the fare and got a quarter in the change that had been painted red. We kept it to remind us of that day. Mom wrapped it in tissue paper and put it in the little plastic pocket..." she paused as she opened the book "...in the guidebook! It's still here!"

She unwrapped it from the tissue paper and held it tightly in her fist before putting it in her pocket. "That's it. As long as I've got that coin Mom's with me."

Linda gave her a hug. "What about the books? You don't want to leave these? Come on let's pack them up – if you don't want them then we can find someone who does."

It took four journeys for Linda to take all the books back up the garden. Before they left for the fifth and final time they sat down for a coffee at the kitchen table. Holly's thoughts, inevitably, were of the morning when everything had seemed perfect until she'd heard the silence behind the radio. *When you walk, through a storm...*

"You know he's taken one plate, one mug, one knife, one fork, one spoon, one dish, one of everything." There was nothing Linda could say. It was so obvious to both of them that Matt had no intention of doing anything for his daughter.

"Thanks for your help." Holly took one of the remaining mugs off a hook and they walked out of the house. Holly locked the door behind her and threw the key into the bushes.

It was not yet eight o'clock.

The change in Holly was immediate. She was talkative, laughing and

134

insisting on making the coffee, toast and orange juice which was the Forster's staple breakfast during the week.

"You've worked some magic clearing the house. She's just like her old self." Pat said to Linda when Holly went to answer the doorbell.

The boys were home.

When Holly left the table an hour later Pat spoke quietly and firmly to her sons. "Holly's been having a tough time, we've been very worried."

"She seems pretty normal to me." Oliver commented.

"Only more so." Linda added. "It's almost as if she's on something."

"She wouldn't do drugs would she?" Pat was concerned "Perhaps all the strain had sent her over the edge."

"I don't think so. Where would she have got them anyway?"

"You, my dear children, are far more likely to know the answer to that than I am!"

As they heard Holly coming back down the stairs Pat added "Look after her, won't you?"

Crispin's reply was heartfelt. "We always try."

But they argued with her when Holly said she wanted to visit her father.

"Get it all over with in one day." She had insisted "Then tomorrow is the beginning of the rest of my life."

"I'll come with you." Linda offered

"I'll drive." Crispin volunteered.

"I'm coming too." Oliver wasn't going to be left out.

"Good luck" they said as she left them in the car.

Holly walked across the wide pavement, through the door between the two shops and up two flights of carpet-less stairs to the door marked 'Eccleston'.

"She'll be OK won't she?" Crispin asked.

"Of course idiot. She's fine."

"I hope so."

They waited.

"Are you sure she's OK?"

"Of course she is."

Five minutes later Holly was fleeing down the stairs.

When he had answered the door Matt had made her stand there while he told her he didn't have a daughter, didn't want a daughter, had never wanted a daughter.

She wondered if he was drunk even though it wasn't eleven o'clock yet.

A son he could have done something with, he said, but a daughter was a drain, a burden, no use at all. Only a pathetic woman like her mother could have given him a daughter. If he had chosen a better wife he would have had a son, someone to carry on his name, someone to make a difference in the world, to fight for the things that were right and proper.

When she had stood there, refusing to run away, he had finally opened the door and allowed her into his flat. He gestured for her to go ahead of him.

As she walked through a doorway she realised she was in his bedroom, the unmade bed, the discarded clothes on the floor, simply adding to her feeling that this was not the father she had known.

She turned back to see what he wanted of her.

He was standing too close to her.

He grabbed her arm. She had to listen as he spoke calmly, almost conversationally "I should have got you used to this by now. I should have started you young. My father always said girl children were only good for one thing. He was right. We learned from him on Rebecca."

He was holding her so she couldn't move, while he was unzipping his trousers. His intentions were obvious.

"That's all girl children are good for. I got no use out of you while your mother protected you but I'll enjoy making up for it now. You need to learn what a man really needs and who better to teach you than your father?"

She hit him as hard as she could but he didn't let her go, he slapped her hard across the face with the back of his hand, his ring catching the corner of her eye. The impact pushed her, unbalanced, backwards, but with strength she had no idea she had she worked herself free and ran out of the flat, down the stairs and to safety.

"I don't want to talk about it." She was not going to give any explanation as she slammed the door of the car. "Let's go."

They all wanted to confront Matt but Holly screamed at them "Leave it. Leave him." Reluctantly, Crispin put the car into gear and drove home as Linda carefully dabbed at the blood oozing from the cut on Holly's face.

Holly went back to Oxford with the boys and Linda but she was withdrawn, there was none of the enthusiasm she had shown that one morning.

"If she doesn't want to talk about it, she doesn't want to talk about it. That's that!"

"But …

"But nothing! She's upset. Nothing's going right for her. We've just

136

got to be here when she wants to talk to us. We can't force her."

"She's just going through the motions as if nothing had happened."

"Well that's up to her isn't it. If she wants to ignore the fact that her father gave her a black eye then that's her prerogative. We can't make her tell us what it was all about."

"But she's been so moody. She answers when we ask her something, she smiles when someone says something funny, she does her share around the house and she hasn't just gone into her room and sulked."

"But she's not really here. It's as if she's been taken over by an alien and has become a programmed zombie!" Oliver tried to lighten his brother's mood.

"Don't be so stupid! She's fine. She's a helluvalot better than she was before we came down here."

Linda and her brothers didn't like to talk about Holly behind her back but they were worried and she wasn't there.

They sat pint jugs in hand. It was Sunday evening and the terrace was crowded even though it was seven o'clock and the pub had just opened. They sat on the wall overlooking the river swinging their legs in the water.

"Where is she anyway?"

"She just left the house early. She didn't tell me where she was going."

"Nor me."

"Not very like her is it?"

"Like she was last autumn. She was withdrawn, miserable and uncommunicative then, and her Mother wasn't even dead!"

"Holly! That's really cruel"

"Well she was a pain. She's just the same now."

"What happened to you two being friends?"

"I dunno. She's changed. We had a morning like we used to be when we cleared out her house, then we went to see her father. What a shit that man is. But we haven't been really close, like we used to be, for ages, not since she starting seeing that shit Graham."

"Does she still do that?"

"I didn't think so."

"She'd have told us wouldn't she?"

"Not if she knows you disapprove of her."

Holly's behaviour was unsettling the three of them, although the weather had been good and they had done all the usual things, it wasn't the same as the previous summer.

"It's my last summer before the real world hits me and it's all being fucked up by her stupid behaviour. It's not fair!"

"When did you start swearing like a trooper?" Oliver tried to sound like a disapproving elder brother.

"Why are you getting at me? It's not my fault we're all having a miserable time."

"It's not that bad." Crispin didn't sound convincing.

"Anyone for another beer? I thought I'd find you here."

"Hi Carl."

When they had all returned to their places on the wall Carl sandwiched between Linda and Crispin, they were still subdued.

"Well were you talking about me then?"

"What?"

"Well you were all talking animatedly when I came and now you're saying nothing. QED you were talking about me."

"No, actually," Linda said coldly, as if there was no reason at all why any one of them would ever want to talk about Carl, "We weren't talking about you. We were talking about Holly."

"Hasn't she got back yet?"

Carl's question seemed quite natural to him but it caused a rash of enquiry.

"Back from where?"

"Have you seen her?"

"Where's she been?"

"Ah." Linda was the first to realise what had been going on. "You've been racing today, haven't you? And so has she, with that creep. You've seen her, them, whatever."

"Yes. Why? What's the problem? I haven't seen her for a few months but I assumed that was because she had exams, and her mum's accident. But yes, she was there, with Graham, he did quite well actually. Surprising really, he came fourth."

"I couldn't give a shit whether he won the fucking Grand Prix what did she say? Was she OK? Did she seem like she wanted to be there?"

"Yes, of course! Why shouldn't she?"

They spent a few minutes explaining to Carl about her odd behaviour recently and her argument with her father. "Well she seemed fine to me, very happy actually. I've not seen her kissing and cuddling with Graham before. They seemed all over each other actually. Sorry Crispin." Carl knew how his friend felt about Holly. "Anyway, you can see for yourselves. Here they come."

They had all listened, stunned, as Graham told them he and Holly were to be married.

"Why?" Was Linda's immediate reaction "You're not, you know, are you...?"

"No of course not." Holly sounded indignant.

"Why then?"

"Because I asked her and because she loves me."

Linda wanted to scream 'No she doesn't!'

Holly certainly didn't look like someone in love.

"Why not just live together?"

"At least while you finish at Leicester."

"You are going to finish your degree, aren't you?

Holly spoke defensively. "Isn't anyone going to congratulate us?"

That evening when Holly got home the boys made themselves scarce so that Linda could talk to her.

"Are you sure you want to go ahead with it? Because if you aren't absolutely certain now is really the time to say so."

"I'm sure."

Linda wanted to hug her friend and say 'don't do it. We all love you too much to let you make this mistake'.

Holly wanted Linda to say 'stop me. Tell me I can't do it. I know I'm making a mistake but I can't go back on it because I haven't any other option.'

But somehow there was a distance between them that could not be bridged, neither could say what they really wanted to so after an awkward silence Linda shrugged and said "Then we'll help all we can. We all will. Of course we will."

Holly managed to get to her room before bursting into tears.

Linda went back to the boys to tell them Holly wasn;t going to change her mind. "Absolutely not! It's crazy. It's madness. She's only 20 for Christ's sake. She's got her finals coming up. She can't."

"He's a creep. He wants something from her. I just know it." Linda voiced the suspicions for all of them "Look at those times he kept showing up, Christmas, New Year, Easter."

"Just before her Mum died."

"It's up to her what she does."

"But marry Graham!" Crispin was horrified

"You sound like Henry Higgins *Marry Graham Huh*!"

"We can't let her go through with it."

"We can't stop her."

"But there are so many reasons why it will be a disaster."

"Can't you talk her out of it Linda?"

"Why would she listen to me?"

"Well you, Carl, she'd listen to you."

"Why would she do that? She's not going to listen to anyone. If you ask me she feels no one loves her and she will be safe and secure once she's married and, as Graham said, he was the one that asked her."

"I'd have asked her."

"We know you would have done, Crisp, but you didn't."

"She never gave me a chance."

Chapter Fifteen

On the morning of Saturday 15th September 1973 a special breakfast was being prepared at the Forsters. Oliver and Crispin sat behind plates of bacon, eggs, mushrooms and tomatoes, though Crispin's appetite wasn't as healthy as normal.

"It's going to be a long day."

"Does she really want to go ahead with this?" Crispin hoped that, even at this last stage, they could persuade her to change her mind.

"She's absolutely set on it." His twin answered. He knew how much it hurt Crispin to see Holly marry Graham.

"How is she?"

"Still in her room, I took up some tea and toast and she seemed absolutely set on it."

"Is Linda with her?"

"She's having her hair done, then she'll be with her. She'll look beautiful, it's a lovely dress."

"That's not the point is it? Weddings aren't supposed to be how pretty people are and how beautiful the bridesmaid looked are they?"

"Aren't they?"

Pat gave Oliver a look that quietened him abruptly. "You will look smart and happy. You will do your jobs as ushers and you will do your absolute best to make this the wonderful day it must be. Holly needs our unqualified support. She will get it. Won't she."

"OK Mum." Oliver answered for both of them.

"We've got two hours before we need to be at the church. Go for a walk or something."

"Why don't they have weddings at ten o'clock in the morning and then no one would have the time to worry. Not having to be there till noon gives so much time to think."

Holly had not wanted to get in touch with her father but Graham had told her she must. He had no intention of paying for the wedding so Matt would have to. She had reluctantly phoned him, expecting a row. She thought he would refuse permission, or if he gave it would insist on a small register office ceremony, or if he agreed to a proper white wedding would refuse to pay for it. But as she talked in a rush "Graham and I are getting married. There's nothing you can do that

141

will change my mind. And I want a decent wedding. Mom would have wanted me to, wouldn't she?" He had agreed. "Yes, sure she would, sure you do."

She asked Pat to be 'honorary Mother of the Bride' and undertake the organisation. Graham sent them a list of names but left everything else to them. As Pat wrote the invitations out, she wondered who all these people were, why they were being invited and what Graham was trying to prove. Try as she might she could not understand why Matt or Graham or Holly wanted to make such a big thing of the wedding when Mary had been dead less than six months.

Some of the invitations were declined.

Holly's grandparents had replied saying they disapproved of the marriage. In a long letter to Pat they asked what she knew of Graham, what had happened to the nice young man who they had stayed with, who had met them at the airport, and asking Pat to persuade Holly not to go ahead.

Carl sent his apologies, explaining he would be filming abroad. Perhaps he could have been in England but the chance of meeting Susannah, or of her seeing his photograph in the paper, was too great.

Ted sent a note saying "Unfortunately I can't be with you. Since I don't have an idea what the young people would like for a present perhaps they can buy something with this." It was attached to the cheque that was for far too much money.

Max replied saying unfortunately both he and Monika had alternative arrangements made for that day. Charles, however, accepted, having argued with Max that he felt he had to go.

But most were accepted.

Maureen Shelton sent a wordy letter of acceptance, referring to the 'old days' and how, although she had only met Alicia's nephew Graham once, she had obviously been wrong in her impressions of him. If Holly loved him there had to be some good in him.

As Holly checked the growing list of acceptances she thought how odd it was that so many of the same people would be at this wedding as had been at Alicia's funeral.

Although it had been only eighteen months ago life had moved on so much for many of them.

On the morning of the wedding Holly looked at her reflection in the mirror on her dressing table, and behind her, her dress hanging on the door.

She liked her dress. It wasn't the chocolate box sort of dress that most people seemed to wear with a tight waist and enormous skirt circling out around her. She had chosen a more elegant, slim line dress that was tight just under her breasts and fell straight to the floor. "Empire line this used to be called miss" the woman in the shop had said. "Very elegant, though not normally worn by one so young." "Well I like it." She had said.

She didn't like her hair. Instead of hanging long and straight, tucked behind her ears as it usually was, it had been styled more formally, swept up into what the hairdresser called a 'French roll' that Holly really did not like. The hairdresser had insisted that it made her look more sophisticated, Holly had taken that as implicit criticism that she was too young to be getting married and had taken against the hairstyle.

"Bugger them," she said, "I'm not too young."

She removed the hundreds of pins and shook her head. As her hair fell more naturally around her shoulders she remembered the day, only two years earlier, when Linda had pinned her hair up and they had taken the school by storm collecting their A level results. *Star Pupils* they had been, she still had the cutting in her box of treasures. She had a brief recollection of Crispin's kiss and how safe she had felt when he had kissed her again in the kitchen in Oxford.

He had seemed interested in her then. She wondered why he had gone off her. Although he'd been friendly enough ever since he had never tried to get close to her again.

She didn't like being rejected.

She sat in front of the mirror in her dressing gown putting on the minimal makeup she had always worn. "Bugger them. I'm not going to be someone I'm not.

"Can I come in?" Crispin appeared at the door, wearing an incongruous combination of Rolling Stones t-shirt and formal morning suit trousers.

"Of course" Holly instinctively pulled her dressing gown around her and tying the belt more tightly around her waist. He saw the defensiveness in her movements and so he didn't go into the room, he just stayed in the doorway, his hand on the door handle.

"Are you OK?"

"Of course. Why wouldn't I be?" She didn't mean to be rude, she knew that no one understood why she was doing what she as doing.

"We, that is Olly and I, we were wondering if we could get you anything. A glass of something? You must be feeling nervous."

"No I'm fine."

"Sure?"

"Sure."

She wondered why he hung around. She didn't feel like company.

"And?" she asked him, prompting him to say what was obviously on his mind.

"Can I come in?"

"You already asked that." This time he went into her room and closed the door behind him. He sat down on her bed, awkwardly, his hands between his knees.

"Come on Crisp. What is it? I've got to get dressed soon."

He didn't say anything for a few moments. He just looked at her. Eventually he said "You are so beautiful Holly."

She wasn't sure what to say. His meaning was obvious. She looked at him and shrugged her shoulders.

"I mean it."

Still he didn't move from the bed and she couldn't move from her seat in front of the dressing table. She looked at his reflection in the mirror and he stared at her.

"Come on Crisp. I've got to get ready." She didn't want him to say what she knew he was trying to say.

"You've got hours yet." He was trying to put off the time when she would put on that dress. He couldn't stop thinking that what she finally took it off she would be married. To Graham.

"Not that long." She was becoming embarrassed.

"Holly" he started "Holly, I've got to say this."

"Don't."

"I've got to."

"Please don't." She was angry with him. Why was he going to say these things now? Now? Why hadn't he said anything before?

"If I don't I'll never forgive myself."

"Please don't. We've always been friends please let's stay that way." It wasn't that she minded, it was just two months too late.

"I've got to say this, Holly. Really. You don't have to go through with this. You don't have to marry him. We can go down to the church and tell everyone that the party is going ahead, they can have the food and the drink and everyone can talk and chat and gossip, but you don't have to go through with the wedding. If your father doesn't like it we'll pay, Oliver and I, we'll pay your father back everything it's cost. We'll make sure he hasn't lost anything. But honestly, you don't have to go through with this. Please. Listen. You don't."

She sat looking at Crispin who still sat on the bed, his hands nervously clasped together, his body bending forwards and backwards in an edgy rhythm.

"I do." She said, aware that those were the words she would have to use in a few hours time in an entirely different context.

"No you *don't*. At least wait until after your finals. Don't do it now.

You don't have to. You can stay here every vac, you've always got a home here. Carl did. We're open house. Mum and Dad love you, we all love you and will be here for you. You don't have to marry him just to have somewhere to live."

She was surprised that he had identified the main reason she had accepted Graham. He had a place she could call home. He had bought a nice newly built terraced house with three bedrooms and a garage and although it didn't have much of a garden there was enough room in the back yard to have a washing line. Graham had bought some new furniture and he kept saying how lucky she was that they were getting such generous wedding presents.

She wanted to use her mother's china, that was still in boxes in the Forster's loft but he wanted everything new. He wouldn't let her fetch the boxes of books and pictures that she had rescued from Number 16 that Spring.

She knew she wouldn't have chosen the furniture he had bought, but she hadn't been given the choice. He had asked her to marry him, she had accepted and then he had taken her to the house that was to be her home that was fully furnished. She couldn't say she hated it because it was the only home she could have.

"I'm going to get married." She sounded more defiant and defensive than she would have wished. "And I'm not going to wait. I've got no need to wait."

"You don't have…"

"No, of course I don't have to. I'm not stupid."

"I didn't mean that." Crispin knew he had handled it all wrong. He had wanted her to know she would be OK, she had people who loved her, she didn't have to marry Graham to feel safe again. He understood she was only getting married because her Mother had died and her father had abandoned her. He just didn't know how to tell her the real reason he didn't want her to marry Graham.

"Well, I'd better go then."

"Yes." She wasn't going to make it any easier for him.

"I hope you're very happy."

"I know."

"The car will be here in half an hour."

"I'll be ready."

"If you're sure."

"I'm sure."

Crispin went downstairs to the kitchen feeling more depressed than he had since he had first heard that Holly was to marry Graham. "She's going ahead with it." He said, resigned to the inevitable.

"Well you didn't think she wouldn't did you?" Oliver replied trying not to understand how much his brother was hurting and how much he might be responsible.

"I suppose not."

They sat down at the kitchen table, coffee mugs in hand, waiting for the time to come when they would have to finish getting dressed and prepare for the ordeal ahead.

Chapter Sixteen

If I had been curious to see the three invitations, carefully addressed to *Mrs Monika Heller, Mr Charles Donaldson and Mr Max Fischer*, I was horrified when I read the contents.

The wedding of his daughter, Holly, with Graham Tyler

So Max had been right. Somehow, in such a short time, Graham had managed to get Holly to marry him.

I phoned Linda. I was quite pleased to have an excuse. I was disappointed she hadn't been in touch since the O'Dwyers had been over from Canada, but then I suppose I hadn't called her either.

She told me the bare bones of how it had all come about so quickly. "I probably wasn't much help," she admitted, "I thought Graham was a complete shit and thought she must be if she liked him at all. I kind of abandoned her. Her father abandoned her. I suppose she felt she had nowhere else to go, no one else to turn to so had decided to marry Graham."

So that was how they had done it.

I asked Linda whether there was any way Holly could know what he was really like.

"If she does she doesn't care."

"She will."

After the service that passed off uneventfully, even though there had been a rash of giggles from some young girls at the phrase 'speak now or hereafter hold your peace', I walked the few yards to the hotel alone. I spent the time observing the motley group of people who had attended the wedding, trying to allocate their relationship to either bride or groom. I had been surprised to see my grandmother with David. I had rather assumed they weren't coming since they hadn't contacted us. I thought that would have been a natural thing for them to have done.

I stood alone in the line waiting to shake hands with Holly's father and congratulate him on his daughter's wedding. There was no sign of Holly or Graham, who had driven off as soon as the photographs had been taken.

As I drew nearer the head of the line I could hear the comments people made to the father of the bride, and his responses. Some guests, aware of Mary's death the previous Spring, spoke kind words of sympathy that he was having to do this without the love and support of his wife. His face was a mask of stoicism and he took their compliments with slight sharp bows of his head.

As I waited I remembered the time I had seen him last, standing on the terrace at Sandhey looking around him as if he owned the house, striding off down the drive without a word to his family or to me. There was something of that same look as he held his hand out and shook mine briefly. There was a knowingness, an assumed superiority about him that I did not like.

I was afraid for Holly in this marriage that I had done nothing to prevent. I knew Graham was not a nice man, but then, it seemed, her father wasn't either.

I was talking to Linda's brothers when the bride and groom arrived some time after all the guests had settled into drinking and talking. Holly looked dreadful. She had obviously been crying and her dress, which I had thought particularly elegant, was badly crumpled.

Crispin and Oliver hugged Holly in turn, I self-consciously kissed her on both cheeks, trying to ignore the smudges around her eyes and the beginnings of bruises on her shoulders.

"Well done Mrs Tyler." Oliver's smile was sympathetic rather than enthusiastic. It was less genuine as he turned to Graham "Look after her, won't you?" I don't think the question was welcomed as Graham made no reply, simply grasping Holly's arm and tried to steer her away from us.

"Holly, are you OK?" Crispin's sensitivity was greater than his brother's.

"Of course she's OK," interrupted Graham "we just got a bit carried away, that's all, didn't we Holl Doll. You know what it's like." And he laughed, in what I can only think of as a lascivious way that simply added to Holly's obvious embarrassment as she realised how many people knew what they had been doing for the past half hour.

"Where's Linda? I need some help from my bridesmaid." Holly tried to sound normal but no one in earshot, not even I who hardly knew her, would have been convinced.

"I'll get her, she's over there, I won't be a moment." I felt I had to be of some use.

As Linda threaded her way through the throng back to Holly and they went, arm in arm, towards the lifts. I made the mistake of putting my hand on Graham's arm as he passed me, obviously intent on following them. It was an instinctive movement, I had no intention of restraining him and I doubt I could have done anyway. "I don't think they need you old chap."

"Screw you." He must have seen me looking at Linda and Holly as they left. "Don't even think about it chummy. She's a randy little tart but she's my randy little tart so you can keep your eyes to yourself."

A few minutes later in the afternoon I was talking with Crispin and Oliver when Graham pulled my shoulder so I had to turn to face him.

"I meant what I said earlier. Touch her and you're dead."

"I have no idea what you mean." I spoke with as much dignity as I could muster though I probably only sounded pompous.

He turned on me, his face no more than a couple of inches from mine. "Shut the fuck up. She's my fucking wife and don't think you can stop me doing what I fucking like with her. I've seen the way you look at her. Week after week you find a way to talk to her. Fancy her don't you? Well no one's going to screw her but me. If I see you anywhere near her I'll fucking kill you."

I wondered what he was talking about. I hardly knew Holly. I'd only really spoken to her once, that evening when her grandparents stayed at Sandhey.

He looked behind me at Crispin and Oliver. "And that goes for you two arsewipes as well."

"I think you've mixed me up with someone else." I said, trying to back away. It was the only explanation.

He thought I was Carl.

He moved away, heading for a group of giggling girls who seemed already to have had too much to drink, leaving me and the twins stunned at his attitude.

"What brought that on?" I was glad the twins were with me.

"He thinks you're Carl." Crispin had no doubts.

"Well, you are very like him." Oliver said, calming, encouraging. Normal.

"Your hair's a bit darker, but he's got the eyes hasn't he Oliver?"

"Pretty much two peas in a pod."

I was still shaking from Graham's onslaught and found it reassuring to talk to Linda's brothers.

"It appears Holly has already had an inkling of what it's going to be like to be married to Graham."

"We'll have to keep an eye on her."

"He's a dangerous man. There's a violence about him."

They told me of Graham's appearances over the past year. "It was really odd. Christmas, New Year, Easter, there he was." As they talked I was thinking that when Graham had turned up at those odd times in their lives, he hadn't wanted to be with Holly, he was showing Matt that he couldn't control him, and, knowing how much Linda disliked him, he was creating a barrier between Holly and her friends.

It seemed he had succeeded.

I was still talking to them when Holly and Linda joined us. "It was my fault, silly really, I spilt a bottle of coke all over her beautiful dress. She had to change."

Only when Holly had left us could Linda tell us the truth.

"She knows she should have listened to you Crispin, even Oliver told her not to go ahead with it, to wait. She knows it's too late. I told her she had to get through today first. When Graham left I tried to tidy her up a bit and told her to try to enjoy the party. We'd see her tomorrow."

"She's married to Graham and all we can do now is watch and wait as it all turns to shit."

"He doesn't care for her, I know he doesn't"

"He's using her. What for, I don't know. There's got to be more to it, everything was done in such a hurry."

I couldn't tell Crispin how right he was.

"You're his cousin aren't you, Charles, you know him better than anyone. What's he up to?"

I couldn't tell them any of what I knew, even if I could have done now wasn't the time or the place.

So I said nothing other than to repeat that I knew Graham was deceitful and devious, that I didn't like him or trust him, and if there was anything they could think that I could do they must just tell me.

"So you're one of us now?" Linda said hooking her arm into mine. "He hasn't got a hope."

I disentangled myself feeling uncomfortable and in many ways as deceitful as Graham, though I told myself mine were the more honourable motives.

For the rest of the afternoon I watched the room closely. More than once I saw Graham leave the room with one or other of the young women I assumed worked with him. I hoped he was simply taking them for a dance in the disco room but it seemed more likely that he was doing something very different. Graham was making it obvious from the beginning that he had no intention of being a good husband.

I was probably the only person in the room who understood why Matt ignored what was going on, not just accepting it but being obviously amused by it. I thought it likely that he was joining in.

"Well that's nearly over." Linda handed me a full glass. I was glad she wanted to talk to me, I didn't want there to be any awkwardness between us and I had probably been more abrupt than necessary earlier on when she had only been trying to be friendly.

"How is she coping?" Perhaps talking about Holly would give us something to share, something we could agree on.

"Regretting, crying."

"Do you know why she's married him?"

"You don't like him either do you?"

"I wouldn't say that. Actually I hate him. Yes 'hate' is the right word."

"I think she was frightened of being on her own. Her mum dying, her father ignoring her for months…"

"He's not ignoring her now is he? This must be costing him a bomb." I swept my arm in a wide arc nearly dislodging a tray of glasses from a waitress's arm where it had been delicately balanced. "Sorry!"

"No harm done."

"If you ask me he's paying for it because he wants her married and no longer his responsibility. This is like his final payment."

"But why Graham?"

I knew why. I knew it was because they had manoeuvred Holly into it, isolating her from her friends. But I wanted to know what Linda thought.

"No one else asked her. If you'd asked her she'd have married you. She would have married anyone to get a home and some security if you ask me."

"So she doesn't love him."

"What's love got to do with it? Of course she doesn't. Crisp tried to talk her out of it this morning. We all think it's a complete disaster. It's one thing in all my life I think I agree with them about."

"I'd hoped that people married for love these days. If she wasn't sure why didn't she just live with him?"

"He asked her to marry him. She seemed to think it was a good idea. She thought she had no one else."

"She had your family."

"We weren't enough."

As I was leaving I bumped into Crispin as he argued with Graham.

"You've been married how long? Three hours? And how many times have you been with another woman?"

"What the fuck's it got to do with you?"

"Holly. She's my friend. You're..."

"Yes I am aren't I? I'm her husband. She's my wife. She has to put up with whatever I do. Lucky me!"

"What about them?" Crispin pointed at the group of girls, giggling in the corner, obviously sharing their experiences.

"Yeah. So what? I had a bet that I'd have it off with them all during the reception. I won."

"What about Holly?"

"Holl Doll? What about her?"

"Don't you care that you're upsetting her?"

"No. Should I?"

Crispin obviously couldn't think of anything to say to Graham that would make clear exactly how he felt. So he hit him.

Remembering how hard Graham could punch I thought I'd come to Crispin's rescue.

"Come on Crispin, time to go home. I think you've had enough." I took his arm, leading him out to the car park where a line of taxis was waiting. Linda must have seen us leaving as she followed us out, thanking me in a rather detached way as she took over the support of her brother.

I needed time to myself to sort out the conflicting emotions of the day, all brought on by my dislike for Graham, so I set off to walk the two miles home.

I thought first about Linda.

Each time I saw her it was in different circumstances, a funeral, a birthday party, a wedding. Each time she was a different person and I decided I rather liked them all. She was opinionated, bossy and had a confidence I could never hope to match, though I had also seen her considerate, loyal and caring. I wondered if she could ever be fond of someone like me.

I knew she had always been interested in Carl. Her parents had made a joke of it at my birthday barbecue.

But Graham had thought I was Carl.

Perhaps we did look more alike now than ever; after all he was getting older and for the past 18 months I had been getting younger. The twins had said I was very like him and they knew both of us. I realised I had probably never tried to know him.

I had always been jealous of Carl but perhaps we had more in common than I had ever thought.

We had both run away from our family albeit at different times and for very different reasons. Carl had run away after he discovered the girl he loved was his father's daughter, I had felt forced to leave when my father went bankrupt and he made it clear there was no room for me in his new home. Nor had there been room for Monika, for whom I felt responsible even then. Max had taken us in, for whatever reason, and had given us a home for more than 15 years.

Perhaps the differences between Carl and I had been emphasised by the people who had taken us in. Where I had found an austere and old fashioned household Carl had chanced on a loving and open-hearted one. As I walked along the beach path I tried not to think what sort of person I would have been if I had had those years with the Forster family. What would Carl have been like if he had had to cope with the mysteries and the secrets of Sandhey? Perhaps his infatuation with Susannah would have died naturally as they grew older.

Finally, I worried about Holly and how she would cope with her marriage. I already knew it was a disaster, and, perhaps, my fault. I should have had the courage to have spoken to Max when we could have changed things. I would have had to own up to eavesdropping on his conversation with Matt but we could have intervened. By not telling him immediately, I knew I had acknowledged in some way that I was in the wrong.

The need to keep Monica safe from her memories had seemed the most important thing. Then.

Now, as I tried not to think what Holly would be going through, I wasn't so sure.

Chapter Seventeen

The first term of Linda and Holly's final year at Leicester passed in a haze of studying and trying to avoid talking about anything that really mattered.

They still shared the flat but they spent very little time together. Graham would arrive every Friday evening and Linda would pack a bag and leave without comment. She was annoyed at always having to get out of their way but anything was preferable to sharing the small flat with Holly and Graham.

She had done it only once. The first weekend Graham had appeared she had stayed, determined that she would not be forced out of her flat just because Holly had got married. But he had criticised everything from the stocks of food in the cupboard to the state of the bathroom.

"It's not your bloody flat and I'm not your bloody slave!" She shouted at him after he had told her that she should go out to get some fresh milk. "We're quite happy when you're not here."

"Well fuck off then bitch."

So she did and whenever there was the prospect of Graham visiting she would leave. She couldn't go to Oxford, now she'd finished with Gerry, and she didn't want to go home so she slept on floors, settees and in baths rather than spend any time with Graham and Holly. She asked Holly once why she didn't go back to her own home at weekends. 'He wants to come here.' Linda soon realised that Holly had no influence over Graham, she also realised that his coming to Leicester was his way of making his power show.

When Linda and Holly did talk they spoke about their coursework, they discussed the answers to clues in their crosswords and who was going to do the shopping. They argued about the housework and the rent. They commented on the war in the Middle East, Watergate and the impeachment of Richard Nixon, the wave of strikes, the royal wedding, the three day week and how they would manage living by candlelight when they came back after Christmas.

But they never spoke about anything that really mattered.

They travelled together back to Cheshire for the Christmas vacation but they said goodbye when Holly got off the train one stop earlier.

On Holly's 21st birthday, she got a birthday card from Graham and wondered blankly whether he had destroyed any others. Even though she knew her father wouldn't have bothered she was sure Linda and the boys would have sent one, and perhaps even her grandparents. But she got only the one, from Graham. She cooked a Christmas meal that they ate when he got back from the pub just after two o'clock. They watched the television and then they went to bed.

It was not the celebration she would have had had her Mother been alive, had she been at home.

Had she had a home.

When she met up again with Linda to travel back to Leicester she said nothing about her birthday. "We called you know. Crispin insisted we call but you didn't answer."

"I didn't want to speak to anyone."

"Are you OK?"

"Fine."

So they didn't talk any more about her 21st birthday or her holiday.

At Easter Linda stayed in Leicester to finish her dissertation while Holly went home. When she got back to Leicester two weeks later she looked tired and depressed.

"Have a good holiday?" Linda asked.

"Shit."

"Wanna talk about it?"

"No."

So they didn't.

At the end of the year they packed up the flat where they had, at least for some of the time, been friends, they divided up the contents as if they were a couple getting divorced. Perhaps, in some ways, it was like the end of a relationship. They were scrupulously polite as they avoided any emotion and emptied the flat that had been their home for three years.

"That picture. Do you want it?"

"Keep it."

"These mugs?"

"You have them."

"I think they're yours."

"Are you sure?"

"Positive."

Graham pushed Holly's bags and boxes, rolled-up posters and clothes on hangers into the back of his car whilst Linda finished the clearing up.

155

They didn't hug each other as they said goodbye. Their lives had been so different for so long.

"Seeya. Good Luck." Linda said as Holly took the final armful of plastic bags out of the door.

"Seeya." Holly replied, trying desperately not to cry.

When she got her results Linda hadn't got the First she had wanted and believed she deserved, she had got a 2.1 but the family gathered to celebrate nonetheless.

"It's rubbish! I've let everyone down. *Everyone* in the family gets a first. I'm a complete waste of space. I've let everyone down!"

"Of course you haven't darling," Pat hugged her as she poured some more champagne into her daughter's glass "You've had a difficult time of it. It was a lot easier for the boys."

"We know you did the very best you could."

"Under the circumstances." Linda concluded gloomily. "It's all Graham's fault. I was doing fine until he pushed his way into our lives."

"You stuck by Holly though, that was brilliant." Crispin was supportive.

"It cost me." Linda was resentful.

All of them were thinking of the very different celebration three years earlier, when they had partied joyfully after the A level results.

It had all seemed so simple then.

"What are you going to do?" Jeff was being practical.

"I haven't a clue."

"We told you not to do Sociology. What the bloody hell does that prepare you for?"

"Sod all." Crispin responded to his brother's question flippantly but Linda gave a more thoughtful answer.

"Holly said she's doing a teacher's training course at Liverpool. I haven't the first clue what I want to do. I suppose it's not too late to do the same. I could keep an eye on her. It's probably better than nothing, it'll fill a year and I don't have to teach at the end of it."

"Those who can, do; those who can't, teach!" Oliver teased his sister.

She aimed a cushion at him.

"And those who can't teach, teach teachers!" Crispin lightened the moment by grinning broadly at his Mother who did just that.

Chapter Eighteen

I was surprised when Linda phoned me in the early summer of 1975 to ask if I'd like to spend a couple of weeks with her and her brothers in Oxford.

We had bumped into each other a few times in the two years since Holly's wedding and had had relaxed conversations about nothing in particular. I always enquired about Holly and so we could spend the time agreeing about our mutual dislike of Graham. It meant that whenever we met we were never short of a topic of conversation.

Linda admitted that the invitation wasn't her idea. Crispin and Oliver, with a little bit of prompting from their Mother, had decided that I should be invited to Oxford that summer. She said they had liked me when they had met me at Holly's wedding, they both thought how like Carl I was and had come to the conclusion that it was their job to get the two of us together.

I wondered whether it could possibly work. I had kept in contact with Carl in an every-now-and-again sort of way, but whenever he called I felt he was contacting me, not for my own sake, but to find out how Susannah was.

"You know they've got an ulterior motive don't you? They think it's time their little sister found a boyfriend, and you seem relatively eligible, at least you're respectable and above board which, they seem to think, is more than could be said for some of the boys they know I've been out with. You can drive me down."

She spoke quickly with a confidence I envied. And I had no chance to argue, even had I wanted to.

As we drove south a week later Linda talked about herself without self-consciousness, perhaps aware that I was actually very interested. She talked of how she had given up on the teacher's training course after only a few weeks despite realising that she would now have no reason to see Holly and no way of checking she was OK. She had decided teaching really wasn't for her and, after a great argument with her parents, had taken a job in the office of a Chartered Surveyor in Birkenhead. "Doing filing, a bit of typing, a bit of this and that; general dogsbody really."

I decided not to use the motorways, it was a lovely day and I wanted to enjoy the drive with the top down as she talked on. "They've got a new machine, a memory typewriter, I'm learning to use, it's like a typewriter but when you type it doesn't only go onto paper it stores a sentence so you can play it back; saves typing anything twice and a helluva lot of correcting fluid. I've just trained two of the partners on it. Not so that they could use it, just so they could know what they could ask other people to do. I'm in charge of the department, we don't call it a pool, which is expanding to four machines, never call them typewriters, and the girls who she had trained to operate them. I'm really enjoying it."

I half listened as I drove. She was happy to chat on, requiring very little in response from me so I'm sure I missed much of what she was saying. Much of the time I was just aware of her enthusiasm as she talked about her job. When I managed to get a word in edgewise to ask whether she regretted not teaching her answer was an emphatic 'Not effing likely'. She then spent about 30 miles explaining how different offices would be in the future, how the relationship between bosses and their secretaries would be different. "Bosses will do all their own typing. They won't dictate to some tarty over made-up female. Women will be bosses too."

"I can type." I managed to say in a break in her monologue. I was quite proud to be able to say that, it was the first time I had felt it was a skill worth mentioning. I had started the courses for all the wrong reasons but I had found I enjoyed the ability to transfer thought to sensible, readable text. My handwriting had always been awful and it was so much easier and quicker to produce my articles now I could type them. So I wasn't just being polite when I said I agreed with everything she was saying.

"Really?" Linda had sounded sceptical.

"Absolutely, I've got my Pitmans Advanced First Class."

"I'm impressed." She actually sounded it. "I really ought to learn to type properly even though the machines do make it all so much easier. I tried a few times but it was bloody difficult. I couldn't take my eyes off the keyboard. It's a lot easier then!"

"I'll teach you if you like, it's a lot quicker to touch type. You might even enjoy it."

"You're quite an unusual bloke aren't you?" She looked sideways at me.

"I hope so."

I had a quick thought of Dani and wondered how she was doing, whether she had started the business and achieved what she had wanted to do. It seemed I was doing most of the things I had set out to do when I had left her in Cornwall and was sorry that I couldn't tell her. We had lost touch after writing shorter and shorter notes for a few months and just about exchanged cards at Christmas.

The morning after Linda and I first slept together we had both been embarrassed that her brothers would know what had happened. "But nothing did happen." Linda argued gently, "OK we slept in the same bed but we didn't *sleep* together."

"No problem even if you did, you're a big girl now." Oliver said as they were all clustered in the kitchen grabbing coffee.

"Well we didn't."

"Why didn't you? Isn't our little sister good enough for you?" Crispin continued in a light-hearted tone.

She threw the paper at him.

I had never been in this situation before. When I had been with Dani in Polperro we had never shared a bed. In the past year I had taken one or two of the girls out for a meal and been invited up for coffee afterwards, but I had never stayed long. That morning, not only had I spent the night in someone else's bed, but her brothers were there for breakfast the next morning. I wasn't sure at all about the etiquette of the situation, so I kept quiet, listening to the to-ing and fro-ing of easy conversation.

It seemed to me a completely different world from the one I had inhabited for so many years, and I liked it.

The fortnight went past very quickly. We spent most of the time doing very little, except read and talk and sit in pub gardens watching the world going by.

The highlights were the evenings Carl came down from Cambridge and we all sat round the table together eating spaghetti bolognaise and drinking good red wine. Crispin and Oliver knew how far apart we had been for so many years and were quietly pleased with their role in bringing us together.

At first we had been distantly civilised, but we had so much in common that by Carl's third visit we were spending much of the evening talking to each other about our work and our plans for the future.

Although we still could not talk easily about Susannah I think I realised something of his feelings for her. He said he didn't want to hurt her more than she had already been hurt; he didn't want to make her life

159

more miserable than it had been.

It was my first inkling that perhaps Carl was as insecure as I was.

By the end of the fortnight any romance I may have had with Linda was over, but we were firm friends. "Just a bit of fun" she said to Oliver, "nothing serious and we'll be better friends for it now we've got it out of our systems. No harm done."

"You realise we're really quite fond of each other don't you?" I explained to Oliver, "I wasn't just fooling around. I'll always be there as a friend for her, and all of you."

"Well that all worked well didn't it?" Crispin had his arms around the shoulders of Oliver and Carl as they said goodbye at the end of our visit. "Our little sister has a friend for life which is far more useful that a 'might be husband' and our adopted brother has made friends with his real one. A pretty successful summer I'd say!"

It was a conversation I had had with Linda and Oliver during that holiday in Oxford that had first given me the idea.

I had been wondering what to do, I needed a project, and talking to Oliver and Crispin I was carried away by their enthusiasm for their work. "Work for yourself old chap. Only thing to do." Oliver had said "We were pretty unemployable really." Crispin had added rather sheepishly. "If we didn't work for ourselves we'd be on the dole, no one in their right minds would want to give us a job with any responsibility."

We had listened while they spoke of visits to the bank manager, start up loans, equipment leases and marketing plans. "It's the only way to make any money you know. We work bloody hard but it's all for us. No lining other people's pockets."

That night as we lay in bed Linda had explained how unusual this enthusiastic approach to hard work was for her brothers and how there really must be something in the idea of having your own business if it gave them so much energy.

I had taken the idea away with me and had thought about it, seriously, but I couldn't think of what business to run. I read the 'business for sale' sections in the newspapers but could come up with nothing remotely interesting. I talked to Max who liked the general idea and suggested a bookshop, but after some detailed discussion I rejected the idea as I couldn't see myself sitting inside all day dusting books and waiting for the occasional customer.

The Sunday after we returned from Oxford I invited Linda and her parents to lunch at Sandhey. I thought it would be useful to have Ted's ideas as well. He had known me longer than anyone and would have a good idea what would work and what wouldn't. The fact that he knew Linda and her family through having kept an eye on Carl all those years helped.

Since it was 'my' meal we ate informally on the terrace during which conversation didn't flag for a moment and a wide range of topics was covered. I could see Ted watching Linda and I, he seemed hopeful that our friendship would become something more than that.

I finally raised the subject of starting a business.

"I need your help. Crispin and Oliver have given me the overall idea but I just don't seem to have any idea of detail. I'm not very good at anything really and there's no way of having a business related to birds so... any ideas? "

"Yes you are," said Linda, "You are good at something other than birds. You can type." She turned to the others continuing "He's very proud of his typing you know. He's a far better typist than I am."

"That would hardly be difficult." Jeff commented drily.

"She doesn't need to touch type, she's got a machine to do all the work for her." I came to Linda's defence, possibly a little too quickly, so I explained "She's told me all about her new fangled machines that are going to make typewriters redundant."

"I didn't say that!"

"Yes you did, just as we were going through Stow on the Wold."

"What on earth were you doing going through Stow?"

"Linda got us lost."

Ted did not seem to be taking much notice of this exchange and spoke seriously. "I know it's not exactly what you might be looking for but it might be interesting. Linda has told you that the business world is changing. We're finding it more and more difficult to get women for the typing pool and I know we're not alone. There's a bureau of sorts in Liverpool but it isn't very reliable and I think it's gone to the wall, but they used these new machines with memories. All very technical really, completely beyond me."

"That's it." I had a moment of inspiration "Linda and I will go into business together. With her experience..."

"All nine months of it." she interrupted modestly

"and my enthusiasm and business acumen..."

"not to mention funding..."

"and Max and Ted's contacts..."

"It can't fail."

"What are we going to call it?"

"You haven't got a business yet, or offices, or anything but you want a name?"

It took several weeks to arrange everything but I think both Max and Ted were impressed with the energy we put into the project. Linda gave in her notice and agreed to work two of the required four weeks. "We'll be sorry to lose you," her boss had said "but we'll know where to come when things get too busy here. Consider us your first client."

An office was found close to the post office and the station. The previous occupants were a firm of auctioneers who were moving to bigger premises and, during the discussions about the property itself I picked up our second client. "It'll be a lot of work each week, you know. There's only two days to get the catalogue finalised. Will you be able to do that? Regularly?"

"Of course, the answer's yes."

Equipment was bought from the bureau in Liverpool that had, as Ted suspected, gone out of business. "Very good value, you know, all less than a year old and hardly used."

Linda and I spent a lot of time with Ted. He was very helpful and seemed to be enjoying himself, frequently ringing during the day with an idea or an answer to a problem.

"I hope it isn't bad luck to take over all this stuff from a failed outfit." Linda commented, it was the first indication I had that Linda was superstitious.

"Of course not. We're a completely different set up. I've got all the figures together. I've been reminding myself hideously of my father. He used to sit at his desk filling out page after page of accounts paper with rows of figures that for him never added up, but for me they will! The frightening thing is I think it's him writing the numbers sometimes. I've started crossing my sevens, something I've never done before. Anyway, my numbers…."

"Whatever they look like."

"….exactly, my numbers, whatever they look like, do add up. Even Ted and the Bank Manager agree."

"We'll need a receptionist. I'm happy to do the typing but I draw the line at answering my own phone." I was not going to be a sleeping partner. When I told Linda she smiled, teasing me 'in any sense of the words'.

"We'll need to do some advertising and then sit back and wait for the clients to queue up at the door."

We worked well together and almost without talking about it, knew what needed doing and which one of us would do it.

"I'm glad we got all that sex stuff out of the way before we started spending all day every day together."

"Me too, though it was quite interesting trying."

"Interesting! I'd thought any other word but 'interesting'!"

"Embarrassing?"

"I was going to say fun."

"This is going to be much more than just fun."

Chapter Nineteen

We didn't consult Max and Monika about our plans for a New Year's Eve Party. I'm afraid I decided it would be a good idea and Linda and I just went ahead and arranged it. The first they knew about it was, as with my birthday barbecue what seemed a lifetime earlier, when they each received an invitation.

I did ask Max's advice about one aspect of the party. "There'll be quite a lot of people; the three of us; Linda and her family. I think her brothers will be around, Carl if he's up." It was left unsaid that Carl would only be there if Susannah wasn't, but we hadn't seen or heard of her for a long time. "There'll be a few clients, Eric and the others from the office at the auctioneers, some of Linda's old colleagues from Birkenhead, Ted and some of the chaps from your firm, Max. The only problem really is Holly. Linda thinks she ought to invite her even though they don't see much of each other these days, but that means Graham and neither of us are keen on inviting him."

Max was firm. "You must ask her. She and Linda have been friends ever since she came to this country and she's had such a difficult time since her mother died. I'll keep an eye on Graham. Leave him to me."

"What about her father?"

"No. Definitely not. I draw the line there."

In the event Holly arrived without Graham.

As soon as I let her in she went straight to Linda, barely allowing me to take her coat. "Can we talk? I know it's not the best time, you've got guests and everything but I've left him." And then she burst into tears.

Half an hour later I wondered what had happened to them and went down to the kitchen. They were sitting on the same side of the table, their chairs close together. Linda's arm was around Holly's shoulders their heads so close that Linda's red hair was mingling with Holly's blonde. I caught Linda's eye as she looked over Holly's shoulder and she shook her head. I backed away, shutting the door lightly behind me. Whatever it was they were talking about it was best left between them.

Linda described the conversation to me later, when all the mayhem had ended. "I've left him." Holly had said "I can't go back. I've had enough. I thought I could last until September but I can't. I tried but I really can't."

Linda let her talk without trying to interrupt. Whatever it was Holly wanted to say she had to have the chance to say it.

"I thought I'd be OK with him, it couldn't be worse than living with Dad but it is. He's vile. He's disgusting. He's a control freak. I can't do anything he doesn't want me to do and I have to do everything he wants. And he's got me sacked."

"It started off all right, he would ask how I was doing and listen while I told him how horrid things were when I couldn't keep order with the girls. He seemed sympathetic and didn't argue too much when I spent so much time in the evenings on lesson plans and marking. I really needed his help, I was so tired and there was always so much to do. He was very good for a week or so, he'd even cook some evenings and bring me coffee. But then he began to moan, 'I'd not done the washing up.' 'The house was getting dirty.' 'When did I last get the hoover out from under the stairs?' 'Had I forgotten he worked all day as well and he needed a rest?' So I tried harder, I stayed up later doing the house after the lessons were planned and the marking done, I wasn't getting to bed till well after midnight and getting up at 6 so I just got more and more tired. Then he complained we weren't, you know, 'doing it' often enough. He said we'd only been married a short time and should be doing it every night. I couldn't! I didn't have the energy. So he said he'd go elsewhere for that. I honestly didn't care. I knew he was going elsewhere since the day we got married. I've only been holding on till we'd been married for three years and I could divorce him."

Linda felt guilty and said something about never having known she was that unhappy.

"You haven't seen me for ages! You've been so wrapped up with your business you haven't given me a thought. I rang you the other day, at your office, and got some girl who said you were busy and would call back – could I leave a number? Well I couldn't I was calling from the callbox at school and I couldn't ask you to call the house. You haven't known how unhappy I've been for years. Since Mom died. You haven't cared what happened to me!"

Linda thought this a little unfair since she had tried to talk that year in Leicester, but realised there was some truth in what Holly was saying.

"I put up with everything he did, all the things he made me do, because I always had this dream. Next year I'd be free. I'd have a job, get a flat, I could divorce him. Now he's lost me my job I can't do any of it."

"I do care, you know. We spent all those years together but we grew apart didn't we? Was it because of Graham? Funny, I always thought that if we ever really fell out it would be because of Carl."

"Well it doesn't seem like you care! Since that summer in Oxford, since, well yes, since Graham." And she burst into tears again.

Linda tried to talk to her, asking gently "You say he got you sacked. What happened?"

Holly had made a real effort to pull herself together and be fair. "It wasn't all his fault, he might have just been trying to help."

"I don't believe that for a moment."

"He knew I was having trouble with one particular girl in the lower fifth, Julia. She'd always whip up trouble with the others in the class and even if they wanted to listen and work she'd stop them by making some stupid remark or laugh and point out how I'd written something wrong on the blackboard. It got so that I couldn't bear lessons with her, and there was one almost every day of the week! Anyway, I told Graham about her, told her how difficult she made everything. I never told him her name! I may have said 'Julia' but I never said 'Julia Robinson'. He must have checked her homework or something and found her name. On the last day of term I was called to the Head's office. It was awful! She was so angry! She didn't raise her voice at all, she just sat there quietly explaining that she was going to have to let me go as she had had a complaint from a parent. I wasn't going to be able to complete my probation. Mr Robinson had phoned. Graham had been to see him and had threatened him! He had threatened that unless Mr Robinson controlled his daughter she would be found to be a thief. Things had been going missing in my lessons, silly little things, pens, small amounts of money, dinner tickets, nothing serious, I shouldn't have told him about it but it was just one more thing I couldn't cope with. I don't blame Mrs Smith for sacking me! I'd sack me!"

There was not much Linda could say.

"Could he have meant it for the best?"

"I wanted to think so. I tried to think so. I cleared my locker in the staff room. It was horrid. They all knew what had happened and no one said 'Happy Christmas' or 'Good Luck'. No one. It was absolutely horrible. I went home and cleaned the house like I hadn't cleaned it for weeks. I cooked a nice meal for Graham so he'd have no reason to be angry, and I waited for him to come home. I wanted him to sympathise, to apologise, to explain; anything to make it easier to bear. I'd worked so hard, I'd tried so hard."

"What happened?"

"He was pleased! He said that now I could concentrate on being his wife, we could start a family. He said it didn't matter! But it did. It does. It matters so much. I knew he'd done it deliberately, to get me fired. He hadn't liked the time I'd been working, he felt I had been neglecting him and he thought this would be a good way to get me to himself. He'd humiliated me to control me. I was so angry I lashed out at him and knocked his glasses off. I'd really tried to hit him! I couldn't believe it! I'm not like that! And then he hit me back so I stamped on his glasses and he really freaked out. It was my fault. I shouldn't have hit him first. He kept saying it was my fault. And it was."

"No, Holly, look at me. No it wasn't. He could have just taken one hit and stopped you. You probably had only hurt his feelings, you aren't strong enough to really hurt him. He didn't have to hit back. Did he hurt you?"

Holly just nodded.

"Are you OK now?"

Holly nodded her head again.

Linda did some calculations in her head. "You will have broken up what, two weeks ago?" she asked "What have you been doing since then?"

"Not much. I couldn't go out until the bruises had died down. We had a quiet Christmas. He didn't even mention my birthday."

"You'll come and stay with us won't you?"

"Can I?"

"Of course. We'd love to have you back. I'll find Pat."

"Don't you call her 'Mum' any more?"

"Since I started work they said it seemed daft so it's first names all round, they've known we've called them Mutt and Jeff for years. It was weird to start with but now it seems quite normal."

"Are we friends again then?"

"We've always been friends, silly, we just went our own ways for a bit."

"It's a lot more than that. There's so much I haven't told you."

Holly began to tell Linda something of what her life had been like for past two years. Linda could only listen in dismay at what she had allowed her friend to endure.

"You were all absolutely right. I should never have married Graham. I knew you would never say 'I told you so' but I knew you would be thinking it if I told you. I'd wanted to go away to the sun for our honeymoon but he had said we couldn't afford it. 'Only if you give up university and get a job Doll.' I hated him calling me 'Doll' or 'Holl-Doll'. He only did it because he knew I hated it. Perhaps I should have given up university. Perhaps I should have done what he said."

"No. You did the right thing." Linda said little, but what she did say she wanted to be unequivocally supportive.

"We spent all that fortnight in bed, Graham said he had to show me what I had to do to give him the pleasure he expected. I'd never thought it would be like that."

"Are you sure you want to tell me this?" Linda asked.

"I wanted to talk to you every day. I wanted to tell you you'd been right all along. I wanted to ask for your help, even go back to live with you. But after those two weeks I didn't think I could ever tell anyone what being married to Graham was like. I would just have to make the best of it."

Linda squeezed her hand if only to say she was still there and still listening. Holly seemed like she was in a world of her own.

"I dreaded going back to Leicester last October. I knew that if I weakened for one moment I would break down and you would know how much I hated my life. And I couldn't do that. Could I?"

She looked at Linda who was feeling more and more guilty for having left Holly to face all this alone.

"I couldn't relax for one moment. All year. I saw a solicitor. He told me to be patient, not to do anything stupid like having an affair but to keep my head down and wait out the three years until I could apply for a divorce. I couldn't believe it couldn't happen any sooner but he assured me that three years was the minimum. He told me to make sure I qualified so I could support herself and most importantly, make sure I didn't get pregnant. I began counting down to 15th September 1976 on that day."

"Why didn't you go to Ted, he'd have found a way to get it sorted more quickly?" Linda knew she shouldn't have said anything that made Holly feel worse than she already did, but she had to ask.

"How could I?" Holly answered Linda's question directly before continuing telling Linda things she knew if she didn't say now she never would.

"Since I left Leicester I haven't been able to do anything right. He's yelled and shouted at me and criticised everything I've done. Unless there's other people around. He had a sheet of paper where he noted everything I'd done wrong and at the end of each week the tally was reckoned and the 'debt' as he called it had to be repaid."

Linda looked questioningly.

"Do you really want to know? Well there was a tariff. If I lost 5 points it was fellatio, if it was 10 points he could bugger me. 20 points I had to have sex with one of his friends while he watched. You really want to know?"

Linda did not.

"I just did as he said and waited for the days to pass."

"Oh Holly. I'm so sorry."

"It got worse." Holly was going to tell Linda everything now. "The first time Graham had told her we were going to spend Sunday with my father I hadn't believed him. I didn't understand how they could be friends? 'Him and me, we've got things to do' was all the explanation he gave. I knew he wouldn't change his mind, even if I could have told him how much I hated that flat. Every visit was the same. He'd drive the three miles so we arrived just in time for them to go out to the pub. I'd cook the Sunday meal and clean the flat though Dad's bedroom was always locked. After we'd eaten Matt would make a show of getting out the key to his room and they'd leave while I cleared up. They never said what they were doing. All I could hear was loud classical music that I'd had never known he'd liked. We'd have tea at five and then we'd leave an hour later. I never spoke to Dad and I made sure I was never alone with him. "

Linda couldn't imagine how she would feel if this had been her life.

"The only Sundays we didn't go to see Dad Graham would set off in his car very early and not get back till late. I had no idea where he went or what he did. I didn't ask and he didn't tell me. I just enjoyed the day on my own. Occasionally he went out on a Saturday evening, as if going to the pub, but when he didn't make me go with him I knew he wouldn't be back all night. I enjoyed the luxury of that time alone, sleeping in the spare room, doing my best to forget what my life had become."

"Why didn't you call? Why didn't you phone and tell me?"

"How could I let you know how much of a mistake I'd made? How could I explain? I just enjoyed those hours being alone."

"But you got a job, he let you do that?"

"He didn't want me to. He didn't want people to think he couldn't look after a wife. He said I should stay at home, looking after him and the house. He wanted me to get pregnant. But I said I had to do a year in a school as part of the course. He said I could do it as long as I gave up then. It was just like I was in gaol for a crime I hadn't committed and I was chalking off the days of my sentence on an imagined cell wall."

Linda looked at her watch, she knew she should be mingling with the guests, but she couldn't let Holly down. She had to keep listening as long as Holly wanted to talk.

"In August we went to Spain with a group of his friends. I hated them but it didn't matter, in a month I'd have my job and some independence. On the last afternoon in Benidorm we were on the beach. We'd been there for hours and Graham was pretty drunk. He had his arm round my shoulders and kept tugging the top of my bikini away. 'S'not fair the others can't see your tits Doll' he said. I kept covering myself up but he kept pulling it down. 'Can't stop me doing any fucking thing I like can you Holl Doll? Not while me and your dad got you tied up tight.' He was telling them all the things he did to me, all about the scale of penalties. They were all laughing at me and there was nothing I could do. 'You should meet her dad' he boasted to his mates 'he's a fucking fascist'. He stood up with the forefinger of left hand under his nose pretending it was a moustache and his right hand stretched in front of him in a fascist salute. He said my Dad used to do it with his sister. He said my Dad knew how to treat women."

Linda didn't like to say she could believe it.

"He pulled at my bikini and showed me off to all his friends. He sat there on, the beach, wiggling his fingers, trying to get them in me. And they were all laughing. I pushed him away. I tried to get him to leave me alone but all he did was say what a 'fucking clever fascist bastard' my dad was."

"Here, Holly, have a drink." Linda could think of nothing to say that could take away the memory her friend had of her humiliation.

"I asked him what he knew about my Dad. When we got back to the hotel I had to ask him. It'd gone on for years. He'd led me on saying he knew more about my Dad than I did. All those Sunday afternoons they spent together. I had to ask what they did, what was going on. I shouldn't have asked him. I shouldn't have, not when he was drunk. It was my fault for asking him."

"What was?" Linda wondered what could be so dreadful compared with what had already happened.

"He told me information costs. I had to buy it. First 5 points, then 10 points. I just shut my mind to what he was doing, waiting for him to tell me about my father. He told me to get him a beer so I got up and went to the cold box we kept in the room filled with bottles of San Miguel. When I got back to the bed he told me to get one for myself. He was enjoying the control, playing me like a yo-yo. I was just waiting for him to be ready. He told me stuff I already knew, he said Dad had been in the Hitler youth, how he had gone to fight for the Germans. But he wasn't interested in telling me that. He wanted to tell me about the Sundays. He said 'your Dad knows so much about people, he knows how to find out all the things they don't want him to know. He's found this rich man who he knows stuff about. But he's stupid Holl Doll, fucking stupid. He's got no idea how to make real money. He's piddling around for peanuts when it's me that's got the real ideas. He'll be pissing around with his hundred quid here and his two hundred quid there while I'll be living it up in Brazil with millions.' I waited for him to carry on. It explained how Dad managed without a job, if he was blackmailing someone. But Graham didn't tell me who it was or what the secrets were that he was paying to keep quiet."

Holly hadn't wanted to believe a word about the millions. The only way Graham could get his hands on millions was through her, and her grandparents. She had been unhappy for nearly two years but that afternoon, for the first time, she had begun to be afraid.

As she shivered Linda made her take another sip of the brandy and she continued.

"He told me what he did every Sunday." Holly's voice was dead. There was no emotion, no reaction to the words she spoke. They were only words.

"He said he spent those afternoons being buggered by my Dad and doing the same to him. He said it felt good, far better than anything I could do for him. He said Dad liked it... He told me what they did. He..."

Linda did not know what to say. She couldn't begin to think what Holly could be feeling.

"I knew when I slapped his face I'd made a mistake. Even when he was pissed he was stronger and more determined than I could ever be. I bit through my lip trying to stay motionless, trying not to think that what he was doing to me he had done to my Dad."

"Oh Holly." What more could she say. "Why didn't you leave him? Why did you stay?"

"I only had a year to go. And I had my job."

It took a few minutes before Holly could continue.

"It was a disaster from the first day. I hadn't slept well the night before. I'd watched the light growing until I could see the colours in the curtains. I hated those curtains. Graham had insisted on driving me to school but somehow he had kept finding things to do to hold us up. He wanted another cup of coffee, he spilt the coffee so I had to change my shirt, he didn't think the shirt went with the suit so I had to change again; and then he couldn't find his car keys. It was like a bad dream when you can't do anything. We were nearly an hour late when we finally left the house. When I walked into the staff room it was empty and I could hear the sound of singing. I was missing the first assembly. I knew Graham had deliberately made me late. I wouldn't be in the line of teachers on the stage at the front of the school, I wouldn't be there to be introduced, as they had told me new teachers should be. It was all wrong. I was standing awkwardly in the middle of the room when the staff appeared. 'Where were you?' 'Late on your first day?' 'What is your name, Mrs what?' I had no idea who was interrogating me."

In the way Holly imitated the voices of the staff Linda could feel her pain.

"I felt like the lowest new girl as I tried to excuse my lateness. I had no time to get my books together. I had no time to find out what room I was in. The first lesson was at 9.15 and it was now ten past. I had five minutes to find out where I would be teaching the two lessons before break and get everything I needed for both lessons. It was impossible!" Holly spoke as if she was living it all over again.

"I had to ask where I could keep all my books when I didn't have a room and no one answered. The staff room locker was hardly large enough to hold my handbag. I'd just have to carry everything around with me, take it home every night and bring what I needed in every day. It didn't just seem like a nightmare, it was one. I was late for my first lesson. It was with the Lower Fifth and they were to become the bane of my life. When I introduced myself I asked their names expecting them to tell me in an orderly fashion, one at a time, but it was the signal for them to start yelling across the room, pretending to introduce themselves to each other. I couldn't control them. I yelled at them to be quiet but it made no difference. It wasn't long before a senior teacher popped her head around the door. 'Everything alright in here?' Of course it wasn't all right but it was the signal for the class to sit down looking like butter wouldn't melt in their mouths, giving all their attention to the empty blackboard. When I said 'Yes, everything was fine' it was so obviously a lie and as soon as the door closed the noise erupted again. I had no idea how to control them, and they knew it."

Holly was speaking as if she was there, she didn't care whether Linda was with her or not, she had to get this all out in the open.

"I shouted at a large girl with a round face who seemed to be the ring-leader who was sitting on her desk, her feet on her chair, her back to me. I begged her to turn around. If she turned around the rest of the class would behave. But she just laughed. Nothing had prepared me for this. We weren't like that at school," she looked at Linda for the first time, "we were never like that were we?" Linda shook her head as Holly carried on living her nightmare. "It took half the lesson to get them to sit down and all I could do by the end of the 40 minutes was to explain what we would be doing in the 24 lessons that term. 24! I had to put up with them 23 more times! I dreaded every one. And then, when the bell rang, they all sat down. They were silent, waiting for me to leave the room. I packed my books in my briefcase and left. One of the loudest and rudest of the class demurely got up and opened the door for me. 'Good morning Mrs Tyler.' I could hear their laughter all the way down the corridor."

"They couldn't all be that bad, could they?" Linda was horrified and so pleased that she had given up her training course if teaching was like this.

"The next lesson was the Upper Thirds. It was their first day too. It should have been better. But it wasn't. I couldn't get any of them to say a word. When I asked a question not one hand went up, I was just faced with 30 blank faces. When I wrote something on the blackboard 30 heads went down to copy it word for word in their brand new exercise books. It seemed like years before the bell eventually went to signal break time and they silently closed their books and put them in their desks. I got through that first day somehow. As I left the woman who had spoken to me that morning reminded me not to be late. 'You will be on time tomorrow won't you, Mrs Tyler, not even the first years are allowed to be late more than once a term.' She hadn't been joking. I hated her, the school and that bloody grey and maroon uniform. I hated teaching and I knew I was never going to be any good at it. But I had to stick to it, just as I had to stick with Graham. Just for a year. And not a minute longer."

Holly could say nothing more. She was exhausted.

I had noticed Linda's absence with Holly but I didn't interrupt them. Linda should have been with her guests but I remembered the funeral when it was I who had left the job of entertaining to others.

I talked to our clients and our friends and wondered what Holly could be saying that was taking so long.

It was an hour before I saw Linda walking down the stairs to rejoin the party.

"She's lying down." Linda said, and then recounted the bare outline of what Holly had told her. It was months before I learned everything but even the brief details Linda told me then horrified me. I had not imagined anything that bad when I had decided that Monika's happiness was more important.

"I asked her if she wanted a job." Linda spoke as she did in the office when she knew she had made a decision that would make other people's workload heavier but knowing she had every right to make it.

"What did she say?" I wasn't sure this was a good idea. Of course I wanted to help Holly but I didn't want Graham and Matt thinking they could get back at Holly through the business.

"She asked if I wanted to employ her."

"What did you say?" I really didn't think this was a good idea.

"I said 'No it wouldn't be anything like that'. She'd work in the office with us not for us. There's so much that she'd be good at. I told her she had a logical mind and an interest in finding patterns in things."

"What did she say?"

"She asked if you'd mind."

"And?"

"I asked was she kidding? You'd be delighted! You know we desperately need someone we can trust and who can take responsibility. She's still got to leave Graham, she still had to extricate herself from their home and marriage." Perhaps she had noticed my lack of enthusiasm as she finished, somewhat lamely "I told her it'd all be all right. Anyway Monika had taken Holly up to her room and given her something to make her sleep."

The guests were mingling. One thing about a New Year party is that everyone has something to talk to anyone else about, even if it's only speculation about the year ahead.

"1976. I wonder what sort of year this'll be."

"A new US president."

"Concord..."

"With an 'e'."

"I bet Liverpool wins the league again."

"Well I'm glad to see the back of 1975, fancy a woman leading the party!"

The guests who knew each other settled in to lively conversations and there was a comfortable hubbub in the room as Linda rejoined our guests. I watched as she worked the room talking to her old boss, Robin, and his wife, to Ted and some other women from Max's firm; she looked and acted every bit the businesswoman.

"Who'd have thought it Charles?" Jeff was looking at his daughter

"What have you done to create this confident and efficient woman?"

"Nothing to do with me." Since I had been working with Linda and since losing something of my aversion to anyone who had a close connection with Carl, I had learned to have a lot of time for Jeff. He said little but he watched and understood people far better than anyone I knew.

"She seems very happy," Ted joined us "I always thought she'd be good at anything she turned her hand to. I see Carl and the boys are here. They all seem well." He looked across the room to where three tall young men were talking politely to several older women who Ted understood to have been Linda's colleagues in Birkenhead.

"They are all well and all doing well. We're proud of all our children, including the adopted one."

"The one I'm surprised at is you Charles." Ted knew he could talk to me in a way no one else could. "You've changed out of all recognition in the past three or four years. You seem ten years younger."

"You've always had a soft spot for him, haven't you Ted? Ever since you managed to get his father to take him away from that dreadful school."

"Nothing to do with his mother of course." Pat interrupted her husband, gently teasing Ted who we all knew had been more than a little in love with my Mother.

"It's nearly five years since her funeral." Ted commented to no one in particular, then turning to Jeff continued brightly "I remember your young daughter and Holly, schoolgirls wearing lovely hats of which Alicia would have approved heartily. They were very striking amongst the grey older folk. Are Holly and Graham here today? I haven't seen them since their wedding, I was sorry to have to miss that."

For the first time since I had known him Ted seemed old as he reminisced. I was pleased to escape when the doorbell rang.

"Is she here?" Graham was obviously drunk. "I'm going to fucking kill the bitch."

"Who?" I knew it was a stupid question but I felt I had to stall for time. I had no idea why a few moments would make any difference; I just wanted the conversation to be more on my terms than his.

"Who the fuck do you think?"

I stepped outside the door and closed it behind me, shutting us all out in the cold porch. "If you're going to make a scene please do it another time."

"Sure as fuck we're going to make a scene." Graham shouted,

pushing past me to ring the doorbell again. "We're going to make a scene like you've never had in this pretty little house of yours."

"Where's Uncle Max?" Matt screamed at me. It seemed they had both been drinking all morning. Max was in the living room with the other guests but I didn't know whether or not Monika was still upstairs with Holly.

I had to stop them getting in, or, if they did get into the house, I had to make sure they couldn't get to Monika. God knows what they would think to tell her. What the rest of his guests heard didn't matter.

But I had to protect Monika.

If they got to her all our efforts to protect her would have been wasted.

All Holly's unhappiness would have been for nothing.

"You're not going to go in." I shouted rather more loudly than was necessary as my suspicions that they were going to make as much trouble as they could were confirmed as they both tried to push past me.

"I beat you up then I can beat you up now."

I offered a silent prayer to anyone who might be listening that someone would notice I had gone to the door and hadn't ushered in another welcome guest. I had to keep them talking, but they were getting physical, barging at me and pushing to get through the door.

"Come back another time. When I haven't got guests. You're not helping anybody. Come back tomorrow and we can all sit down and talk."

"And Rebecca will be miles away!"

"We want to talk to Rebecca!" Graham shouted as loudly as he could at the still closed door. "Open up!" he was banging on the door with his fists.

And it opened.

"Can I help you?" Jeff and Ted now stood in the doorway and I noticed behind them Pat ushering other guests who had any proximity to the door away into the lounge.

"You can let us in. I want to talk to my fucking Uncle Max!"

"Come on in. He's in his study. I'll show you."

"I think they already know the way." I wondered what Ted was up to as he caught my eye and I understood from his look that I shouldn't worry.

As Ted opened the door I understood.

Max was in the room, sitting at his desk, and alongside him were Carl, Crispin and Oliver. With the three of us the odds were definitely on our side.

"You wanted something?" Max addressed his nephew.

"He wants to speak to his sister." Graham answered.

"I wasn't addressing you. And neither of you will be talking to anyone. You are not welcome here. The police have been called and you will wait here for them. I understand you assaulted Charles Donaldson."

When he got no reply he picked up his pen and began to write.

"You can't do that." Graham wasn't used to being told what to do.

After a lengthy pause Max looked up "What is it you say I cannot do?"

Max got no reply other than the ringing of the doorbell. Crispin left the room, returning very soon after with two uniformed policemen.

It did not take long for them to arrest Graham and Matt and lead them from the room. It was remarkably straightforward.

"Let's get back to the party. Charles, go and bring Monika back down. We suggested she didn't come back down until one of us went up to fetch her. We told her Graham was at the door and that she must stay with Holly just in case he broke through our defences."

I went up the stairs and knocked on the door of the room that in all the years I had lived at Sandhey I had never before presumed to enter. "Monika? It's me."

"Come in. Be quiet though, she sleeps."

I went in and sat down in the window seat, I hadn't realised quite how shaken up I was from the doorstep encounter. As I tried to pull myself together I looked briefly around the room. I didn't mean to be inquisitive or rude but I did notice a picture on the far wall. I couldn't see it properly but it seemed to be a dirty brown piece of paper with pale writing on it. It seemed out of place. Taped to it was a newspaper cutting. I could only make out the headline 'Star Pupils' but it meant nothing to me. All the other pictures were traditional landscapes.

"Is he very angry?"

"You could say that he was very angry indeed, as was her father. He was there too."

"They have gone now?"

"They have gone. The police came and they have gone." I didn't add that I was sure, as soon as they were released they would be back.

I looked out of the window at the view over the golf course towards Millcourt, the house I had lived in when I was a child. Max and Monika had been my only family for so long, but in the past few months I had got to know others; Linda, her brothers and, of course, Carl. I realised that, despite the violence of the past hour, in a strange way I was happy.

All the way through the scene in Max's library, when I had stood with Crispin, Oliver and Carl I identified with them. Not with Max. The wave of amazement at how my life had changed passed almost as soon as I recognised what it was.

"I hope Linda's OK. I must go down. I just needed a minute."

I turned towards Monika but I caught sight of Holly, lying asleep on the bed. Her blond hair was straggling across the pillow; her eyes were closed but I could see where her makeup had run in streaks down her cheeks, just as it had on the morning of her wedding.

I thought I had never seen anyone so beautiful in my life.

I wonder what Monika must have thought.

She must have watched me staring, for far too long, at the young woman in her bed.

Chapter Twenty

Immediately after the New Year's party I discussed with Max what we could do to help Holly.

"If what you thought is true he'll have to do something while she's still his wife."

"She must immediately change her will and tell Graham she has done so."

"Would that hold up? In court I mean? He is her husband. He could fight it."

"We would have to make sure he didn't wouldn't we?"

"We must warn her."

"The police will keep them until Monday. I've told them we intend to press charges of threatening behaviour and assault. I don't think we can claim anything else at this stage. And they won't be out of action for long."

"Holly's quite safe at the Forsters for the moment and when she starts work I'll make sure she's never alone in the office. But we can't be sure she'll have someone with her every minute of every day. What do we do when they are free 'bound over to keep the peace' as, no doubt, that's all that will happen to them?"

"We must go back to basics, put ourselves in their minds. They have done very well with their little plot. Graham married Holly as we suspected he would. No doubt she has made a will leaving all she has to her husband. That would have been done some time ago so what I fail to understand is why the marriage has gone on for so long. I had expected things to happen sooner."

I was remembering our conversation after the O'Dwyers' visit and it made me feel guilty again that I had done nothing to protect Holly. I had agreed to trade her unhappiness in order to keep Monika's secrets. I could not let it continue if it meant risking her life, no secrets could be worth that. I had to persuade Max to do something.

"Why do you think nothing has happened? It's over two years now. Why have they just been sitting doing nothing?"

"It seems reasonable to assume that, had Matt had his way,

everything would have happened very quickly. He has no reason to delay. So it must be Graham who is holding things up."

"Why would he do that?"

"Perhaps there is a marriage worthy of the name."

"Never!" I couldn't believe that Holly had stayed with Graham willingly. "She hates him, she's hated him from the day they married. You should have seen what she was like when she arrived at the reception. God knows what he did to her during that drive from the church."

"Then perhaps he has made it worth her while. Some men can be very, how do I put this, very persuasive."

"You mean he controls her? She can't get away?"

"Either that or he makes it attractive to her to stay with him."

"You mean he's so good in bed she doesn't want to leave?" I didn't know how else to put it.

"It happens."

"Well I don't believe it."

"Then why was she with him all that time?"

"She was told she had to wait three years before she could start proceedings."

"Who told her that? Silly girl. She should have come to us." He said as an aside before he continued, as if discussing with himself the answers. "Matthew has wanted things to move faster than they have. That is what I believe. He has been pushing for them to finish the business but Graham has stalled. He has wanted his access to his wife to continue."

"That's a strange way of putting it."

"To a man like Graham the ability to control, to have such power over someone, is addictive. He has been unwilling to give that up. For as long as Holly let him control her he has continued the charade. Graham made the mistake of letting it go on too long. He began to believe in his own power to hold her where he wanted her. I apologise for suggesting she stayed with him willingly. I have no doubt she stayed not one minute longer than she felt she had to. I don't believe a word of this 'leaving because he had me sacked' she left because she realised she was in danger. She had worked it out for herself."

"How did she do that?" It made sense. I had thought the excuse about the job a little feeble in the face of all the other things she had had to put up with.

"Perhaps he grew over-confident, let slip one word too many, made one hint too clear of what he intended, of what he knew about her family. She is a bright girl underneath it all."

"But now she's left him. There's no reason to delay any more in fact they've got to get a move on. The O'Dwyers... "

"You are quite right, The O'Dwyers. If Graham's going to get the money they've got to have passed it on to Holly in the first place. That means..."

"...in a very short time either Graham or Matt will have to go to Canada."

"Indeed. I believe it is now time for us to intervene."

I wondered why Max was willing to get involved now when he had resisted any idea of protecting Holly three years earlier.

If we had done something then Holly would have been spared so much.

"Why now but not then?" He did not answer my question.

"We will separate them. Divide and rule; separate and weaken."

"How?"

"Leave that to me."

I suppose it was inevitable that once Holly started work we would have to spend a lot of time together, and, in spending a lot of time together we would become close. I found I could relax with her as I had with very few people in my life. I tried not to look for signs of Monika in her but it was difficult. There were looks and mannerisms that were so familiar.

I spent several days explaining the work to her and showing her the rudiments of typing. I gave her all the books of exercises I had acquired for my evening classes and we worked on them for a couple of hours in the evenings after the girls had gone home and while Linda caught up on the paperwork. She insisted that she had to be faster and more accurate than the girls who were working for her. She was serious about getting to know more than they did as soon as she could. 'I'll never get their respect if I can't do anything any better than they can.'

I realised it was beginning to grate with Linda that Holly and I spent so much time together, perhaps she felt we were shutting her out a bit. I tried to explain about protecting her from Graham but since I couldn't tell her the whole truth my explanation must have seemed rather lame.

"Did you ever sleep with Linda?" Holly asked me one evening when we were working late together.

"I'm not sure how to answer that."

"I'll take that as a 'yes' then."

"Not really. It depends what you mean by 'sleep with'. Yes, for a while we slept together, but I'm not sure you would say we had 'slept together'."

"Are you saying you were at it all night every night and never got any sleep?"

"No!" I wasn't used to having this sort of conversation. "No. I'm saying we slept in the same bed but we never 'made love'. Do you think I'm odd? It wasn't something I really wanted to do, it was nothing to do with her but I just didn't want to do it. I'm just not cut out for sleeping around. I just don't want to do it with someone if they're not going to be around forever."

"You're still a virgin?"

I like to think the silence I maintained was dignified. In the end I felt I had to say something, though I managed not to answer her question.

"I didn't think her motives were right. I know that sounds pompous but I think she liked the idea of sleeping with me because I reminded her of Carl and to make him jealous."

"That's a bit unfair on you isn't it? She doesn't know you very well does she?"

I asked her what she meant.

"Well you try so hard to do the right thing, especially things that don't come easily to you. You're shy, you're great when you know someone…"

"But…"

"But nothing. She didn't know when she was onto a good thing. That's all."

A few days later Linda cornered me. "What are you up to with Holly?"

I had to say I had no idea what she was talking about.

"You spend a lot of time with her, not just all day but in the evenings."

"I'm teaching her some of the stuff she needs to know." I probably sounded too defensive.

"Yeah yeah…" She sounded as if she read another meaning into what I had said.

"I like her. She's having a tough time."

"You're not falling for her then?"

I was very defensive now. "I'm not falling in love with her, or 'anything'. No. Nothing like that."

"Probably a good thing considering she is a married woman and no doubt her husband would be delighted to make trouble for anyone who did."

"I'm hardly likely to forget that am I?"

"Well try not to. If you do it might just land you, me, the business, all of it in a whole pile of trouble."

"Sorry." As I spoke it I realised I had no idea what I was apologising for.

It all came to a head on a day that had started at seven in the morning as we had the day to complete a particularly difficult job. We were all exhausted when Holly finally handed me the large envelope to drive to the clients just in time to meet the critical five o'clock deadline. Holly and Linda were going to wait for me to get back before closing up.

I later had two very different versions of their conversation while they were waiting for me to return and I tried to work out what had really happened.

Holly was worried that I was taking longer than I should have, I had been gone an hour and delivering the packet should only have taken half that.

They apparently had a heated discussion about the need to have done everything perfectly if the contract, for which this was a trial run, were to be given to us. Holly said that she hadn't spotted anything wrong and it was her job to check.

Linda contradicted her, it was her responsibility on such an important job, she should have looked at it. It was too important not to have had her check it.

Holly was hurt, she felt Linda didn't trust her. Linda had said, yes but if there were anything wrong ultimately it was her problem not Holly's. If work had to be redone it was Linda that would lose, Holly was going to be paid whether it was right or wrong. It made no difference at all to Holly, Linda argued. She alone should have been given the work to approve.

Holly tried to ignore the way Linda was making their employer-employee relationship very clear by saying there was probably a perfectly good reason why I was delayed. Maybe they were so pleased they wanted to go over some additional work.

By 6.30 they were both beginning to get worried. Holly suggested they phone the client. Linda said that was stupid, perhaps I had gone straight home. Holly had argued that I wouldn't have done that as I'd have known she'd be worried. That annoyed Linda who had contradicted her 'we'd be worried' and told Holly to go home. Linda could have a very annoying edge to her voice at times and in making an issue about the difference in their positions she served only to upset Holly even more.

"You'd better call him yourself since I can't be trusted to do anything right."

As I opened the door I realised in my enthusiasm to tell them my good news I had pushed Holly against the wall behind it.

"Holly? Are you OK?" I pulled Holly out from between the coats and the wall. "They were very pleased. I mean *very* pleased. They wanted to go over various jobs you know 'can you do this?' and 'surely you'd need more time to do that?' I was doing instant quotes. I hope I haven't let us in for more than we can handle."

I was surprised at the atmosphere in the room. I had thought they would both be really pleased and I got no response at all.

"What's the matter? It's masses of work. We'll be busy for months. No need to worry about the phone not ringing Linda." Still there was no response. "What's going on?"

Holly seemed to recover soonest. "That's fantastic. Well done. We'll handle anything they can throw at us." And she grinned at me.

"That's better!"

It was only when Holly moved to her desk, and my arm dropped, that I realised it had been resting around her shoulders since I had pulled her from behind the door. She turned her desk diary towards her "When do we start? How's it going to work? How often is it?"

"Hang on you two, whose business is this anyway? Look at you Holly! You've worked here a month. And you Charles. This isn't just you two you know." She was angry, and upset.

"Two. I've worked here two months." Holly was defiant but on being rewarded with one of Linda's diminishing looks she ended lamely "You said one."

"Whatever. You've only just come in and now it's your business! Well it isn't. It's mine."

"And mine." I gently reminded her, "It's *our* business Linda." I spoke quietly but, I hope, with authority. I did not want this scene to get any more acrimonious.

"It was my idea!"

"Come on Linda, we're not arguing. But we *all* put a lot into it. None of us could do it without each other or the girls. We're a team and a damned good one."

"I'm sorry, I'm just tired. It's been a long day."

"Come on, let's go over the road, have a few drinks. We should be celebrating."

I tried to get things back on an even keel but the words that had been spoken were not easily forgotten.

As usual Linda did most of the talking in our early morning briefing the next day.

"Charles, you've been great with Holly but she needs to get on her own now, especially with all this extra work. I'll spend less time out of the office. Holly I'll help you more, we can let Charles get on with his stuff."

Linda was gently manoeuvring Holly and I into positions where we wouldn't be working together as much. I had to admit she was doing it quite cleverly. And she was right. Maybe Holly and I were getting too close. Maybe Holly was jumping into something while she was vulnerable. She was still married and we mustn't give anybody the idea we were an item or her husband, or her father, might get nasty. Linda was absolutely right.

But Holly still needed protection.

I spoke up for her, arguing with Linda that Holly had fitted in really well, she had learned so much so quickly and she did really seem to enjoy it. She got on well with the girls and managed to get far more out of them than Linda, or I, did. I supposed it was because she was still learning herself and so she understood what it's like not to know everything. The girls cut short their lunchtimes because she asked them to, she didn't tell them as Linda or I would have done. And she sat down and worked with them, she didn't sit in her office isolated and away from everything, as Linda did. She answered their problems as they arose rather than waiting until several had built up and they'd got in a muddle. She saved so much time and we got a much better result in the end.

We couldn't do it without her.

"I think we should look at the arrangement we have with Holly." I ignored Linda's warning frown. "It was perfectly appropriate for her to be an employee when she first joined us, but she has shown herself to be far more useful than, say, Lorraine and she's only earning a bit more."

"I think we should talk about this between ourselves, Charles, come to a decision and then talk to Holly. Don't you?" Linda tried to stop me but I thought it was time I stamped something of my authority on the business, Linda had not only been making assumptions about Holly's role, she had been making assumptions about mine.

"No. I think we are all good enough friends to talk about it openly. I think Holly should come in with us. Commit herself."

"Become a partner? With us? You're joking!" Linda wasn't just angry she was livid. "Holly, please go out. I need to talk to my partner alone." Holly looked from Linda's anger to my determination and decided to leave. "I've got some work to do." She said rather weakly and left us to it.

"How dare you spring that on me! Surely it was something we should have talked about first! The last thing I want is another chief. You know the saying 'too many chiefs and not enough indians' well if we do as you suggest we'll had three chiefs and four indians. It won't work."

"Why not? She's shown her worth. I don't think it's right that she's lumped with the girls when it's clear she's with us. They know her status is different, I'm simply thinking we should make it formal."

"More than 'simply thinking', you've decided haven't you? Whatever happened to our partnership? Aren't we supposed to be equals? How can you make this decision without even talking to me? I don't believe you could do this!"

"I thought you would realise how right it is." I had been prepared for an argument but trusted that Linda's sense of justice would prevail. "Let's look at the pros and cons."

So we talked it over.

"We depend on her, this way we won't lose her."

"But can we afford her?"

"You know how difficult it is to get good staff how on earth would we find someone as good as Holly if she left? This way she won't."

Linda could think of no argument to counter the logic of the situation. It had always been a tactic of hers in arguments with her brothers that when they had won the sweeping general argument she would settle on the nitty-gritty and tie them in knots on the details, often ending up with them thinking they had lost the whole thing. She tried that tactic now.

"What would her package be? What percentage of the business would she get? What would we charge her for it? How would she raise the money anyway? How would it affect her divorce?" Linda listed some of the details that would need to be cleared up, but I wasn't to be deflected.

"So you do agree in principal."

"Well, yes, I suppose so. But you still should have talked it over with me first."

"Right then let's get her in and ask her what she thinks. We could have been having this argument for nothing if she doesn't want to join us anyway."

But she did want to join them and it was confirmed with self-conscious handshakes and hugs.

"We'll get Ted to sort out the details. I bet he's been wondering what took us so long. "

Linda was quick to forgive me, or maybe she was just trying to build bridges, and the following Sunday I was invited to lunch with her family. It was a full house, the twins and Carl, the girls and me along with Jeff and Pat.

It felt like a family lunch should and I was again reminded of all that I might have missed and that Carl had gained. But the difference the last three years had made was that now it didn't depress me, I didn't dwell on it feeling that I had missed out. We were friends now and I think we were both relieved at that.

Jeff answered the phone as we were helping clear away and his voice was unusually low so we couldn't overhear the conversation. All we heard was "No, I'll tell her. Don't you worry. Is there anything we can do? Oh dear."

"Come on Holly, I need to have a word with you on your own."

"What is it Jeff? What's happened? "

Holly followed Jeff out of the room. All conversation stopped, no one quite looked into anybody else's eyes, knowing that it was not going to be good news.

When they came back into the room Holly spoke matter-of-factly "It was a car crash. He was drunk. No one else was involved. It was his own fault. He was well over the limit, skidded on some ice and hit a tree. He hasn't driven on ice for years. I didn't even know he had gone to Canada. It's Dad. He's dead."

As Linda and Crispin immediately went round the table to hold her I remembered how Max had said he would 'deal with' Matt. At the time I had imagined there would be a problem with immigration stopping him from leaving for Canada.

Surely even Max couldn't engineer a car accident in Toronto.

But it was very convenient.

As we all re-grouped in the sitting room I took hold of both her hands. "Tell me what I can do."

"What we all can do." Crispin looked at me as if I had no right to be doing any comforting whilst he handed Holly a large glass of brandy.

"Don't worry. Any of you. I'm fine. I'm glad. I'm not sad at all. It was just a bit of a shock."

"There'll be the funeral to sort out." Linda, ever the practical one, "Will it be in Canada? Will you want to go over?"

"I don't know. I haven't a clue. Where do I start?"

"Just leave it to us." I made the point of not excluding others this time. "We'll call Ted. He'll know what's best."

"And then there's the flat. I could take over the lease."

I don't think I was the only one who wondered how she felt she could possibly live there.

Chapter Twenty-One

Holly didn't go to the funeral that was held the following week in Canada, she spent the time clearing out his flat.

Ted had quickly made sure there were no problems in her taking over the lease but it was going to take a great deal of work to turn it into her own place, getting rid of everything that reminded her of him and facing up to all her dreadful memories.

She insisted on being alone as she began to work through his belongings room by room, the silence broken only by the music playing on the radio.

She threw all his clothes into a plastic sack to take to the dump. She looked through the bookshelves to see if there was anything she would like to keep but it was filled with science fiction and murder mysteries, so she put them in boxes to take to the second-hand bookshop. Everything in the small kitchen she threw into plastic sacks for the tip.

She was going to start from scratch.

She left the desk till last.

She was not surprised to find no pictures of her Mother. There was nothing that told of the years they had had together, nor were there any photographs of her.

It was as if he had had no family.

She opened the drawers one by one and placed all the papers on the floor. He had said he was writing a book, but there was no sign of anything approaching a coherent narrative.

There were cuttings, paper notes and exercise books whose pages were filled with his almost illegible writing. One page stood out particularly clearly. It had been ruled carefully into columns. One had a number of dates and next to the dates were sums £500; £700; £250. So Graham had been right, he had been blackmailing someone. It had to be Max Fischer. He would have been the 'rich man' Graham had talked about in Benidorm.

No wonder he had no need of a job.

The newspaper cuttings and photocopies of newspaper articles were all about Max and the Donaldsons. The words that stood out from the pages of writing were 'Charles' 'Alicia' 'Max' 'Monika'. As she turned the pages those names appeared everywhere. She read extracts trying to piece together what her father had been doing, what he thought and what Graham had had to do with it.

Leafing through all the cuttings she couldn't find the one of her and Linda. There was no sign of *Star Pupils*.

She glanced through the books, she would sit down to read them in detail another time, but she picked up enough to realise her father had been studying the household at Sandhey. There were notes about *MF, MH* and *CD*, against dates and times with details of their movements. *CD/MH to Lighthouse. 10am. 2 hours. Every other Wed. MH Liverpool 5 hours Mon. Can we do anything with those kids?* This last sentence was crossed out.

Then there were notes that showed he had been in the house. *CD man's room. Nothing to give the game away.* What game she thought? *MH Shit. Is RR. Map.*

Holly picked up another book *O'D brilliant. Have to get rid of GT prat. Thinks he can do me out of what's mine. Thinks I don't know.* There were pages that seemed to be about Graham and her grandparents. She would have to read this all later, carefully.

She picked up a small bunch of old photographs held together with a rusting paperclip. They were of groups of people she had never known. There were more envelopes filled with scraps of paper with writing in English and in German.

One of the drawers was locked but she found a screwdriver in one of the sacks she had been taking to the dump and forced it open.

Inside the drawer was another file. All the papers it contained were in German which she had no way of understanding, but there were a number of small black and white photographs of young men in uniforms. On the back of one of them were names, roughly lining up with the figures on the other side.

Berndt   August   Mattieu

She picked up one photograph. There were six figures lined up against the backdrop of a stone wall; a tall man on the left, an elderly couple, two tall boys and, on the extreme right, a young girl. Slowly she turned the photograph over to see if names had been written on the back.

They had.

Maximilian   Vater   Mutter   August   Mattieu   Rebecca

She sat looking at the photograph for a long time trying to make sense of it. She had realised that *Mattieu* was her father when she had seen that first photograph. August must be his brother. That was what Graham had meant. She hadn't realised that August was a first name. Graham must have been making sure her Dad knew he knew.

She looked long and hard at the faces of *Vater* and *Mutter*, her grandparents.

He wasn't Canadian. He *was* German, just like Graham had said. Then she turned her attention to *Maximilian* and *Rebecca*. Rebecca must be the sister of Mattieu and August.

As she looked at the photograph she felt a prickle in the skin of her arms which quickly spread to her neck and her knees; the whole of her body shivered with the sense of recognition.

She could see her own face in the face with the screwed up eyes, the head slightly angled as it faced into the low sun.

A phrase came to her mind 'The child is father of the man'. She hadn't understood how that could be, but she did now.

The young faces, looking out towards the camera on that sunny day nearly 50 years before, were unmistakably those of Max Fischer and Monika Heller.

And the face of Rebecca, of Monika Heller, was her own.

She checked back through the pages she had been reading '*MH=RR*'. Monika Heller is Rebecca... Rebecca who?

A jumble of questions was barely forming in her mind when she heard the knock on the door. Someone, soon, was going to have to give her some answers.

Chapter Twenty-Two

"Hi! Holly! We're here!"

Linda and I walked in on a room filled with boxes and black plastic sacks with Holly kneeling on the floor by the desk surrounded by piles of paper, a small black and white photograph in her hand.

"What is it?" I reached her first as she handed me the photograph and turned it over so I could read the names on the back.

"Oh Shit."

I didn't think Linda heard anything as she had started picking up sacks.

"Come on, down to the car, we've got to get this lot to the dump." Obediently Holly picked up far too many bags and boxes, she couldn't possibly carry them all down the stairs so I pocketed the photograph and took some of the bags from her. "Let's get this lot down to the car and to the dump before it closes."

As we carried all the bags down from the flat and loaded up the car Holly's mind was definitely somewhere else.

"It's too late now to go back to the flat, fancy some supper?" I tried to sound casual and tried to include Linda in the invitation, but she chose to be left out.

"You two go, I've got some work to catch up on." Adding pointedly "Someone has to do it."

"Come off it Linda, Holly's had a rotten day. We'll be back into it tomorrow, don't worry."

We dropped Linda off and drove in silence to Sandhey.

It was only as we walked through the hall that Holly said what had been on her mind since we had walked in on her. "Give me the photograph." She said and I obediently took it out of my pocket and handed it to her.

"What do you know about all this?"

"Not a lot. But some of it's beginning to fall into place."

"Graham said that my father was a Nazi. He seemed to know an awful lot about him. Was he? He must have been. There were other photographs, boys in uniform."

I tried to keep her quiet. Monika must not overhear. "Let's wait until we can talk to Max."

"What about Monika?"

"No, she won't be involved. We'll talk to Max."

"You'd better shut the door." Max said as we walked into his study and Holly wordlessly held the photograph up so he could see.

"Well?" she asked on the verge of tears but trying hard to sound as if she was in control "I found it in my father's things."

Max took the photograph from her and held it under the light. "What's it all about?" Holly wanted some reaction, any reaction. She expected more than this silent investigation. "What's going on?"

Max looked at us as if he was weighing up what he should tell us, how much he could get away with. We both knew I had already discovered his relationship with Monika, we both knew Graham had read those same papers and we could assume that Graham had told Matt everything he had read. But what else had he read that I hadn't? What was it that Max was not telling me?

Max opened the drawer of his desk and took out an envelope I recognised. He carefully shuffled through the papers and pulled out a small photograph album. Opening it at a page from where, both Holly and I could see, photographs were missing, he carefully placed Holly's photograph on the black paper and fitted it between gold corner holders.

He held the small photograph album in his hand and started to talk conversationally.

"Why did Graham steal this photograph? Of all the photographs why did he find this one with us all in it? I wonder. The photograph was taken by Berndt, I never knew his family name, he was a friend of August's. I had handed him my new camera and explained which button to press and for how long as the boy had never taken a picture before. It was her 7th birthday. I gave the picture to my sister on my next visit, but she never liked it. 'Who is that old lady. It cannot be me.' She had said. Were there others?" Max turned to Holly who took an envelope from her pocket and handed it to him. I sat watching him as he looked through his memories.

"You've seen all these then?" he eventually asked Holly, still intent on not giving anything away that he didn't have to.

Holly nodded.

"I am going to have to tell you things I had hoped never to tell any living person. I have written it all down to be read after my death but now I am going to tell you; and trust you will tell no one who does not need to know."

He addressed himself to Holly. "You are correct, my dear, I am Maximilian and Mattieu is, was, your father. The older couple are your father's father and mother. I will not call them old because when this photograph was taken neither was yet 50. She was my sister. It follows that your father was my nephew and you are, therefore, my great-niece."

Holly didn't ask how long he or I had known any of this and, if we had known, why we had said nothing.

If Max had hoped to divert Holly away from the young girl whose birthday it had been, standing with her screwed up eyes, staring into the sun he failed. "And the girl?"

"She was your father's sister, Rebecca." Holly realised he would say no more unless he had to so she pressed him.

"You say 'was' but she's still alive isn't she?"

He hesitated before replying with such a weight of sadness in his voice. "Yes. She is still alive."

But he wasn't going to voice the final link.

"What happened to August?" Holly diverted the subject hoping that, if on less difficult territory, Max would talk more freely. He obliged.

"Mattieu and August were young and impressionable. When this photograph was taken they would have been about 14 and 15 years old. August was the elder of the two, but he was not the leader. He went where his brother dictated even if it meant neglecting the farm that, one day, should have been his. Mattieu didn't like the hard life on the farm but was not bright enough to use education, which was the only legitimate means of escape. They became involved, as all young boys did in those years, with organisations that gave them mud coloured uniforms and sticks of wood that they could pretend were guns. They marched up and down the square in the village full of their own importance and egging each other on into acts of greater and greater stupidity. What one day was harmless became the next dangerous. The young uniformed ones began to bully and argue with their elders. Any person who disagreed with the nonsense they spouted from their ugly mouths was at first laughed at, then shouted at and then hit. Yes, Holly, August became one of those boys, along with Mattieu. It wasn't long before they only ever wore their uniforms and refused to work on the farm. They had decided they were too important for that."

He paused, as if taking himself in hand. Max had been speaking with more passion, feeling, involvement and finally distaste than I had ever heard. It was as if he was part of the events of which he spoke.

"When the Germans invaded..."

194

"Weren't you in Germany?" Holly interrupted.

"No, Austria." I answered quietly for Max, whose expression indicated that he couldn't understand how such a question could be asked. "I am not a *piefke*." He spoke the words as if spitting.

"When the Germans invaded they left to join the army. Both boys went leaving their parents…"

"and young sister." Holly added. "Where were you?"

"… and went to war." He finished, ignoring Holly's question for as long as he could.

"Where were you?" she insisted.

"Me? I ran away." Perhaps Max was still trying to distract Holly from asking about Rebecca. "To my eternal shame I ran away."

This time, when he paused, neither of us interrupted. Max took a sip of his wine, savouring it before bearing something of his soul and offering hostages to fortune. Unusually he had offered none to us.

"You see, it was not a good time to be Jewish. Not very Jewish you understand, just a single grandparent in the dark recesses of our family tree. But enough to be considered tainted by the ignorant bullies who had taken over the world. Enough to bear the brunt of a nation's fear and resentment and hatred."

He took another sip of his wine, drinking it as if it was the last drop he would ever touch.

"I was studying at the *Universität Wien*, the University in Vienna, I was lucky enough to be enrolled in the School of Law there. My father was not a farmer, he was a shopkeeper, a man of the middle classes and he wanted me to do well. I had advantages that were not open to my sister's family. I left the university in 1930 and began to practise law in the city. My parents hadn't wanted Ingrid to marry Johannes." Max paused, as if surprised at how easily the names came to be spoken. "He was a good enough man in many ways but he was a farmer and they considered her to be marrying beneath herself. They never saw her after her marriage instead they asked me to keep in contact with the family and tell them how things were for their daughter and her children." He could not keep the bitterness from his voice and he knew we had heard it, so he paused for another sip of the wine before continuing.

"I was quite successful as a lawyer and I enjoyed the metropolitan life. I met many English and American people in Vienna and learned their language. I was not political but after 1934 life was very difficult for anyone who did not allow himself to pretend to be. This was something I could not do. It was obvious even then that there would be a war, whatever the politicians let the people know. Austria was in Germany's pocket and it was just a matter of time. I arranged for my parents to leave for France and I made sure my friendships with the English and Americans were sound. I persuaded Johannes to leave his farm and take Ingrid and Rebecca away with others of their village to Switzerland. Our country was invaded soon after."

"So you ran away." Holly had been listening closely, trying to slot this individual account into the impersonal history she had learned.

I sat fascinated at learning, after so many years of friendship, more about this man. I had never asked Max about his past. I had wondered, of course, but I had never felt confident enough to ask questions that demanded answers. As Holly was now doing.

"I ran to England. I won't regale you with tales of adventure and bravery but I did have a war some would say was 'interesting'. Suffice to say my knowledge of Austria and of languages was very useful to the Allied cause."

"But, you bought the firm." I knew that much about Max' history. Everyone had commented on how this refugee from Eastern Europe had bought the firm in 1941.

"Not immediately. I had lived here for two years before I bought Roberts & Jones. I lived in Millcourt you know? I sold it to your parents when I moved here. I had married Elizabeth, who I had met when I first came over to England."

"You had a daughter, Veronica. I remember her." I was drawn into his recollections.

"She was not my daughter. Elizabeth had been married before. She was a widow. She had a child, born three months after her husband had been shot down. I was indebted to her brother and agreed to look after them both. I was always very fond of her." I wasn't sure whether he meant Elizabeth or Veronica.

"She died didn't she? Whooping cough. It was when Mother left."

"Yes, Charles, Veronica died. There was nothing I could do."

In the silence that followed I remembered I had had the whooping cough at the same time, but had survived, thanks to Monika.

Holly asked a question I would never have had the nerve to ask. "How could you afford all that? I don't know much about it but I can't think it would be easy to get money into this country. Not during a war. You must have had a lot of it to afford to marry and to buy a house and a business."

I expected Max to brush the question aside as impertinent or to ignore it. The last thing I expected was his answer.

"I stole it."

I was trying to understand how I could know so little about him when I had lived in his house for so many years.

Max seemed so matter of fact about it, so unrepentant as he continued. "All you see around you, all the money I have given you, Charles, all the respectability I have purchased has come from stolen money. I can only excuse myself by saying that had I not stolen it the Germans would have."

"You mustn't tell us if you don't want to. I'm sure you will have had good reason." It was so out of character for him to talk so openly when he had no need to that I had to give him an opportunity to stop, but he didn't take it.

He continued as if relieved these things were out in the open, or perhaps he simply wanted to deflect the conversation from more painful issues.

"I had many clients in Vienna, many wealthy people who entrusted their documents to me, the keys to their safety deposit boxes, the deeds to their properties, that sort of thing. I had access to them all. Many of my clients were going to be persecuted by the Nazis. It was inevitable that they would lose their wealth and their position. Nothing was going to stop that. Even before I left some had disappeared, running away, leaving their keys and their papers. So I forged documents, sold the properties that weren't mine, emptied the deposit boxes of their cash, their silver and jewellery. I only made use of the property of people who had run away, I took nothing from the brave who stayed. I knew if I got away and had money with me I could do far more good than if I ran away without. I have always tried to use the money well. I have tried to help people.

"You have helped people." I had to say. This must have been what Graham had read, that I had not seen, why Max paid the blackmailers money. It wasn't any fear of being called queer, or even his relationship with Monika.

It wasn't to protect others.

He had paid money to protect himself.

"What happened to my father?" Holly asked quite gently. I hoped Max would regain some of his normal bearing, I didn't like the way the telling of his story had diminished him.

"Ah yes, Mattieu." He said, as if bringing himself back from somewhere he had not wanted to be. "Mattieu and August joined the

197

army, quite willingly. They joined the Austrian Army and were subsequently conscripted into the German Army. I have to say I know little about their war though I believe they served together until the end."

"What happened to August?"

"He died. He was killed just as the war was coming to a close."

"But Dad survived."

"He survived, somehow he found his way to Canada where he apparently took the name of a Canadian soldier who died in the same skirmish that accounted for August."

"If you don't know, what do you think happened?" I asked. Max looked at Holly, who was still sitting her brows knitted in concentration.

"It was the very end of the war. There was no glorious victory ahead for the Germans. I think perhaps they argued about what they would do after the war. Perhaps August wanted to return to the farm, perhaps he was injured and Mattieu knew they couldn't both escape to the west. I think he may have been killed in that skirmish with the Canadians, but for whatever reason Mattieu was on his own. Perhaps he killed August. We cannot know for sure."

"I think Graham knows. I think Graham talked to Dad and knows." Holly blurted out. "He called my Dad a 'murdering Nazi bastard'. Why would he say that if he didn't know? They must have talked about it. So Dad got to Canada and met Mom and came over here to live and, just by happy coincidence, happened to come to live in the same town as his uncle."

"Of course it wasn't coincidence. He was looking for me. He wanted to find me."

"And his sister?" she asked almost slyly, continuing without waiting for his answer. "That must have been why he took Mom on those holidays in Austria, before we came over here. He must have been trying to track you down, you both down."

Max sat in his chair, his arms on the armrests, his hands together, as if in prayer, his head slightly bowed as he came to the inevitable point.

"Yes Holly, Monika is, indeed, Rebecca. She is your aunt, your father's sister but you must never, ever, tell her that. You must never give her knowledge that would destroy her." He was pleading with her, he wasn't ordering, he wasn't making someone do what he wanted through the sheer force of his personality. He was pleading with her.

"You do not know how hard her life was, how hard her war was, how she has tried and finally succeeded in removing so much from her memory. Don't I beg you, bring it back. She must not know while I live."

"Holly, he's right. Monika has so many reasons to forget her family and you absolutely must not bring it all back to her."

Holly rounded on me, standing up and shouting "You knew!"

"No! I didn't! I promise!" I lied.

"You must have! Stop lying to me!" She was staring at me, her eyes narrowed in a look of disappointment that I recognised as being pure Monika. She turned on Max "How can you say I can't tell her! She's got a right to know!"

"You're being selfish now Holly. She doesn't need to know. She mustn't know. It would harm her beyond anything to have all those memories dredged up. You must not tell her. You must swear not to tell her."

"Charles is telling you the truth Holly. He did not know. I have never told him." As he glanced at me I wondered if he could see my embarrassment and read in my face that somehow I had known. "It is I you should be hitting out at. I knew that your father was Mattieu my nephew and Monika's brother."

"And you didn't say anything? You didn't welcome us? You didn't help us when my Mother died? You did nothing?"

"I did nothing" he agreed.

"Why not?"

"Because he was afraid for Monika, Holly, don't you see that?"

"Stop sticking up for him!"

"I'm not, I'm just saying he couldn't tell anyone, you must see why."

"Well I don't."

"You must not tell her."

"Then tell me why not! Tell me what's so goddam awful!"

"You don't want to know." I said with finality. There was no way Max was going to let Holly read the papers I had read, learn the things about Monika I had learned by reading them.

"But I must know."

"I see so much of myself in you." Max said wearily. "You will not go without the truth." He paused as Holly looked at him, she was not going to give up. "He raped her, many times, he and his brother and their friends abused her when she was a young child." He held up the photograph that had been on the table by his chair all this time. "Probably that day."

"How do you know?" She instinctively came to her father's defence "You can't possibly know that!" But she remembered what he had said

199

to her that day she had first visited him at his flat and she knew it was the truth.

"To my eternal shame and regret I did not know at the time. If I had I would somehow have stopped it. She told me when we first met again, after the war. She didn't know who I was, she didn't recognise her Uncle Maximilian, why should she? She had only been 8 years old when she had last seen me. It was ten years and they had not been easy on her. She did not even know her name when she talked of her childhood to the sympathetic army officer who befriended her and arranged for her repatriation to England in the winter of 1947. That gentleman has always felt too guilty to tell her who he was. He has never told her. She still does not know and she will not know until he is dead. Do you understand?"

Weight and authority had returned to his voice, but there was also an urgency for us to understand his pain. We were both silenced by the strength of his sense of dishonour. "You swear that you will not tell Monika who you are and who I am?"

Holly pursed her lips and nodded assent, aware that there was so much she could not know or understand.

Frustrated by Max's control she turned to me, "You knew. Why didn't you tell me about Dad?"

"I didn't know. I really didn't know. I only knew about Monika's past I had no idea who your Dad was, who you were."

"Charles is telling you the truth, my dear, he didn't know." Why did I think Max knew I was lying?

"So what am I to do?" She seemed beaten.

Someone once told me years before that truth was an absolute thing. If you chose to know truth you couldn't pick and choose which bits of it you learned. Holly had wanted to know everything, and now she wished she did not.

"What am I to do now? My Dad wasn't anything I thought he was. He wasn't Canadian he was Austrian. What does that make me? He was a nazi, he probably murdered his brother as well as my mum, is there anything else I should know?" There was the slightest hint of sarcasm in her voice "I really would like to remember him as he really was."

Max was going to say nothing. I should have said nothing. I shouldn't have ignored his frown and the barely perceptible shake of his head as I began.

"He was a shit. He and Graham were both shits. They were just using you to make money, through Max, through your grandparents, through me. It was all about money. He was only ever after your money. That much was obvious from when your mother died. They were just using you. Both of them were shits."

"And what does that make me?" Holly's voice was small. They were confirming what she had already learned but to hear it from someone else was more than she could take. "What does that make me? Their prey? Their victim? And you knew. All along you knew. And you did absolutely nothing."

"Of course I knew but you wouldn't have listened! You *didn't* listen. Crispin tried to talk you out of it. Linda tried. *You didn't listen.*"

"But what about since then! That was years ago! You've been talking behind my back, everyone laughing at me for being a poor little victim. You knew I was unhappy but everyone else's happiness was far more important. Your bloody secrets were far more important. You let me put up with all that to keep your own bloody secrets. And now somehow it's changed so we can all help poor little Holly. Well I don't need your help. I don't need any of you. Thanks! Thanks for nothing. Oh yes. There is one thing to thank you for. Thank you for the history lesson. And thanks for showing me that just as I've found out I have family I am really more alone than I have ever been."

She turned and walked out of the room.

I let her walk out.

I wish, above everything I have ever wished in my life, that I hadn't.

"Oh shit."

"What possessed you to say those things?" Max sounded weary. "How could you be so crass?"

"I don't know! I just couldn't bear it that he was getting away with it! It was all about Matt but Graham was just as bad!"

"You still would have been best advised to say nothing."

"How am I going to face her in the office tomorrow?"

"*Take no thought for the morrow; for the morrow shall take thought for the things of itself. Sufficient unto the day is the evil thereof.*"

"Thanks."

The next morning I arrived at the office to find Linda fuming.

"What did you say to that girl last night? And don't say 'what girl'?"

"Why?"

"She didn't come home last night and she's just phoned to say she won't be in for a few days. She knew we'd understand because of all the stuff she has to do clearing up after her Dad. Well I don't understand. She was fine yesterday evening, well almost, but now she's all upset about him. What did you say to her?"

"It's complicated."

"Well complicated or not we're going to have to do without her 'for a few days' and it would be nice to know why."

"I think I upset her."

"Well that much was pretty obvious. Is it a permanent upset? Is she likely never to want to see you again? Are you going to be able to work together? It's not that long since she was the greatest thing since sliced bread and the business couldn't do without her!"

"Sorry. I'll go round tomorrow if she doesn't come in."

The atmosphere in the office was not good throughout the day. Neither of us was in a good mood and Lorraine and the girls relaxed, knowing that their work wasn't going to be as closely scrutinised as usual. I could hear them talking and laughing far more than was normally acceptable. It just made Linda and I more irritable.

The next day wasn't much better. We had both hoped one day off would be enough and Holly would turn up for work as usual. She was too conscientious to be away for longer than was necessary.

"Have you called her?"

"No, not today, maybe tomorrow." I knew she was at her father's flat. I had walked round the previous night to see if there was a light in the window. I didn't like to think that she had run away entirely. Or had gone back to Graham.

"Don't you think it would be a good idea?" Linda could sound very condescending when she chose.

"No." I didn't want to argue with her. I wanted, so much, to go back to the Sunday we had all had lunch together, just before that phone call from Canada.

There were two jobs that only Holly knew about and that was to be my excuse when I went round to the flat on the morning of the fifth day. It wasn't really an excuse, the work was getting urgent and no one but Holly had any idea about what was really required and we could hardly call the client. When she hadn't called in by ten Linda and I argued about who should go to see her. It was one of the few arguments with Linda that I won.

She was at the flat. I knocked on the door, which was ajar, and when I got no reply tentatively walked in. There was the sound of a radio playing loudly and the overpowering smell of paint. I looked into the room with the desk, it was still there, the drawers still open and paper strewn around the floor, now organised into small piles.

I wondered what else she could have found.

Apart from the desk the flat appeared empty. All the furniture had gone. I walked back along the short corridor that linked all the rooms of the flat, into what had been the living room.

Holly had her back to me. She was sitting on the floor concentrating as she painted the skirting board. I watched as she meticulously painted along the edges and filled in between. It was easy to see what she was doing as she was replacing old cream with a lurid shade of orange. I looked around and realised that she had painted half the room in brown, orange and purple. I couldn't believe she liked it, she must be trying to make some kind of statement.

She had still not realised I was there as I stood silently watching her.

When you walk through a storm
Hold your head up high
And don't be afraid of the dark
She began to sing gently along with the radio.
At the end of a storm there's a golden sky
And the sweet silver song of a lark
I waited silently watching her every movement as she painted.
Walk on through the wind
Walk on through the rain
Tho' your dreams be tossed and blo own
She began to emphasise every syllable, making the familiar words ugly.
Walk on, walk o o o on, with hope in your heart
And you'll ne ver walk a a lone
You'll ne ver walk a a lone
She started to sing more loudly, tunelessly.
"Wo ork on Wo ork o o o on with hope in your heart
and You'll Ne ver Walk a alone
Then she wasn't singing, she was shouting a statement
YOU'LL NE E E VERWALK A A LONE.
She sat up, stretching. I noticed there were tears on her face, but she wasn't crying. I really wished she had had a speck of paint on her nose and I could walk over and clean it off and we would kiss and make up.

It always happened like that in films.

"Shit! How long have you been here?"

"Not long. I didn't want to interrupt you."

She had seemed quite pleased to see me but then she remembered and grew cool.

"I was OK. You shouldn't creep up on people."

"I did knock but you didn't hear me."

"I'm busy."

"So I see."

"What do you want?"

"There's some work no one can get on with until you tell us what's needed. I've got the file here."

"OK, I'll make some coffee and we can go through it."

We talked business whilst she boiled the kettle and drank the coffee. I didn't mind what we talked about as long as we were talking about something.

"If that's all I'll get back to decorating."

"Do you really like the colour scheme?" I had hoped that would lighten the conversation, she would say 'No, it's crap.' But she didn't laugh or joke about it. She explained briefly that the decorators had had a sale "No one wanted those colours. There were cheap."

I looked across at the tins, there were oranges and browns, greens and purples. Not more than one tin of any one colour. The flat was going to be disgusting when she'd finished. Perhaps that was what she wanted.

"What do I tell Linda?"

"What about?"

"About when you're coming back to the office."

"I don't know."

"If it's me you want to avoid. I'll stay away for a bit."

"No it's not that. I just need some time to get my thoughts together."

"I thought we had something."

"We might have had," she ignored the importance of the admission she was making "but I've got to get this place fit to live in, and there's so much paperwork to do and Ted thinks he can get the divorce going now so there's all that to worry about, and…"

"Please Holly. Stop talking. Tell me. Am I wrong?"

I tried to explain to her how I'd felt since she had left Sandhey the other evening. I tried to apologise for having been so stupid, selfish and arrogant.

"I don't want to lose you."

"We've had nothing to lose."

"I thought we had. I thought you could be thinking the same."

"Well you're wrong."

"No I'm not." I wasn't going to let her get away with that. "I may not have a great deal of experience with women…"

"Like I have with men you mean."

"No. That's a cheap jibe and you know it's not true. Stop deliberately misinterpreting everything I say. I haven't known many women at all, but I do know when people like me and when they don't. I have a lot of experience of people not liking me and you aren't one of them."

"Perhaps I've just joined them."

I wanted not to believe her.

"We'll have to sort something out then won't we? At the office I mean." I couldn't believe she would want to leave. It was all just beginning to come together. "It's all my fault. I'll stay away. You go back in. You enjoy it. You're good at it. We can be polite can't we? Just not spend any time together anywhere else."

"You're sounding as if we're breaking up and we were never together to break up were we?"

"Weren't we?"

"It was close." She admitted and I was sure I didn't imagine the wistfulness in her voice.

She came back to the office the next day and through the rest of the Spring we managed to maintain some sort of a working relationship but when, at the end of the day, I went home or to the pub with Linda, Holly went home alone.

Neither of us liked it, we were both worried about Graham, but she wouldn't listen to either of us.

No one enjoyed the work as much as we had through the winter. In those months everyone had pulled together and got on with everyone else but now there was less of a fun atmosphere, two of the girls decided they had had enough and gave in their notice and we had great difficulty in replacing them. One or two jobs didn't go as well as they should have done and Linda had to visit the clients to promise that the same errors would not happen again.

It was inevitable that she would blame Holly.

I spent less and less time in the office and we found that, where we had always agreed about work and how it should be tackled, we were now arguing about just about everything. More often than not we barely spoke a word to each other throughout the day and, of course, the business began to suffer and clients began to make other arrangements.

At the end of May Linda had had enough, she phoned me and told me to come into the office on Friday evening after the office shut, we had to talk. Everything had gone on long enough.

"But it's my birthday dinner, I've got to be at home."

"Tough."

I turned up at six o'clock unsure what to expect. Since Linda had called I had been wondering what could be fixed by talking. I sat down opposite Linda and Holly. No one said anything for some time until Linda started the ball rolling by remembering the winter and how much fun we'd had and asking us to tell her why it had gone wrong. She asked a simple question. "What happened? You've never told me? You dropped me off that evening and you were both fine and then suddenly it's all turned to shit. Why? I've put up with this for weeks now and the business is suffering. We've got to sort it out."

"It's personal." I said.

"That much is bloody obvious! Is it fixable?"

"Probably not." Holly sounded very definite.

"Stop me when I start going wrong. 'Charles fancies Holly, Holly fancies Charles'." She paused briefly and I was reminded of the section in the marriage service 'or hereafter forever hold his peace' when she continued "Neither of you have stopped me so that much must be true. What's the problem then? Apart from the obvious fact that you're still married Holly, but that's never stopped anyone in the past."

"It's complicated." I wasn't prepared to explain.

"So you've said but it seems pretty damned simple to me."

"Can I talk to Charles alone?" Holly seemed to acknowledge the need to sort things out. "OK. Linda?" I added my voice to Holly's, we had spent weeks avoiding facing up to the way we were harming the business.

"Great! Communication at last!" and Linda left the room thinking all might now be OK.

Holly turned to me and told him what her problem wasn't.

It wasn't that I had ridiculed her for being stupid in marrying Graham; it wasn't because I had known about her father and hadn't told her; it wasn't because she didn't love me.

"Then for Christ's sake Holly what is it?"

"Ever since I met Linda and the Forsters they've talked about your family. Carl is as much part of their family as he is yours and we all talked about you. I can't remember a time when we didn't know about you and Max and the rumours about your family and how you had always been in love with your Nanny. It was always a bit of a laugh I suppose. Carl was never part of it, don't blame him. It was just a case of 'everybody knows'. When I got to know you better I realised you felt a lot about Monika, loved her in some way I couldn't understand – not as a mother, not as a sister, but certainly not as a lover. It was one of the interesting things about you. Graham always said you were gay but I knew that wasn't true. Since New Year you have been so good and kind to me and I saw something in you I've never seen in anyone, certainly not Dad or Graham, and I was falling in love with you just as I knew you were falling in love with me. I was so jealous when Linda told me about last summer in Oxford. She told me how you slept together and all the boys accepted you as a couple. I couldn't believe how hurt I felt and I had no right to. I was married to Graham, 'we', 'you and I' didn't exist, but I was still so jealous. I really thought it would work out, I'd get divorced, we'd be free to get together and we'd live happily ever after. On Leap Day I nearly asked you to marry me. I could have made a joke of it if you'd said no, but I really thought you might say 'yes'. But then Dad died and everything went wrong."

She drew breath. I hadn't moved and I knew I was looking at her as if she was the only thing in the world.

"And then that bloody photograph. I realised that evening that the only reason you loved me was because I am so like Monika. It's Monika you really love. You've always loved her. I just remind you of her, I'm just a younger more eligible Monika."

I couldn't believe that she actually meant it.

I got up to cross the room to hold her but she shied away. "If we ever got together Charles, it'd always be Monika you were seeing."

"No it wouldn't!"

"It would! She was more important to you when you found out about Dad and Graham's plans. She was more important to you then. What's changed?"

How could I convince her? I had no idea. How could I explain what I really felt?

"So I'm going to leave the business." She continued without waiting for me to find an answer. "I know I've let you down. I've let you both down. But I can't go on being here with you or without you. I'm a complete mess. I haven't been able to do anything. I haven't touched the decorating for weeks. There's still paint pots and rubbish all over the flat. I just can't do it anymore. I can't think. I can't work. I've got to get away. Sort myself out."

"It's not Monika, it's you."

"I'm not listening. I don't believe you. Linda! You can come in now."

As Linda came back into the room she looked at my face and realised things had not gone the way she had hoped. She must have been convinced that we would get together and everything would be 'back to February again'.

"I've got to leave Linda, I'm so sorry. I've learned a lot and there've been good times but I must leave before I ruin your business for you. You were doing so well before I came along! Get back to where you were before New Year. I'm so sorry. I've gotta go."

And so Holly left us.

Chapter Twenty-Three

Oliver was surprised when he answered the phone and it was Holly, asking if she could stay with them in Oxford for a while; surprised and not a little worried.

They had talked about what they could do for her after the scene at Linda's New Year's party. Crispin had wanted to take Holly down to Oxford then, 'out of harm's way' he had said. He said he thought it would be sensible to 'get some miles between her and Graham'. But before he had had a chance to ask her Linda had offered her a job and she had agreed to stay up in Cheshire.

"You're being stupid." Crispin told his sister "She needs to get away and we'd look after her, make sure that little shit didn't get anywhere near her."

"She's fine here. And she'll have a job, keep busy. I'll look after her."

"At least let me talk to her, suggest it. You never know she might think it's a good idea."

"She doesn't need options at the moment, She needs to know what she's doing and," Linda said firmly, "having a job and living with us is the best thing for her."

"We can give her a job, she could help us out at the workshop."

"She's not going to want to work with all that grease and noise. She'd be far happier with us."

"Just because we're engineering doesn't mean the place is greasy and dirty. The exact opposite, we have to keep it clean and she'd love it."

All his arguing made no difference, Linda had made up her mind and Crispin was given no chance to talk to Holly.

Now, four months later, Oliver and Crispin discussed what they could do.

"Who knows what harm has been done to her by working with Linda and Charles?"

"I told her it wouldn't work. It was too soon. Holly needed a break and a few months with us would have given her breathing space."

"The last thing she needed was Linda telling her what to do all day every day."

"Well at least we can do something positive now."

"Just don't get too involved, will you Crisp? She needs friends not..."

"I know. I know. 'Wait'. 'Be patient'. You all always say that. Well one of these days..."

She had always enjoyed her visits to Oxford but Holly soon found living in Jericho and being part of that community was very different from being with students in a bed-sit. They agreed on their first evening that the twins would share most of the chores in the house but she would do the shopping, the cooking and the washing up.

She loved walking into town every day to wander around the covered market talking to the butchers and the greengrocers as if there was all the time in the world. They had, at first, made the mistake of assuming she was a tourist but she soon let them know she knew the price things should be. Some mornings she would sit at a café drinking iced tea and listening to the real tourists discussing the country that, she realised, she now thought of as home.

For the first time in years Holly had time to herself, to do the things she wanted to do. She knew which pub the twins always had their lunchtime pint at and, if she felt like it, she joined them sitting in the cool dark bar looking at all the idiotic paraphernalia that was attached to every square inch of the ceiling and the walls. But she knew that if she didn't meet them there it wasn't a problem.

They never criticised anything she did and she began to understand what it was like to be appreciated. After every meal the boys would thank her saying that was 'the best meal we've had since, well, yesterday!' It became a standing joke, one amongst many.

It was difficult for Crispin not to tell Holly how much he cared for her and how much he wanted to look after her. Oliver warned him to keep away until she was more settled 'the last thing she needs is more complication in her life. Give her time. If it's right it'll happen if it isn't it won't.'

But Crispin found that very difficult as Holly walked around the house in bra and pants as if it was the most natural thing in the world.

"She's practically our sister," Oliver said, "she thinks of us as Linda's brothers, almost her brothers, she doesn't see you as a man, as such"

"Thanks."

Oliver wasn't sure he was being fair to either of them, but he wasn't prepared to lose his brother to someone who, although perfectly friendly, didn't seem to care about him especially anyway.

Most days Holly walked along the canal. She and Linda had often walked along the tow-path on their summer visits but they had never bothered to talk to the occupants of the houseboats. Now Holly began with cheery 'good-mornings' which soon developed into discussions about the weather and then conversations that would last as long as everyone wanted them to. It was cool alongside the canal and she loved talking to these people who knew nothing of her and wanted nothing from her as they sat in their deckchairs on the flat roofs of their boats and she idly watched the water coursing through the lock gates and out into the River Thames.

The summer was becoming a long and hot one and as the days passed she began to take note of the falling levels of water in the various channels. On the days she didn't feel like talking she would find some shade under a tree and sit and read. She had forgotten how much she loved being in the sun and this summer of 1976 was something special.

Linda wrote to her regularly, scribbled postcards or short notes arrived every few days telling her how things were in the office. She didn't reply, thinking there wasn't much she could say that Crispin and Oliver weren't reporting anyway.

As the city emptied of students and filled with tourists she wondered if anyone from home would recognise her if they passed her in the street. Her skin was a deep bronze, her long hair had been cut short and she knew she was losing the drawn, haunted look she had had for so long.

It was three weeks before she could talk to the twins about anything that mattered.

"It all went wrong when Mom died." She had said to Oliver one evening as they sat on the pavement outside the pub. "I was fine up till then."

He listened sympathetically, wondering how much of her pain was down to him for warning his brother away from her. He dismissed the idea. It had never been the right time, however good they might have been together. And it wasn't the right time now. He was sure of that.

"You need time to get over all that. You've had a rotten few years, parents dying, rubbish marriage, no support from anyone."

"I feel like I'm hiding my head in the sand. I haven't earned any money for weeks. I've abandoned the flat half decorated. It's such a mess. I just went down to the hardware store and bought whatever tins they had on offer. They're god-awful colours! I got rid of all the furniture and need to get some more."

"You can stay here as long as you like you know." Crispin arrived and handed them each another glass.

"But my life's just on hold."

"Why not?" Oliver backed up his brother "Stay as long as you like, the longer the better. We'll hate getting back to having to do our own cooking and washing up."

"But I've run away haven't I? I suppose I'll have to face up to it all one day."

"We all have to run away sometime. We ran away here, we didn't go back up north when we'd graduated, we hung around here doing our own thing which was definitely not what was expected of us. Everyone has to run away sometime."

"It's perfectly OK you know."

"That's not the same. You're doing so well, you've got your lives together, you know what you're going to do for the next few years."

"We haven't got everything right, you know, we haven't even got proper girlfriends let alone wives. And the worst thing is we're 30 next week and we still live with each other. A lot of people think that is very odd indeed."

"You've got years yet, don't get married for the wrong reasons."

They all left that comment hanging leaden in the air as they consumed more pints of ice cold lager or as near ice cold as the Landlord could produce in the heat.

Eventually Holly asked them what they were going to do to mark the 'Big Three O'.

"Are you going back up north?"

"No, hadn't thought of it really, rather gave that up when we got passed 21. Mutt and Jeff will send a card and a present and we'll phone them and thank Mum for the pain we must have put her through x number of years before, that sort of thing. But we can't just drop everything at work like we used to when we worked for someone else so we won't be going up."

"You should have a party here. Get Linda to come down, Carl, all your mates from the pub, the blokes from your work, it'd be fun. I'll do the food, you do the booze. Come on! You've got to do something."

"Could do."

"Possible. What day of the week is it?"

"Sunday."

"We'd have to have the party on the Saturday so we'll all have time to recover."

"Right then. It's on. Hey guys..." Holly caught the attention of a group of drinkers whose names they just about knew "Party, next Saturday, round the corner, 10a. Be there!"

"Holly! We hardly know them" Oliver tried to restrain Holly, "We don't want millions of hangers on."

"The more the merrier!"

Where all the people came from and how they heard of the party Crispin and Oliver could only guess as the house filled up and overflowed onto the pavement outside.

Holly spent the evening in the tiny kitchen at the back of the house pouring wine and beer into plastic mugs and paper cups for anybody and everybody. Most of the men tried to chat her up but she was well practised at preventing unwanted attention. She had long ago taken off her wedding ring but she had put her Mother's ring on her engagement finger and she would wave it in the face of anyone who got too friendly and if anyone asked who the lucky man was she would wave vaguely in the direction of Crispin or Oliver who were never far away. She knew they would back her up.

But it was neither Crispin nor Oliver who rescued her at around 2 in the morning from one particularly persistent drunken attempt to grab her and plant beery kisses on her neck.

"Go away you prat! You're pissed." She was shouting, trying to make him hear she was serious over the noise of the music.

"An' you're gorgeous, here, gissa kiss."

"Piss off !" as she tried to push him away he staggered against the table upsetting all the cups and mugs on the table so the flat booze with disintegrating dog ends spilt over Holly.

"Piss off! You're disgusting!"

"Here! Gissa kiss gorgeous." He was not going to give up without a fight, so it was a fight he got.

Holly had never punched anyone before in her life.

She had hit out at Graham but they were more slaps than punches, but this time she pulled her arm back over her shoulder and formed her right hand into a fist, remembering from somewhere in her mind that she should keep her thumb on the outside so she didn't break it, and she thrust her arm forward towards the idiot's face with such force that she hurt her shoulder as she connected with his nose.

It couldn't have hurt him very much as he was anaesthetised by alcohol but it stopped him in his tracks. He backed away, not forgetting to pick up one of the few remaining full mugs of lager on the table.

"Bravo! Couldn't have done it better myself!"

"Carl! We didn't think you were going to make it."

"Got back from the airport, got your message on my flash new answerphone and got straight in the little car. I drove like a lunatic here hoping I wouldn't miss the party. It seems I got here just in time for the best punch I've ever seen a lady lay."

When Oliver eventually woke up the next morning and made his way down stairs he found assorted people asleep in all the rooms in the house.

Hearing voices from the kitchen he gingerly picked their way over legs and arms that may or may not have been attached to each other, headed for the sound of laughter.

"Coffee? You look as if you need it."

Holly was standing wearing the shortest of shorts, a t-shirt that barely covered her and a pair of yellow rubber gloves. In one hand she held, at arms length, a bin bag.

"It's been like that game, you know, where you drop a pile of sticks down on the table and have to pick them in turn without moving any others. I've been going around the house with this," in her other hand she held a long handled stick that had pincers on the end operated by a lever at the top, "picking up mugs and cups and bits of fag end trying not to wake anyone up! We've been taking it in turns to see who can get the most without someone grunting or farting or turning over! This is the third sack load."

"Once you get rid of all the bodies we'll give it a hoover round and you'll never know there's been a party here at all. Oh," Carl added almost as an afterthought "Happy Birthday."

"God yes! 30! Ancient."

"Not so much of that. I'm already there you know."

Carl had done nothing on his 30th birthday nearly two months earlier. He had been in Spain working and had barely given it a thought, which was partly why, tired as he had been the previous evening, he had driven the 40 or so miles from his home to join Crispin and Oliver to celebrate theirs.

"Bloody successful bash that." Oliver planted a kiss on Holly's cheek. "Thanks old girl. We wouldn't have even thought about doing it if it hadn't been for you."

"Thanks Holly." Crispin appeared at the kitchen door and wanted to kiss Holly as well but there wasn't room for another in the small kitchen. "Make sure you're around for our 40th won't you."

"Of course! Try and keep me away."

She smiled. She was happy.

She was in a tiny kitchen with three good looking men who any girl would have given their eye teeth to have been with. And they all cared for her, maybe not in the same way, but they all liked her and wanted her to be happy. Unlike ...

She brushed away the shiver that she always felt when she thought of Graham and how she had ignored their warnings and married him. That was the past. She hadn't heard from him for months. Ted had said he had moved and was being very cooperative with the divorce. Graham was the past. Once the divorce was behind her she need never think about him again.

He couldn't spoil her life now.

Not when she had friends like these.

"We'll leave you to your Cinderella and Buttons act." The twins helped each other over some supine bodies and up the narrow stairs.

Carl felt he and Holly were the only ones with any energy that morning. He kicked and nudged the hangers on who had stayed overnight awake and urged them out of the door while Holly cleared up what seemed to be hundreds of plastic glasses and paper plates.

"Why does this always seem so appetising at three in the morning?" She asked conversationally as they filled the black sacks. "It's disgusting."

"They should ban smoking." Carl added as he decided the only way to dispose of an ashtray that was swimming in a golden cocktail half beer and half nicotine, was to throw the whole thing into the sack.

Holly watched him. "Yuch. That's totally disgusting."

"Have you ever smoked?"

"Absolutely never. Disgusting habit. There's nothing worse than having to kiss a man who's been smoking. Ban it."

"Done!"

For a few moments as she remembered Graham's breath. She had always hated the mixture of alcohol and stale cigarette smoke. The memory was so vivid she could almost taste him and shuddered before shaking her head and getting back to the task in hand.

"You're very domesticated." Holly said when she and Carl eventually sat down in the cleaned and tidied empty house "Most men would have left all that to me."

"I don't think I've ever been accused of being 'most men'."

"Well you definitely aren't."

"I'll take that as a compliment then."

"Like I did when you all said I wasn't American any more?"

"You know what we meant."

"Of course I did."

She wondered what Linda would have thought of the ease and familiarity between her and Carl that morning.

When the twins eventually reappeared Carl handed them each a mug of coffee. "I know it's hot but we're going to make today special."

"Sunday lunch. That's all I need." Oliver sounded less than enthusiastic as he sat sprawling on the sofa. Carl deliberately misinterpreted him "Of course it is. It'll do you both good. Good roast, all the trimmings, a walk by the river then an afternoon drinking Pimm's. It'll be a real celebration."

"Of course it will." Crispin didn't sound convinced.

"A few cups of coffee and you'll both be fine."

An hour later they piled into Carl's Jensen and headed south out of Oxford towards the small village pub by the Thames.

"Dorchester. It sounds like it should be a big town, a city with a cathedral, not a tiny village." Holly shouted above the noise of the engine as they approached the village.

"There's two."

"Two what?"

"Two Dorchesters."

"Why?"

"Because."

Conversation with the twins was limited but the rush of fresh air in the open car completed what the coffee had begun and if only for a few seconds at a time they were able to forget their hangovers. By the time they sat down to eat they had forgotten them completely.

The lunch went well.

"Good idea Carl." Oliver admitted as he ate the roast beef and Yorkshire pudding as if he hadn't eaten for weeks.

"But definitely not the best meal we've had all summer." Crispin added looking at Holly.

"It's OK Carl, don't look so downcast. He's joking." Holly put her arm in Carl's and briefly rested her head on his shoulder. "It was a brilliant idea."

Conversation never flagged as Carl brought the others up to date with his next television series and the twins detailed their plans for developing their engineering business. If Holly was a little quiet as the others talked so animatedly about their plans and their successes, she contributed enough for them not to notice.

"Time for a zizz I think." Crispin was feeling weary and after the food and wine was almost asleep. "I think I'll go into the garden and sit in the shade and relax a bit." "Me too." added Oliver, normally the one with less stamina anyway. "You two'll be alright on your own for a bit?"

"We'll be fine. Don't worry about us, it's your birthday you can do exactly as you want."

The two brothers left the room and headed for the chairs set out under the trees on the grass that was being kept green by the gentle stream of water from the sprinkler. It was probably its rhythmic whoosh whoosh that sent both of them to sleep almost as soon as they had sat down.

Carl stood up, walked round the table and pulled Holly's chair out as she stood up.

"That's nice. No one's ever done that."

"Ever the gentleman." Carl replied chivalrously "What would you like to do with this lovely afternoon Holly? Sit in the garden with us elderly gentlemen?" Carl didn't seem enthused with the idea of joining the twins.

"I thought I'd go for a walk around the churchyard."

"It's an Abbey, I think"

"Does that make is an Abbeyyard?"

"Probably not. Can I come with you?"

"Why not?"

They crossed the road and, passing a chattering group of women milling around by the tearooms, walked into the quiet haven of the churchyard. Holly loved to look at gravestones and wonder about the lives of the people buried beneath. She didn't do this in a morbid manner, it was more her way of paying tribute to the people long dead and of remembering her mother whose grave she had never seen.

"Oh how sad!" She drew Carl's attention to one particular tomb "Look at all those children, and so young." She quietly read out the names and ages of the children whose short lives were noted on this weathered stone. She felt angry that some of the names were so worn she couldn't read them. It was so unfair the lives of those children wouldn't even be marked by their names being spoken aloud.

Carl took her hand and led her to one grave. "Exactly 200 years ago today." He was not surprised to see tears filling Holly's eyes, so he didn't let go of her hand, nor did she draw it away herself.

They walked through the network of graves and stopped at the corner of the building looking down a slope to the river.

"It's just so beautiful."

It may have been the quiet serenity of the spot, or maybe it was because they had had a lovely morning together, but whatever the reason Carl bent his head to kiss her lightly on the lips. "You're not so bad yourself."

It could have meant nothing.

"Come on, let's walk."

Still holding hands they walked slowly back through the gravestones, along the path and towards the river. Despite it being a lovely sunny Sunday afternoon they soon found an area where there were no other people.

They followed a path through the long grass without speaking. It was as if they both sensed the inevitability of what they were about to do.

Carl wasn't in love with Holly. He hadn't been in love with any of

217

the girls he had made love to in the past few years. He loved, and always had loved, Susannah. But since he had no idea when she might decide she needed him enough to overcome all the barriers that separated them he found no difficulty in enjoying the company of others. As long as girls found him attractive and he didn't hurt them or let them get emotionally involved he couldn't see why not.

Holly knew she wasn't in love with Carl now, perhaps she never had been attracted to him for any other reason than she knew Linda wanted him. She had always known he was Susannah's. Or Linda's. She had never really wanted him to be hers.

She had no idea what she really felt about Charles. Sometimes she missed him so much it was a physical pain, at other times she hated him and how he had been able to lie to her. She saw so much of Charles in Carl, they had the same beautiful blue eyes. She would have loved to have met their father.

Neither Carl nor Holly was in love with the other but they made love that hot Sunday afternoon. Carl had learned the art well, and he knew he was a caring, gentle lover. He knew it was his role to give pleasure as well as to take it. He knew when to be gentle and when not to be; he knew where to touch and where not to; he knew how to arouse and how to fulfil.

To Holly it felt like she had never been made love to before. This, she decided, was what they had all talked about, had all dreamed about, what all those songs were about, what magic was about. Graham had not cared about her feelings, and it had been many months since she had even pretended to enjoy sex. But this was different. This wasn't 'sex' this was 'love making'.

Afterwards they lay in the sunshine, both smiling.

"Thanks."

"That's an odd thing to say."

"I mean it. Thanks."

"Thank you too"

"No, I mean thanks for more than just the last, what?" she looked at her watch "20 minutes. Thanks for restoring my faith in men."

"Is that the first time since..." He left the question unfinished, it should never have been started but she didn't seem to mind.

"Yes. I was never unfaithful to Graham, God knows why, but I wasn't. Christ!"

"What?" he asked in alarm as she had sat up sharply.

"I said his name without flinching! I've not been able to think of him or say his name without panicking and now I have."

"Time, you know, it does work in the end."

"And a good ... well what we've just done!"

He pulled her down towards him and kissed her again.

"One more time then."

An hour later they had rejoined the twins and were sitting under the shade of the tree in the hotel garden drinking tea and eating scones and jam.

"Did you two have a good walk?" Crispin had noticed the grass stains on the back of Carl's shirt and couldn't believe they would have done anything together.

"Terrific, it's so beautiful down here. We went through the churchyard, sorry 'Abbeyyard', and down onto the water meadows, there's miles of them. It was so cool." Crispin was relieved, Holly didn't seem embarrassed or secretive, they had, after all, just been for a walk and sat down on the grass to enjoy the countryside.

"We did a lot of talking, and I've decided it's time I thought about not sponging on you two any longer."

"We love you being here, don't we Oliver?" Crispin tried to keep the panic out of his voice. He had been patient. Again.

He hadn't tried anything before she went to university, then he had lost her to Graham. He had been waiting for her to get her divorce, he was giving her time to decide what she really wanted to do after her disastrous marriage. He hadn't wanted to take advantage of her when she was low. Now he was losing her again.

"Of course. You know you're welcome to stay as long as you like." Somehow Oliver's invitation was less genuine than Crispin's.

"Sooner or later I've got to face getting my life together. My divorce will be through soon and I'll be free to be me again."

Crispin wondered what had gone on down by the riverbank. What had Carl said, or done, to change Holly's plans. This morning she hadn't said anything about even thinking about leaving.

"The bank's being paying the rent but I'm going to have to earn something soon or they won't pay up any more. I reckon I must already be overdrawn. There's probably loads of letters on the mat waiting to be opened. I hate not opening bills."

"Come and work for us, there's loads you could do at the workshop, there's all the admin, I know we're no good at that." Crispin knew he was talking too much but it felt like he had this one last chance to make her change her mind.

"I've already got a job. I know I let them all down terribly in the Spring but I'm better now. I can cope now."

"Why did you run away?" Crispin asked. He knew it was too late, he should have asked before. He didn't really expect an answer now.

Holly couldn't explain to these men who she knew so well, all the feelings of resentment and betrayal she had experienced when she had found out about her father. How she felt so let down by Charles, who she had thought she might have loved. She couldn't explain any of it to these men who she cared for in such different ways, so she ignored the question.

"I will try to be more sensible, but it's a risk!" she tried to laugh, but wasn't entirely successful.

"We'll miss you." Oliver had been watching the three of them, as he often did, and probably saw more in Holly's mood than his brother could.

"Only because you'll have to do your own washing up."

"Why else."

"Anyway, now you two have woken up is it time for a drink? I'll get them."

"I'll help you." Crispin jumped up.

As they walked in towards the bar Holly put her hand inside the crook of Crispin's arm and hugged him to her. "You know you and Olly have been great. I love you both so much for helping me out, but it really is time I took myself in hand."

"You could have talked to me you know, anytime." Crispin felt hurt. Even though he had almost persuaded himself that she and Carl had not been up to anything that afternoon he couldn't help feeling jealous that she must have spoken about her life with Carl and not with him.

"I know, silly, but I didn't did I?" She hugged his arm and leant up to give him a playful kiss on his cheek.

"I tried to talk to you, you know, the morning of your, you know, your wedding." He was embarrassed and uncharacteristically diffident.

"I know. And you were absolutely right. I really wish I'd listened to you. I really do."

"So do I."

"But I didn't and here I am 'picking myself up, dusting myself down and starting all over again' thanks to you."

As they carried the large jug filled with ice, fruit and alcohol out into the garden Crispin told Holly that if she ever needed a friend to talk to he was always there, he'd always listen and try to help.

"I know."

But he knew she would never call him.

She would only ever see him as Linda's brother, almost her brother and he felt immeasurably depressed.

"Here you go boys," Holly said rather too loudly as she filled their glasses. "Cheers".

They all drank to a 30th Birthday that would be remembered for such different reasons.

Chapter Twenty-Four

When she opened the door to the flat Holly expected to be pushing a month's worth of mail across the floor, but the door opened smoothly. She had expected to face the paint pots and stepladders she had left in the dining room, but there were none. The weather had been so hot for the month she had been away and she had expected to find the flat stifling with the stink of paint still lingering, but the air in the flat was fresh.

She was stunned when she walked into the living room. It was completely immaculate. There was a sofa and chairs, a table against the wall with a vase filled with fresh pink and white roses, there were pictures hanging on the fresh magnolia walls, lovely, slightly provocative prints of gypsy girls.

She went into her bedroom. It had been decorated too and completely refurnished although her father's desk was still there. She tried the locks, they were secure; she found her key and opened it, relieved to find all the papers as she had left them.

In the bathroom everything had changed. Gone were the horrid green bath and basin, replaced with white and there was a shower. On the floor, instead of a dreadful black white and red lino she had hated, was a beige carpet. On the window ledge was another vase of roses.

The whole flat had been transformed.

As she went around the flat opening all the windows she wondered what had happened, and how...? And who...? She walked back down the short corridor to the new table where she had seen all her mail laid out in neat piles labelled BILLS, DIVORCE, BANK, LANDLORD, WORK, RUBBISH.

Turning on the radio absent-mindedly she sat down, deciding to tackle the LANDLORD pile first.

There were three letters. She checked the postmarks and opened them in chronological order. It was the order in which they had been arranged anyway.

The earliest was a letter dated the day she had left, explaining that the Landlord was selling the building but that the tenants, which apart from Holly were two old people in the flat above and the two shops beneath, would all be safe from eviction. Their tenancies meant that they could not be thrown out immediately but the new Landlord wanted them to know that he had no intention of evicting anyone, nor increasing their rents.

The second letter was from Ted Mottram. The thought crossed Holly's mind that this had been miss-filed by the mysterious organiser, this should be in the DIVORCE pile. But as she read the letter she realised that was simply a coincidence, his firm was acting for the new Landlord. The letter explained that essential refurbishments were to be made to the property and that, if she was not in to give access on a certain date they would have to force entry but would ensure the lock remained unchanged. It continued saying the Landlord believed that the change in ownership would serve only to improve the facilities and status of the building. There was no sign in Ted's letter of the name of the new landlord but Holly didn't care. It seemed that that explained the changes in the flat.

It was the third letter that explained the roses.

Dear Mrs Eccleston,

She was mildly surprised at the salutation. She had reverted to her maiden name as soon as she had left Graham but she was normally called 'Miss'. She had always preferred 'Mrs' and had mentioned more than once to Charles and Linda that she wished the English worked as the Europeans did and people were given the title 'Frau' or 'Madame' or 'Señora' simply when they reached maturity without necessarily advertising their marital status.

It is with great pleasure that I inform you of my recent purchase of your building and hope that you approve the decoration and other improvements made to the property in your absence.

I want to assure you that all your belongings have been treated with the greatest respect through this refurbishment and have been stored in boxes that you will find in the spare bedroom.

If there is anything you wish to know about the ways in which the new ownership of your building may affect your tenancy please do not hesitate to contact me directly.

Yours faithfully,

Holly was completely unprepared for the signature and the handwritten note at the bottom.

Charles Donaldson

PS Welcome Home!

She held the letter at arms length knowing she could react in two ways.

She could feel her space had been invaded, she could feel that he was hounding her, taking over her life; she could resent him for the power he had over her and feel that there was no hiding place; she could hate him.

Or she could love him for what he had done.

She could appreciate the care and forethought that had gone into the transformation of the flat which had obviously been done with her in mind; the expense he had gone to so he could help her; she could understand it for what it was meant to convey.

That he loved her.

She wasn't sure how to react so she walked back into the living room. The photograph of her Mother was on the mantelpiece and looking at it made her want to trust Charles, made her want to believe that all this wasn't to control her, it was to show how much he cared.

He hadn't contacted her in the month she had been away, he hadn't phoned or written, but she now knew he had been thinking of her all the time. He must have started this process well before she left. He couldn't have done it all in one month. Why hadn't he told her?

That letter, apart from the PS, was as formal as it could be.

Still, she allowed herself to think, he had left flowers all over the flat and the windows had obviously been opened every day through the continuing heat wave. So maybe he wasn't being completely impersonal.

So many thoughts ran through her mind, trying to make sense of what had happened, and what she should do.

When you walk through a storm, hold your head up high

For much of the life that she could remember she had had to do things for herself. Her parents had had their own problems and, though they had rarely fought in front of her, she knew they had been unhappy together. She understood that even better since her own marriage.

At the end of the storm is a golden sky

They had fed her and educated her and probably loved her in their own ways, but she knew she had never been the most important person in either of their lives. When she had married Graham she had thought that perhaps now someone would do things for her, make her the centre of their world.

Walk on through the wind, walk on through the rain

She had wanted to be loved and cared for. Perhaps she was being unrealistic; perhaps you could never be the only important person in someone's life. Perhaps, even if you were, it would be too much of a responsibility.

But now, it seemed, she was. Charles had done so much, no one had ever gone to so much trouble for her.

Walk On, Walk On, With hope in your heart, and You'll never walk alone.

She became aware of the song on the radio, she listened to the words, and, as every time she listened to that song, she felt the tears running down her cheeks.

She wanted to believe her mother was talking to her. She knew it was stupid, she knew she was tired and emotional, but that didn't stop her wanting it not to be a coincidence.

You'll never walk alone.

She took the photo from the mantelpiece and kissed it.

"Thanks Mom."

It was getting late. There was still bright sunlight streaming through the windows but the sun was low and, looking at her watch, she realised it was after nine o'clock.

She went back to the kitchen and opened the new fridge. There was milk, butter, bread, water, oranges, some cheese, cold meat and salad and a note.

Just in case you don't feel like shopping today. See you in the office Thursday morning? Please?

It was written in Linda's easily recognisable, childishly round handwriting.

Holly poured a glass of the creamy milk.

The other piles of post would have to wait, she had some coming to terms with herself to do.

The next day, the last day in June, Holly unpacked all her belongings from the boxes in the spare room and made the flat her own. She phoned Crispin to say he wasn't to worry, sorry she hadn't phoned yesterday but it was late when she got back. They were on the phone for a long time, talking as though he didn't love her and she didn't know how he felt. She told him about the transformation in the flat and got the idea that he had already known; he told her how everyone at the pub was devastated that she had gone without saying goodbye, especially 'some bloke with a wonderful black eye'.

"Bye Crispin, love to Olly."

"Bye Holly, Good luck. We're always…"

But she had hung up.

She faced the BILLS pile on the dining room table and found that there weren't many. Perhaps she hadn't been away so long after all, it just seemed that way. In the BANK pile was a statement that showed her that her salary had been paid in full for May and June. She'd have to talk to Linda about that. In the DIVORCE pile were several letters detailing dates and with various forms to sign. Everything seemed to be going smoothly. The final letter, with a hand written addition at the bottom, was from Ted.

Don't worry, my dear, everything is going according to plan,

Graham Tyler is being unusually co-operative. Please call me when you get home.

They were all so sure she'd come back.

Perhaps she had been the only one who had doubted it.

The RUBBISH pile appeared to be just one letter from Graham. She recognised the handwriting and saw from the postmark that she had only just missed getting it before she had left for Oxford, though she couldn't make out the place it had been posted. She nearly didn't open it. It was short and to the point.

I just heard about your father. Shame.

He was a bit of a failure though wasn't he?

Now, I suppose I'll have to do the best I can on my own.

It occurred to Holly that many things had gone on in the background that she would never know about, that she didn't want to know about, to get Graham off her back.

But this letter filled her with foreboding. She remembered her fears for her grandparents and for herself.

Perhaps he had not given up at all.

It was some time before she could turn to the letter in front of the WORK label.

Welcome home.

We hope you enjoyed your holiday. Now you have no excuses not to get down to some hard work. We have all missed you and you will notice some changes – hopefully for the better.

Can we just consider that you've had this year's and next year's holiday in advance? You'll come back won't you?

We need you!

It was signed by both Linda and Charles.

Perhaps Graham couldn't touch her after all.

There were people who cared about her, were looking after her, and would always look after her whatever stupid things she did.

Charles would protect her.

If only she would let him.

The next morning Holly got up very early and enjoyed the luxury of the shower. As she stood under the lukewarm water trying to cool down, for it was already over 75°, she thought of Charles. Very few people, drawing up the specifications for re-doing a bathroom, would have thought about a shower, unless they had wanted to please the person who would be using the bathroom.

She dressed more carefully than she had for weeks.

She had a calf length loose cotton skirt that she had bought in the market in Oxford. It was a mess of maroons blues and whites and she had loved it. It made her think that she was a 1960s hippy, carefree and facing the world as if it weren't a frightening place. She had nearly worn it the previous weekend when she had gone down Dorchester with the twins. And Carl.

Now she was glad she hadn't.

It held no memories. It was fresh and new.

Like her life.

As she walked the mile or so to the office she was preoccupied trying to remember all the things she thought she would never need to know again; how to operate the machines she had been so adept at; all the clients' names and the work they required, always supposing she hadn't managed to put them all off through the Spring.

She was really looking forward to her fresh start, to seeing Linda again.

And Charles.

Holly was so lost in her own world that she didn't notice the man walking several yards behind her along the wide tree-lined road. He had been waiting outside the flat, as he had the day before, leaning against the doors of the telephone box, half hidden from view. She could have seen him if she had been looking for him, but of course she wasn't.

He followed her at a distance, watching her body move as she walked, wondering again why she had cut her lovely long blonde hair.

That made him quite angry as he thought of that hair brushing against him, of him holding her head, making it swing slowly from side to side, brushing over him, arousing him.

It would be very different having sex with her now.

But he was sure he'd find a way to enjoy it.

Chapter Twenty-Five

I was in my room in the office while Linda went round switching on fans, opening windows, getting everything ready for the day. I was under strict instructions not to appear until she said it was OK.

When Holly walked in she looked up as if it had only been a day since they had seen each other and there had never been any problems. "Love the hair."

She poured two plastic mugs of water from the cooler and handed one to Holly.

"This bloody weather, it hasn't let up for ages. Had to get in all these fans even though they blow all the paper everywhere and we have to weigh everything down. We always want a hot summer and then when we get one all we do is complain. No such thing as air-conditioning here. Not worth it usually. Oh! I'm wittering on aren't I? I always do that." She paused for a moment and topped up her cup from the cooler.

"It's so good to see you!" Holly was overwhelmed by the welcome "I've missed you. I've missed you for years really."

"Come on. Don't get all serious. It's all history. 'Today is the first day of the rest of your life' as they say. We've got a staff meeting at 8.30. I've asked everyone to be here early so we can bring you up to speed with who's who and what's what."

"Everyone?"

I listened as Linda enthusiastically explained all the changes a month had wrought on the business.

"Absolutely. Lorraine has left. I don't think it was a surprise and she got herself a fantastic job in Liverpool. I think she preferred to be in a bigger office with shops just round the corner every lunchtime. We've got Luci now. She's absolutely brilliant. You'll love her. She's just spent a year travelling in Canada and the States and Charles found her looking through the job adverts while working behind the bar in the Derby. Saved no end of agency fees. But she's really very good. She spent loads of time temping in Canada and used all sorts of new fangled machines and she's got so many brilliant ideas. Although she's only been with us a couple of weeks but it's as if she's been with us for ever."

Seeing the worried look on Holly's face she continued rapidly "Don't worry, she's not going to take anything away from you, just add to all your training. We've taken on one or two other people because we've got one or two strange clients. Completely different sort of work. We still do the memory typing and what we should now call 'word processing' but we're getting into other stuff. We're doing translation and I'm looking at new machines that will do a lot more than these." She waved her arm dismissively at the desks. "Anyway, time enough for all that when the others come in."

She slowed her talking down, looked more serious and asked "Are you really OK about this? About Charles I mean. I know you two had the most awful row, but is it all OK now?"

"I don't know really. I think so. I hope so. I haven't spoken to him since … since May. But I've done a lot of thinking and I'm looking forward to seeing him, talking to him, thanking him. You know what he's done to the flat and everything?"

"Of course! He told me all about it but stressed it was purely a brilliant business opportunity. Good morning Charles."

Linda kept up the business front for a few moments after I came out of my office. "Those flats were in a dreadful state and I got them for a really knock down price, with sitting tenants. It's purely an investment."

She must have seen the look Holly gave me. It was a slow smile, beginning with her eyes and spreading, almost as an afterthought, to her mouth.

"I'll go and check the… um … yes."

And Linda left us to it.

As Holly got into the swing of things at work I tried to keep everything between us on a purely business footing. We were as we had been in the early part of the year when the three of us enjoyed the hard work during the day and a little relaxation in the evenings.

Linda helped by making sure we spent very little time alone.

Holly and I spoke of work and of the weather, neither of us said anything about anything important. Sooner or later, I knew, we would have to face up to difficult subjects but for the time being we both seemed to be happy to put that moment off.

In those two weeks I mentioned neither Max nor Monika and no one mentioned Graham or Matt.

And I left it until the very last minute before mentioning that Susannah had come home.

I was extremely wary of inviting Holly to Susannah's graduation party, a party Max was determined to give her 'for Alicia's sake'. I didn't think she would want to go back to Sandhey, I couldn't imagine she would want to meet Max, or Monika. But I didn't want not to ask her in case she found out and felt hurt. I didn't think I could win either way I decided to ask both of them. Perhaps I could have done it more graciously.

"I don't suppose you'd like to come to Susannah's graduation party? It's next Wednesday? Well, it's not really a party, more champagne and canapés in the garden for the select few. Both of you? Don't feel you have to if you don't want to."

"Bloody hell. Susannah's back." Linda didn't sound very enthusiastic.

"Don't you want us to go?" Holly must have picked up the hint of some reluctance in my voice.

"Of course I do. It's just that you might not like it. It'll be stuffy and formal. It's Max's party not mine."

"We might liven it up a bit then."

"What do you think Linda? Shall we accept his kind invitation?"

"We'd love to come." Linda agreed. "Just make sure you don't leave us to talk to the grown ups!" I hated being teased.

Holly came to my rescue by asking "It's odd that I've lived here five years and I've never met her."

"Yes you have," Linda reminded her "at the funeral."

"I don't remember."

"That was the last time I saw her too." I think I surprised them. "It was my fault. We argued. I went to Cornwall and she went away saying she wouldn't come back till she'd sorted herself out. She wanted to get a proper degree and now she has."

"Have she seen the children? How are they?"

"He's seen them every other Wednesday for two hours at ten o'clock." Holly answered.

I looked at her questioningly. "You don't want to know." She answered my unspoken question.

I tried to concentrate on my answer to Linda "Not yet. They're growing up. Bill, the youngest is 7; Josie, the eldest she's 12, nearly 13. We go to see them most weeks for an hour or so."

"I've been visiting them too, every so often." Linda had never told me about her visits even though I had known about them almost since she first went.

"I wondered when you'd get round to telling me. They often talk about this energetic bubbly lady with red hair who comes to visit them now and again. I've always said 'a friend of your mummy's' when they asked me who it was though I knew it must be you."

"I don't go very often. It's just that Carl…"

One, maybe two years, before I would have said "What's it got to do with him?" feeling an area of mine had been invaded but now I understood far more. Carl was always going to be interested in Susannah and her children, however much she hated the idea, were part of her. Now I was able to accept that I felt none of the old pangs of jealousy. "I suppose he wants to keep in touch with Susannah in any way he can."

"Yeah. I just tell him how they're doing, what interests them, you know, that sort of thing. Just in case…"

"…just in case he ever gets to know them himself you mean. I wish you'd told me, we could have gone together." I had no reason not to be generous.

"When did Susannah last see them?" Holly was curious.

"Jack's 4th birthday. 1st August 1971. "

"Jeez. That's as long as I've lived here. It seems forever ago and she hasn't seen them all that time?"

"No. Not once. She's been living in the south."

"But she's coming back now?"

"Maybe she's grown up."

"Well we'd love to come. Will we know anyone other than you?" With only the slightest of pauses she continued. "Apart from Max and Monika, of course." Sooner or later they would have to be mentioned, I was glad she had the courage. I didn't.

"Ted, he always comes to important family occasions, it's just a small party really, close family. We don't want to scare her off again."

"Carl?" Linda asked and I tried not to notice that Holly looked interested in the response.

"I sincerely doubt it. They've avoided each other one way or another, for more than 15 years. We haven't seen him for a while, I think he's spent a lot of time in Spain. We keep in touch by letter more than anything, though he did phone a couple of weeks ago to say he's back in the country."

I kept looking at Holly and tried not to be worried when I saw her blush.

I forced enthusiasm. "We'll leave Luci in charge and have the afternoon off. Champagne will be served on the terrace at noon."

"We'll be there."

Chapter Twenty-Six

Neither Charles nor Linda went into the office that morning. Charles had rung Linda to say "We're off to see the children. They've broken up now so I'm just going to check everything's OK."

"We?" Linda asked, surprised. "Is Susannah going with you?"

"No. Ted. He comes along sometimes to check on the house, the nanny and to make sure everything is as it should be. Want to come with us?"

Holly wasn't included in the invitation but she didn't mind; Linda knew the children, she didn't, and in any case, someone had to stay in the office.

It turned out to be a very busy morning. She had had every intention of stopping work at eleven. This would have given her plenty of time to change, put on some makeup and walk the mile or so to Sandhey by noon. At a quarter to twelve she was still fielding phone calls and leaving instructions for Luci and the girls for the afternoon. She very nearly rang Sandhey to say she was sorry she couldn't make it after all, she was too busy. It was after twelve when she ran out of the office, past the station, through the crowd milling around outside the sweetshop and down to the promenade.

She stood leaning against the railings, looking out over the estuary to Wales, panting as she to tried to get her breath back. She decided she should calm down. It would be better to be a few minutes late than to arrive breathless and dishevelled.

Passing the sweetshop had made her think about all that had happened in the years since she had been kidnapped by Linda, how her life would have been so different if they had caught a later train, if there had been a taxi outside the station, if her mother had had her way and they had gone to see the house in Formby instead of the one in West Kirby.

Enjoying the cooling sea breeze on her face she turned away from the busy prom and headed along the path towards Sandhey.

She remembered the day she had walked that same path with her parents. How angry they had all been with each other on the afternoon of Charles's birthday barbecue four years earlier. She gasped as she had a vivid memory of her Mother walking along this same path. How quiet she had been. How unhappy. Her father's mood had been very different. Angry, yes, but confident and aggressive.

She hadn't really wanted to go to a party that day but now she was looking forward to an afternoon on the lawn at Sandhey. So much had changed, but it was the same place, and many of the same people. Watching the house as she walked, seeing the colourful umbrellas in the garden getting closer, she knew she was lucky. Even if she couldn't acknowledge them as family, she was glad to have them as friends.

She would be meeting Max for the first time since their argument back in March. He'd know everything that had happened and that could be embarrassing but Charles wouldn't have asked her if he thought there would be a problem.

She had to trust him.

And she would have to meet Monika. How would she be able to stop staring at this woman she hardly knew, who was her aunt? How would she be able not to say anything? How could she forget what Max had said about how she was treated? She understood why she had to say nothing and she was not so selfish as to want to do something that could cause so much hurt. Charles knew Monika and what she was capable of knowing.

She would have to trust that he knew best.

With all the other people on the path Holly wouldn't have been aware of the man who had been following her since she left the office.

Graham had struggled at first to keep her in sight, but once she turned onto the beach path he knew where she was going and he took his time, careful to keep a good distance behind.

He was confident that even if she turned around she wouldn't see him. Even if she saw a man she wouldn't see *him* as she wouldn't expect him to be there.

And Graham knew that people only ever saw what they wanted to see.

Chapter Twenty-Seven

As Holly rounded the corner of the house I saw her walk past Ted who had arrived just before her. I saw her trying to catch his attention to say hello, but he was looking down from the terrace at the tall, beautiful woman standing on the brown grass below him.

Susannah, champagne glass in hand, turned as if she had felt his gaze and walked up the steps towards him.

I walked over to Holly, diverting her from Susannah for the moment. They would have to meet, but not until Holly felt more comfortable.

"She's beautiful. So smart."

"She looks just like I remember my mother. She was beautiful too."

"She makes me feel so unsophisticated."

Holly looked down at her bright cotton skirt, bare brown legs and white sandals.

"Don't think you're not beautiful too."

I led her across the lawn to join the others.

An hour or so later we were playing an aggressive game of croquet when Holly said she hadn't seen Susannah for a while. "Inside with Max I think." I said as I aimed at a hoop "Catching up on things probably. She seems to be showing some interest in the kids at last. We've taken a lot of photos over the past few years so she can see what she missed." I tried not to sound bitter.

"I'm going to have a word with her. You OK here for a while?" Since she had been back Susannah and I had had little chance to talk. I didn't get back from work till late and had gone in the mornings before Susannah came down to breakfast. I thought this afternoon would be a chance to build bridges.

We sat in the kitchen telling each other something of our lives since that argument at our mother's funeral. I wondered when, if ever, we had had a conversation with no tantrums, no misunderstandings and no tears.

"You've changed Charles, you're a much nicer person than you ever were. I actually quite like you."

"We've both changed, Susie." I noticed that she didn't yell at me for calling her that.

"Perhaps we've both shrugged off what our parents made us and been able to become what we should be?"

"Are you going to see the children?"

"Are you going to tell the blonde American you're in love with her?"

"I will if you will. But how do you know that I love her?"

"It shows a mile off. Good luck Brother of Mine, have better luck than I have." She turned to leave the kitchen only to bump into Holly.

"Go for it girl!" She said as she passed her. "Although he's my brother he probably is quite dishy. Now."

"Hi." I hoped I sounded less foolish than I felt.

"Hi. Look I wasn't listening in, I just came to get some ice."

"Don't sound so guilty! Susie and I didn't say anything you couldn't hear."

"Not even that last bit?"

"I'd like to have told you properly, I'd like to have been outside in the moonlight with you, sitting on the sand or walking along the edge of the water not standing in the kitchen with the table between us when I said 'Holly, I love you' for the first time but if you had to hear it like that then you had to hear it like that."

"Do you?"

"Holly, I do, really, love you." and I kissed her.

I am not sure how we got through the rest of the afternoon.

I didn't want to let her leave my side in case she disappeared so I held onto her hand as if, were I to let it go, everything would fall away to dust.

Linda couldn't stop smirking and I'm sure Ted smiled far more than he had ever done at any of our family do's.

When Monika joined us, smiling, she kissed Holly on both cheeks. "I am so pleased my dear. I have waited a long time to see my Charles so happy."

Even Max looked long and hard at us both before saying "Love is never easy, dear children, but respect it and it will repay you one hundred fold."

All we were doing was holding hands but everyone was talking to us as if we had got engaged.

When the children had been taken home and the few other guests had left, Holly and I were left sitting on the terrace with Susannah and Max. I was wondering whether, if I walked her home, Holly would 'ask me in for coffee'. What would I do then? What would she be expecting me to do? Would I disappoint her? I couldn't help wishing I had a little more experience of the situation.

Max interrupted my worry by announcing "Holly, my dear, you will be sleeping here with Charles tonight will you not?"

For an old fashioned man Max could sometimes be surprisingly forward.

Not knowing how to answer I looked at Holly, who looked surprised, embarrassed, and a little frightened.

"I am a gentleman who likes formality. You are all probably aware of that." It was difficult not to smile. "I like events to be celebrated. I like births, marriages and deaths to be noted, I like people's passing to be talked about. I do not like events to be swept under the carpet."

I wondered at his ability to say that in all seriousness, but I suspect he was not thinking of events such as murder and blackmail.

"Life events, rites of passage, should be marked. In the old days where I came from men and women did not sleep together until marriage. They slept with other people," he smiled mischievously, "but they did not sleep with the person they were to marry until the union had been blessed. Where I came from young people were shown their bed, they were undressed and their first union was a public event. No! No! Do not worry." He must have seen Holly's look of horror and continued with only the briefest pause. "I did not want the event to go unmarked. Nowadays there is no such ceremony for when people first give themselves to each other. There should be. I am proud that Charles and Holly will show their love for each other under my roof. I am proud that Alicia's son will not be underhand about this. It is not a thing to be furtive about."

He stood up, ushering Susannah away, aware that it would be far easier for us if they were not there to watch us go inside and upstairs together.

The following Sunday, the last Sunday in July, we were reading the papers in Holly's flat. We had decided, after that first morning, that it was less embarrassing if the nights we spent together were not at Sandhey.

Holly had been made very welcome at the breakfast table, but she couldn't ignore the smiles that passed between Monika and Max, nor could she ignore Susannah's grin whenever she caught her eye. I remembered what I had felt like that first morning in Oxford with Linda and decided it would be far easier if I never put her through that ordeal again.

"Come on, we can't stay indoors all day. Let's go to Hilbre."

We found the local paper and checked the tide times. We had an hour to start the walk across the estuary before the treacherous tide would start rolling in, especially lethal on a hot sunny day when people's minds were far away from the dangers of the tide.

As we walked along 'millionaire's mile', the wide tree-lined road flanked by large detached houses in their equally well maintained gardens Holly grabbed my arm. "Isn't that Carl? There, in that yellow sports car?"

I just caught sight of him as he turned off the road into the drive of Millcourt.

"You're right, there can't be many people who drive flash cars like that. Why he chose it I don't know. He's usually so quiet and reserved." I was joking but Holly looked at me as if she wasn't sure.

"He's gone into Millcourt." She obviously didn't understand the significance until I explained. "That's where Ted lives."

"I didn't know that. No wonder he always seems to know what everyone's up to."

I began to tell her something of my history. "I used to live there, before it was split into flats. My father bought it from Max at the end of the war, I was two or three years old. That makes me sound very old doesn't it?"

"Not really, you're only ten years older than me."

"and a half."

"Funny that he bought it from Max." I hadn't really thought about that. Holly must have seen something in my face because she didn't pursue it.

"It must be odd, living in the same place all your life."

"Not all yet. I might yet live somewhere else."

"You know what I mean."

"Well yes I was born in West Kirby, lived in Meols then moved a couple of miles to here when I was two, then Mother left us, then I went to school, then I came back, then Carl and his Mother moved in, then I had a big argument and then I moved all of half a mile across the golf course to live with Max." I tried to make light of it but realised how sad it sounded.

We were standing, hand in hand, looking across the road, through the open gates in the high stone wall at the lovely grey house covered in creeper.

"Were you happy there?"

"Never." That wasn't strictly true but this was no time to tell Holly that the only times I was happy had been the ones I spent with Monika.

"I wonder what Carl's doing up here. He usually lets me know when he's coming, to check…"

Holly finished the sentence for me "…to check whether Susannah's around?"

"Exactly." I was fascinated. Last week Susannah had seemed so different, so in control of her life and here was Carl.

I wondered if they were finally going to sort themselves out.

"Do you think they've made it up?" Holly was obviously thinking the same thing.

"I don't think they've got an argument to make up. I think they just never seemed to understand each other at crucial times. They wanted to say the words but the right ones never came out. I always thought they'd end up together. They were so close even when they were children together. Soul Mates. They were inseparable then."

"Leaving you out?" She seemed to understand one of the reasons people thought we had not liked each other.

"It didn't help."

"Funny to think you've had all this security of being in the same place all your life but you had such an unhappy childhood."

"Odd really, rather than unhappy. There were strands which were happy."

"Come on, we're getting too serious." Holly flirted with him, running her finger up and down his bare arm. "I love men with brown arms and rolled up shirt sleeves. It's such a turn on."

"OK. Let's go. No doubt we'll find out what's happening when we get back."

So we left thoughts of Millcourt, and of Carl, behind us and carried on walking hand in hand down the shady side of the road.

"They're lethal, those sands." I said as we set out, amongst the last of many to leave the slipway on that sunny afternoon. "It's not unusual for people to drown if they get caught out. The water comes in very fast and from unexpected directions. Susannah nearly managed to kill herself, but then she was crossing the wrong route, and Carl's father did drown."

I had confused Holly, "I thought…" I saw what she was thinking and answered her unasked questions. "Carl's Mother married and her husband brought Carl up as his own. He probably never knew Carl wasn't his. Not many people knew that Carl was my father's son."

"They must have done! You're so alike in so many ways."

"I think we're more alike now than ever but if they knew they never said anything."

"They will have done. You just never heard them."

She was probably right.

"I was always jealous of him. I thought Carl was so lucky, he had everything, he was the golden boy, he never had any problems, he sailed through childhood, and he always had Susannah."

"Now you've got me." She pulled me round to face her suddenly serious. "It's not a short term thing this is it?"

"I hope not. It's taken me long enough to make you realise how I feel so it's up to you really."

"I hope not too." And she stood on tiptoe to kiss me to show she meant it.

"Come on," when I stopped to draw breath, "we're getting left behind. There's not many people behind us." I turned around "In fact there's no one behind us. Come on, I think we'd better get a move on." She picked up on the urgency in my voice and realised that we were well behind the last stragglers heading towards the island. "Let's walk!" and there was urgency in my voice.

We were never in any real danger, it was a busy weekend afternoon and there were volunteers keeping an eye from both the island and the mainland to make sure no one got into difficulties, and any rescue required would be quickly undertaken. I knew that, but such was my heightened sense of responsibility towards Holly that I was not going to put her in the slightest possible danger. I had never felt so protective about anyone since I had stood up to my father when he wanted to throw Monika out of our home.

As we had expected the islands were very crowded, but we did manage to find a small area of sand that was relatively quiet and isolated.

"Have you told me everything you know about me and my family?" Holly spoke after we had rubbed sun tan lotion into each other and had been roasting in the sun for a while. It was almost as if she had been rehearsing the words. "I don't think we should have any secrets from each other any more."

I sat up and replied as I would have done when giving instructions in the office, "Two kinds of knowledge, that we can tell people we know and that we can't. Firstly, public knowledge. You are the son of Matthew and Mary Eccleston both deceased."

"Uncontroversial" she took his lead and answered formally with a nod of her head.

"Now the difficult bit. You are the daughter of Mattieu Rebmann, deceased, the niece of Monika Heller, previously Rebecca Rebmann, and the great niece of Maximilian Fischer."

"Will we ever be able to tell anyone?" She had dropped the falsely formal voice.

"I have promised Max, no one will know of his relationship to Monika until after he is dead. I don't think even Ted knows."

"Graham knows."

"Max has made sure he never gets in a position to tell anyone. He's made it worth his while to keep schtum."

"He's been bought off?" Holly asked "That explains a lot. Has he been 'bought off' me as well?"

"It seems to have been all part of the same deal. It had to be."

"I don't care how it was done, I'm just glad to get rid of him. I just don't like the idea of him winning, of him getting something for nothing."

"I don't call giving you up 'nothing'."

It was a few minutes before we continued talking.

"We've gone over who I am, who are you?"

I put on my office instruction voice again "I am Charles Arnold George Donaldson, elder son of Arnold and Alicia Donaldson, both deceased; sister of Susannah Donaldson (sometime Parry), half brother of Carl Witherby, uncle of Josie, Jack, Al and Bill Parry."

"It's odd Susannah had all those children before she was the age I am now."

"She had too many too quickly, it did her so much harm but they're super kids. You will meet them properly one day."

"Can I come with you? When you next go to visit?"

"I don't know." I was doubtful. I had been prepared for Holly to tire of me quickly and end this relationship that was in its infancy. I had half expected her to be horrified that she had slept with me after Susannah's lunch and never want to see me again. I was so surprised that we were here, four days later, getting to know each other better. Although she still seemed to like me I couldn't introduce her to the children. They would become fond of her and then, when we broke up, they would lose her. I couldn't risk that. They had had so much to put up with in their short lives.

"Perhaps in a few weeks."

"You're not sure of me are you? You're not sure we're doing the right thing?"

"Of course I am! It's you I'm worried about."

"You think I'm going to get this far and just dump you?"

"Probably."

She made a small fist and gently hit my arm. "You are sometimes very stupid you know. I'm not going anywhere."

We lay back down in the sand, our arms wrapped around each other, just happy to be together in the sunshine, with at least three hours before we had to walk back to the real world.

Holly couldn't settle.

"I need to tell you something."

"Anything I need to sit up to hear?"

"Probably"

So we untangled our arms and legs and sat up.

As she sat there Holly seemed to be turning something over and over in her mind. I realised she didn't know how to start.

"What is it Holly? It can't be that bad."

"All your family relationships, all mine as well, they've all been wrapped up in lies haven't they?" She didn't expect an answer but I nodded anyway.

"We don't want to get into a relationship that's going to last and then find it's all based on another lie do we?" I couldn't imagine what it was she felt she had to tell me.

"I mean are we going to be together for a long time? Are you serious? I'm not sure I should be asking this or even whether I want to or could commit to anything. Oh I'm making such a mess of this!"

I wondered if I could make it easier for her.

"Look Holly, I don't mind waiting. It's all happened so quickly. You need time. I won't ask you to marry me for, oh, at least a month." I hoped she'd laugh but she didn't.

"You may not want to when you know what I've got to tell you."

"Well I can't know that until you tell me what it is can I? It can't be that bad surely."

"Not bad. Dumb."

"Well it can't be that dumb then."

"The longer I leave it the worse it'll be. At least if I tell you now we've only wasted a few days."

I was beginning to worry. At first I had thought she was going to tell me something silly or embarrassing now I realised it could be serious though I couldn't imagine what could be so bad. "You OK?"

"Fine."

"Not an easy thing to tell me then?"

"No."

"Are you sure you want to?"

"Absolutely."

"OK I'll hear what you have to say but only if you listen to something that is difficult for me to tell you. Deal?"

"Deal."

"Right. I'll go first." I had to keep her here with me. I couldn't lose her. Not now. I knew I had to tell her something so personal that she would know that what she had to say couldn't be as bad.

"I ran away from school once. I hated it. I was bullied. Everyone hated me because I wet the bed." It was the only thing I could think to tell her. "I started when I was 6 years old, just after my Mother had left us and we'd all been ill. I didn't stop wetting the bed until I was 21. It stopped me from going to university, it stopped me from leaving home. It stopped me from having girlfriends and sleeping with them. Everyone thought that was because I was gay but instead it was because I wet the bed and didn't know how to cope on my own."

Holly looked at me hard. She must have realised I was trying to make light of something that had hurt me deeply for much of my life but she could have no idea what it cost for me to tell her.

"That must have been tough."

"I couldn't have got through it all if Monika hadn't helped and understood. She was good to me, you know, and when I was young I really did think I loved her and would always love her. Which I will. But it's not the right sort of love to want to be with someone all your life. I only found that out recently. For years I thought she was the love of my life. I was wrong. I was so wrong about that and other things too. For years I always thought sex hurt people, I always thought it was something that people did to, not with, another. I know I was wrong there too."

I kept talking, trying to put her at her ease. I was probably just making it more difficult.

"I was a virgin, you know. Last week, with you, that was my first time. I slept in the same bed as Linda for a month but we never did do anything. It wouldn't have been right." At last I got a response from her.

"You almost told me that before, but hasn't there been anyone else?"

"No. I never found the right person. I knew you were that person but I had to wait until it was right. Until..."

This was getting more and more difficult, the more I said the worse it got. I told her how I had realised I had spent most of my life being wrong. I had been wrong about my mother, my step-mother and my father, even Max and Carl. In the end I ran out of words.

"I slept with him." She probably hadn't been listening to what I had said at all as she had made herself say the words.

I looked at her, knowing exactly what she meant but mouthing the question anyway. "Who?"

"Carl."

"I thought you must have." That was clearly not the response she had expected. "Thanks for telling me though. It shows that you and I won't have any secrets at all. Will we?"

She shook her head. "How did you know?"

"Well. It was Oliver really. He rang Linda at the office to say you were coming back home. Linda was out and so he got me. I asked why you were coming home. He told me that you and Carl had spent the afternoon walking by the river the day you'd decided. He said you were different when you got back. He said it was like an enormous weight had been lifted from your shoulders. He was quite lyrical. He said you 'shone'. Those were his words 'you shone'. He said that he'd seen Carl have that effect on other women he'd slept with."

"Oh."

I'm not sure whether it was a sign of deflation caused by my calmness at her revelation or disappointment that Carl seemed to sleep with a lot of women.

Neither of us seemed to have a clue as to what to say next.

The sun continued beating down on us, we listened to the shouts of laughter of children playing on the beach and paddling in the water. We heard the dull sounds of transistor radios. We watched the birds as they wheeled and turned around in the bright sky. Holly ran sand nervously through her fingers.

"It doesn't matter you know. I thought you probably had been with him right from the first day you came back and it doesn't matter. It doesn't change me and it hasn't changed you. It honestly really doesn't matter."

She didn't answer because I was kissing her and she was kissing me back, though she had to break off quickly because she couldn't breathe. "It's pretty difficult to kiss and cry at the same time!" so I handed her my handkerchief and waited while she wiped her eyes and blew her nose before kissing her again.

"Thanks for telling me. It can't have been easy."

"We won't ever have secrets from each other will we?"

"Never."

"Promise?"

"Promise."

So I kissed her again.

An hour later we set off hand in hand to walk back across the sands towards the red-bricked buildings on the shore.

"Chalk and cheese. We're chalk and cheese. That's why we get on so well. We're different nationalities for a start."

"You're ten years older than I am." She joined in the game.

"You're blonde and I've got dark hair."

"I've been married before and you're a confirmed bachelor."

I let that pass.

"I've lived here all my life and you've only just arrived."

That seemed to exhaust the differences. "What about the similarities?"

"We're both human?" She asked as if to emphasise what had gone before. I liked her sense of humour.

"We're both orphans."

"Neither of us have any real close family."

"We've both been lonely, frightened, miserable, unhappy, uncertain, unsure, lost, alone and friendless."

"This is getting too heavy."

"OK OK. We both like our work."

"That's a point, we'll be together all day every day, no getting away from each other when we've had enough!"

"Actually, that is a point we'll have to think about. We must be careful not to shut Linda out, look what trouble that got us into in the Spring."

"We'll be super-professional, super-efficient and we'll never use the office desks for anything other than their designated purpose!"

"So it'll be OK on the office floor?"

And again she made a small fist and thumped me on the arm before grabbing hold of my hand and snuggling up to me as we walked back across the sands.

Chapter Twenty-Eight

The next day was an important one at work. At the end of the week the company would have completed its first year of trading. "I'll give it 25 years to make my million and then I retire. 2001. A whole new millennium." Linda had sounded as if she was joking as she led the regular Monday morning meeting when we three partners did our best to plan the events of the coming week. But we all knew she was deadly serious. "We've got to get the books together now, everything hunky dory for the accountant. He's coming to check us out at the end of the week so I'm going to be busy in here adding and subtracting"

"And getting through at least 15 pots of correcting fluid by the look of things."

"It's important! Everything's got to add up and look right."

We went through the work in hand and the regular jobs that we knew would be coming in, trying to anticipate which clients might spring a surprise project and what staff we had to do what work. It was very similar to many of our meetings.

"I must say, you two are doing a remarkable job of pretending you're not together."

"We're not going to embarrass people during office hours. You will tell us if we're being too familiar won't you."

"You can count on me! But honestly I think it's great. The girls are so pleased for you, Luci said they won't giggle and tease you any more than they would tease each other!"

All day Thursday we pored over the ledgers, making sure everything added up.

"Do you need all these? I mean it's only a small business and you've got eight, no nine, files and three books and God knows how many packets of bills and slips.

"It's all got to be done right and we don't want the Inland Revenue thinking we're trying to get away with anything."

"We know. What time do they arrive tomorrow?"

"10, and it's a 'he' not a 'they'."

"Do we know who the 'he' is?"

"Yes, I met him at his office. Ted recommended the firm and took me round a week or so ago."

She saw the look that passed between Holly and me. "Oh yeah?" Holly sounded very American sometimes.

"You were both busy, doing other things, at the time."

"Sorry. We did rather leave you to it."

"No problem. It is rather my fault we've got the business in the first place."

The next morning we were all in the office early.

Holly commented that Linda looked particularly smart in a fresh white shirt, navy linen skirt and, for the first time since the end of May, high heeled shoes. 'She's even wearing make up.' Holly whispered. She and I were in the informal clothes that had become the unofficial uniform of the office that summer, denim shorts and t-shirts.

As soon as the accountant came into the office Holly caught my eye and mouthed silently 'gorgeous'. Ramesh Kambli was a very good-looking man. He walked straight to Linda and shook her hand.

"Good morning Miss Forster."

"Linda, please. Mr Kambli"

"Ramesh, please. And these are Mrs Eccleston and Mr Donaldson?"

"Do call me Holly."

"And Charles."

It was all so formal but perhaps because Holly and I were in the early stages of finding out what it was like to be in love our understanding of what was going on between Linda and Ramesh was heightened.

Perhaps we just read signs which were not very subtle.

While he was punctilious in his politeness to Holly and me, at every opportunity Ramesh turned back to address Linda, who didn't stop smiling.

"I'll get the drinks. Tea? Coffee? Water?" Holly offered, I suggested she needed help and we managed to leave the room and reach the kitchen before we started to laugh.

"Was that electricity or what?" Holly was "No wonder she kept quiet about him!"

"I think we might see quite a lot of Ramesh." I agreed "Let's just finish these drinks and then leave them to it."

At the end of the day it was a group of four that went over the road to the pub for the winding down session and we took the opportunity to find out more about Ramesh.

Linda didn't have to ask many questions but she was very interested in the answers.

Through the course of the four rounds of drinks we discovered that Ramesh was 28 years old, had been born in London but his family had originally come from Bombay where his grandfather, uncles and cousins still lived. They were all accountants. 'It's just something everyone in the family can do. I will have the choice, when I reach 30, to stay in England or to go to Bombay and take over the office there. I am the oldest grandson, the eldest son of the eldest son.'

"Will you have the choice in other things?" Holly was always forward and I was worried he was take offence, as, I noticed, was Linda, but he answered openly and without embarrassment.

"I am lucky, my family will let me choose my wife, as they will let me choose other things in my life, we're not as traditional as some."

Unusually I found I had a lot to talk about with Ramesh. A shared interest in cricket breaks down a great many barriers and Linda seemed miffed that he spent more time talking with me that evening than he did with her. I made up for it in her eyes by inviting him to the barbecue we were holding at the weekend for all the girls in the office, their boyfriends or husbands and families to celebrate the business's first birthday. When she heard me inviting Ramesh I didn't get the glare I had expected. She seemed quite pleased at the prospect of seeing him again.

It was a very lively party that Sunday. The weather continued to be unusually fine and sunny and we had arranged plenty of things for the various children to do. Max had arranged for a swimming pool to be installed and there was plenty of food, which Monika had insisted was her responsibility even if I did have to show her how to cook on the barbecue. She seemed to enjoy it.

There had been many parties and gatherings of one sort or another at Sandhey over the years but that afternoon was unique in many ways. Perhaps the most important difference was that, for the first time, Susannah, Carl and her children appeared, and acted, as a family. Jack and Al almost looked like twins, although Jack was nearly a year older they were the same height and build and had their father's blond hair and blue eyes. Bill was dark and of slighter build than his brothers and he was as different from his brothers in temperament as he was in looks. Josie continued to act as her brothers' surrogate mother but there were signs of her relaxing into a long overdue childhood. She held Carl's hand and pulled him towards where her brothers were playing with the croquet mallets and balls and persuaded him to show them all how they should play properly. It was apparent that he had spent a lot of time with them in the past week as they were comfortable with him and he with them.

I exchanged glances with Susannah who was also watching her children with Carl and we smiled, the arguments of years set aside, if not forgotten.

Watching them, Pat and Jeff worried how their being together would affect Linda. "She's always thought he would be hers one day, it caused so many problems with Holly."

"It doesn't seem to be worrying her one bit! Who is that gorgeous young man with our daughter?"

Linda and Ramesh were sitting close to each other on the wide wall, their feet dangling over the edge, their backs to the party in the garden as they looked out towards the sea.

"No idea. Charles? Holly? Who's that with Linda? Anything we should know?" Jeff leant across to ask.

"Ramesh Kambli, our accountant. They've known each other all of a week and don't seem to have stopped talking the whole time."

"It can't only be work they're talking about."

"He's probably explaining the rules of cricket."

"That'll take a lifetime."

"You never know!"

"Good grief! Have you got them married off already? How long did you say they've they known each other? She's never spoken of him at home."

"Three days or so, that we know about anyway."

"Sometimes that's enough."

"I hope any relationship lasts at least until next July, July 7th 1977 that's all I'm asking. He might invite us to Old Trafford for the Aussie Test, he was saying his firm always gets tickets. I want to see us regaining the Ashes."

Jeff was always interested when there was cricket to talk about.

"You look pleased with yourself Max." He turned to Max who had joined us, seeming more relaxed than he had for a long time.

"I like Ramesh," Max spoke without preamble "I have spoken with him many times and know his family. He is a strong minded, intelligent man who will keep Linda in check. That is if their friendship develops." He had already decided that that would happen. "I hope they have less of a rocky road than theirs." He nodded in the direction of Susannah and Carl. "I have never been totally comfortable with that relationship but I know better than to fight the inevitable."

"What about Holly and Charles?" Pat asked Max in all seriousness, while she looked directly at me with mischief in her eyes.

Despite the lightness of her question Max answered as if Holly and I were not part of the group he was addressing. Perhaps it was the only way he could say the things he wanted to say. "I have no such qualms about Charles. I have watched him change and grow as a person over these past months. I know him well enough to know that he will only be happy when he knows he is needed, and it is clear Holly needs him." I hugged Holly to me, Max's continued approval, though in many ways irrelevant, was important to me.

I walked Holly back to her flat that night,. We were the last to leave the garden and took the short cut across the golf course, carefully keeping to the fairways we walked in the moonlight, tired after the effort of being sociable all afternoon. After a few minutes I stopped and pointed in the direction of a dark house with large windows standing out with no curtains drawn and light pouring out into the blackness.

"That's Millcourt. Those rooms, on the first floor, that's where the Nursery Floor was, the room to the right of the big one, that was my bedroom. When they divided it into flats Ted bought the one on the first floor."

"What a strange thing to do when he must have known your family when it was their home."

"He's always been almost a part of the family. I've seen less of him since, well, since you got back from Oxford, but he is still the one person you can always rely on to get things done. He was in love with my mother, he's always looked after me and Susannah when he could."

"When you'd let him."

"I think it was so sad, he loved her for so long and I'm not sure she ever knew. If she did she never did anything about it."

"You love me don't you?"

"You know I do."

"Would you like to do something about it?" she asked provocatively, pulling me down towards the grass.

"I think sand might be a little less prickly and more private." Though it was difficult to imagine why anyone would be on the golf course this late I led her to the protection of the nearby bunker.

Chapter Twenty-Nine

After they finished their coffee, they kissed goodnight and Charles left to walk back to Sandhey.

Holly lay in bed remembering the gentleness and joy of making love with Charles. She could still feel the dampness between her legs and the gentle throbbing within her reminded her of the satisfaction, both emotional and physical, she felt because of him. She was so lucky, she told herself, the future was looking good, work and life was falling into place for her. 'For the first time in your life, you're actually happy.' She spoke out loud as she lay waiting for sleep to come, looking forward to tomorrow.

At first she wasn't concerned when she heard the noise of a door opening, Charles must have decided he wanted to sleep with her that night after all. He had said how much he looked forward to bringing her a cup of coffee in bed in the morning, having breakfast and planning the day together. She put her hand between her legs to still the anticipation that was building within her.

But Charles hadn't got a key.

Perhaps she had left the door ajar, she knew she was a bit too relaxed about that, especially when she knew the outside door was locked and the Lockwoods were in the flat upstairs.

But the Lockwoods were away.

Perhaps she had better check. But before she could get out of bed she saw a figure framed in the doorway.

It took only a moment for her to realise it was not Charles.

"Hi Holl Doll. Chummy left you alone tonight has he? Well it's a good thing I'm here to keep you company. Wouldn't want you to get lonely."

She didn't have time to move, she could barely pull the sheets around her before he had reached the bed. He didn't bother to undress fully, simply unzipping his trousers, pushing the sheet aside leaving his arm across her neck and forcing himself into her. He ejaculated fiercely within seconds.

"I love it when someone's already loosened things up. No need to force through unwilling flesh. Chummy left you soft and sweet didn't he. Shame you cut off all your hair I'd have liked to wipe myself clean on it like I used to. I'll have to find something else."

He held her down very firmly as he rubbed himself on the sheet, forcing her to see how powerful and unspent he was. She knew she could not fight him off, she had never been able to in the past. There was no point in screaming, there was no-one else in the building and besides, she had already decided, no one was ever going to know.

She neither said nor did anything to argue with him as he pushed himself into her again, this time taking several minutes before working himself up to his climax. As she lay as still as she could she remembered the patterns of his assaults. He would take longer each time until he was no longer urgent for gratification and then he would turn her over and try something different. 'That's not rape', he used to tell her 'it's indecent assault, at least it might be if we weren't married. But we are so you'll have to put up with it like the pathetic little bitch you are.'

She was determined not to respond in any way, she couldn't relax as she worried her body would begin to remember how much it had enjoyed the experience of such a short time before and instinctively respond. She concentrated on the grains of sand on her back, still sticking to her. She must not let her body think this was the same thing at all. If she didn't respond perhaps he would leave her and go away. He would like her to get upset and angry. Not arguing may be the way to make him get bored and stop. She must give him nothing.

She didn't try to scratch him with her nails. She didn't squirm and resist. She didn't touch him or try to fight him off at all as he entered her again.

He held his arm across her throat as he manoeuvred his clothes off and lay naked next to her, making sure the whole length of his body touched hers.

Then he started again.

"Playing dumb are we Holl Doll? Think I'll go away if you stay quiet? Well I'll do all the talking. I learned a lot from your father. He told me what he did to women, he enjoyed that. He started young, he did, with his sister, Rebecca, that's Monika to you in case you didn't know. Gang banging he called it. Practising with his mates on the nearest thing available. He told me what they did to the women they came across in the war. He gave me all sorts of ideas of what to do to get pleasure out of a lump of flesh, dead or alive. Imaginative, your father was. Carry on playing dumb Holl Doll. I'll just carry on doing what I want."

And he did.

"It'd be in this room, before it got tarted up. Over there he'd sit and show me what he did. Every Sunday afternoon he'd get his prick out. Your Dad had a big prick Holl Doll. I told you that didn't I? Knew what to do with it as well. Taught me a thing or two how to treat women. And men. I needed those Sundays. You were too soft and willing. Your Dad now, he was good, a bit of a challenge. I need a challenge."

She didn't move other then when he moved her, or when she had to because she couldn't breathe for her face in the pillow. At times he would pull out of her and lie with his arms around her shoulders, in a mockery of a loving embrace. Whenever she moved he held on to her tighter, his fingers kneading into her flesh, preventing her from getting away.

Then he would talk, conversationally.

As if she wanted to listen.

"I followed you this afternoon, I watched your arse in that swingy little skirt as you walked along the path to your party. I got quite a hard on thinking what I've done to that arse. Why do people call it 'making love' Holl Doll? I've never 'made love' to you. I've fucked you and buggered you but I've never 'made love' to you. It was so fucking easy to get you to think I was 'in love' with you. You stupid bitch.

"I bet that wog has a good go at Linda. Wily Oriental Gentleman my arse. I bet he's no gentleman when he's got a little white girl between his legs. He's probably on her now."

She didn't listen as he told her what he thought they would be doing, what he would be doing if it were him.

"I got used to having you available whenever I needed it. I didn't think you'd have the guts to leave me though. I thought you'd managed to ditch that red-headed cow years ago. I really thought you wouldn't leave me when you had nowhere to go. Then those interfering queers had me and Matt arrested. They thought they'd bought me off, chummy and that German poof, they made me sign papers that they were stupid enough to think I would take any notice of. As if they'd stop me if I wanted to see you again, Holl Doll, they weren't worth the paper they were written on. I suppose they thought Croydon was far enough away from you doll. They arranged the house, a job and everything. They must have spent a fair few bob to get rid of me. But they made one big mistake. Know what that was doll?"

He didn't wait for an answer, perhaps he knew he wasn't going to get one.

"They were stupid. They thought I'd be bound by some idea of honour. So I let them spend all their money setting me up nicely and I played the good boy and let them think I was doing what they told me to do and all along I'd got this plan. Don't you want to know what the plan was? No? Well this is it doll. I'm going to get something back for all my investment. I don't want to think I've wasted the four years I've spent with you Doll. You wouldn't have wanted me to waste all that time would you? You'll have a lot of money one day Doll. Millions. And that would

251

have been mine. Your dad fucked it up. He was supposed to get rid of the O'Dwyers, then I'd get rid of you. But the fucker got pissed and killed himself. It was funny really. It was already too late. Your fucking lawyers had made sure I couldn't get a penny. I didn't tell him though. He thought as long as it was all done while you were still married it'd be OK and he'd still get his cut. So he killed himself for nothing."

Graham leant up on and put his arm across Holly's throat and gradually put weight on it. He took his arm away from her neck, rolling on top of her so his face was inches from hers.

"There's no point in killing you now Doll so you don't need to be afraid. I'm just making the best of a bad job."

He rolled off her and ran his fingers slowly down her body until they were amongst the moisture and warmth between her legs. "I need a bit of recovery time, this'll have to do for now."

"I've been following you, you know. I've kept an eye on you all through the Spring, watching you in Oxford with those twins. Did they have you at the same time? Now that'd have been fun to watch. Then wasn't the time to let you know I was watching you. It wouldn't be long before you'd know you hadn't seen the last of me. I was just picking the right time. When you were happy. That would be the time to have you. I wanted you to be happy so I could show you. While I'm around you never will be. I've been following you, checking up on you, making sure you didn't do anything I didn't approve of. You're still my wife and I wasn't going to have you screwing around.

He stopped talking and looked down at her. She was lying with her eyes shut. "Open your fucking eyes bitch! Look at me when I'm talking to you." She opened her eyes, trying not to see, but it seemed to satisfy him as he began to talk again in a conversational tone.

"I nearly went to the party, they couldn't understand why I was paying for drinks while they would have been free round the corner. Nice car that shit Carl's got isn't it. Goes fast. Had difficulty keeping up even in my new van. Still, you had a lovely afternoon didn't you? I'm glad you enjoyed yourself, both times."

Holly almost reacted, she almost lost the grip she had on herself not to make any move, not to say or do anything that would recognise that he was in her room, in her bed, in her. She was not going to let him know he was winning.

"Then you came back here. It's been easy spying on you. You've never noticed the van parked outside have you? Tied up in your own little world, you've been. Haven't noticed me watching you have you doll? Then that Sunday you went for a walk. I didn't fancy it, too hot. So I came in here instead. I came in and lay in your sheets, went through your drawers, you always did keep all your pants neat and tidy didn't you, even the ones you'd worn. I wanted you to lie here and not know I'd come on these sheets. I liked the idea of you fucking chummy in the same bed. Not knowing. Now I want you to know."

He turned her over and started again.

She had to keep her mind busy. She must not think about what he had said. She must not think about any of it.

She had to concentrate on other people. Monika. Think of Monika. She'd lived with this for years. How she must have suffered so much more than this one night. This was not a stranger, or her brother. Holly made herself remember that the man who was repeatedly raping her was a man she had willingly shared a bed with for nearly three years.

He was doing very little that he had not done many times before.

She tried to think of the sunshine and walking across the sands, but turned her mind from that as she didn't want to think about Charles.

She thought about her work but it was better to concentrate on something small and insignificant. She pictured a keyboard and concentrated on each key in turn. 'one, shift one is exclamation point; two, shift two is double inverted commas; three, shift three is pound sterling sign, in America the pound number sign... eff gee aitch jay ... slash shift question mark'.

She found that if she focused on that she didn't think what Graham was doing to her.

He could do what he liked with her body.

He was not going to do it to her head.

He left her as it was getting light.

After he had gone she got up, stripped her bed and pushed the sheets into a black plastic sack. She showered until the water ran cold.

She made herself look in the full length mirror. She didn't look any different, he had not marked her badly. He had always been clever that way. There were bruises on her shoulder where he had braced himself as he bore down on her but if she wore a shirt with sleeves for a few days no one would notice. Would anyone know what had happened by looking at her? She thought not. She would just have to keep away from Charles for a few days but that wouldn't be a problem until Friday, by then she would be less sore. And any marks would have gone.

She just had to act as though nothing had happened.

And she nearly got away with it.

Chapter Thirty

We had a good week at work. Holly and I kept our distance, as we had the previous week, but I knew she was not unhappy with me as I would catch her looking at me and we'd smile at each other. She did seem a little withdrawn and quieter than usual. I hoped I hadn't upset her, though I couldn't think what I could have done. She had been perfectly happy when I had left her on Sunday night.

I asked Linda whether she noticed anything about Holly, whether she thought she was acting a little oddly. "Perhaps it's that time of the month."

"I hadn't thought of that." There was so much I had to learn about being close to a woman. I remembered my months in Cornwall, Dani had always become moody and irrational, she had tried to explain why. I hoped Holly would feel comfortable talking to me about it soon enough.

It seemed the obvious explanation when one minute she said she didn't want me to go back to the flat after work that week and the next she asked if I would stay with her every night even though we had talked about this and agreed that we wouldn't sleep together during the week. Then the next she wanted to stay with me at Sandhey, she said the flat was too stuffy. But we had talked about that too, and had decided it wouldn't be a good idea, it was quite a full house with Susannah and the children.

So I stayed with her every night that week and, although we slept in the same bed and were physically very close, we didn't make love. She always wore pants and a shirt, I never saw her naked. This seemed so odd as I had got used to her wandering about the flat with next to nothing on.

I had no idea how long these things could take so I didn't ask her. Perhaps ten days was pretty average. In a week she seemed back to her normal self.

Every night after work we would either adjourn to the local with Linda or pile into the Daimler and drive to a pub in the country. Ramesh was getting into the habit of joining us most evenings even when he wasn't actually working at our office, and we saw a lot of Susannah and Carl in the last weeks of the seemingly endless summer of '76.

Holly and Linda would talk with Susannah while we men argued the finer points of the recent test series and the dire performances of the English team against the rampant West Indians. Ramesh happily recounted the events of the recent Old Trafford test and the humiliation of seeing England bowled out for 71 runs, 'and that included 19 extras' only for the West Indies to score 411. "Why don't you all come to Old Trafford next Monday. It's a Bank Holiday, the Roses match. Be my guests."

"What? All of us?"

"Why not?"

We had a long day at the cricket in Manchester. Ramesh was the perfect host as he introduced us to his family.

Linda had had some worries that she would not understand Ramesh's mother, but she soon discovered that, in many ways, the Kambli family's English was far better than her own. Mrs Kambli spoke to us of her home in Bombay. "We are very lucky, we have a lovely apartment on Malabar Hill. We look across the bay to the Queen's Necklace, that's what we call the lights around Marine Drive, the road around the bay. It is an ugly, busy, noisy road to be on but it is truly beautiful at night from above." She had then taken Linda's arm and squeezed it in a very familiar way. "You will come to visit us I know. Ramesh will so enjoy showing you our home and our beautiful city."

In the small box we were able to hear conversations that perhaps we should have ignored but I couldn't help listening in as Linda and Ramesh whispered conspiratorially in the corner. I nudged Holly to listen too, but she seemed miles away.

"They are pushing you too quickly, I know, but they say I am getting older and if I don't find a woman for myself they will have to do it for me. I think they have a cousin in mind but I am resisting. They have always said the choice is mine but perhaps I haven't found someone quickly enough for them. Would you mind if I use you as a little camouflage? It'll keep them from nagging me. You don't have to read anything else into it. Unless, of course, you want to."

He had sounded surprisingly diffident but I noticed Linda taking his arm before answering "As long as it's not only camouflage it's OK with me, for as long as you like."

I believed his reply. "It is definitely not only camouflage." I hoped Linda did too.

Holly had been quiet all day.

She hadn't said a word as we drove down the East Lancashire Road towards Manchester, though I was probably driving too quickly she didn't complain and didn't tell me to slow down. She looked decidedly pale when she had the welcoming cup of coffee and didn't eat any of the buffet that had been prepared for lunchtime. Perhaps the spices were too strong and the food too unusual.

She wasn't as interested as I thought she should be in what was going on in the match and when I asked if she was OK she just said it was very hot and cricket wasn't really anything she had ever known anything about. I tried to explain something of what was happening as Lancashire were bowled out with an hour to spare to hand victory to Yorkshire, but I got the impression she wasn't listening.

She still hadn't perked up when we got back to Sandhey, it had been a long day and she had every reason to be tired. She wanted to go home as it was getting late but since Carl was due to go back to Cambridge after the Bank Holiday we all sat in the garden having a farewell drink.

I had thought it would be a sad occasion marking the end of an unforgettable summer when so much had gone right for us all. But Susannah didn't seem depressed at the impending separation and I realised she had been very upbeat all day.

"I'm the last of us to reach 30. You were years ago Charles, but we've had Carl's, Crispin and Oliver's and now mine all this year."

"I've got a while to go." Linda commented, I'm not 30 for 7 more years. God 1983! That's nearly 1984!"

"Well anyway, as I was saying before being interrupted by the younger generation, 30 is a milestone and I'm marking it by moving to Cambridge. All five of us are moving to Cambridge to live with Carl."

"About bloody time too!" Crispin got up and held out his hand to Carl which he shook as old friends do when they're trying to hide their emotions. Oliver clumsily hugged Susannah and took his turn to shake Carl's hand and then the children were ushered into the garden by their nanny. "They'll be a handful. They'll take a lot of looking after."

"I know, and I'm really looking forward to it."

"My ready made family." Carl hugged Josie and stretched his arms around Bill, Al and Jack who all looked suitably embarrassed.

"Carl's going to be our Dad" Bill had gone over to Charles who was sitting on the steps which ran down to the lawn and taken his hand. "You don't mind do you Uncle Charles?" he asked with all the seriousness of his years. "We'll still love you and Aunty Monika. You'll come to see us won't you?"

"Of course we will Bill. Try and stop us!"

"Aunty Monika?"

"Of course dear, and you'll come up and visit us."

When the Nanny had ushered the children away to their beds Monika spoke quietly, in the way she had, that made everyone stop their own conversations and listen to what she had to say.

"None of you have given any thought to the woman who has looked after those four children in the cottages opposite the old cinema for the past five years. She must have loved them, She has cared for them as well as any woman could even though she must always have known there would come a time when she was no longer needed, either because the Mother returned or the children grew up. It is not easy to accept. The more time passed the less likely it would have seemed. So she would have grown to love them as if they were her own. Now you have told her she is no longer needed. She will have to think about another family, will she love them as much? Will they love her? She will never know if young Josie ever remembers her, or whether Bill ever gets to like his brothers more, or if Jack and Al do as well as they should do at school. She will not know those things, or any other, about the children she has loved as her own for five years."

I wondered what Monika had been trying to tell us of her own feelings. She had seen her own charges grow up and now we were all leaving her.

Susannah, being entirely practical, replied somewhat indignantly "She's got three months money and can stay in the cottage until she finds another position. We didn't have to do that for her." I frowned at my sister, she had missed the point entirely, but she ignored me, continuing regardless, tactless. "It's part of being a Nanny. You are part of a family, then you're not. So you move on. She'll probably start looking after an elderly gentlemen, marry him and end her days living happily in a large comfortable bungalow in Prestatyn."

Without a word Monika stood up and went back into the house.

"How could you?" I snapped.

"How could I what?" she replied, completely oblivious to the hurt she had caused.

I realised she hadn't changed so much in her time away and wondered whether Carl had any idea what he was letting himself in for.

By the end of September not only had the summer ended but it seemed to have been raining for weeks. The quiet summer workload, when the business had 'ticked over quite nicely' as Linda told anyone who asked how things were going, had accelerated as schools went back and offices filled with people wanting typing.

Despite all the work Holly seemed pre-occupied. She seemed very tired in the mornings, it was all she could do to get out of bed in time to get ready for work. She seemed tired out all the time and, most unusually for her, she snapped at people when they asked her perfectly reasonable questions.

After a week Linda finally cornered me in my office.

"I've been wondering how to mention the subject." She began, which immediately made me wary. "Holly couldn't be, you know, pregnant could she?"

I couldn't answer for a while, such a mixture of emotions came all at once. Relief, I had worried she was ill and this would seem the answer; worry, why hadn't she said anything to me; and joy, I had honestly wondered if I was ever going to be a father. It was wonderful news. I corrected my thoughts. It would be wonderful news.

"Not impossible I suppose." I finally answered.

"Do you want me to talk to her?"

"No. Thanks. No I'll talk to her tonight."

"If she is…" Linda left the question incomplete.

"I would be over the moon! It would be the best thing." I looked at Linda who looked relieved "You didn't think I'd leave her to it did you?" I was hurt.

She smiled "Just checking."

The rest of the day took a very long time to pass.

I waited until after we had had supper and Holly was looking through the papers to see what, if anything, there was to watch on the television before asking nonchalantly "Holly, are you OK?"

"Fine thanks." She answered distractedly.

"No I mean really OK?"

She still didn't understand what I was getting at. "Yeah, fine, a bit tired but OK. Of course I'm OK."

"I don't think you are. You're so tired, the girls in the office are making comments about it. They say you always had so much patience but now you snap at them and won't explain things calmly and long-sufferingly like you used to do. They're gossiping about you being pregnant."

"Well you know what we think about gossips don't you." she said shortly. "They're talking rubbish as usual."

"Come on, Holly, that's not like you.

258

"Well I'm not. I can't be."

"Forgive me if I show ignorance of these things but I did think what we had been doing most nights actually could lead to that end."

"Oh don't be so fucking pompous!"

She had never talked like that. I hated it. I really didn't want to argue.

"You're so fucking right all the time aren't you? Well piss off home. I'll see you tomorrow."

Perhaps it was that time of the month again. I made a note to keep a check.

"I'll go if you want me to."

"Fucking well do."

I had to ask again, this was so unlike her. "If you're sure."

"Fucking well am."

She stormed out and headed for the bedroom, so I folded the newspaper, turned the television off, wondering whether I should go in to see her, sit on the bed, tell her it's not a problem, cuddle her, tell her I loved her.

But I didn't.

I should have.

And I went home when that was exactly the wrong thing to have done.

Chapter Thirty-One

Holly sat down on the bed and grimaced. She went to her bureau and took out her diary. She opened it at the bookmark.

"Shit!" she whispered, "Oh shit shit shit!"

The bookmark was in the week ending 20th June. Three months ago. She hadn't thought as the summer had progressed and so much had happened in her life. She just hadn't thought. She had been so happy, had had so much on her mind.

She just hadn't thought.

She'd been on the pill, of course, when she had been with Graham and she hadn't stopped taking it, though she had missed the odd day now and again, especially in Oxford when it hadn't seemed necessary. She had often missed months, but never this long. He must be right. She must be pregnant.

She heard the television go quiet and the door shut. She had pushed him away, just when she needed him to be sitting here with her, his arms around her shoulders, saying he loved her.

She was pregnant. He would be overjoyed. He would think it was his. He'd make a good father.

But was he? If she was three months gone it could be Carl's. But what if she was only two months gone?

It could be Graham's.

She gave a short involuntary gasp at that thought. That would be too much to bear and she slumped on the floor, her diary in her hand and prayed. "Please God. Please. Not Graham. I can handle it if its Carl but not Graham. Please make me three months. Please. I'll never lie to anyone ever again about anything. I'll be the best Mother ever."

She put her hand on her stomach. She had felt funny for a few weeks, not sick, not ill, just odd. How could she have been so blind? Of course she was pregnant.

She had always thought of herself as different from the girls she had seen at Leicester who slept around. She had never wanted to be like that. But she was pregnant and the father could be one of three men.

She wrapped her arms around herself and rocked backwards and forwards. This couldn't be happening to her. How could she tell Charles? What would he do? What should she do? "Oh shit!"

"It's a shame you've been on the pill Mrs Tyler, it usually helps to determine birth dates if we know when your last period was. The pill rather confuses that. Judging by the size I'd say it's either a small three months or a large two months. Difficult to know which, but you are definitely pregnant. Congratulations."

The doctor peeled off his rubber gloves and threw them in the bin he had opened absent-mindedly with his foot. "Now fill in these forms and give them to my receptionist on your way out."

He showed no emotion at all, it had been all so normal for him.

She went straight back to the flat.

What if the doctors said in the end she wasn't three months gone, she'd have to have an abortion and how would Charles feel then? And she couldn't tell him about Graham.

He would want to know why she hadn't trusted him enough to tell him immediately. They had promised not to have any secrets but some things just couldn't be told.

She would have to go over everything that happened that night again and she had nearly managed to forget the pain and the humiliation and pretend it had all happened to a different person.

When the phone rang Holly knew it would be Charles so she made herself answer it, however much she didn't feel like talking to him.

"It was all so matter of fact. I suppose he's given that news to hundreds of women, it's nothing special to him."

"But it is though isn't it?"

"You sound happy." She spoke as if talking to herself.

"Why shouldn't I be? Holly listen to me. I've been thinking. Ever since last night I've not stopped. I want to marry you Holly, I want us to be a family. Please?"

"You want to get married? You want to marry me?"

"Don't sound so surprised! Of course I want to marry you! I nearly asked you that day we went to Hilbre. I've nearly asked you a hundred times but the moment was never right."

"But you didn't did you? You must have always found a reason not to. And now you're only asking because of this."

"I was waiting for you to ask me."

Holly didn't answer, she didn't laugh as he had expected, she was just silent at the end of the phone line.

"Are you OK?"

"No."

"How long?"

"Must be two maybe three months."

"And you didn't know?"

261

"No idea. Didn't think." She couldn't say more than the odd word. She didn't want to cry. She didn't know what she felt. She just knew that if she said anything more she would cry and she wasn't going to do that.

"What about, you know, the pill?"

"I forgot a few times."

"Don't you have to forget a lot?"

"Didn't think. Didn't think it could happen to me."

"Well it looks likes it's happened to *us*."

"But you saw the timing! Think about it!"

"So?"

"I need to spell it out? My last thing. June. What happened at the end of June?"

"You were in Oxford."

"And I slept with Carl! I told you."

"But you must have had a 'thing' since then surely?"

"No. I would have moved the marker in the diary."

"So it could be either of us."

"I suppose."

She couldn't believe he was laughing.

"I'll tell you something to put your mind at rest. Carl can't be the father."

"Why not? Why are you so sure?"

"Because he's had the snip. He did it when he was young. He told me ages ago the he never wanted children, he had some stupid idea that it would not be a good idea for him. He's had a vasectomy. So you see you don't need to worry."

But she did anyway, for a reason she could not tell him.

"So?"

"So what?"

"In case you've forgotten I asked you to marry me. Why aren't you screaming and laughing and yelling 'yes' down the phone?"

She thought of the only thing she could say "I'm still married. My divorce doesn't come through for weeks. I can't get engaged while I'm still married can I?"

"Of course you can! We'll need time to make arrangements and be ready as soon as you're free."

"Why? I'd be no better off. I'd be out of the frying pan into the fire."

She regretted the words as soon as she had spoken them. She hadn't meant to be so bitter, so hurtful.

"I'm sorry." Charles broke the silence before it had lasted an eternity. "It's my fault. I've asked you too soon, you're still coming to terms with everything. Shall I come round?"

262

"No!" she knew she sounded hysterical.

"You need to be on your own. I'll phone in the morning. Lie down, get some rest, watch television, read, do anything but please think about it. I do so want to marry you. You. Not our baby. I want to be with you all our lives. I have loved you since I don't know when, it's not the baby that's making me ask you. I love you. Please please think about it."

She put the phone down without saying another word.

She felt more alone even than during those days after her Mother had died and her father had shut her out of his flat, this flat, than every night she had laid next to Graham in their bed, than the day she had left him and had walked and walked and ended up at the party in Sandhey.

More alone even than when she had found out what her father had been and when she had learned how much Charles could have done to help if he had wanted to.

She knew now that not only was she alone but there was no one left she could possibly tell about what had happened to her.

She wanted to talk to her mother more than she could ever have imagined. She wrapped her arms around herself and rocked backwards and forwards. She wanted her to be alive, she wanted to talk to her, she wanted to be hugged and comforted as if she were a child again.

Where was that red quarter? She needed to hold the coin that her mother had given her. She had taken from the New York guide book and had carried it around with her for months. Then she had put it away, frightened she'd lose it or Graham would realise how important it was to her. If he'd known he would have thrown it away.

Where was it? She had to find it.

With increasing urgency she searched her drawers to find the small red coin. It became a matter of such urgency she wasn't bothering to close or replace anything as she searched through all the pockets of all her clothes and found nothing. She finally went to the old cigar box she used to hold silly little bits and pieces that reminded her of places and times. It was there, under the yellowing cutting of *Star Pupils*. She knew she would never have thrown it away.

She held the coin in her hands as if it was the most important thing in the world. She gripped it until its imprint was embedded in the palm of her hands. She cried her eyes out in relief that she had found the single most important memento of her Mother, of her childhood, of herself as she had once been and would be no more.

She went to bed, closing the curtains and carefully checking the door was still locked. She had to shut herself away from the world. She lay in bed listening to the wind in the lime tree outside the window. It was nearly October.

Where would she be in a year's time? Would she still have Charles or had she thrown him away for ever. Would she have a baby? Who would the baby look like? She tried not to think of anything, anyone.

The street lights were still glowing orange through the curtains when the phone rang.

She jumped up and ran to pick it up.

"Charles?"

"No Holl Doll, it's your husband not your lover."

She listened without response as he talked "Just to let you know you are still my wife. Lover boy's not with you tonight is he? I'll stop you being lonely. You still owe me. The other week was good, doll, but it wasn't worth millions. For a few more days you're my ..."

She didn't say a word as she put her finger on the phone to cut him off and then, after a few moments listened for the dialling tone. Could she call Charles? She couldn't bear the thought that Graham might be outside, watching her. He must be close by – how else would he know she was alone. He must be watching the flat. He's probably just outside in the phone box.

She pulled the wires out of the wall and ran to the front door to check the bolts again. She dragged a chest of drawers across the floor, ramming it as hard as she could against the front door.

He must not get in.

A few minutes later the door bell rang but she didn't answer it. It rang again, and again, and she sat with her back to the door with her fingers in her ears. "Go away. Go away. Go away." she screamed silently in her head.

She rushed through the rooms of the small flat turning off all the lights ending up in the spare room at the back. She huddled in the corner, her arms wrapped around her knees rocking backwards and forwards waiting for the noise of the doorbell to go away. Her eyes were screwed up with the concentration of fear.

Eventually the ringing stopped.

She knew he wouldn't have gone away. He would be trying the fire escape. He could be climbing up and breaking one of the windows. Had she left the kitchen window open? The bathroom window? She rocked backwards and forwards, her body held rigid, her fists clenched, her nails digging into the flesh of the palms of her hands.

He had to go away. He just had to.

She couldn't hear anything. It was quiet. But she knew he would be back. She had to stay here, rocking, safe.

Charles turned away from the door and slowly walked back across the golf course wondering what had gone so terribly wrong.

When she woke up she was cold and stiff. She wondered for an instant why she was curled up in the corner of her spare room and then remembered.

All was quiet.

She wanted some coffee. It was still dark. She wasn't going to turn a light on. She felt her way along the hall, bumping into pieces of furniture in unfamiliar places.

She could hear the rain battering against the window panes and the wind whistling round the edge of the building. She stopped herself from thinking what it would be like to watch the waves thundering against the sea wall at Sandhey.

As she sat with the coffee mug in her hands more and more cars went round the roundabout, their lights reflecting round the ceiling. After a while she didn't see the lights any more. She could see the colour and the patterns of the curtains.

The night was over and he hadn't come.

She crawled over to the window and, sitting to the side of the window so she couldn't be seen, stared through the gap between the curtain and the wall. She could see a corner of the pavement and the zebra crossing by the roundabout. She sat willing Charles to walk round the corner and cross towards the flat. Perhaps he would drive over, hold her and keep her safe. Perhaps the tenth, the twentieth car round the corner would be his. She sat holding her empty mug as she counted the cars. But he didn't walk round the corner, and his car didn't drive up into the parking bay outside the flat.

She crawled beneath the window to see if she could see the road in the other direction.

There was a red van parked there.

Graham had a van. He hadn't said what colour.

It had to be him.

She backed away from the window and crawled across the floor. She thought about closing the curtain more, if she could see out someone might be able to see in, but she didn't want to move them. If anyone saw the curtains moving they would know she was still inside.

She had been stupid staying in her dressing gown and slippers all day.

She crawled into her bedroom and picked up clothes from the floor. She put them on, as many as she could, three pairs of pants, tights, trousers, t-shirts, sweat-shirts. She had to have as many clothes on as she could.

She was stifling but it was worth it.

When he broke into the flat at least he wouldn't be able to get in her body.

She didn't turn on any lights.

She kept boiling the kettle and drinking mug after mug of coffee, she ran out of milk and carried on drinking it black. She found she had wet herself, the warmth quickly turning cold.

She was shivering. She couldn't light the fire. He would see the light and know where she was. She was aware only of being cold, of her own misery and the noise of the wind and the rain.

More coffee. More warmth as she wet herself. More cold.

She ignored the door bell when it rang, she covered her ears with her hands and rocked backwards and making herself sing in her head the words *'when you walk through a storm hold your head up high and don't be afraid of the dark la la la la la la la la la la la la la la la la la la la la'* as she made low and tuneless humming noises to keep from hearing the bell and eventually it stopped.

Through the night she sat, rocking backwards and forwards, crawling to the kitchen whenever she finished each cup of coffee to make another. She must not sleep.

There were no curtains on the window of the kitchen so she put the kettle on the floor. He must not see her. She must not sleep.

She must be awake when the door was broken down, when Graham forced open the door open and tried to rape her again.

It was light again, she didn't know how many times it had been dark and light.

She crawled to her bedroom. The floor was covered with her father's notebooks and photographs. She remembered searching through the desk for her coin.

The coin. She mustn't lose the coin.

She looked frantically for the coin until she remembered where she had found it the day before, or was it a few days before. She didn't know how long ago. She gripped the coin in her hand as she looked again at the photographs of her father's family. She looked at the pages and pages of notes he had written when he had been spying on Max and Charles and Monika.

Just like Graham was spying on her now.

Graham would have a book, all her movements would be written down in a diary. She knew he was looking at her as she sat on the floor in her room. There was no way she could escape him.

He had said he'd never let her enjoy his money. Whatever she did in her life he would always be there.

She crawled to the bathroom.

266

He would never leave her alone.

She reached up to the shelf and her hand found the packet of razor blades.

He would never leave her in peace.

She took one out.

He had won.

She looked at the razor blade in her hand. It would be so easy and it would be the end of it.

She had no idea what time it was when she heard the crashing of the door being broken down and voices.

She looked around her. She had fallen asleep.

She was in the bathroom.

Her clothes were soaking.

She looked, uncomprehending, at the razor blade held in her hand.

She had only been asleep a few seconds.

There were voices, so it wasn't Graham on his own, he was coming with others just as he had said he would.

Gang bang he had called it.

That's what her father had done to his sister with his friends. Now Graham had brought his friends and they were all going to take their turn.

She didn't care who saw her shadow through the curtain she stiffly stood up, moving as quickly as she could to the kitchen. She pulled at a drawer and looked at the knives inside. Thinking very carefully she looked at all the knives before choosing the longest. Backing into the corner she held it out in front of her as she heard the voices coming closer and closer.

"No sign of her here."

"Try the bathroom"

"Not here Sir."

Why were they being polite to each other, they've broken into her flat to rape her and they're calling each other 'Sir'. She was confused, she stood in the kitchen waiting for them, her hand waving the knife in front of her, she reached down to pick up the kettle still hot with boiled water. It was held to the wall by the cable and she yanked it hard until the plug came out of the socket and she could stand, knife in one hand and kettle in the other.

This time she would protect herself. This time she would fight. This time he would pay.

"No sign of her here, are you sure she's here?"

The voices were getting nearer. She tried to work out how many there were, three? four?

"What about the kitchen?"

And suddenly the door was filled with people, she shut her eyes and flung the kettle at them screaming for them to go away.

"Holly for Christ's sake calm down."

She flashed the knife blindly in circles around her. They had to keep away. She was screaming at them, "Leave me alone. Leave me alone. Don't touch me."

"Holly. Calm down. It's me, Jeff."

They didn't seem to be coming near her. She hadn't felt them touch her. But she wasn't taking any chances.

"Go away! Leave me alone."

"Holly. Put that knife down!"

She took a while to work out whose voice it was, she tried to listen as it continued calmly, but she could hardly hear it through the screams.

"Holly, open your eyes, put that knife down. It's me, Jeff. Holly for Christ's sake stop screaming. Constable, leave me with her. She'll open her eyes soon and she won't need to see a stranger. Holly listen to me. Whatever it is that has terrified you it's gone. It's me, Jeff." He spoke gently, clearly and rhythmically. "Quieten down. Open your eyes. You're quite safe now."

Slowly she opened her eyes but it was some moments before she dropped the knife weakly in front of her.

He opened his arms to her and held her close to him, rubbing her back as he had done with Linda when she had been a little girl and had been upset. "There there. You're safe now. There there." He half turned and motioned to the policemen that they could leave them. Holly was no longer a threat to anyone as Jeff held her rigid and motionless.

It was several minutes before he edged her gently out of the kitchen into the living room.

"Now Holly, you must sit down. You needn't tell us what has happened. If you want to you can tell us when you are ready but just sit down. Look around you. You're home and you're safe. Charles is outside with Linda. Would you like to see Linda?"

When he got no reply he carried on talking calmly and reassuringly. He managed to get her to sit down though she didn't relax, she sat with her back rigidly straight, not moving, but her eyes darting around warily, looking for any movement.

"Pat's getting some tea, the kettle seems to be OK, lucky the water wasn't too hot and you're such a bad shot." He tried to make a joke of it but Holly didn't seem to have heard him.

"We were all so worried about you. Charles came round last night saying you'd been on your own for days and hadn't answered the doorbell or the phone. He was so worried. He thought you may have harmed yourself somehow, fallen in the shower or something." He added quickly in case she misunderstood but he needn't have worried, she could hear nothing but the ringing in her ears.

"He is so very worried about you. He loves you very much and he doesn't understand why you're so desperate. Being pregnant isn't the end of the world you know. If you don't want it you don't have to have it. If you do you can. We'll all support you whatever you decide to do. And it's your decision Holly darling. You must know that. Talk to me Holly. Say something."

Holly started to rock backwards and forwards, her arms wrapped around herself.

Holly looked up but didn't react when Pat joined them, placing a tray with three mugs of tea on the table.

"I wish she would cry Jeff. Something terrible has obviously happened to her and she's bottling it all up. Go and tell the boys and Linda to go home. I'll stay with her. She'll tell us in her own good time."

"Come on Holly, drink this." And she gave her the tea laced with crumbled sedative.

It didn't matter whether it was the drugged tea or Pat's calm presence that brought Holly back from the brink but ten minutes later she was sitting more normally, sipping the last dregs from the mug. She still hadn't said a word.

"You don't have to tell us what the problem is, but is there anything we can do to help?"

Holly finally showed she had heard and shook her head.

"Was it anything Charles has done?"

Holly shook her head vigorously looking round wildly, struck with panic that he might be blamed for anything.

"We didn't think it could be." Pat's calm voice overcame Holly's panic. "Well who has upset you? I refuse to believe that just finding out you're having a baby is sending you into the dismals like this." It was always Pat's way to understate problems.

Holly didn't respond.

"Holly, dear, if you don't tell me I can't help you."

But Holly really couldn't tell her and just shook her head.

Then she fainted.

Chapter Thirty-Two

She woke up in an unfamiliar bed. I watched her as she became more aware of her surroundings, seeing the pink check curtains and hearing the crying of babies.

I had spent the last hour trying to understand how they could possibly think it right to put women who had had miscarriages so close to the maternity ward.

"Hi there. Welcome back." I didn't know what else to say.

"What happened?"

"Have a glass of water first, then we'll talk." As I poured the water into the plastic cup I pressed the button to alert the nurses.

"Why aren't you in the office?"

"Because." I couldn't believe she thought anything could be more important than her.

"What's happening?"

Holly had made to get out of bed but clutched her stomach as she was hit by a terrible cramp. She looked enquiringly up at me.

I couldn't say anything, I didn't need to tell her. She knew.

A man in a white coat, who seemed far too young to be a doctor, pulled the curtain aside picking up the chart from the bottomn of Holly's bed.

"Well, Mrs Tyler isn't it? Awake now are we? Good. Here. Take this." He handed her a pill and waited while she swallowed it. At no time did he wait for an answer from Holly or from me.

"Your wife's had a miscarriage, Mr Tyler, but you mustn't worry, it's all cleared out now. There shouldn't be any problems. You're both young and fit. You'll have another in no time." He spoke as if Holly were not there. I was about to ask how long she would be in hospital; could he get something for her pain; would he look at us when he talked to us, but he just wrote something on the chart, clipped it at the bottom of the bed and left without another word.

I sat holding her hand as we both listened to the sound of babies crying.

"Are the others here?" she asked after a while.

"Of course, they're all waiting to hear you're OK."

"Go and tell them they can go. I'm OK. I'm awake." She turned away from me but I didn't leave until I heard regular breathing and realised she was asleep.

As I walked past the desk at the end of the ward the doctor was laughing with one of the nurses. As he saw me pass he said "She'll be out for a few hours, come back in the morning. There's a decent pub over the road if you need a few pints."

I ignored him as I walked towards the waiting room.

When I came back into the ward the next morning Holly was sitting up in bed. I noticed she had brushed her hair. She seemed a lot brighter.

"Hi."

"Hi." She said, almost shyly.

I handed her a cup of brown liquid and we sat looking at it, unable to look at each other. It was a few minutes before I eventually spoke.

"What was all that about? Please Holly, if you never tell me anything ever again please tell me what that was all about."

She shook her head.

So I sat with her, trying to find the right words to say.

"Was it me?"

She shook her head again. "No." she spoke very quietly.

"The baby?" I couldn't ignore what had happened. Anyway I was grieving too. She must have realised how much the baby meant to me. Even though it had been mine for only three days.

"What was it then?"

When she didn't reply I couldn't push her. I reached out for her hand and sat, holding it between both of mine as she failed to find any words.

"Was it Graham?"

I knew from the tightening of her hand that I had guessed right.

"Graham's been to see you?"

She nodded.

"When? Tell me. Talk to me. Please."

She frowned slightly, as if trying to remember something precisely.

"Was it recently? Last week?" I tried not to push her.

Eventually she spoke "After the party."

"Which party?"

It wasn't as if we had had so many.

"Birthday."

"The firm's birthday? That was ages ago!"

"Why didn't you tell me? Why didn't you say anything?"

When she didn't answer I dropped her hand and stood up. "What happened Holly? Look at me."

She flinched so I sat down again. I should have realised she was still so vulnerable but I had spent five of the most difficult days of my life, living with such a variety of emotions and I needed some answers.

"Please Holly. I know you're devastated. You've just lost a baby but please remember I've just lost my baby too. We've lost our baby, I can't lose you as well." Perhaps I was being too harsh. Perhaps I was just as frightened as she was. "Please, Holly, Please. Tell me what happened."

She spoke the words in such a flat voice I wasn't sure I had heard her correctly. In a voice devoid of any emotion she told me how he had spent that night, how he had raped her over and over and over again and done things to her she couldn't even talk about. How he had said it wasn't rape as she was still his wife.

I asked her the only question I could "Why didn't you tell me? We said no secrets."

"How could I? What could you have done?"

I felt so helpless at the defeat in her voice that I could only shake my head.

"I couldn't tell you." It may have been five minutes or twenty when she eventually spoke. "We were so happy."

I knew by 'we' she meant us. I knew she had never been happy with Graham but she had spoken in the past tense.

"We will be happy again." I had to tell her, she had to know, I wouldn't leave her. "I love you." Sometimes it is most important to say the simple things.

"I know." And we were quiet again.

I was thinking about what Holly had said. For five days I had been worrying about why she had been so distraught at being pregnant and now I realised the reason.

"You didn't know who the father was did you? It wasn't just me or Carl was it, it was me, Carl or Graham? You could have handled Carl until I told you it couldn't be him and so it was me or Graham."

As I watched her tears I knew I had, at last, worked something out correctly.

"I wouldn't have minded, you know. I would have brought up the child, even if it was his. But you couldn't could you? You would have worried every day whether the baby was his but you couldn't get rid of it because it could have been mine. Oh Holly! Why didn't you tell me? We could have worked it out together. We could have done."

She spoke at last. "How could I have killed it if it was ours? I couldn't. But if it had been his how could I have lived with it? I couldn't. And then…"

"And then what?" he prompted after she didn't finish.

"He phoned."

"When? When did he phone?"

"He said he was going to… going to have one last … one last… He said I'd cost him millions. He said I was going to have to pay for four years of his life. I couldn't let him. I couldn't."

"You didn't answer the door because you thought I was him."

She nodded.

"And you were alone all that time, thinking he was outside. Oh Holly I'm so sorry. And you'd taken the phone off the hook so he couldn't call. And I thought it was because you didn't want to talk to me."

She let me take her hands again and she held on to them for all she was worth.

"Oh Holly, I love you so much."

But I couldn't ask her to marry me.

Not while that man was free to move about. As long as he was around Holly would not, could not, be either safe or happy.

So that evening I talked to Max.

"It didn't work, buying off Graham." And I recounted what Holly had told me. He seemed very distressed.

"He won't go away, Max. I can't protect her from him."

"No you can't. You are right. I underestimated him. I believed he was only motivated by greed but there was more to it wasn't there. Give a man power over another and he will never want to give it up. In many ways Graham was the son Mattieu never had, they were alike in so many ways. But I can protect her now. I will now do the right thing."

"What is that?"

"It depends, my dear boy, on what you understand by 'right'." He picked up the old fashioned phone and dialled a number he obviously knew well.

As I went to get up and leave him to his phone call in private, as I had for so many years he stopped me "No, don't go away. You will want to hear this." He turned his attention back to the call as the number answered

"Max Fischer." He said nothing more, then he waited, not catching my eye but frowning as he looked towards the bookshelf to my right. Whoever he had phoned they knew where to direct the call. I heard the old authority in his voice, I realised it had been missing for some time. It was only a few moments before he continued "We need something a little more permanent for GT."

Obviously there had been conversations between these two about Graham in the past.

Max's next contribution to the conversation surprised me.

"A long prison sentence?"

I couldn't keep silent. "We can't put Holly through a court case." Max said something I didn't catch into the phone and spoke to me as if to a child.

"She doesn't have to."

"Well what else has he done?"

Max was being patient with me. "He doesn't have to have done anything."

"But how then?

"I believe you can leave that up to me."

Max was speaking to me as if I knew nothing about anything; perhaps I didn't.

"David. What do you suggest?" There was silence for a short time as Max listened. "Yes, probably you are right. I agree." As he put the phone down I realised there had been no hello, no goodbye. The conversation was one between two men who were used to making arrangements such as this. It was all so businesslike.

"That is dealt with. Graham will no longer be a problem to anyone."

I knew Max had influence and power but I hadn't realised he was so ruthless. I couldn't think what to say so I simply raised an eyebrow in admiration.

"Sometimes, my boy, you are so very like your Mother."

He stood up and opened his wine cupboard. A ritual he had always performed when something momentous was occurring.

After placing two glasses on the table he sat back.

"I am merely re-paying my debt to you."

I must have looked as though I did not understand.

"I have been indebted to you, yes, indeed, indebted."

He seemed to be thinking as he spoke, worrying about whether he should entrust me with more of his secrets, and what that might lead to. "You have held my secrets, you have had knowledge that has caused people you love much pain. For that I apologise. I hope by removing the sources of that pain I make your life easier."

"Matt." I prompted. "Not you?"

"We couldn't allow him to carry on."

"You had to protect the O'Dwyers, I understand that."

"He was getting too close to truths that must remain buried …" he hesitated. I felt sure he was going to say 'until I'm dead' but the just said "…for a while."

"Believe me, he was a very real threat not only to me but to you and to your Holly. He was greedy and arrogant. As he killed his wife, so would he have killed his daughter if it meant getting hold of her grandparent's fortune. He was blackmailing me, what about you need not know. And if you pay off blackmailers they keep returning for more. I had hoped that by paying him it would divert his attention from others. It did not. I hope he suffered. He deserved to suffer."

"Do you do a lot of this?" It was the only thing I could think to say.

"I used to, during the war. My old contacts have remained useful. I have been useful to them, sometimes they help me in return."

"David?" I had been curious, and I had to ask though I fully expected Max not to answer. I knew it was a common name but I remembered when the man who is my grandfather had walked into the drawing room on the evening before my Mother's funeral Max had looked at him as if he knew him. There had been a controlled but definite look of recognition passing between them.

"That David?" I repeated the question.

Very rarely had I ever seen Max not know how to control a situation. Everything we had ever said to each other had been on his terms. He would begin and end conversations as he wanted. But this time he didn't know what to say, so he said nothing, he leant down to unlock a drawer of his desk and took out an envelope which he handed to me.

"Read."

Charles,

It is the evening of your mother's funeral and perhaps I am feeling a little maudlin but there are some things I think you should know. Maybe not now but when the time comes.

"I knew there was something, at the funeral, at the wedding. I thought you must have known him. And then at Holly's wedding they didn't come to stay with us. That was odd. You needed to keep your distance didn't you?"

Max dipped his head in agreement.

"You met him in the war?"

Max nodded briefly again.

"Can you talk about it?"

"No. There are some things that will not be known. There is no need. Nothing would be gained."

"Can you tell me how you can just call him up and a man is dead?"

"No."

"You can't explain how I happen to be living in your house all these years and you have never told me that you have known the man who is my grandfather for the best part of 40 years? And don't tell me it is 'coincidence' because I won't believe you."

"I have told you before you are correct to distrust coincidence. I don't believe it exists."

"Then how?"

"David knows some things of my past I don't want anyone to know." He began but I couldn't help interrupting.

"About the money? The pictures?" He nodded briefly, almost distractedly, then continued.

"He arranged for me to buy the firm, he arranged for me to buy Millcourt. It is because of David that I am here."

"Why here?"

"Because Alicia was here."

"I don't understand." How could I have done?

"David wanted me to take care of his daughter, to look after Alicia. It's quite simple really. David saw his daughter, the daughter he could never acknowledge, embarking on a marriage that he could only think was going to bring her unhappiness. There was nothing he could do to stop your mother marrying your father but he could make sure there was someone close by who could help her whenever she needed help. Provide for her and her family." He paused and looked deliberately at me. "I believe I kept my promise."

"And when you took me and Monika into your home it was the two strands coming together?"

"Indeed. I know you have come to believe that it was Monika I felt responsibility for and that I had no choice to take you on as well but in truth, yes, it was both of you."

"Why did you never tell me?"

"That, my dear boy, I cannot answer because I do not know. Perhaps I have been so used to secrecy."

"Is there anything else I should know?"

276

He smiled, but gave me no answer.

"I'm going to ask her to marry me." I eventually spoke the words.
Max had relaxed. "Of course she will say yes."
"If she does, we'll be family."
"Convoluted, but yes we will be family."
"Monika will be my aunt."
"I think she would be very happy with that."
"But of course I will never be able to tell her."
"Of course you won't."
And I didn't.

Finale

22 years later, on November 29th 1998, three months after Ted had phoned me, the family was gathered in the study of Sandhey for the reading of Max's will.

Holly looked across the room at me, now 56 years old, as I stood behind Monika. Carl stood close by with his arm loosely resting on Susannah's shoulders.

With little preamble Ted began to read from the papers on the desk in front of him that had seen so much drama over the years. I was not the only person in the room with memories of talking to Max as he sat behind it.

"I, Max Fischer, being of as much sound mind as I have been at any time in my life wish to make the following clear, to you all, you who have been a part of my life for so long."

Any light murmur of conversation was silenced; all the young ones fell quiet at the tone of voice and the seriousness of the occasion.

"I begin with a quotation Exodus Chapter 34 Verse 7

"Keeping mercy for thousands, forgiving iniquity and transgression and sin - and that will by no means clear the guilty - visiting the iniquity of the fathers upon the children, and upon the childrens' children, unto the third and to the fourth generation."

I can see you all now, pondering that quotation.

Well Charles, Carl, Susannah you are the second generation. Arnold and Alicia, Maureen and Kathleen, they were the first to suffer from the actions of their parents."

The names meant little to most of the people in the room.

I looked across the room at Holly, whose eyebrows were furrowed in a way that I had loved. She wouldn't remember Maureen and she wouldn't know who Kathleen was any more than Josie and the boys did.

"Susannah, your children are the third generation. I know you and Carl have given them all the love they could possibly need to end the sequence. If God wills it the pain will end now."

I could see Linda thinking 'that's all he knew'.

I wondered when he had written those words. It was obvious much had been kept from him in his declining years, or perhaps he just had chosen not to see what was in front of him.

278

"For you all I would say 'Do not judge them too harshly for things they could not know'. Much of this is not your responsibility. Do not blame yourselves."

Most of the gathered company would have their own ideas of what Max had been referring to. For my part I thought 'but I did know. I can blame myself.'

Ted paused briefly before continuing.

"The first and most important bequest for you all is this book of Ted's. Read it carefully, learn from it."

The people in the room all turned towards the table in the corner, for the first time perhaps realising that the parcels were all the same size. Children and adults alike had rather assumed they were small gifts outside the remit of the will.

Only Ted, myself and one other had known what they really contained.

Their glances turned away from the table towards Ted as he began speaking again.

"Learn to forgive your elders their mistakes for they make them either unwittingly or through weakness.

My second bequest is an explanation..."

I looked around the room, every person was listening rapt as Ted read the words Max had written about his family. With a dawning realisation of what was to follow Holly couldn't help but turn her gaze towards me as I looked straight at her. 'At last' she mouthed and I half shook my head in answer.

She looked at Monika who was listening unblinking as Ted spoke of things she thought were long forgotten.

Ted read that Max had given his niece a map, how after the war that map had meant she found her way to Britanny, how he had found her there.

"Your real name is Rebecca Rebmann. You are my dear niece – but I could never tell you for all the memories I knew it would bring up to mention it. As we grew older together I knew your knowing our relationship could not make us any fonder of each other. So I let it be."

It was still only half the truth.

And as Holly looked at Monika she could see no surprise, no shock or despair on her face.

After the reading of the will was concluded people were talking in urgent but hushed tones about the disposition of Max's assets. I watched Holly walk across the room towards us.

She interrupted Monika unapologetically, talking directly to her.

"You knew didn't you? How long have you known?" She could not keep the hostility from her voice.

When Monika replied he spoke firmly and with as much bitterness as Holly had expressed.

"I have known since the very earliest days. I was not very clever in many ways but there are things I will always remember and I knew when I saw his hands, resting on the sea wall as we watched the tide covering and uncovering the unterseeboot. They were my father's hands. There were memories but they were unclear and I knew I did not want to live with them. So I didn't try. For years I was content with my life and that people should know me as Monika. Then I saw a photograph in the paper. A girl I recognised even though the name, Holly Eccleston, meant nothing to me. I met that girl called Holly and the man called Matt. Then I saw those same hands again. How could I not know?"

"You knew but you said nothing? Ever?"

"I said nothing because nothing was said to me."

"When you saw the pain around you?"

"I saw no pain."

"And me? You were happy never to tell me you were my aunt?"

Her anger and resentment subsided. Holly raised her shoulders and let them drop in a gesture of helplessness. Keeping those truths secret had cost so much and it had all been a complete waste.

Monika had known all along.

"You see an old woman when you look at me. You see my roundness and my grey hair. Well I saw much when I looked at you that day on my bed, asleep. I saw my hair. Although I had always worn it plaited but I had loved to brush it at night and in the morning. I saw my young self in you. I did not know why you had come, what you wanted from me, but I knew who you were. I waited and I watched."

"But you said nothing. Why say nothing?" I felt something of Holly's pain.

"I said nothing because nothing was said to me." She repeated as if it were a mantra.

"All that pain. For nothing. You let us go through all that for nothing." Holly spoke with a quiet anger.

"Whose pain? You think only of your own pain. What of the pain of others? That doesn't matter to you does it? You were all so sure I could not know. You must have thought I was stupid. You did think I was stupid. All of you look at me and what do you see? No one has tried to know me, not even you Charles. So I waited for someone to ask me what I knew and tell me what I had forgotten. I wanted someone to tell me who I really was. But you didn't tell me. It was you who said nothing. Not me."

"Why is it impossible for anyone in this bloody family to tell the truth?" Holly turned on me, knowing she had no answer for Monika.

"Because sometimes it is easier to lie?" I gave an unsatisfactory reply.

"Whatever the cost?" Holly looked directly at me as she hadn't looked at me for years.

"Whatever the cost." I confirmed with finality.

I watched with such sadness as she turned, walked away from us and after hesitating slightly as if wondering whether it was the right thing to do, collected her parcel from the table and walked out of the door alone.